GU

IMMO

(epic fantasy series)
Wreckers Gate: Book One
Landsend Plateau: Book Two
Guardians Watch: Book Three
Hunger's Reach: Book Four
Oblivion's Grasp: Book Five

ALSO BY ERIC T KNIGHT

CHAOS AND RETRIBUTION
(sequel to Immortality and Chaos)
Stone Bound: Book One
Sky Touched: Book Two
Sea Born: Book Three
(BOOK 4 SPRING OF 2018)

THE ACTION-ADVENTURE-COMEDY SERIES
Lone Wolf Howls

THE ACTION THRILLER
WATCHING THE END OF THE WORLD

All books available at Amazon.com

For news about new releases, plus
bonus content and special deals:
Join my Readers Group

Follow me at:
ericTknight.com

Guardians Watch
Book Three of
Immortality and Chaos
by
Eric T Knight

Copyright © 2018 by Eric T Knight
Version 2.0 6/2016
ISBN-13: 978-1986038348
ISBN-10: 1986038343

Author's Note:
To aid in pronunciation, important names and terms in this story are spelled phonetically in the glossary at the end of the story.

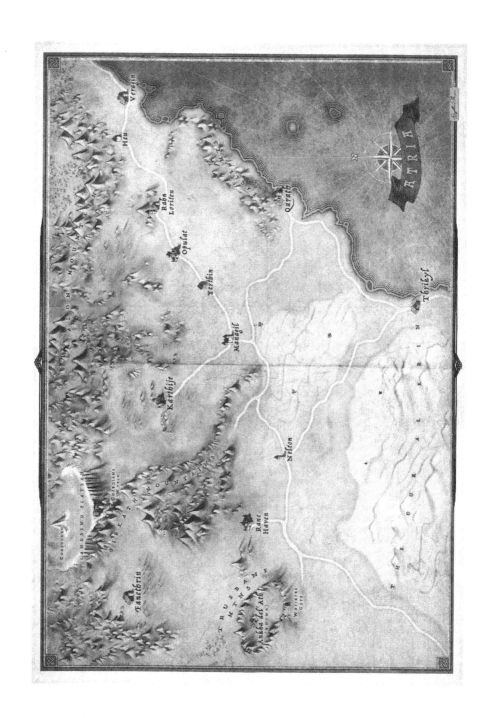

For Dylan
My first born
Always know that I love you
and I'm proud of you

PROLOGUE

In the beginning, the world was new and raw. Primeval seas crashed against nascent cliffs while mountainous thunderheads dealt torrential rains that scoured barren stone with torrents of angry water. No eyes looked on this new world. No creatures scurried across its surface. There was no will, no thought, no purpose.

Until the day when the first of the beings arrived, crashing down out of the sky in fragile-looking pods that cracked open upon impact, spilling their passengers onto the lifeless world. These beings awakened slowly. They were shapeless, nameless, without memories or form of any kind. They were blank as newborns, remembering no past, knowing no future.

In time, these beings divided into three groups, based on their basic natures. Some were heavy creatures, slow of thought and action, ponderous and weighty. Others were fluid, sliding across the broken surface of the world, gathering in the low places. The last were nearly invisible, flighty and rapid, unable to finish one thought or action before racing onto the next.

One of the heavy group looked down at the stone it sat on one day, then reached down with what passed for an appendage and scooped some forth. Wonder glowed in its eyes, for the stone was like clay in its grasp, and it could shape the stuff, even sink into it with only a thought.

The others looked on, wary and interested. Others of the heavy, ponderous type began to poke at the stone as well. Those who were fluid of form prodded the stone in only a desultory fashion, disappointed, until one among them slid across the stone to the edge of a vast sea that foamed and muttered to itself. The being slid into the water and a wordless cry of delight arose from it. It gestured and a wave arose, taller than the rest, crashing against the shore, clawing its way almost to the gathered creatures before sliding back.

1

A third being, one of the flighty ones, looked at the stone, then at the sea. Nothing showed on its blank face. Then what might have been its head tilted back and it looked into the sky overhead, surveying the massed clouds. With a leap and a cry it soared upwards, faster than the eye could follow. In moments the clouds had trebled in size, dark and fearsome as the eye of winter, and tongues of lightning flicked down to stab at the stone.

Thus were the three Spheres delineated, Stone and Sea and Sky, and the beings that dwelt within them named themselves. Those of the Stone became known as *pelti*; those of the Sea became *shlikti*; those of the Sky *aranti*. They were the Shapers. The world was their playground, the power that suffused the Spheres yielding to their every whim.

In time they would be called gods.

They were the First Ring, the first to arrive on the new world, and the greatest, but they were not the last. More would follow, until Stone and Sea and Sky frolicked with these ageless beings, each moving through its Sphere, endlessly bending and folding and shaping.

In the Stone, the *pelti* sculpted cliffs as high as the clouds, mountains whose stone faces reflected every color of the rainbow. Volcanoes that blotted out the sun and rained ash.

In the Sea, the *shlikti* raised up mountainous waves that washed across entire continents. Mighty rivers that roared down the mountains, eagerly returning to the sea.

In the Sky, the *aranti* howled down rainstorms that turned the planet black, cut only by nonstop flashes of lightning.

The Sky took water from the Sea, snatched it away and raced with it into the heavens, then hurled it back at the land. The Stone absorbed the Sea, hiding it away deep in its bowels. The Sea carved away the Stone with its infinite patience.

Theirs was an existence unburdened by mortal chains of pain and consequence. They neither aged, nor died. They felt no pain, nor even conceived of its existence. Their pride was boundless. They taunted each other, stole from each other, fought and forgot. Over and over, endlessly. It was a timeless, endless existence.

But they could not escape boredom. In time it beset them all, made them quarrelsome. And, at last, one of the First Ring, a *pelti*, began to wonder. Despite all it could do, it was empty. What was the point of it all? True, the very bones of the earth yielded to its slightest whim, but to what end? The only motive came from it and its brethren. There was no real change, no real growth.

And thus it was that this one Stone Shaper conceived of a new idea. Of another Sphere, yet not a Sphere, that could change and move on its own, that could go beyond the limited imaginations of the Shapers, that would Shape *itself*.

This one Shaper sat alone, away from the others, and pondered this new thought it had. Pondered for a time that humans would have called eons, but which meant nothing to it or its timeless brethren. And slowly, very slowly, a new idea began to form.

It bent, and scooped forth raw Stone. To this it added Sea and Sky, taking from the Spheres and forcing the three together. Then it breathed on this new concoction, adding some of its own essence. Its creation stirred. The *pelti* was pleased and turned to show its brethren.

Behold. I bring you Life. It is formed of the Three, and so makes a new.

They gathered around, curious at first, and then concerned. In their multitudes they watched this new thing. It did not have the robust nature of the Spheres, could not be called such, was more a Circle. The time they spent was only moments to them, timeless beings that they were, but time enough for vast changes in the short-lived world of Life.

The first to speak was a First of the Sea, a *shlikti*.

We do not approve. This steals from our Sphere to make its very being. Destroy this thing now.

But the one who forged the Life demurred. *It moves and changes on its own, without our motivation. It is fascinating. See?*

Indeed, in the time they had spent pondering, the new Circle had grown and changed. Some types of it now covered much of the land, green and brown that grew across stone faces and up mountains, stretched tendrils down into the water and up into the air. Other types had spread into the oceans, some anchored at the bottom, some floating free. Most Life was so slow-moving as to be almost motionless, but some swam in the water, ran across the land, or soared in the air.

We should watch it longer. See what it does, the *pelti* said. *It is new, and different.*

We should destroy it. It is outside us, and therefore dangerous.

So conflict seemed imminent until the *pelti* who shaped the first Life said, *We have not heard from our brothers in the Sky, the* aranti.

What say you?

The *aranti* raced and skittered around the Life, sniffing and listening. *It is bad and good,* it said at last in its many voices. *It is, and yet it is not. We do not care.*

Still the Sea would not be assuaged and it rumbled in its crashing green voice, threatening and complaining. *It takes from us. It takes from all the Spheres without respect. It has broken our law.*

Then the Shaper of Life spoke yet again:

But see. Its taking is very short. True, it takes from the Three, but only for a short while. See how it dies? Then does it give up what it has taken, back to the Three, and all is made complete again.

So it was that the Shapers allowed the intruder to exist among them: Stone, who watched over and nurtured in its own rough way. Sky, who cared less and forgot more. And Sea, who watched, ever sullen, nursing bitterness toward the intruder.

From the writings of Sounder Treylen

ONE

Macht Wulf Rome, the man known as the Black Wolf, feared far and wide by his enemies, fierce and ruthless in battle, sniffled and wept openly. Tears poured down his cheeks and gathered in his great, bristling, black beard before dripping onto the breastplate of his distinctive black armor, smearing the dried blood splashed there. He leaned aside and blew his nose onto the floor, then wiped ineffectively at the tears with the back of his hand. The room around him was packed with sweating, shouting men. Curses and smoke filled the air. They surged around Rome, pressing on him from all sides, but he paid them no heed, his attention focused on his opponent and several small objects lying on the table before him.

Lucent sat opposite Rome on the other side of the table. He wasn't as tall as Rome, but he was considerably older and the years had packed weight on his frame so that he was bigger around. A great deal of muscle lay hidden under his fat—a fact which many young soldiers had discovered to their chagrin when they faced him in the practice yard. He leaned back in his chair, his legs sprawled out in front of him, a broad smile on his face. His nose was red, the broken blood vessels attesting to too many years of hard drinking. A tankard of ale sat on the table before him. "Are you ready to give up then, Macht?" he boomed. His voice, honed by decades as a sergeant in the army, easily cut through the din. "There's none will think less of you for doing so." He leaned forward, setting his meaty forearms on the table. The glint in his eyes was mocking. "Except me, of course."

"I'm not giving in," Rome said, grabbing his own tankard and taking a long draught. The ale didn't seem to help at all. Lucent was a blur through the tears. "I've only just started."

"Too true," the fat man replied with a laugh, slapping the table. "You've only had four," he said with disdain. "My youngest is a babe of five and he eats more than that for breakfast."

Rome wiped at the tears once again and tried to think of a proper retort, but nothing came. Realizing he couldn't put it off any longer—not if he wanted to preserve some self-respect in the middle of this debacle—he picked up another of the tiny orange peppers from the bowl in the middle of the table. The shouting and hooting from the crowd doubled and money changed hands as odds changed and bets were placed. Grimacing, he stuck it in his mouth, bit it off at the stem, and started to chew. Fresh tears started and his face darkened to a new shade of red that bordered on purple. "I think I'm getting used to them," he gasped, tossing the stem down with its four brothers before him and grabbing his tankard.

Lucent already had a dozen stems in front of him and there wasn't a tear on his broad face. The people of Managil called them scorpion peppers and now Rome knew why. He'd been stung by a scorpion back when he was stationed at the outpost near the Crodin lands. In retrospect, he didn't think that hurt as much as this. Something seemed to have stung the entire inside of his mouth, his throat, and even his stomach. Why had he ever let Lucent goad him into this? Why didn't he just keep his mouth shut when Lucent started bragging about how many of these he could eat? He'd known the man for twenty years now. Lucent didn't brag unless he could back it up.

It all started earlier that afternoon. Lucent was training some of the new recruits and he was venting his frustration with them by yelling at them. That was about when Rome happened by and he'd made some comment about how surely young, strong men should be ashamed of themselves for letting an old, fat man kick them around. Of course Lucent responded to the insult by calling Rome out and naturally Rome just had to grab a practice sword and take him up on it. One thing led to another. One moment Rome was taunting Lucent and clowning for the recruits and the next moment Lucent backhanded him in the nose—which was where all the blood on his armor came from. Somehow one thing led to another and here he was, sitting in a tavern eating scorpion peppers.

A new wave of heat struck Rome and he started coughing. He didn't have to be a genius to see this was going nowhere good. In the beginning there'd actually been a few bets placed on him winning this contest; now they were just betting on when he'd give up. If he had any sense at all, he'd quit now. There was nothing to gain here.

Instead Rome took another pepper from the bowl, nearly knocking it on the floor in the process, and stuck it in his mouth. This time he didn't even try to remove the stem. What difference did it make? It was the only part of the pepper that didn't hurt.

Across from him Lucent shook his head. "You're a stubborn man, Macht. A stubborn, stubborn man."

"Want to give up now, old man?" Rome croaked. "I can see you're having second thoughts." In fact, he could barely see at all. The pain in his mouth was bad enough but it was the tears that really bothered him. A leader shouldn't be crying in front of his men. But he couldn't seem to help it. He didn't think he'd shed this many tears in his entire life. There was a fresh tankard by his elbow and he grabbed it like a drowning man.

"I am," Lucent said with mock gravity. "I'm wondering what kind of fool's calling himself my king!" he yelled. The room burst into laughter. Men whooped and slapped each other on the back.

Rome coughed again, felt the horrific mess in his stomach start to come up, and somehow fought it back down. This was going south fast. He really should quit before it got any worse. It was the only halfway sensible thing to do. He couldn't win. His mouth opened to say the words but just then his vision cleared enough for him to see that Lucent had stood up and was thumping his chest, playing to the crowd.

Rome ate another one.

The crowd cheered. More money changed hands. Hands patted him on the shoulder. Other hands set a fresh tankard of ale down before him. Rome leaned forward, grabbing it with both hands as a fresh wave of pain roared up from his stomach and out through his nostrils. As he did he saw with relief that there was only one more pepper in the bowl. Maybe there was a way out after all. But just then a barmaid wormed her way through the crowd. She carried two tankards in one hand and another bowl of orange peppers in the other. Rome groaned. Fortunately the sound was lost in the din. It was looking like he'd made a serious mistake.

The crowd parted again and there was Tairus, shaking his head. The short, stout man yelled at a nearby soldier and a moment later a chair appeared. He pulled it up to the table and sat down. Leaning in close to Rome he said, "You're a damn fool, Rome."

He said it low enough so no one else could hear over the crowd, but somehow Lucent did. Or maybe he just guessed. Either way, he guffawed, slapped the table again and dropped into his chair. "I tried to tell him to quit, but he won't."

"Bad things are going to happen to your stomach," Tairus said. He was wearing chain mail and his face was sunburned. He'd been at the training grounds outside the city, working with the soldiers they'd picked up from the other kingdoms during the summer campaign.

"Ain't it the truth," Lucent intoned.

"To say nothing of your arse," Tairus added.

"Didn't you eat a couple of these with me one time?" Lucent asked.

"I did," Tairus said gravely. "Two days I was running to the privy. I wished I was dead."

"And you only ate two," Lucent said.

"It's not that bad," Rome said. He wasn't sure if they understood him. His words were kind of garbled. He wiped at his eyes again. "I think I'm getting used to them." This time when they tried to climb up out of his stomach he thought he was going to lose the battle.

"Help me out here," Rome heard Tairus say to Lucent. "He won't quit."

"I was only having fun."

"There are openings on the city watch. We need more patrols in the Warren." The Warren was the meanest part of Qarath.

"No need to be nasty," Lucent grumbled. Abruptly he stood. "I submit!" he yelled. "I submit!"

A chorus of curses and threats met this statement. Lucent's face darkened and he turned on the crowd. "Some of you have trouble with this, we could go outside and discuss it up close like."

He wasn't yelling anymore, but every man in the room either heard what he said or caught the gist of it. The room went quiet and there was a lot of mumbling and averted eyes. Nearly every man in that tavern had faced Lucent on the practice field. He'd been training new recruits for years and he'd cracked a few of their skulls. Nobody trained the pups better, but no one was quite as mean. No one wanted Lucent mad at him.

Lucent sat back down. "All in good fun, eh?" he said to Rome.

"I never had so much fun," Rome replied. What he wanted to do was look in a mirror and see if his mouth was blistered, but instead he took another long drink of his ale. "Any time you want to try again."

He missed the dark look Tairus gave Lucent, but all Lucent did was laugh and say, "I think I've learned my lesson, Macht."

Rome stood up. "I think I have a meeting."

Outside, Tairus pulled a square of cloth from his pocket and handed it to Rome, who used it to wipe his eyes and blow his nose. When Rome offered it back to him, Tairus shook his head. "You keep it."

They walked in darkness for a few minutes, boots crunching on the cobblestoned street as they began the climb up the hill to the palace. Tairus scratched his neck, looked up at the sky and casually said, "You just don't know when to quit, do you?"

"It's not something I've ever been good at," Rome conceded.

"You're going to pay for this tomorrow," Tairus said.

Rome shrugged.

"It's not going well with the new soldiers," Tairus said. Since they returned from the summer campaign in which they'd conquered Managil, Opulat, Yerthin, Rahn Loriten and Hen, effectively quadrupling the size of their army, he'd been personally overseeing the training and integration of the new troops. "The men from Yerthin don't get along with those from Opulat. Those from Rahn Loriten don't like Opulat either. In fact, they hate each other. They won't back each other up. Each wants to be in the front in any kind of action. Fights break out all the time. It's not just the men either. Today I had to get between their commanders. They drew swords on each other during the midday meal. I thought they were going to kill each other."

Rome spit on the street, wishing he could spit out his tongue at the same time. When would the burning stop? "Knock them down to sergeant. Promote someone else."

"It's not that easy, Rome. The men won't just follow anyone. Those men are respected by their soldiers. The men will follow them. I need to find a way to work with them."

"Don't they understand what's going on?" Rome growled. "Melekath's just waiting to swallow us all. They need to put aside their stupid feuds."

"You're right. They do. But they won't. They've been fighting each other lots longer than they've been fighting Mclekath. Besides that, Melekath's out there somewhere." He gestured at the horizon. "He's not even real to them. This is real to them. This is here and now."

"Split them up?"

"Sure. Why didn't I think of that?" Tairus spat on the street. "I tried. I really did. But then I discovered that those from Rahn Loriten

9

hate those from Hen, who hate those from Yerthin even more. Gods, Rome, there's not a one of them gets along. If we weren't using wooden swords in the mock battles I don't think a one of them would be left alive."

"You'll get it worked out," Rome said, clapping Tairus on the shoulder. "You're good at that sort of thing."

"I just hope you're not planning on marching this army anywhere soon. Or fighting it. Or doing much of anything with it."

"I sent someone to Karthije to talk to Perthen about allying with us against Melekath."

"I'm sure that will go well. Kings love to share power," Tairus said drily.

"But surely he will see that he's got no choice. My army is bigger than his now. By a lot."

"So you're saying that he'll choose to be sensible and surrender instead of throwing his soldier's lives away?" Rome nodded. "Have you forgotten Rix already?"

Rome sighed. "No. I haven't forgotten him."

"Perthen knows you don't want to lose the soldiers necessary to take Karthije. He'll use that against you."

"He'll be sorry when he looks out his window one day and sees Kasai marching down the road."

"Sure he will," Tairus agreed. "He'll know he made a big mistake. But it won't help us any by then."

"So you think we should march on Karthije?"

"No. I don't. We're still stretched thin after the summer campaign. We can barely feed our army here. I don't know how we'd feed them on the road."

"So all we have left is talk."

"It's what kings are good at." Tairus cracked his neck. "If we can wait through the winter, get these men trained and our supply lines straightened out, by spring we'll be able to whip Karthije and it won't matter what Perthen wants. What does Lowellin say? How close is Melekath to getting free?"

"I don't know. I haven't seen Lowellin since we got back to Qarath."

"What about Quyloc? Hasn't he talked to him?"

Rome shook his head.

"And he's supposed to be our ally?"

"At least he's still helping the Tenders with their *sulbits*. I guess that's something."

"I trust them only slightly more than I trust Lowellin. If we survive this, they're going to be a problem."

"I agree with you. Quyloc's keeping an eye on them. He says they're getting stronger fast."

"So our new army is at each other's throats. Our allies are completely untrustworthy. We don't know how long we have before Melekath is free. Am I missing anything?"

"You forgot about Kasai."

Tairus groaned. "I was hoping that was just bad information."

"I don't think so. Perganon swears by his sources." Perganon was the old librarian. He had a loose network of informants in a number of kingdoms. The one in Fanethrin had recently sent news that one of Melekath's Guardians, Kasai, was gathering an army. Even more disturbing was how that army was being gathered. Bands of soldiers led by men whose eyes had been burned out were scouring the entire northwest. Everyone they caught was asked a question. Those who answered correctly were spared and joined the army. Those who didn't were burned.

"You think Kasai is coming here?"

"Either that or the Gur al Krin, to be ready when Melekath gets out."

"Has there been any more news? Does Perganon's informant know how long until Kasai's army is ready to march?"

Rome shook his head.

TWO

Quyloc opened his eyes and what he saw shocked him.

He was not in his bedroom in his quarters in the palace. He was lying on the ground, staring up at thickly interwoven tree branches. The light was all wrong. All at once he knew where he was and he sat up quickly.

He was in the *Pente Akka*.

How did he get here? The last thing he remembered was going to bed. Oddly for him, he'd fallen asleep quickly for once.

He looked around. He was in a small, grassy clearing. There were huge trees in every direction, their trunks covered in moss, their leaves blotting out most of the light, casting the world in gloom. Ferns grew everywhere, along with mushrooms as big as his head. He was in the jungle, though it was not nearly as thick or as wet as the jungle he'd gone into before, when he killed the huge beast and made a spear from its tooth.

He looked around. There was no sign of his spear.

I'm not here, he told himself. He had no memory of going to the Veil or passing through it. This had to be a dream.

He heard something in the distance, breaking limbs as it came. It was closing fast.

I'm not here.

But he could not entirely convince himself of that. It all seemed too real for a dream. And whatever was coming sounded big.

He closed his eyes and visualized the Veil, picturing it in every minute detail. When he opened them, it was there, a grayish-white, gauzy web, superimposed over the jungle background, stretching out of sight in every direction.

But he no longer had the bone knife to cut an opening.

The crashing grew louder.

He threw himself at the Veil, hoping to tear his way through. But there was nothing there. He passed right through it. It was no more substantial than fog.

He was trapped here.

He took off running, animal fear overriding everything else. Whatever was coming, he didn't want to see it. He burst through clumps of ferns, jumped over rotting, fallen trees thick with orange and yellow fungi. He didn't choose a direction. He had no destination but away.

But it was no use.

As hard as he ran, he could hear his pursuer getting ever closer. He broke through a screen of ferns and into another clearing. This one had a small hill in it, strangely free of trees or other growth save thick grass. On top of the hill was what looked like the ancient remains of a wall, the stones almost completely obscured by moss.

He ran up the hill and jumped over the wall, then crouched behind it.

The jungle went silent. Had his pursuer given up? Was it sneaking up on him? After a minute he peeked over the wall. There was no sign of movement. Had he imagined it all? Slowly, he stood up.

Something, some intuition, made him turn and look behind him.

The hunter stood there.

Completely black, it was manlike in shape and stood head and shoulders taller than him. Its head was an inverted wedge in which two red eyes gleamed.

This was no dream. This was a nightmare. This thing before him had nearly dragged him into the *Pente Akka* once before. Lowellin's warning came back to him:

It wants you alive.

The hunter opened one hand. Quyloc tried to step back, but the wall blocked his way. The skin on its palm began to bubble. Quyloc stared in horrified fascination as small, black things wormed their way out of its flesh. Tiny wings unfurled from them and buzzed.

A second later they launched themselves at him.

Quyloc slapped at them, but there were too many and they were too fast. They swarmed around his head, so thick they completely blacked out his vision.

He felt a sharp pain as one bit him on the upper chest—

And opened his eyes. He was lying on his bed in the dark, drenched in sweat. There was a stinging sensation on his chest.

Gasping, he sat up and fumbled with the lamp on the table beside his bed. He got it lit and carried it with shaking hands over to a mirror hanging on the wall.

There was nothing there, no bump, no redness.

It had to have been a dream. There was no other explanation.

Quyloc picked up the spear from where it lay on a table and went out onto his balcony. Dawn was spreading in the east. The wind off the sea was cold. Far below, the waves crashed against the foot of the cliffs.

It *was* a dream, wasn't it?

What if it wasn't?

He hadn't been back to the *Pente Akka* since he made the spear. It had been a tremendous relief, knowing he'd never had to go to that cursed place again.

It *had* to be a dream. Otherwise, how did he leave, without some way to cut through the Veil?

He felt cold and sick inside. Had the place found some new way to get its hooks into him?

"You did it. You found your weapon."

Quyloc jumped in surprise, then turned around. "I wondered when you would show up again."

Lowellin came forward, the black staff gripped in one hand. He looked as unremarkable as ever, like an ordinary old man with short, white hair and plain clothing. But there was something in his face that belied that. It was stone, made to look like flesh, but lacking something vital, the lines and creases that inevitably mark a face as it ages, gives it depth and personality.

"That's close enough," Quyloc said, stepping back. He had the spear in both hands, angled across his chest, ready.

"I only wish to see the weapon closer."

"Or you think to take it from me, now that I secured it for you."

Lowellin's stone face hardened fractionally. "Don't be a fool. If I wanted to take it don't you think I already would have? What door or lock can stop me?"

He was right. Lowellin seemed able to appear anywhere he chose. But that didn't mean he wasn't playing a deeper game.

Lowellin folded both hands on top of his black staff. "The weapon is not for me to wield. It is for you."

"I thought you didn't care whether I succeeded or not, now that the Tenders are doing so well with their *sulbits*."

Lowellin went to the balustrade and stared out over the sea. "The Tenders are becoming a powerful force, it is true. But...new developments have forced me to reevaluate my plans."

"Or is it just that you're worried I might use it against you?"

Lowellin's head turned and there was a look of pure, elemental rage in his eyes. A moment later it was gone, hidden away once again. "So it has occurred to you that a weapon powerful enough to threaten Melekath could also be used on me."

"Yeah, it has."

Lowellin's next words surprised Quyloc.

"Do you know what I am?"

"The Tenders think you're a god."

"But you don't think that."

"I'm starting to think there are no gods."

Lowellin gave him an inquiring look. "Go on..."

"I've been spending some time in the library. Perganon showed me a book written by a Sounder long ago." Sounders were people who worshipped the sea and claimed to be able to speak with the creatures who dwelled in it. They were presumed to be extinct now, ruthlessly exterminated by the Tenders during the time of the Kaetrian Empire. "The one who wrote the book told an interesting tale of beings that fell from the sky. He called them Shapers, and said that one day they would be called gods. I think you're one of those, a Shaper, probably a *pelti* from the Sphere of Stone."

Lowellin nodded. "Interesting. But then, they are only words, are they not? They do not change the fact that I am immortal and possessed of powers you have no comprehension of."

"True. Nor do they change the fact that this weapon, here in my hands, can kill you. So let us say, instead of immortal, that you are ageless."

Lowellin cocked his head to one side. He seemed genuinely curious when he asked, "What do you hope to gain by threatening me?"

"What do you hope to gain by coming here?"

Lowellin nodded, as if Quyloc had provided a real answer. "We still face a common enemy. Whatever you may think of me, *I* am not a threat to end all life on this world."

"Yet we have only your word that Melekath *is* a threat to do that."

The anger returned then, Lowellin's hands tightening on the staff. "You know of the Guardians, what they are doing. Kasai in the northwest, raising an army. Gulagh in Nelton, enthralling people. You've seen the effects of the poison that they have introduced into the River itself, people dying, being driven mad. An entire city, Veragin, found dead of it. Can you look at all that and still doubt me?"

"I don't doubt that Melekath is a threat. The question is how much of a threat *you* are."

"I spoke of new developments. I have learned something recently, something that makes our situation even more dire than I previously realized. You saw the clouds of smoke and ash in the sky to the north. Do you know what caused it? It was caused by the death of Tu Sinar, one the gods—or Shapers, if you will—who imprisoned Melekath."

Quyloc couldn't be sure, but he thought he saw a flash of real fear in that stone face before it was hidden quickly. Interesting. Did Lowellin fear that what was used on Tu Sinar would be used on him?

"How did Melekath kill him?"

Lowellin moved to one of the chairs and sat down. "He used creatures taken from the abyss."

Quyloc sat down as well. "What's the abyss?" he asked wearily. Wasn't it bad enough they fought a god?

"It is a place at the center of the world. A place whose very nature is anathema to this world."

"And Melekath was able to take creatures from there and use them to kill another god?"

"Not Melekath, one of his Guardians. I believe those creatures will be set loose on the rest of the gods who imprisoned him, now that he knows what they can do. *Now* you see why I am here. I admit that I dislike you immensely. I admit that you angered me and I gave up on you, left you to live or die on your own. Patience has never been a virtue I aspired to." His depthless gray eyes bored into Quyloc. "But none of it matters now. We have to fight together or we're doomed."

He pointed at the spear. "That weapon might be our only chance. Somehow, against everything that I would have thought possible, you killed the *rend*, a creature nearly as powerful as the *gromdin*, the being which rules the *Pente Akka*. That one act changed everything. That weapon is powerful enough to kill even Melekath, especially if you hit him as soon as he emerges from the prison."

Quyloc looked at the spear. The slightly curved tooth, nearly as long as his forearm, was melded seamlessly to the shaft, which had once been a piece of wood, but now looked more like stone.

"We have no more room for petty bickering," Lowellin said. "It's time to put that behind us."

Slowly Quyloc nodded. "How does it work?"

"I don't know for sure. All I know is that the *Pente Akka* is poisonous not just to flows of LifeSong, but to the power of the three Spheres of Stone, Sea, and Sky as well. It is why I cannot wield it."

"Then how come I can?"

Lowellin shrugged. "I don't know."

"There's one other problem." Quyloc told him what had happened during the night.

When he was done, Lowellin said, "And there's no mark on your chest where you were bitten?"

"No."

"You must have been dreaming."

"Do you dream?"

Lowellin gave him an odd look. "I don't sleep."

"If I keep having dreams like that, I won't sleep anymore."

"Don't worry about it. There's no way you can be dragged into the *Pente Akka* against your will. Nothing inside there can reach across the Veil, even though the *gromdin* desires nothing more than that."

"Why me?" Quyloc asked, though he knew the answer. "Why is that place so interested in me?"

"Because you have proven your strength. The *gromdin* has trapped others in that world before, but they weren't strong enough and died before it could draw enough Song through them to shred the Veil. You might be the one it needs to succeed. Additionally, by killing the *rend* you have proven yourself a threat. No doubt the *gromdin* would like to eliminate that threat."

"So by succeeding I've just made myself a target."

"Yet another reason why we need to work together."

"You're sure it was just a dream?"

"Of course I am. I've been studying that place for millennia."

"This isn't going to be like the last time, when there was that chain attached to me and the hunter almost pulled me through the Veil?"

"That happened because of the wound those birds inflicted on your spirit-body. The wound let some of your Life-energy drain out into the place. There was no chain, actually, that was just the way your mind interpreted it. It was simply your Life-energy—Selfsong,

17

to use the Tender term—that was slowly draining out of you. That can't happen this time because you didn't actually go there."

"I hope you're right."

Lowellin got up. "I need to learn more about the creatures the Guardian used to kill Tu Sinar, so I won't be around much. Keep that weapon safe and do not use it. You remember what happened when you killed those assassins with the bone knife."

Of course Quyloc remembered. Some sort of hole opened into the *Pente Akka* and through it he saw the *gromdin* for the first time. It wasn't the sort of thing he could forget even if he wanted to.

"How long do you think we have before Melekath finishes breaking open the prison?"

"A few months at least."

"That's something."

Lowellin left without replying, walking through the door into Quyloc's quarters. When Quyloc followed him a moment later, Lowellin was gone.

Quyloc looked at himself in the mirror again. There was still no mark from the bite. Lowellin must be right. It must have been a dream.

Quyloc needed to talk to Rome. He should be in the audience chamber. Twice a week he spent the morning there, listening to the problems of his subjects. If he hurried, he could get there before Rome started.

There was already a long line in the hall outside the chamber, but Quyloc saw with relief that the doors were still closed. That meant he'd be able to speak to Rome without having to listen to any supplicants. Rome was fussy about being interrupted, said he'd made an oath to himself to never forget his people. Once Quyloc needed to talk to him and had to wait while some old woman told Rome an endless story about her pigs that kept getting into her neighbor's garden. Most of her story was just rambling nonsense and Quyloc would have sent her on her way after just a few seconds, but Rome sat patiently through the whole thing.

As usual, there was a wide variety of people in the line, merchants, farmers, shopkeepers, tradesmen. At the very front of the line was a beggar, his shoes little more than rags, pants and shirt torn and badly stained. Next in line was a noblewoman wearing a satin dress, her hair piled up in a towering, powdered mass on top of her head.

The beggar was talking excitedly to the noblewoman and—Quyloc had to look twice to be sure—waving about a dead possum as he did so, using it to punctuate his words. The noblewoman had backed as far away from him as the line would allow and she had a scarf shoved tightly up against her nose, while her eyes darted this way and that, following the possum's progress. Beside her was a middle-aged manservant who kept trying to interpose himself between his mistress and the beggar, but every time he did so the beggar shifted to keep an unobstructed view of the noblewoman.

The guard at the door opened it for Quyloc and he went through into the audience chamber. During Rix's reign there'd been a throne on a high dais at the far end of the room. Not his official throne, but still a fairly imposing piece of furniture.

Early on, Rome tipped the throne over so it crashed down the steps and broke into several pieces. Then he'd had the dais torn out.

"I won't sit above my people like some kind of god," he'd said. "When they come see me they'll look me in the eye."

Now there was a large, comfortable chair for Rome, with a couple of other chairs facing it.

When Quyloc entered the room, Rome was just sitting down. To the side was a small desk where his secretary sat with parchment and ink, ready to jot down whatever Rome needed him to.

"Quyloc!" Rome boomed. "Good morning! What brings you here? I thought you hated this."

"I just spoke to Lowellin."

Rome's smile faded. To his secretary he said, "Wait in the other room for a minute, will you?" The man bowed and scurried out. "Sit down. What did he say?"

"You remember that cloud of smoke to the north?"

"How could I forget? It looked like the end of the world." Ash was still falling on Qarath.

Quyloc rubbed his eyes. He felt terribly tired suddenly. "It might be."

Rome sighed. "I don't like the sound of that."

"Lowellin says it was caused by a god dying." Quyloc decided that he'd explain to Rome about Shapers at a different time. Now didn't seem like the best time.

Rome gaped at him. "Did I just hear you right?"

Quyloc nodded grimly. "A god. Dying."

Rome looked pained. "Which god?"

"Tu Sinar."

"I don't know that one. Maybe Lowellin is wrong."

"Tu Sinar was one of the Eight, the gods who built the prison. Lowellin says he was killed by one of Melekath's Guardians, Kasai."

"How? How do you kill a god?"

"The Guardian used some creatures from the abyss."

Rome groaned. "What creatures? What's the abyss?" He rubbed his temples. "I already know I'm not going to like the answer."

"The abyss is some place at the center of the world. I don't know anything more about it except that it's basically poisonous to everything in our world. I don't know anything about the creatures. I don't think Lowellin does either, which is why he's putting a lot of effort into finding out."

"So what does this mean for us?"

"I don't know yet. Not exactly. All I know is that it has Lowellin worried enough that he actually came to me and made nice."

"I thought he hated you."

"He does. But he hates Melekath more."

"Don't you ever have any good news?"

"I do. The spear—the *rendspear*—is apparently a powerful weapon, more powerful than he'd thought I was capable of making. Maybe powerful enough to kill Melekath."

"That's good. Very good. So we just need to be there when the prison breaks open and you stab him and we're done. Right?"

"Something like that."

"Did Lowellin say anything about how long we have before Melekath is free?" This was something he and Quyloc had talked about quite a few times. They'd even considered sending scouts into the Gur al Krin to see what they could learn, maybe set up some way to relay the information back to Qarath relatively quickly.

"He said we still have time. He thinks at least a couple of months."

"There's another bit of good news. We still have a couple of months before the end of the world," Rome said with a chuckle that sounded forced. "Do you think Lowellin is really going to work with us?"

"I do. He looked…worried. He was hiding it, but I think he's afraid."

"I still don't trust him at all, but as long as he's got the same enemy as us…"

"I agree."

"Is there anything else?"

Almost, Quyloc told him about what happened last night, but then he shook his head and left the room.

After all, it was only a dream.

✗ ✗ ✗

After Quyloc left, Rome called to the guard at the doors to go ahead and let them in. As the beggar stepped through the doorway, he tripped suddenly and fell down. While he was still rolling around trying to get up, the noblewoman and her manservant hurried up to where Rome was sitting.

"My Lord Macht," the woman said, curtsying deeply.

"Did you just trip that man?" Rome growled, glaring at the manservant.

"Absolutely not," the noblewoman said. "They may have gotten their feet tangled together, but Hessman here would never stoop to such a thing."

"I didn't ask you," Rome replied without looking at her. "Well, did you?"

The manservant paled. "I…uh…"

"Go to the back of the line."

"What?" the noblewoman cried. "That's outrageous! We've been waiting since sunrise! I demand—"

"What is it, *exactly*, that you demand?" Rome said in a low, ominous voice.

The noblewoman fell back, her hand to her throat. "Nothing," she whimpered. As she and her servant hurried away, she could be heard berating the man.

"I heard of a place where once a year the servants and their masters switch places for a day," Rome said to his secretary, who was just taking his seat. "What do you think of that?"

"Splendid idea, Macht."

"Are you just saying that because I'm the macht, or do you really think so?"

The man hesitated. Rome could see that prudence was wrestling with what he really wanted to say. Finally, prudence lost. Maybe he was finally getting through to these people that he wasn't like old King Rix.

21

"Would that include you, Sire?" the man ventured with just a ghost of a smile.

"I hadn't thought of that," Rome admitted. "Maybe it's not such a good idea."

The beggar stumbled up then. His long beard was matted and his eyes were very red. "Sir, Macht, sir," he said, his words slurred. "I 'ave something to tell you, something I saw."

Rome gestured to him to continue.

"Last night, down by the Pits, I was..." He tapered off. "What was I doing again?"

"Does it matter?"

"No, not really." The man looked down at the dead possum in his hand with a surprised look, as if just noticing it for the first time. He held it to his nose, sniffed it, then made a face. "It's been dead awhile," he told Rome seriously. "Probably not good for eating anymore."

"Is that why you're here, the dead rat?" Rome asked.

"It's not a rat. It's a possum."

Rome looked up and saw the chamberlain approaching with a guard, clearly intending to remove the man. Rome waved them off. Sure, the man smelled bad. He was definitely drunk and probably crazy. But he had a right to be heard too. Still, there were others waiting. "Get to the point," he told the man.

"I saw a woman down there. She was hiding behind this wall. Then a man came by, name of Sots, at least that's what we called him. Probably not his real name. Poor old Sots," he said, wiping his eye.

"The point," Rome reminded him.

"She killed him. She killed old Sots."

Rome sat back in his chair. "This sounds like a matter for the city watch."

"Wait! I haven't told you the worst part!" He fixed his bleary eyes on Rome. "It was *how* she killed him. When he came by, she jumped out and grabbed onto him. She didn't hit him or anything but he just sagged down on the spot without a struggle or nothing."

"Are you sure she didn't stab him?"

The beggar shook his head vigorously. "I snuck up close to see and I..." He broke off. He was shaking visibly. "You don't have anything close to hand to drink, do you?" he said in a loud whisper.

"No. Get on with it."

"There was these two things. They jumped off her and onto him. Things the size of rats, but with too many legs and all the wrong color. I think...I think they was sucking his blood or something." He passed a shaky hand across his brow. "I thought you should know, what with all the weird stuff happening now."

THREE

The five Tenders stood wide-eyed in the midst of the bustling throng outside the gates of Qarath, clinging to each other. People streamed around them, sweating, pushing. Everyone seemed to have somewhere they needed to be, fast.

"Look at all these people," Donae said nervously. "I never thought—"

What she thought was never clear because right then a pig squealed, a man yelled, and two pigs ran right through their group, nearly knocking Karyn down. Cara caught her arm and held her up.

"How are we going to find the FirstMother?" Cara asked. Leaving the Haven without Siena and Brelisha seemed like a worse idea every day. They should have found some way to convince the two older women to come with them. They were lost without their leadership.

Cara's thoughts went back to the day the messenger came to the door of the Haven. He was a young man in leather, riding a drooping horse. The days of hard travel showed in his face. He stood at the door of the Haven that afternoon holding a simple cylinder. It was Cara who met him and when she tried to ask him what it was, who it was from, he simply shook his head and trudged back to his horse. "Don't know. Don't want to know," he said over his shoulder. Without looking back he mounted and rode away.

Cara took the message cylinder back into the Haven and gave it to Brelisha, who was sitting in the common room. Brelisha took it like a woman who already knew what it said. She unsealed it and shook the parchment within into her hand. Taking it over to the sunlight spilling through the window, she opened it and read for a moment. When she was done she stood very still, looking out the window for a long moment before telling Cara quietly to gather the others. When Cara returned, Siena was reading it. She looked grim, but unsurprised.

"It's from the FirstMother. In Qarath." Brelisha sat in a chair to her left, her hair pulled back into its usual stern bun, her hands folded carefully over one knee. She kept her gaze averted, careful not to meet the eyes of any of the women.

"She commands us to go to her."

"But why?" Karyn asked. "What does Melanine want with us?"

"Melanine is no longer FirstMother. Now Nalene holds that title."

"What happened to her?"

"It doesn't say," Brelisha cut in, still without looking at any of them. "It doesn't matter. She commands our presence. Only one thing matters for you all now."

"What do you mean?" Cara asked. "Isn't she summoning all of us?"

Now Brelisha did look up, but she looked only at Siena and they shared much in that glance. Neither answered her.

"But why does she want us to come?" Karyn persisted.

"Melekath," Brelisha said simply. "His shadow rises and she would have the Tenders join together to face him."

"But how?" Cara asked. "What can we do?"

Again Brelisha and Siena shared a look. "Lowellin," Siena said simply. "The Protector has returned. He reforges the Mother's Chosen."

"But this is wonderful," Donae breathed. Beside her Bronwyn was nodding in agreement. "It means…it means the Mother has forgiven us." Her voice trailed off and tears stood in her eyes.

"Apparently," Brelisha said. She did not seem impressed.

"How soon will we leave?" Donae asked. She looked like she wanted to walk out the door right then. Considering she was the one who was most frightened by the things that were happening—she would barely leave the Haven to use the privy—she looked like a woman reborn. There was a ray of hope and she was anxious to follow it.

Siena and Brelisha exchanged another look. Siena took a deep breath and said finally, "This is my home. I'm not going."

Brelisha put her hand on her old friend's shoulder but she wouldn't meet anyone's eyes. She just frowned and shook her head.

"But you have to come with us. We're a family…" Cara couldn't finish.

"I will not take up this fight," Siena said softly. "Not like this. I'm sorry," she said, seeing the look on Cara's face.

"Listen to me," Brelisha said. "You five stick together. Whatever happens, just take care of each other…"

"We just have to ask someone," Bronwyn said, jolting Cara out of her reverie. "It's the only way we'll find the FirstMother." The tall, dark-haired Tender, only a few years older than Cara and Netra, always presented an image of self-contained confidence, but she didn't look so confident now. Her head swiveled, trying to track everyone in the crowd at once and failing. There was a sheen of sweat on her face. She ran her fingers through her long, black tresses and then frowned when they got tangled. None of them had bathed in some time.

"But we don't want anyone to know what we are," Donae put in. "Remember what happened in that little town." Their fourth day after leaving the Haven they had entered a little town. Somehow the people had guessed that the solitary group of females was made up of Tenders and in no time a small mob had gathered and was confronting them, blaming the "witches" for the poison spreading across the land and talking of cleansing Atria of them. They'd had no choice but to hike up their robes and flat out run.

"Let me handle this," Owina said. She was the oldest of their little group, already in her sixth decade. Despite her years, her plump face was barely lined. The gentle smile that seemed always to lurk at the edges of her mouth had always comforted Cara. Alone of all of them she did not look overwhelmed. Cara realized that Owina might have even been to Qarath before. She was already approaching middle age when she joined the Tenders at Rane Haven and she had never spoken of her life prior to that. There was something almost regal in her bearing, the way she spoke and moved, that hinted at a past in the upper crust of society. She might have been a wealthy merchant's wife, or even one of the nobility. Cara and Netra had spent hours when they were little girls imagining that Owina was an exiled princess who had to flee to the Haven to escape a cruel stepmother.

Owina's eyes fell on an old couple skirting along the edge of the crowd, out of the worst of the current of humanity. They carried small packages and seemed untouched by the general chaos. What made them stand out was that they were headed for the gates and most of the other people were heading away.

"Pardon me, good sir," Owina said, touching the man gently on the forearm. "If you could spare a moment for lost travelers."

26

The old couple paused and looked up at her. Both were bent with age, though their movements did not look decrepit. The old man beamed at her. "Lots of those these days, sure enough."

Owina nodded her agreement. The Tenders had seen many other people on the roads in the past days of travel, nearly all of them heading to Qarath and each bearing more outlandish rumors. Most seemed to concern a vast army rising in the northwest and people being burned alive.

"We seek a residence."

"And whose might that be?" Both pairs of eyes stared curiously at her.

Owina looked around, then ducked her head and spoke softly. "The Tenders."

"Really?" The women tensed, but the couple's demeanor did not appear hostile. "Would you be Tenders then too?"

Owina opened her mouth, then drew a breath, clearly unsure. "Ah..."

"Of course you are. And we standing here like ingrates." To the Tenders' astonishment, the old man removed his hat and bent his head, while his wife managed a slight curtsy. The Tenders stared at them as if they had just grown wings.

"You...you..." Owina could not quite get the words out.

"I'll get someone to take you. You don't want me to take you. I walk too slow."

"Okay," Owina managed, her composure returning somewhat. She shot a look at the rest of the group but none of them had anything to offer. "We would be most grateful."

"It's we who are grateful," the old woman said. Her dress was old, but it was clean. Her eyes were very blue and very bright and they sparkled as she smiled. "Bless the Mother for sending you."

At these words Owina lost the power of speech yet again and could only manage a nod of acknowledgement. Her small hands nervously smoothed the front of her brown robe, quite stained and wrinkled from traveling and sleeping on the ground. All the women looked the same. It had not been an easy journey. Only once had they slept indoors, in an abandoned farmhouse they passed. But that night had not been pleasant, due to the large bloodstains on the walls inside the house. There were no bodies, no real clues as to what had happened at the place and the women had spent exactly no time speculating on what happened, trying to avoid even looking at the stains. Still, despite the rough travel, Owina's hair was brushed and tied back neatly.

The old man started to accost a passing laborer when a voice suddenly boomed, "Make way! Make way! Stones for the Temple! Make way!" He was a big man, armed and dressed in leather armor with a plain white cloak thrown over his shoulders. With him were three others, also in white cloaks, clearly guards. Behind them were two wagons, drawn by teams of eight horses. The wagons groaned under the weight of huge, cut stones and the horses were drenched in sweat.

For a crowded street, it emptied quickly, as people actually ran to get out of the way. The Tenders had no choice but to be shoved to the side with everyone else where they watched as the wagons slowly passed.

"Whose temple is it, I wonder?" Karyn said, scratching her head. Her brown, curly hair, usually a frowsy cloud around her head, had clumped badly during their days of travel and she was always scratching it. "Probably Protaxes. The nobility in Qarath worship him, I believe."

People were moving back into the street now and the old man was apologizing profusely to the women for "being rattled and scrapped about like that" while the old lady seemed to be trying to pat the wrinkles out of Owina's dress, as if they had only just happened during the crush instead of during long hours on the road.

The old man seized the arm of a broad-shouldered young man wearing rough, homespun clothing who was hurrying by. "Here, young man. Take a moment and escort these women to the Tender estate."

The young man shook his hand off and started to retort angrily when his eyes fell on the five women and the old man's words finally sank in. Instantly his manner changed. "Of course," he babbled. "Of course. All manner of 'aid and assistance,' like the FirstMother says. I'll do no less." He bowed deeply, twice, and then straightened, but avoided looking at the women directly.

"He'll see you on your way, then," the old man said, patting Owina's arm. "You'll be right." The old woman took Owina's hand and pressed it to her cheek for a second, then dropped it with a whispered blessing when her husband hissed at her.

They began following the young man, who seemed unable to figure out how fast to go. At first he started off too fast and was leaving them behind, but then he shot a look over his shoulder, realized what was happening, and came to a stop. When they caught up to him he started walking so slowly that Bronwyn finally said, "Getting there today would be preferable to tomorrow." Whereupon he picked up speed, but kept shooting looks over his shoulder every little bit.

"I have no idea what is going on," Owina said finally.

"Clearly, times have changed," Karyn said, peering around squinting. She was quite nearsighted and it had been years since she'd had a decent pair of spectacles. She had an ancient pair, but one lens was spider webbed with cracks and she only put them on when she had to. "Our order commands more respect than previously." She was their scholar. Only Brelisha knew more about Tender history than Karyn.

"But why?" Donae asked plaintively. She seemed to be perpetually flinching before a hostile world. She was a small, dark-skinned woman with large eyes and very fine, almost childlike features. Almost every night since they left the Haven Cara had heard her crying in her sleep. She had lost weight too, so that her robe hung on her like a sack. Cara took hold of her hand and gave it a squeeze. She couldn't think of anything else to do. She never could.

"I don't know why," Bronwyn announced, "but if it gets me a bath tonight, then I like it." She scratched her head then looked at her fingers with annoyance, as if they were responsible for the constant itching.

"Perhaps it is our temple they are building," Karyn suggested, then let out a self-deprecating laugh to show how seriously she took such a possibility.

"Sure, and we'll be living in a grand estate like nobility," Bronwyn added. "Where servants bathe us every day."

Overhearing their talk, the young man shot them another wide-eyed look over his shoulder and seemed to be seriously considering bolting, then settled somewhat as Owina gave him a reassuring smile.

"It isn't much further," he blurted out, then lowered his head as if regretting his outburst.

They continued on and the crowds grew thinner, the homes and businesses beside the street ever more grand. The road angled upward, drawing ever closer to the imposing tower that stood at the apex of Qarath, with its back to the sea. The higher they went, the quieter the women grew as their tension increased. This was so far outside the realm of anything any of them had expected that they felt overwhelmed by it.

They came to a wide, brick-laid street lined with palatial estates. The estates seemed subdued, with no activity other than a guard or two stationed out front by the gates. All except one, that is. The gates were flung wide at this one and there was a steady stream of people coming and going. None of them looked like nobility. It seemed to be mostly workmen. To one side was a short line of women of varying ages. They were dressed in a variety of clothing, from simple homespun cloth to fine woolen garments. They seemed to be waiting to get in. Their guide stopped and pointed at the place.

"That's it, then," he said softly, then hurried away so quickly they didn't have time to thank him.

They approached tentatively, still not quite sure they could believe their eyes. The Tenders lived *here*?

"This is going to be better than sleeping on the ground in every way," Bronwyn announced. She shifted the pack on her back and groaned. "The straps on this thing are killing me."

Now Cara could see that there were three women standing clustered together just outside the gates. They carried an air of authority about them that was completely at odds with the women who waited to get in. All three wore white robes. Strangest of all, all three were bald. One of them turned and Cara gasped when she saw a familiar, forbidden shape hanging around her neck. Donae saw it at the same moment.

"That's a Reminder!" she said excitedly. "The others have them too." She paused. "But that means…why are they *bald*?"

Cara's hand went to her hair and from the corner of her eye she saw several of her sisters do the same.

"We won't know until we find out," Owina said calmly, setting her shoulders and leading them forward. "They might be from an outlying Haven, like ours."

"Clearly not like ours," Bronwyn muttered.

They were almost at the gate when one of the women noticed them. She gave them a quick look and pointed at the line of women waiting at the gate. "New recruits wait over there." She was starting to turn away when she seemed to realize something and turned back.

"You are Tenders, answering the summons, aren't you?" Her bald scalp was sunburned and Cara felt as if she couldn't stop looking at it.

"From Rane Haven," Owina answered. "We came as quickly as we could."

The woman looked them over. "Is this all of you?"

Owina nodded. "We are a small Haven and…we have lost sisters recently." Cara noticed that she neglected to say anything about Brelisha and Siena refusing to come along.

"I am Velma," she said with an apologetic smile. "The FirstMother's aide. Anouk here will show you where to go."

Anouk was a skinny woman with freckles and a mouth full of crooked teeth. Like Velma, she was bald, though a bit of stubble had crept back. "It's good to have you. As you can see—" she motioned at the line of women at the gate "—we have no shortage of women seeking to join us. But they're mostly useless." She made no effort to keep her voice down and several of the women in the line heard and frowned at her. "We can use all the soldiers we can get."

Cara blinked and looked at her sisters. *Soldiers?* She had a sudden image of them wearing armor and carrying spears and it was so ludicrous that she smiled. But Bronwyn and Karyn looked very serious and so Cara swallowed the smile and followed Anouk onto the estate. The estate doubtless looked very different than it had under its former owner. Most of the grounds showed signs of neglect, the lawns and flowers turning brown. Several long, rough wooden buildings had been recently erected on one of the lawns and two more were rising next to them. Workers streamed everywhere. Small groups of bald women in white robes hurried here and there. Anouk led them to one of the rough buildings.

"You'll sleep in here." She eyed their packs critically. "At least you didn't bring much with you. Some arrive with a wagon load of their past. The FirstMother hates that. She makes them burn it the first day."

She led them inside. Since the building only had one window and the shutters were closed, the interior was dim. The ceiling was low and Bronwyn had to duck to avoid cracking her skull on a rafter. It was all one long room, with a row of cots lining both sides and a narrow aisle down the middle. On several cots lay folded white robes with dull metal Reminders on top.

"Those are the ones that don't belong to anybody yet," she said. "Pick whichever one you like. Strip off your old clothes and put on the robes. Throw your old clothes in the barrel outside by the door.

They'll be disposed of. Put on the Reminders. No other jewelry. When you're changed, I'll take you over to get your heads shaved."

Donae made a strangled sound and Bronwyn said, "You mean *everyone* has to—"

Anouk smiled and it had a harsh edge to it. "Don't go thinking you're special. We had to do it—" she leaned close "—so *you* have to do it."

She left the building and the women stared at each other. "I'm not sure this is better than sleeping on the ground," Bronwyn said. She was looking ruefully at her hair.

"Well, we do what we have to," Owina said, choosing a bed and sitting down. "At least no one has to worry about washing her hair for a while. That's a benefit, isn't it?"

FOUR

Cara was dreaming of home when the banging started. Netra had just returned and she was telling her how much she had missed her when suddenly she was thrust rudely into the waking world by a horrible noise. She jerked upright and stared through bleary eyes at the tall Tender who was walking up and down the narrow aisle between the rows of cots, holding a metal pot in one hand and whacking it with a long metal spoon.

Dazed, Cara swung her feet down to the cold stone floor, unsure for the moment where she was or even who she was. The dream scattered in bright warm fragments. The cots were so close together there was barely room to stand between them. A lantern sat on a shelf at one end of the room and all around her were other women of all ages groaning and rubbing their eyes. Karyn had the cot on one side of Cara and she was one of the few women who had not risen yet. The tall woman leaned over her and gave her a hard smack on the arm with the spoon. Karyn yelped and sat up, her eyes distant and unfocused. On the other side of her was Owina. The older woman didn't look nearly as regal as she normally did, probably because she was bald.

Sick memories flooded back and Cara reached for her own hair. And was rewarded with nothing. The long blond locks she had been so proud of were gone. For a moment Cara thought she would weep.

But she would not do that. She must be strong. It was what Netra would want. Netra would show up one of these days. She would return, and Cara wanted her old friend to be proud of her. She wanted her to see how she had overcome her fears, how she was a real part of the fight against Melekath. So she pulled her hand away from the rough stubble on her scalp and stood up.

There wasn't much to do as far as getting ready. Like the other women, Cara had slept in the same plain white robe that had been issued to her yesterday. Each woman had two of them, but not night shirts or any other clothing. The material was coarse and itchy and Cara scratched herself as she searched under the bed for her shoes, rough sandals just like all the other women had.

Then she was stumbling out into the predawn along with several dozen other sleepy women. They filed into the estate house and for a few moments Cara forgot her misery as she took in the place. She'd been in the place last night, for dinner, but it still impressed her. They entered through huge, heavy double doors bound in brass. Tile underfoot displayed detailed paintings of birds and flowers. Thick columns reached upwards. Huge arches led off into shadowed halls. Nooks in the thick walls showed where statues had once stood. It was somewhat forlorn, with the rugs, art and furniture stripped from the place, but it was still impressive and far beyond anything Cara had ever been in.

She and her sisters from Rane were the only ones awed by the place though. The rest rubbed their eyes, yawned and passed down the one hallway that was lit. They ended up in the same dining hall, dominated by an immense table, where they had eaten dinner the night before. Breakfast was thick, tasteless oatmeal and an apple, which at least was sweet and crisp. The women set to their food quickly, uncertain under the stern presence of the heavyset woman who sat at the end of the table. Her Reminder was gold, but other than that she was dressed like all the others.

"That's Nalene, the FirstMother," the woman next to Cara said, when she saw her staring. There was a lean, hungry look about her and she seemed nervous. "Favored of the Protector. The first to take the *sulbit*."

"What's a *sulbit*?" Cara whispered. She and the other Tenders from Rane had been put to work right after their heads were shaved. They'd had dinner with the other Tenders, but talking at mealtimes was discouraged and when they got to their living quarters the other Tenders just lay down and went to sleep, so exhausted were they by the day.

The woman gave her an odd look. "You'll find out soon enough. There's no doubt about that."

She turned out to be correct because a few minutes later the FirstMother stood up and began to pace along the long dining table. When she did, every woman in the room ceased eating and watched her, the way a bird in a cage will watch a cat that has suddenly jumped up onto the table where the cage sits. She stopped on the opposite side of the table from where Cara and her friends sat and looked at them.

"Welcome to Qarath," she said. "Welcome to the war."

Her words sent a chill through Cara. Though she knew that was what they were here for, it still sounded unbelievable. They weren't soldiers. They were women.

"You are no doubt wondering what we, mere women, can possibly do against Melekath. Am I right?"

Along with the rest, Cara nodded.

"We will fight with these, our *sulbits*." The FirstMother pulled her sleeve up then and Cara and the others gasped when they saw what was there.

It was the color of old bone and it was about as long as her hand. It had four short, almost vestigial legs, a long tail, and a blunt, rounded head with two tiny black eyes.

Cara looked around and saw that a number of the other women there, probably about twenty altogether, had *sulbits* also that they were holding out in the palms of their hands. None were as large as the FirstMother's and the smallest was about the size of a tadpole.

"Melekath will not find us helpless, will he?" the FirstMother asked.

There was a rumble of agreement from the other women.

"I said, Melekath won't find us helpless, *will he?*" she said, much louder this time.

"No!" the women yelled.

The FirstMother nodded and turned back to them. "Soon, you will receive a *sulbit* as well. But now it is time for morning worship. Stand tall, my sisters. Stand strong. Let the people of Qarath, of all Atria, see that they need not fear. Let them see that the Tenders of Xochitl are ready for the fight."

They walked in double file through the city streets, Cara and the other women from Rane Haven in the back. Along their sides and at the rear marched guards in ring mail, each armed with a short sword, each with a Reminder emblazoned on the breast of his white cloak. Cara glanced at her sisters as they walked. These women were all she had left in a world that made less and less sense. Bronwyn, tall, determined, aloof, lost in her own world. Owina, older, with an erectness and propriety in her bearing that spoke of nobility in her past. Donae, so determined to please everyone that she could never make up her mind about anything. Karyn, the keenest intellect among them, sharp-eyed and thoughtful and prone to argument.

So many were behind her now. Gerath had been the first she lost, killed by Tharn when she and Netra traveled to Treeside. Brelisha and Siena had chosen to stay behind. Jolene had gone off on her own. She just walked off one day and never returned. Didn't take as much as a change of clothes with her. They'd been able to track her as far as a canyon which led down out of the mountains, but there her tracks had disappeared into the soft sand.

And, of course, Netra, who Cara missed every day. The pain of her leaving was still sharp. Cara dealt with it by talking to her. She did it every day, imagining the two of them sitting somewhere peaceful like the bench under the mesquite trees behind the Haven. In her imagination Netra listened carefully and laughed often while Cara told her everything that had happened since she'd left. Cara never allowed her hope to dim. Netra would return some day, when she had done what she needed to do. All this ugliness would end and the two of them would again sit under the trees and talk.

The morning was crisp and almost cold and Cara shivered in her robe. It was surprising how cold her head was without hair and it took real effort to avoid touching her scalp, yet again, to see if her hair really was gone. She wondered briefly why the Tenders needed to cut their hair to fight Melekath, but decided quickly that it was not important. The FirstMother must know what she was doing. It was Cara's job just to go along and do what she was told.

As the women made their way through the streets, people came out of their homes. Many just stood and stared and Cara shivered again, for there was such fear and desperate hope in their faces. Others began to follow until there was quite a crowd behind them. Almost on its own her hand moved to the metal Reminder that hung around her neck. When she and the others from Rane Haven finished changing and went to get their heads shaved each of them had had the Reminder hidden under her robes. Whereupon Anouk had told them that they did not have to hide who they were any more and they were to wear them proudly.

Now she wasn't so sure. The look in the people's eyes, like starving dogs circling a wounded deer, was frightening. They were desperate, and that desperation was fixed too closely on Cara and the other women. Tenders who wanted to grow old peacefully did not flaunt what they were. Too much hostility still lurked beneath the surface. She began to slip the Reminder back into her robes.

"It's not like that anymore," the Tender beside her said. It was the same hungry-eyed woman who had spoken to her at breakfast. "They know we are all that stands between them and Melekath."

Slowly, Cara released the symbol and nodded. She still felt uncomfortable, but as they continued through the city streets she saw that the woman was right. No angry words were directed at the Tenders. None in the crowd sought to hinder them in any way. She saw men removing their hats and lowering their heads, women curtsying, even people falling to their knees, hands reaching up in supplication.

The crowd following them had grown quite large by the time the Tenders arrived at their destination, a square near the edge of the city. A number of buildings along one side of the square had been razed and a large, stone building was being erected in their place. Even this early, workmen were already swarming over the site, climbing ladders, hurrying along scaffolding, pulling on ropes that wound through pulleys, raising blocks of stone into the air. She stared at it wide-eyed for a moment, unsure what it all meant, then realized this must be where the carts laden with stone she and her sisters had seen the day before were headed.

The Tenders arrayed themselves in a double line in front of what was going to be the front entrance to the building. Behind them was a simple wooden platform with steps leading up to it. The FirstMother climbed the steps to the platform as the guards who had accompanied them fanned out to form a barrier between the Tenders and the growing crowd.

"Wonderful, isn't it?" the hungry-eyed woman next to her said. Cara found herself wishing the woman would leave her alone. "Can you imagine? All this for *us*! And to think only a short time ago we lived in dirt and were spat on by trash."

Cara edged away from her somewhat, though she tried to be discreet.

"It was right here, in Seafast Square, that the FirstMother, Mulin and Perast faced a monster from the sea and destroyed it."

Cara gaped at her without replying. *A monster from the sea?* How was that possible? Surely the woman was exaggerating.

As the sun peeked over the horizon, the FirstMother began to speak. She spoke of the coming darkness and of the Tenders who stood between the people and Melekath. The crowd grew larger and Cara began to understand why the guards were there.

There was a hunger in the crowd, as if it was a single animal that crouched before them. But no animal could exude such desperate, frightened energy. This animal had a great need and it was a need that only the Tenders could satisfy. What made the animal terrifying to Cara was wondering what would happen if the Tenders could no longer supply what it needed. She had a sudden image of the crowd surging forward in a massed wave, tearing the few women who stood before it into pieces as it sated its fear and its need on their blood. She fell back a half step. The meager guards would be able to do nothing.

There was a hand on her elbow. It was the hungry-eyed Tender. "Don't be afraid," she said. "Isn't it wonderful?"

After the service Cara found herself beset by the Tender again as they were standing in a loose group, waiting to return to the estate. She was an odd woman, only a few years older than Cara. One shoulder seemed lower than the other, as if something heavy had fallen on her when she was a child. But oddest of all was her gaze. The way she fixed her eyes on Cara was almost voracious. It was as though she could draw Cara in with her gaze and devour some essential part of her, something she lacked that Cara could supply.

"My name is Adira," she said, taking hold of one of Cara's hands in both of hers and not letting go. "I came from Talkir Haven, near Veragin." She said the names as if she expected Cara to recognize them. Cara shook her head. Adira frowned and continued, "Veragin was a cursed city. They worshipped Gorim."

"I've never been to Veragin," Cara said. "I've never been anywhere until we came here. I only got here yesterday." She realized she was babbling, but the woman's stare made her uneasy.

"Just as well," Adira said, still fixing her with that intense stare. "Everyone's dead there. It was only the justice they deserved." She gave Cara an odd, sly smile.

"Everyone in the city is dead?" Cara stuttered.

Adira snorted. It might have been a laugh. It was hard to tell. "Every one of them. People think it was some kind of disease, but I think Xochitl did it to punish them for worshipping a false god."

Cara stared at her in horror. "I can't believe the Mother would do such a thing. What about the children?"

Adira shrugged. "Too late now. All dead."

Cara pulled her hand from the woman's grasp and looked around for someone to help extricate her from this conversation, but she saw none of the women from Rane Haven.

"Everyone on the wrong side is going to pay now," Adira continued. "We're going to make sure of that. That's why Xochitl gave us these." She reached into her robe and pulled out her *sulbit*, held it up to Cara's face.

Uneasily, Cara took a step back. The thing was the size of Adira's thumb, its color the dirty white of old snow. It had no eyes or mouth that she could see. It squirmed there in Adira's palm.

Adira's eyes narrowed. "What's wrong?"

"I just...I'm a little afraid of it is all."

"Aren't you a Tender? You said you were a Tender."

"I am."

"Then what are you afraid of? Xochitl wants us to have these so we can kill her enemies. The Protector says so."

Cara nodded, her eyes fixed on the thing. Something about it made her profoundly uneasy.

Adira thrust it in her face again. "Touch it. Prove you're not afraid of it."

Cara reached out with one hand, trying not to let it shake, and touched the *sulbit* with her fingertip. It was smooth and soft, and just a little bit cold. She relaxed a tiny bit. It wasn't so—

The thing recoiled under her finger, rearing back like a snake about to strike, revealing a tiny, open mouth. Cara jerked back with a cry.

Adira frowned. "What's the matter with you?"

Cara was trembling all over. "It tried...it tried to bite me!"

"Ridiculous," Adira replied, looking at it closely. "It hasn't moved at all."

Cara stared. The thing was motionless as before, its smooth surface unbroken by eyes or mouth. "I guess I imagined it."

"You'll see once you get yours. You'll love yours just as I love mine. It talks to me, you know. I can hear it inside."

"Okay," Cara said. She didn't know what else to say.

The call came to line up for the walk back to the estate. As she moved away, Adira whispered, "I think we're going to be friends. I like you."

FIVE

"So you probably have a lot of questions," Velma said. The Tenders from Rane Haven were gathered around her on the grounds of the Tender estate.

"What, exactly, is a *sulbit*?" Karyn asked, peering nearsightedly at her. "I have never come across any mention of them in all the books I have read."

Velma frowned, her nose wrinkling. She scratched her sunburned scalp. "I should have known you'd ask that one first," she said ruefully. "The truth is I don't know. I've wondered the same thing myself. All I know is that you go up into the ruined temple in old Qarath and Lowellin is there and he pushes you *beyond* and then this black thing wraps around you and takes you to the River and that's where you get your *sulbit*. It's some kind of creature that lives in the River." She paused and looked at them uneasily. "Does that help?"

"I have even more questions than before," Bronwyn said.

"Oh dear," Velma said. "I knew I should have had Anouk do this. She's lots better at it than I am, but the FirstMother has been saying I need to be more involved or what kind of second-in-command am I so I thought…"

"Who is Lowellin?" Donae asked.

"He's the Protector," Velma said, nodding vigorously. She seemed happy to be asked a question she could answer.

"*The* Protector? From the Book of Xochitl?" Karyn asked.

"The same one. He's come to get us ready to fight Melekath." Velma's smile disappeared and she looked down. "Though I don't know if I'll ever be ready. I'm really very bad at controlling my *sulbit*."

"Can we see your *sulbit*?" Bronwyn asked.

"Of course. Here it is." Velma reached inside her robe, then frowned. "Where did it go?" she murmured. She started patting herself down. "I know it's here somewhere, I can feel it, it's just, it moves sometimes and oh, this is so embarrassing..." She patted her left arm and her face lit up all at once. "Here it is!" She reached into her sleeve and pulled it out triumphantly. "That's a bad *sulbit*," she told it. "Hiding from me like that."

The other Tenders all moved closer to get a better look at the thing but Cara stayed back. Touching Adira's *sulbit* had been enough for her for one day. As if thinking of the odd woman summoned her, she looked off to the side and saw Adira standing by one of the rough wooden barracks, staring at her. Cara turned away.

"Was it scary, going to get it?" Donae asked. The small woman was looking at Velma's *sulbit* with horrified fascination.

Velma looked around to make sure no one was listening, and lowered her voice. "I was terrified. I thought I was going to faint." She put her *sulbit* back inside her robe. "But I'm afraid a lot, so that probably doesn't mean anything. The FirstMother says I need to stop acting like such a baby."

Donae shivered. Owina patted her on the arm. "It's okay," the older woman said. "I'll come with you if you want."

"Oh, the Protector doesn't allow that. You have to go alone."

Donae gave Owina a stricken look. "I'm sure it's perfectly safe," Owina told her.

"As long as what happened to Lenda doesn't happen to you," Velma blurted out, then clamped her hand over her mouth.

"What happened to Lenda?" Donae fairly shrieked. "Who's Lenda?"

"I'm sorry," Velma babbled. "I'm not supposed to talk about her."

"I think it's too late for that," Bronwyn said sternly.

Velma looked all around, then lowered her voice to a whisper. "Lenda was—*is*—a little simple, you know? Like a child in a woman's body. She just couldn't handle her *sulbit* and it...it..." She broke off. "I shouldn't have said anything. You shouldn't worry. You'll all be fine."

"*What* happened to her?" Bronwyn said. Her voice was calm but authoritative and Velma melted under it.

"It took control of her. She ran away."

The women of Rane Haven stared at each other, grappling with the implications of her words. Donae spoke first.

"I want to go back to the Haven!" she wailed.

"Nonsense," Bronwyn said. "It's too late for that."

"But I don't want one of those things controlling me."

"It's not like that," Velma said. "You can do it. If I can, you can. Believe me. It's just that…well, they don't know how to move around when they first come out of the River. The Protector says it's because they don't have bodies there. So when they want to do something, like when they're hungry, they try to get you to do it. But you'll learn how to control it, just like I'm learning. You just have to be firm. It's hard when you first wake up but most of the time it's okay." She stared at them earnestly, willing them to believe.

"What happens when you wake up?" Donae asked.

"It's nothing, really. When you're still sleepy and not really there yet sometimes your *sulbit* can make you do things. But don't worry, because mostly they just want to feed on your Song."

"They *feed* on your Song?" Donae shrilled.

"It's just because they're hungry. They're always hungry. That's why we feed them every day and as long as you do and you learn to control them it's really not much of a problem."

"I don't want something that's going to try and eat me during the night!" Donae said, her eyes very large.

"Your *sulbit*'s not going to eat you," Velma reassured her. "It would have to be much bigger and stronger before it could do that."

"They're going to get *bigger*?"

"This isn't going well at all. Forgive me. I shouldn't have said anything."

"Back to what you said before," Karyn said. "I take it to mean there's some kind of mental link between you and your *sulbit*."

"I guess. At least, I can feel it there, in the back of my thoughts. In some ways it's really kind of comforting, like a friend who's always there."

Donae didn't look convinced at all.

"There's other good things too," Velma added. "I can hear Song all the time now, and I never could before. I can go *beyond* easily. I can't really take hold of a flow and fire a Song bolt yet, but one of these days I'm sure I will." She didn't actually sound sure to Cara, more like she was trying to convince herself.

"What is Song bolt?" Karyn asked. She was clearly fascinated by all this.

"It's when you bleed Song off a flow and then let it build up until you can shoot it at something, kind of like a little lightning bolt. The Protector says we're going to use them on Melekath." She looked

42

around at all of them. "Does that help? You're not still frightened, are you?"

Most of them shook their heads but Donae said, "I still am. I don't feel any better at all."

"Stop being a child," Bronwyn told her sternly. "You're a Tender, aren't you?"

"Yes," Donae said meekly.

"This is a war. It's not supposed to be easy. It's going to be hard. It's going to be frightening."

"Okay."

"But you have us. We're all here with you. We're all going to help you." She looked at the rest of them. "Aren't we?"

"Of course we are," Owina said, and the rest echoed her.

"I just don't want to go first," Donae said.

"I'm sure you won't have to," Owina said.

"*I* want to go first," Bronwyn said. "I'm excited." Cara wasn't surprised by that. Bronwyn had always been bold and confident. She was like Netra in that, just not as rebellious.

"It looks like some Tenders are going to feed their *sulbits*," Velma said. "Let's go watch. You'll learn a lot."

They walked over to where a group of Tenders were standing around a bull shatren. A tall, dark-skinned woman was in charge of the group.

"That's Mulin," Velma said softly. "She was one of the ones who killed the sea monster. Her *sulbit* is already very strong."

Mulin pointed to one of the Tenders and said, "You first."

The woman, plump with red hair, walked up to the bull hesitantly.

"Remember, don't let your *sulbit* feed until I say to," Mulin said. "This is an excellent opportunity to exert control over your *sulbit* and teach it who is in charge. Begin when you're ready."

The red-haired woman took her *sulbit* out of her robe and held it in the palm of her hand. It was quite small, hard for Cara to see from where she stood. Though it didn't move, it seemed to her that she could feel it become suddenly alert.

"Move your hand until it is only a couple of inches away, but no closer."

The red-haired woman moved her hand closer, closer.

"That's enough," Mulin said.

At first Cara thought the red-haired Tender didn't hear her because her hand kept drifting closer. But then she saw the strain on the woman's face and knew she was having trouble.

"Fight it," Mulin said. "Remember that you're in charge."

The woman's hand shook and she bit her lip. Still her hand drifted slightly closer. She put her other hand on the bull and with a great effort managed to pull her hand back a couple of inches.

"Good," Mulin said. "Hold it there. Hold it." She waited a minute, then said, "Now, move it closer again."

This back and forth went on for several minutes and then Mulin said, "Now for the hard part. You're going to let it feed, but you have to be ready to stop when I tell you to. Are you ready?"

The red-haired woman nodded but didn't look at her. All her concentration was on her *sulbit*.

"Go. But do it slowly, at your speed, not its."

The woman's hand shook as she let it move slowly toward the bull. She turned her hand over and pressed her *sulbit* against the animal's back. The bull's head jerked up and it bellowed.

An unpleasant feeling started in the pit of Cara's stomach as the *sulbit* began to feed. Her knees grew weak and she staggered to the side, bumping into Karyn. She heard voices speaking to her but they seemed very far away. A great dizziness was growing in her and she blinked, trying to clear her vision.

The next thing she knew she opened her eyes and saw a ring of faces staring down at her with concerned looks.

"You fainted," Karyn said, as if she were pronouncing a diagnosis.

"Are you okay?" Owina asked.

"Of course she is," Bronwyn said, extending her hand. Cara took it and she helped her to her feet. "You're probably just still tired from the long journey here."

"I don't think so," Cara said. She felt nauseated and still wobbly. She didn't have to look to know the woman's *sulbit* was still feeding. More than anything she just wanted to get away. "If I could just sit down for a minute."

They led her over to a bench and she sank onto it gratefully.

"Someone get her some water," Donae said. But she made no move to get any and neither did anyone else.

"What happened?" Owina asked.

"I don't know. I just felt dizzy all of a sudden and then…"

Karyn felt her forehead. "You don't have a fever."

Velma said, "Here comes the FirstMother."

Everyone went quiet and they parted as the FirstMother walked up to Cara.

"She fainted when the *sulbit* started to feed," Velma told the FirstMother.

"I'm okay now," Cara said, struggling to her feet.

The FirstMother looked her up and down. "How long have you been a Tender?"

"Since I was five, FirstMother," Cara said dutifully.

"Do you understand the seriousness of what faces us?"

Cara nodded. "I do, FirstMother."

"Tharn killed one of our sisters," Donae said, then looked uneasy at having spoken.

"Your vows," the FirstMother said. "Do you take them seriously?"

Cara stood as straight as she could. "I do, FirstMother. No sacrifice too great."

"Good. This is only a momentary weakness. Getting used to the *sulbits* can be difficult at first."

Cara lowered her head. "Yes, FirstMother."

"You are young and strong. Xochitl needs you. The land needs you."

"Yes, FirstMother."

The FirstMother turned to Velma. "She will go tonight to get her *sulbit*. Make the necessary preparations." She turned back to Cara. "Are you ready?"

Cara opened her mouth and when she spoke she meant to agree. She really did. She was Cara, the one who always did what she was told. Netra was the rebellious one. Instead she said...

"No."

The FirstMother gave her an incredulous look. Several people started talking at once. Bronwyn said loudly, "She's just tired from the journey, FirstMother. I am happy to go first."

Ignoring Bronwyn, the FirstMother asked Cara, "*What* did you say?"

Cara was as surprised as anyone. She looked at the FirstMother. She looked at the others, women she had lived her whole life around.

"If she could just wait a day or two," Owina interjected. "She just fainted. She isn't thinking right."

The FirstMother ignored her too. Her gaze was piercing, painful.

Cara took a deep breath, knowing what she was going to say next would have painful repercussions, but also knowing there was no other answer she could give.

"I will not take a *sulbit*."

"She just fainted!" Donae cried.

"To be clear," the FirstMother said, "you would refuse this weapon, brought to us by the Protector himself, to aid in the fight against Melekath. Is this correct?"

Cara swallowed, looked at the others around her. She wanted to say yes. For their sakes she did. But she just couldn't. She wasn't sure why.

"It is," she admitted.

The FirstMother's face darkened and for a moment Cara thought she would strike her. "And why have you decided this? Are you afraid?" The FirstMother's tone made it clear how she felt about the fears of others.

"I think so," Cara admitted, then, "Yes, I am."

"Fear can be overcome," the FirstMother grated. Her *sulbit* had poked its head out of her robe and was staring at Cara with its shiny black eyes.

Cara nodded. Then she swallowed as she tried to find the words. "I didn't say no because I am afraid."

The FirstMother's eyes narrowed. "Tell me why you said it then."

Cara wished suddenly that Netra was there. Netra would know what to say. She was the strong one. But Netra wasn't there, so she said the only thing that came to mind. "They seem wrong to me."

"They are *wrong*?" Nalene growled. "The weapons sent by the Mother to save us from Melekath are *wrong*?"

Cara couldn't breathe. What was she doing? Was she making a terrible mistake? She thought of Netra again. "What if they don't?"

Veins were standing out on the FirstMother's forehead. "What if they don't *what*?"

"What if they don't come from the Mother?" As soon as Cara said the words she knew that was what bothered her. She wasn't even sure what she meant, but she knew she'd said what she really felt.

"The Protector brought them to us. He is Xochitl's most trusted lieutenant."

Now the confusion returned and Cara lowered her eyes again. "Yes. He is."

"Yet still you refuse him?"

Tears started in her eyes and Cara had a moment to feel disgusted with herself. Why did she always cry? Why was she so weak? Why couldn't she be more like Netra? "I do." A moment later she added quietly, "I'm sorry."

"I should have you removed from these grounds immediately."

"She has nowhere to go," Owina said softly. "She can't possibly journey back to the Haven by herself."

The FirstMother looked at Owina, then back at Cara. She stepped forward and put her face close to Cara's. "Very well. Since you are a Tender, I will let you stay, but..." She held up one thick finger in front of Cara's face. "You can no longer sleep with the rest of the Tenders and you will not wear the white robe or the Reminder. You will not speak to the Tenders and they will not speak to you. If you are going to stay here, it will be as a servant."

Cara lowered her head once again. "Yes, FirstMother."

The FirstMother spun on her heel and strode away.

Cara stood there in a daze, feeling as if all the air in the world had just been sucked away. Did that really just happen? Surely someone else had just done that, not her.

"Why did you do that?" Donae's voice was shrill and high pitched with fear. Karyn was beside her, shaking her head. Behind them loomed Bronwyn, her face stern.

"I...don't know."

"Is it because of the shatren?" Karyn asked. "Because you know I've been to a slaughterhouse before and the animals there are much more cruelly treated—"

"I don't think that's it," Cara said. Her tears were receding and she was starting to feel tired.

"Then go to the FirstMother," Bronwyn declared. "At once. Tell her you're sorry. She seems a fair woman. She'll understand."

"We'll go with you. We're your family," Donae said imploringly.

"I'm sure she'll forgive you," Karyn added.

"I don't think you should wait." Donae actually grabbed her arm.

Gently, but firmly, Cara removed Donae's hand from her arm. When she looked up at them she was surprised to find that her eyes were clear. The tears were gone and in their place was a small kernel of resolution. "No. I made my decision and I'm sticking with it."

"But that makes no sense," Donae said.

"You're not thinking clearly," Karyn added.

"You're just upset. So much has happened. Maybe if you don't have to go first," Bronwyn added.

Only Owina said nothing, simply looking at her with sad eyes.

"Stop!" Cara held up her hands and to her surprise they went quiet. She looked at them, really looked at them, and suddenly she realized something. They were just as frightened as she was. So much had been lost. Netra was gone. Siena and Brelisha, the two women who had guided and shaped the Haven for so many years, were gone. They had lost their home. Chaos raged around them. This, the five of them, was all they had left. This tiny family was their last stability. And the thought that they were about to be fractured even more scared them all.

In that moment of clarity, Cara suddenly realized what these women who were her family would do: they would shun her as the FirstMother had decreed. They could not risk doing otherwise. With the realization came a sudden, sharp glimpse of how much it would hurt, how alone she had just made herself. She decided in the same instant that she would not hate them for it. She loved them and forgave them and let them go all in the same moment. This was her decision and she alone would bear it.

"I am sorry, but I have decided this. I will not take one of those things." She did not attempt to convince any of them of her reasons or ask any of them to change their minds. She was still too unsure of her own reasons. She only knew that her decisions felt right to her, however much pain they would cause her.

The repercussions were swift in coming.

Bronwyn was the first. She stepped back and folded her arms. Her face hardened. "So it's goodbye then."

Karyn shot her a look, then stepped back too, giving Cara a stiff nod.

Donae hesitated, still trying to cling to Cara, but a look at her sisters decided her and she turned away hurriedly.

"Goodbye," Cara said, and now she thought she would surely lose to the tears as three women as close to her as any family turned and walked away.

That was when Owina stepped in and enfolded her in a deep hug. "Stay true to yourself, Cara. And know that we still love you, however it might seem."

Cara hugged her back, and then she did cry.

"You're supposed to come with me," someone said, and when Cara turned away from Owina she saw Adira standing there, frowning. "I'll show you where you sleep now."

Cara fell into step behind Adira and they started across the estate. First they went to the rough barracks that she had slept in the night before. Adira handed her a shift made of the meanest cloth. "Put this on. Leave your Reminder and white robe on the bed. Don't touch anything. And hurry."

Wordlessly, Cara did as she was told. When she was done, she followed Adira from the building and along one of the many stone footpaths that lead to the back of the estate. Ahead she saw a neat stone and wood cottage and felt momentarily better. That would not be a bad place to stay. But her hopes fell a moment later when Adira took a fork on the path that veered to the right. Tucked away, almost at the back wall of the estate, was a tiny, rude hut, the sort of place where gardening tools would be stored.

"You sleep here. You eat here. When you're not working, this is where you stay." Her orders finished, Adira just stood there, staring at Cara.

Finally, Cara said, "Is there something else?"

Adira scratched at her damaged shoulder, started to say something, changed her mind, then said, "I don't think we're gonna be friends after all." Then she left, and Cara was alone.

Six

Rome was sitting in a small room just off the kitchens. It was a place for servants and other staff to eat, out of sight of the nobility and the wealthy. Rome liked eating here. He could stop in unannounced, holler into the kitchen for some food, and have something hot in front of him in no time. It was far better than eating in his official, formal dining hall where there was actually a servant who stood at the door and whose job it was to announce Rome when he entered the room. Announce him! Usually there wasn't a soul in there. Why in the world did he need to be announced to no one? And if there was anyone in there, they knew who he was without being told. It was all just stupid. And it took forever to get food there also. He had to wait while they brought him a spoonful of this and a flake of that. A man could die of hunger waiting for something solid to appear. And it wasted his whole day.

Which was why Rome liked this room. The food was quick. It was solid. No one bothered him with fanfare. Why, some of the servants who worked and ate here were finally getting over their fear of him and would actually talk to him like people instead of frightened mice. All in all, it was a great system.

Except for today. Today Rome was just digging into a great pile of meat and gravy when Opus, the chief steward, walked in. Just like that Rome knew the fun was over. He set down his knife. "I am betrayed." He glared at the three servants who were also sitting at the table eating. "Which one of you told him?" he growled. "I told everyone not to tell him."

All three paled and shook their heads.

"None of them told me, Macht Rome," Opus said smoothly. He was dressed as neatly as ever in black and white, with the wolf's head emblazoned on his breast. Every hair was in place and his thin mustache looked almost painted on. His expression was smug and smooth as well. "It is my job to know."

"Of course, it's your job to know. Can't this wait?" Rome asked, gesturing at the steaming food before him. He'd been up since before dawn, meeting with the weapon smiths, talking with the stable master about the horses, overseeing weapons practice in the yard. He was starving. "Can't we set up a meeting or something?"

"Which you would conveniently forget?"

Rome sighed. Opus had him there. That was exactly what he would do. He did whatever he could to avoid the pompous little man. More than once he'd turned a corner in the palace, seen Opus in the distance, and taken off in the other direction. It was hardly dignified, he realized, but the way he saw it he was doing it for Opus' own good. One of these days the steward was going to make Rome too angry and he'd just up and break his neck. Neither of them wanted that.

Rome resumed eating, already telling himself not to get angry, no matter what Opus said. He was only a servant. There was no need to let the man get under his skin. "What is it then?"

"I have taken the liberty of having your possessions moved from the tower to your proper quarters in the royal suite."

Rome stopped with a forkful of food halfway to his mouth, feeling the heat rise in his neck. All resolutions about not getting angry disappeared. "You did *what* with my *what*?"

"I had your clothes and other sundries moved to your actual chambers. Really, Macht Rome, it is time you stopped skulking in the tower and showed the people you are a proper ruler."

"You're saying I'm not a good ruler?" Rome's tone was low and dangerous.

Opus paled slightly and took a half-step back. But he had prepared his battle plan as thoroughly as any general and he would not flee the field so easily. He straightened the tight jacket he wore and brushed an invisible speck from his lapel. "These are frightening times, Macht. There are things the people expect of their leader. You lead men in battle. You know how important it is to show your soldiers—"

"I get it," Rome said, cutting him off. He gave his chief steward an appraising look. The man had planned this well. Caught him when he was eating, knowing that way he wouldn't run off in the middle. Then stuck him with a jab about his responsibility to his people. It was a brilliant strategy, really. Opus was a dangerous opponent, indeed.

"You win. I will move," Rome sighed. He picked up his fork again.

"A servant will show you the way when you are done eating, Macht," Opus said smoothly, bowing deeply and moving for the door. Was that a hint of a triumphant smile on Opus' face? Yes, Rome decided, it was. Opus had won this round and he knew it.

"I don't need a guide," Rome said, trying to salvage something from his defeat. "I've been there before."

"Ah, yes," Opus replied. "The rooms you have been *sleeping* in." Some time ago he had elicited from Rome a promise to sleep in the palace part of the time, instead of always in the tower. Rome had never actually slept in the palace, though he pretended to. What he actually did was go in once in a while and mess up the blankets so it looked like he'd slept there. "Those were not actually the royal suite."

"What? Those weren't the king's quarters? Why did you tell me they were?"

Opus bowed. "I was concerned that you would be..." He hesitated for just a moment. "Uncooperative. If you saw the true quarters. They are somewhat more opulent than you prefer."

When Rome had finished his food a silent servant led him down hallways and up stairs, through anterooms and across galleries, until he was thoroughly turned around. "I'll never be able to find this place again," Rome growled. "I don't think I've even been in this part of the palace before. Why is this Bereth-cursed place so big?"

The servant shot him a frightened look over his shoulder and scurried on.

Opus appeared suddenly at the top of a short flight of stairs. Behind him were open double doors. "Right this way, Your Majesty."

Rome fixed him with a glare. "What did I say about that 'Your Majesty' clatter?"

Opus lowered his head in recognition of the rebuke, but the faint smile did not leave his face and Rome had to stifle the all-too-familiar urge to throttle him. Rome clumped up the stairs and into the open doors, where he stopped and stood with his mouth open. "You could stable horses in here," he said at last.

That got to Opus. A stricken look appeared on his face. "But you won't, right? You'll leave the horses outside? I don't think you could get them up the stairs."

"Oh, I can take a horse anywhere," Rome assured him with a huge smile. It felt good to have the balance shift back to him. "I can show you right now if you want."

"No, Macht," Opus said weakly. "I have never doubted your abilities. I only meant that I thought the horses would prefer to remain with their own kind."

"Sure you did."

The room Rome found himself in was massive. On the far side were more double doors, opening to a long balcony with potted trees and flowers on it. On one side of the room was a giant bed, buried under a mound of silken pillows and tassels. There were four large wardrobes and thick rugs on the floors. But what drew Rome's attention first was the mirror. He walked over to stand in front of it. It was very large, taking up a great deal of the wall, and enclosed in an ornate, gilt frame. Below it was a long table with drawers. On the table was an impressive array of combs, brushes, bottles of scented hair oil, powders, scissors and a few things Rome didn't recognize but might have slipped up here from the torture room in the dungeon.

"Look at that mirror," he said with a low whistle.

"It is impressive, is it not?" Opus said with pride. He actually caressed the frame.

"That's not what I was thinking. What's it for?"

"Well, I…" Opus stumbled, at a loss for words. "It is for looking at yourself, Sire."

"Waste of time," Rome announced. "I already know what I look like. I'm not likely to forget, am I?"

Opus looked around, saw that the servant had fled and realized he was on his own. "Of course not."

"No wonder Rix was such a miserable king," Rome continued. "If he spent all day in here staring at himself." He began pawing through the implements laid out in neat rows on the table. "I won't be needing any of these. Useless, useless." He came on a large brush with a silver handle and picked it up. "I could brush Niko with this." Niko was his favorite horse.

With a small cry Opus plucked the brush from his hand. "Please don't jest so, Macht. This is very old. It was a gift from the king of Karthije over a hundred years ago."

But Rome was already moving on, surveying the four wardrobes. "All my clothes put together won't fill one of those," he said. "I guess I could use one for my armor and weapons. That still leaves two. Even if I brought my saddle and all my tack in I'd still have one left over."

"Oh no, Macht," Opus assured him, moving swiftly to the first one and throwing the doors wide. "These are already full. You can leave your saddle in the stable, I assure you."

Rome pushed past him and leaned into the wardrobe. "What's this? Clothes? Who has this many clothes?"

"They are yours, Macht."

"Mine? When did I order all these?" Rome asked suspiciously. He pulled out a bright red shirt with two rows of silver buttons, wrinkled his nose and tossed it on the floor. "I can't believe I'd ever get drunk enough to order this."

"They belonged to the late king, Sire. Of course, I have had them all cleaned and altered so that they will fit you."

"Why would I want that old tyrant's clothes?" Rome pulled out a yellow shirt with ruffles on the sleeves and let it drop on the floor as well.

Opus struggled to find firmer ground. Like any general, he could tell when he had lost the initiative and was on the defensive. "You never ordered anything else so I didn't know what to have made for you. And attire such as this is extremely expensive. I know you are a thrifty man so I thought it wiser to refit than repurchase."

Rome paused and grunted. "That makes sense." Opus straightened. "But I still don't want all this. Here, let's make some room for my stuff." So saying, he took a big armload of clothes out of the wardrobe. Looking around, he saw no good place to put them so he simply dropped them on the floor.

He went to the next wardrobe and opened it. The first thing he saw was the shoes. Dozens of them on little shelves filling the bottom half of the cabinet. They were in all colors. Some had buckles, some had stripes, and some seemed to have small stones set in them. "God," Rome breathed. "These are awful."

"The latest fashions, Sire."

"Not to me. What's in here?" The top half of the wardrobe had little doors covering its contents. Rome opened them and nearly staggered backwards. "What in Gorim's blackest nightmares are those?"

"Wigs, Sire. Made from the finest maidenhair." Opus said it wearily, clearly knowing what reception he would get.

"Wigs, eh? I thought something crawled in here and died." Rome took one gingerly between his thumb and forefinger, and pulled it out. It was blond and curly. Rome gave it a little shake, as if expecting it to come to life and bite him. Then he tossed it back and turned around.

"Well, I will stay in here, if that will make you happy, Opus," he announced. "But you'll have to get rid of this stuff. Give it to some orphans or toss it out to let the dogs chew on. I don't care. Now, I have things to do."

"But you haven't seen the other rooms," Opus protested.

Rome stopped and swung around. "Other rooms, you say?" His eyes fell on closed doors on either side of the room. He shook his head. "Another time, maybe."

SEVEN

"Just more of the same," Quyloc said. He was sitting at his desk, Rome across from him. After leaving Opus, Rome had gone to his office to speak with him and Quyloc was telling him about his latest meeting with the delegation of nobles. It was always the same three nobles, led by Lord Atalafes. Ever since Rome left with the army on the summer campaign they'd been coming to see Quyloc every few days.

Quyloc ticked the points off on his fingers. "They're unhappy because they weren't consulted before you went on the summer campaign. They're unhappy because none of them hold any rank in the army. They're unhappy because they are not part of any of the decision making."

"It sounds like they have a lot to be unhappy about."

"I'm getting really sick of seeing their faces. I wish I had an excuse to arrest the lot of them."

"Your informants haven't found anything pointing to who was behind the assassination attempt?" Rome asked. The night of the Protaxes ceremony, two men had infiltrated the palace guards and tried to assassinate Rome. Quyloc killed them both with the bone knife.

"Nothing. They covered their tracks too well. But I'm certain Atalafes was one of them. He's their leader. There's no way something like that happened without his knowledge and consent. If you'd just let me arrest him and question him—"

"Not without some evidence," Rome cut in. "I won't be like Rix. While I'm macht no one, *no one*, gets arrested without evidence. I'm not a tyrant."

Quyloc sighed and Rome could see how irritated he was. They'd had this argument too many times before.

"I understand your desire to adhere to the law, Rome, but what will happen to that law if they succeed next time? Because there *will* be a next time, you can count on that. And if they succeed, your precious law will mean nothing because they will regain power and things will go back to just what they were before."

"That's a chance I'm willing to take."

"But is it a chance you're—"

Quyloc broke off abruptly and froze, staring over Rome's shoulder.

"What is it?" Rome asked, looking over his shoulder. There was nothing there. He looked back at Quyloc. His old friend hadn't moved. He leaned forward, over the desk. Quyloc's eyes were open, but they were utterly blank, empty. He waved his hand before his face, but there was no response.

"Quyloc?" Then, louder. "Quyloc!"

Still nothing. He grabbed him by the shoulders and shook him, but Quyloc didn't react.

What was going on?

Then Quyloc blinked. He looked around, but there was no recognition in his eyes at first. Gradually, he returned to himself and put his hands on his desk to steady himself.

"What the hell just happened?" Rome asked.

"I was there."

"Where?"

"The *Pente Akka*."

"Just now? But you were here the whole time."

Quyloc was bent forward, rubbing his temples. "I told you, my physical body doesn't go there. My spirit body is what goes there."

"Yeah, which makes no sense to me and never has. I don't really care either way. Explain to me what just happened and explain it in a way that I can understand it."

Quyloc sat back in his chair and looked at him. "I don't know what just happened. One moment I was talking to you, and the next I was in the *Pente Akka*. I could hear something coming for me."

"How did you get out?"

"I'm not sure. It was like, from the corner of my eye I could see the Veil and there was an opening in it—probably the one I came through—and it was closing fast but I threw myself at it and somehow I made it out." His gaze was haunted. "If I hadn't made it, I'd be trapped there. I'd never get out."

"But why wouldn't you just leave the way you did every other time?"

"Because I didn't have the spear to cut the Veil. Without it I can't get out any more than anything else in there can."

"A whole lot of what you're saying I don't understand. If you need to cut the Veil to get out, don't you also need to cut it to get in?"

"No, I don't. For some reason, from this side I can just step through. But to get out I have to cut an opening."

"Okay, if you say so, I can accept that. But how did you get there to begin with? Didn't you say you have to picture the Veil in your mind or something to go there? Did you do that by accident?"

"No, I didn't do it by accident. I try not to think about that place at all. The place terrifies me. I never want to go there again."

"So something on the other side is doing it, something's dragging you through."

"I think it's the hunter." Quyloc proceeded to tell Rome what happened a couple nights before, how he was there in his dream and the thing stung him.

"Why didn't you tell me this before?" Rome asked when he was finished.

"Because I thought it was just a dream. Lowellin thought so too."

"Obviously it was more than that."

"Yeah."

"What are you going to do?"

"For starters, I'm not going there unarmed ever again." Quyloc stood up and went through the door into his quarters. When he emerged a minute later, he was carrying the *rendspear*. "I'm keeping this on me all the time."

"That works for now, but it doesn't solve the problem."

"You don't need to tell me that."

"I'd say this all has to do with whatever stung you. Somehow it poisoned you or something. The venom is giving the hunter a way to get a hold of you."

"That's what I'm thinking," Quyloc replied.

"So then the question is, how do we get the venom out of you?"

"I have no idea."

After Rome left, Quyloc opened his shirt and looked at the spot on his chest where he'd been stung. There was still no sign of a bite; the skin was unbroken and normal-looking.

He had his spear, but at what cost? Would he ever be free of the place or was it just a matter of time before it trapped him?

EIGHT

Cara paused in her work and sat up to rub her back. She was scrubbing the stone foot paths of the estate, a task clearly designed more for humiliation than anything, as the stones' appearance did not noticeably change with the scrubbing. They also seemed endless, running here and there over the entire expanse of the estate. Her hands were red, her knees and back were sore and there was nothing to look forward to but more of the same. She was working on one of the walkways near the front of the estate, not too far from the front gate, so when the Tenders emerged from breakfast and headed out for the morning service, they passed fairly close to her. Cara looked up as they approached.

At their head was the FirstMother, who did not so much as look at her. Behind her was Velma, who gave her a sorrowful look before turning her face away. Adira stared at her with those intense, burning eyes, an unreadable expression on her face. Near the end of the procession were her friends. Owina looked at her sadly, Karyn seemed not to notice her, and Bronwyn gave her only a short, distant look. At the very end of the line was Donae. She had her hand pressed to her chest and a dazed look on her face. She must have received her *sulbit* last night. It looked like she had been crying.

The women filed out the gate with their phalanx of guards and it occurred to Cara that she didn't have to do this. She could put the brush down and walk right out the gate too. She wasn't a prisoner. They wouldn't stop her.

But in reality there was nowhere to go. She had no friends or family in Qarath. What blood family she'd had was lost in the distant past. There were still Brelisha and Siena, back at Rane Haven, but that wasn't really a choice. She could never travel that far alone. She might as well be a prisoner for all the options she had.

Cara went back to work, surprised that she did not feel more upset about this realization. The truth was she didn't want to go anywhere. Owina, Donae, Karyn and Bronwyn were still her family. That hadn't changed. They had chosen differently than she had, but the facts didn't change. No, she wanted to be here, where she was. This way she could still keep an eye on them. She didn't know if there was anything she could do, but she could at least be here for them.

Cara worked mindlessly for some time, letting the monotony of the work lull her. She was hardly aware when the Tenders returned from the morning service, so lost was she in her own world. It was later, pushing midday, when a commotion at the front gates drew her attention.

Larin had never dreamed leather armor could be so hot. He always thought the soldiers in their leather armor with the rows of metal studs looked strong, powerful. He never thought they were just hot. But he was. Sweat was dripping down his back, gathering under his arms. And the armor chafed too. He was going to have blisters on his shoulders, he just knew it. He shifted the long pike he held to the other hand and reached up under his armor, trying to shift it to a better position.

"Stop fidgeting," Haris hissed. Haris was the other guard on the gate to the Tender estate this morning. "You're supposed to stand still. Don't you know anything?"

"But it's making sore spots," Larin whined. "And I'm sweating. Can't we move into the shade?" The shade was just a few steps away, retreating up to the wall. When they'd first gone on duty a couple of hours ago the shade had stretched clear out to the street. Now it was behind him, and not doing him any good at all.

In answer, Haris slapped Larin on the back of the head with his free hand. "You're here to guard the gate, you nin. Not the wall!"

Larin rubbed the back of his head where Haris had struck him. It didn't hurt, not really. But it was embarrassing. "You're always acting like you're better than me," he complained. "We both signed up on the same day." Larin had come to town with a wagonload of potatoes for the market. Dad hadn't come with him that time, on account of his having a bad ankle from where he stepped in the gopher hole and Ma stayed at the farm to look after him and the little ones.

He'd gotten barely halfway to the market when the wagon got stuck in a huge mass of people gathered in a square and cheering. Larin liked crowds, so he stood up on the wagon seat and craned his neck to see what was going on. Some woman was giving a speech, telling how she and the other Tenders would protect them all from the bad things that were coming. That sounded fine to Larin. He'd seen the people streaming in from the west along the road in front of his parents' farm, and some of them had told him stories. He knew something was going wrong. When the woman finished talking, she said how she and the other women needed strong men to protect them while they fought the badness. Well, Larin got down off the wagon on the spot and pushed his way up to the front. Weren't many who were bigger or stronger than Larin, his folks were always telling him. And he wouldn't mind getting away from the farm either. Dad was always yelling at him and Ma treated him like he was some kind of purblind idiot.

"Maybe we did," Haris replied. "But they put me in charge. Do you remember why?"

"It coulda happened to anybody," Larin said sullenly.

"But it didn't. It happened to you."

So he broke a door. The door to the barracks he shared with two dozen other guards. He thought it was locked. He thought they locked him out to make fun of him. And when he yelled at them to let him in and they all just laughed, he got a little heated. He finally put his shoulder into it and smashed the thing clean out of the wall. That was when the others pointed out to him that the door opened outwards. It wasn't locked; he was just forgetful. It could have happened to anybody.

"I still don't see why we have to stand here in the sun."

But Haris wasn't listening. He was staring at the women approaching the estate.

There were three of them and they came striding up like they owned the place. The one in the lead was dressed in a red robe. Behind her, the other two were dressed in bright yellow robes slashed with black. They appeared to be twins.

When the lead woman's eyes fastened on the two guards, both men took an involuntary step back. Haris's pike dipped. Now Larin really wanted to go stand by the wall. He wanted to hide there, actually. But he remembered his duty. He was here to guard the Tenders so they could concentrate on fighting Melekath.

He stepped forward, one hand held out to stop the women's advance. "Here now," he rumbled. "You can't come in here without permission."

Two utterly cold eyes stared into his. They weren't like human eyes at all. No emotion or feeling at all there that he could read. He flinched before them, but he didn't lower his hand.

"We have business with the FirstMother," the woman in red said without slowing.

Larin reached to grab her shoulder.

She stepped inside his grasp and one hand flashed up towards his face. In the moment before she struck him, Larin saw something glitter from the end of her finger. Then there was a small stinging sensation in his neck and everything went black.

"FirstMother, come quickly!"

Nalene was in her quarters on the top floor of the mansion, working at her desk, when the young Tender arrived breathless at her door. "What is it?" she asked sharply. No doubt it was something minor, a shortage in the kitchen perhaps. Sometimes she wondered if any of them were capable of anything.

"It's...there's someone come to the gate, asking for you," the girl said, and she was hardly more than a girl, with pale blue nervous eyes and pimples.

"I'm busy right now. Tell them to wait.'

"I..." The girl shifted nervously from one foot to the other, but she made no move to leave. "They're not like anyone else. I think you want to see them."

Nalene looked up from her desk and gave her a sharp look. "Did you not hear me?"

The girl hung her head. "I did." Still she did not leave.

With an irritated sound, Nalene got up. The girl backed out of the way as Nalene brushed past her.

As Nalene approached the front gate she saw one of her guards, the big, dumb one, lying on the ground. Standing near him were three women in brightly-colored robes. The woman in red must have heard her because she turned and looked at her. Even from a distance something in her cold, emotionless gaze was unnerving and Nalene faltered for just a moment, before recovering herself.

"He is not dead. Only sleeping," the woman said as she approached.

Nalene looked down at the man, saw the faint rise and fall of his chest. Because of her *sulbit*, it took only a small effort to hear his

Selfsong emanating off him. It sounded healthy enough. "What did you do to him?"

"I taught him not to touch what he does not know. Now he knows. He will be more careful next time." There was a large, red welt on the guard's neck.

Nalene crossed her arms and tried to appear calmer than she felt. Her *sulbit* was a comforting presence curled around the back of her neck, just under her robes. It was awake, watching the woman in red warily. It too sensed something different about her. "You were asking for me." She made it a statement, not a question. However unusual this woman and her companions were, she needed to know that the FirstMother was not a woman to be ordered about.

The woman in red made no reply at first, only stared steadily at her. Some kind of beetle crawled out of the woman's robe and disappeared into her long, black hair. She didn't appear to notice. Behind her the two women in yellow were as motionless as statues, gazing at Nalene with the same unnerving lack of emotion. Everyone around them—the other guard, the Tender in charge of new volunteers, a short line of new volunteers, two workmen with heavy carts—had stopped what they were doing and were staring.

"What do you want?" Nalene hated how thin her voice sounded. She should be in charge of this situation. This woman should be shaking in her presence, not the other way around. A large, heavy moth flapped around Nalene's face, its wings brushing her. She recoiled, slapping at it ineffectively. She had always loathed moths.

"You are the FirstMother."

The moth flapped away and Nalene could again focus on the woman. "Of course I'm the FirstMother. Are you blind?"

"Are *you*?"

Nalene blinked at her. She could get no read on this woman or her companions. The Song coming off them was muted. What little she could hear gave her no clues. With no real clue as to how to proceed, she fell back on angry bluster. "I don't have time to stand here and play games with you, whoever you are. If you won't tell me why you're here, then leave. I have things to do."

She had no sooner finished speaking than she felt something crawling up her leg. She looked down to see that she was standing on an anthill. Ants were boiling everywhere. When did an anthill show up here? Slapping at her leg, she jumped back to get out of it. The woman in red followed and stood right where she'd been. She didn't seem concerned about the anthill at all.

"We are here because you summoned us."

"I *summoned* you?"

"I am known as Ricarn. These are my sisters, Yelvin." The two women behind her appeared identical in every way, both with long, flowing black hair, strangely white skin and dark eyes that might have been black.

A sudden realization hit Nalene. "You're *Tenders*?"

"Of the Arc of Insects."

"But you're...your Arc disappeared in the early days of the Empire."

"Correction. It was the rest of our sisters who disappeared, consumed by their hunger for power. It was then we chose to remove ourselves to a quieter place, to avoid being caught in your fall."

"How did you know to come? I sent no messengers—"

"We have our...friends. We learn much from them."

She raised a finger and pointed. Nalene felt something on her hand. It was a wasp. She shook her hand and it flew away.

"Then you are welcome here," Nalene said, trying to recover her balance. She felt certain the woman was laughing at her inside, though nothing showed on her face. "We need all allies we can get in the fight against Melekath." She turned to the Tender who was screening the women who were lined up to become Tenders. "Anouk. Leave those women there for now. Show our sisters to their quarters and get them their robes and haircuts."

"We do not need quarters. We are quite comfortable outside," Ricarn said. "Nor do we require clothing and our hair suits us as it is."

Nalene felt her anger rise and she welcomed it. Anger blunted feelings of discomfort, feelings of unease that might be fear. "It is not a request. It is an order from your FirstMother," Nalene grated. She felt her *sulbit* slide forward, its skin cool against her neck.

"You are not our FirstMother," Ricarn said coolly. "We do not follow your orders."

Nalene felt her face grow red as her anger burned hotter. She could feel the others looking at her and knew they watched closely to see how she would respond. How much of her authority might be lost, right here, right now?

"Is it necessary to do this now?" Ricarn asked softly, as if she could read her thoughts. "In front of so many?"

"You speak this way to me, Xochitl's chosen representative? What else shall I do?"

"Perhaps it is as you say, that our Arc disappeared long ago. If that is the case, then it follows that we are not actually Tenders, and thus not under your dominion."

"What are you talking about?"

"Would it not be better to treat us as close allies rather than as subjects?"

Nalene thought about this, then gave a curt nod. "For now," she agreed. "But we are not done with this."

"No. I suppose we aren't. What do you call the creature on your shoulder?"

Nalene's hand went protectively to it, though Ricarn had made no threatening move toward it. "It is my *sulbit*. A gift from the Protector."

"Yes, the Protector."

"He has been sent by the Mother to aid us."

"And these creatures are his aid."

"They are. With them we will be able to stop Melekath."

"There is no other way then."

"No. There isn't."

"Then you must do as he says."

"We do it willingly, happy to serve the Mother anyway we can. You'll understand, once you take a *sulbit* for yourself."

Ricarn gave the merest shake of her head. "We have no need of them."

"You would refuse the Protector himself?"

"We answer only to Xochitl."

"Then why are you here? What use can you be?" Nalene challenged.

"That remains to be seen," Ricarn replied, completely unperturbed. "With your leave, we will find ourselves suitable accommodations on your grounds. And we will discover how we can help in the fight."

NINE

"We found another one, FirstMother."

Nalene stopped and turned around. Mulin and Perast stood in the hallway behind her. It was Mulin who had spoken.

"Not here," Nalene said. "Let's go outside and walk." She wanted to make sure no one overheard what the two Tenders had to say. It was still predawn and the Tenders were starting to file into the dining room for breakfast.

When they were outside Nalene led them along one of the many stone footpaths. It forked, and she started to go right, but then she saw the girl who'd refused her *sulbit* scrubbing it so she went left. What she wanted was to find a bench they could sit down on because she suddenly wasn't feeling so well, but there didn't seem to be any on this path. Finally, she just stopped and faced them.

"Drained, like the others?" Nalene already knew the answer, but she had to say something.

"Yes, he was. At least I think it was a he. It was hard to tell from what was left." Mulin sounded shaken. Perast looked pale and she was biting her lip.

"How many does that make?"

"At least five. That we know of," Mulin replied. She wiped her forehead and Nalene saw that she was sweating, though it was still cool. "There could be others. The streets of Qarath run thick with rumors. It is impossible to follow them all."

"Did you see...*her* anywhere?" It was hard for Nalene to say Lenda's name out loud. She still felt guilty. Despite what Lowellin said, Lenda *did* matter. Whatever happened to her was Nalene's fault. She should never have let the girl go for her *sulbit*. She wasn't strong enough to handle even one of the creatures and now she had two.

The two Tenders exchanged looks. "From a distance," Mulin said. "We were by the river, down near Merchant's Bridge. We saw someone climbing up the side of a building on the other side of the river."

"Climbing up the side of a building? Are you sure it was Lenda?"

"Yes. We could hear her Song, only…"

"What?"

"It has changed. Her SelfSong is different. There's something else woven into it."

Changed. Lenda's *sulbits* were changing her. Into what? What was happening to her? Nalene felt sick.

"FirstMother," Perast said, "we could see her *sulbits*. They were on her back and they were big. The size of cats." She broke off and lowered her eyes. Mulin took over.

"We think they were the reason she was able to climb the wall so easily. It was not something a normal person could have done."

Nalene fought to hide how upset she was. "Keep looking for her. Find her. *Help* her."

"What if we can't? Help her, I mean. Should we…" Mulin was unable to finish the sentence.

"No!" Nalene said sharply. "There has to be a way. I don't want her harmed." She said this knowing that if word got out there was a rogue Tender killing people it would hurt the Tenders' standing in the eyes of the people.

But right then she didn't care.

TEN

Quyloc was exhausted. The strain was getting to him. He never knew when the next attempt would come, but already three times he'd been dragged through into the *Pente Akka*. He had to keep his spear always in hand for when that happened and he'd learned to listen for the faint crackling noise warning him that it was about to happen. So far, every time he'd been able to react quickly enough, summon the Veil, and flee before anything attacked him, but it had been close a couple of times and each time it got closer. It was like the hunter was getting better at it.

Sooner or later he was bound to make a mistake. It happened while he was eating. He set down the spear for just a moment to smear butter on a piece of bread. He heard the faint crackling noise, just a fraction of a second before the world began to shimmer and fade. Instantly he grabbed for the spear and got hold of it just in time.

He was back in the jungle, thick trees crowding all around, the hum of insects in the air.

He was about to summon the Veil when there was the faintest rustling sound overhead, the sound of something heavy dragging along a limb.

He acted instantly, without looking to see what it was, throwing himself forward. There was a hiss of air as something struck at the spot where his head had just been.

As he hit the ground, he tucked and rolled, letting his momentum carry him back to his feet and spinning around. In the same motion he brought the spear up before him, and set his feet wide, his weight on the balls of his feet.

A huge snake, its head as big as his, hung from the limb he'd been standing under. It was green tinged with yellow and its dead, reptilian eyes fixed on him, its tongue flicking out.

Then it recoiled and struck at him again. Quyloc twisted to the side, the open fangs scarcely missing him.

Before the snake could recoil he struck, burying the point of the spear into the soft spot just behind the snake's jaw.

The snake hissed and jerked back, so fast he almost lost hold of the spear. It fell from the tree as it thrashed in its death throes, its body easily forty feet long and as big around as a man's torso.

Quyloc saw movement from the corner of his eye and turned his head to see yet another snake gliding along a thick limb toward him. He heard hissing on both sides.

Without waiting to see anymore he pictured the Veil in his mind, then slashed an opening and dove through.

On the yellow sands, under the purple-black sky, he paused and looked back. He could see at least four snakes converging on the spot he'd just left. One of them was closer than the others and Quyloc realized with alarm that although the cut he'd made in the Veil was sealing rapidly, it wouldn't be all the way closed in time.

The snake's head flashed forward and it got its head in the opening just before it closed. It twisted this way and that as it fought to get the rest of its body through the opening.

Quyloc stepped forward and slashed downward with all his strength. The blade cut through the snake's skull easily, nearly cutting its head in half. As it thrashed wildly, he reversed the spear and used the butt to jam it back through the opening. A moment later the rent in the Veil was sealed.

Before Quyloc left the borderland between his world and the *Pente Akka*, he noticed that the spot on his chest where he'd been stung was itching. When he touched it he felt a bump there.

He closed his eyes, pictured his office, and returned there. Back in his office, he walked into his personal quarters and stood in front of the mirror.

There was no bump on his chest, no mark of any kind.

As the adrenalin wore off, Quyloc began to feel really tired. He went out on the balcony and sat down on one of the chairs and thought.

Clearly the hunter had some way of watching him. There was no way it was just coincidence that he'd been pulled through into the *Pente Akka* just after he set the spear down. Nor was it a coincidence that there was a snake just in that spot, ready to strike at him. It was a planned ambush.

So why didn't the hunter pull him through earlier, before he realized he needed to keep a hold on the spear? And how was he able to escape the last time, when Rome was with him in his office?

It had to have something to do with the sting he'd gotten. It must be spreading through him, getting stronger. As it did so, the hunter was better able to see him, to drag him through at just the spot where it wanted him.

Quyloc began to glimpse just how truly dangerous his predicament was. There was no way he could be constantly alert. Sooner or later he was going to make a mistake, and it would be his last.

ELEVEN

Nalene sat on the balcony outside her quarters. There was a low table before her with one chair on the other side of it. The chair she sat in was very simple, but compared to the one on the other side of the table it was a throne. That one had a crack down the middle that had a tendency to pinch the sitter, and one of the rear legs was shorter than the rest. This made it unstable and the result was that anyone sitting in it had to be conscious of her balance all the time. Failure to pay attention could easily lead to a new seat…on the floor. Only a few days ago Velma forgot herself while giving a report, leaned back without thinking, and fell on her back. Nalene thought the chair dealt out useful lessons in humility and alertness.

The balcony wrapped completely around the top floor of the estate house. From it she could look down on the grounds and observe her Tenders while they trained. There was almost nothing on the estate that she could not see, almost nowhere that was safe from her gaze. She liked it that way. She suspected that the estate's previous owner, the late, unlamented Lord Ergood, had felt the same way. Perhaps the man had not been a total idiot.

It was hard to sit there. She had to work to resist the urge to pace. She could not completely deny the fact that she was nervous, and that angered her. She didn't like being afraid. The source of her fear was Ricarn, the Insect Tender, who was hopefully even now on her way here. She'd dispatched Velma to find her and bring her for a talk.

"But FirstMother," Velma had said uneasily, her hands twining around each other restlessly, "that woman makes me nervous. Can't I send one of the others?"

"No, I don't want one of the others to fetch her. I want you. And I want you to do it exactly as I told you."

"But what if she won't come?" Velma was getting dangerously close to whining. In most ways she was a suitable second-in-command. She did what she was told and she had almost no inclination to think for herself. But there were times when Nalene truly regretted giving her the position.

"That is not an option. Her presence is requested by the FirstMother of her order. The request is delivered by the FirstMother's personal aide. You will make sure she complies and at once."

"But the *bugs*. I'm allergic to bees and wasps. Spiders too, I think. What if she turns them on me?"

"That will not happen. She may have some small influence over insects, but she certainly cannot command them like servants."

"But the other women say—"

"If you say 'but' one more time, I will put you to work at the front gate sifting through the latest batch of worthless girls and give your position to Anouk. She, at least, knows how to follow orders."

"Yes, FirstMother." Velma lowered her head. There was some kind of discolored blotch on the top of her scalp. Nalene wondered if it had always been there, hidden by her hair, or if it was some kind of rash from the sun. Being bald wasn't always the most pleasant thing.

"Go now. And hurry. I have much to do."

Now Nalene sat waiting, hoping that Velma actually was successful in bringing Ricarn here. It would look bad if the others came to think the FirstMother had no control at all over the Insect Tenders. Already she had had to spread word—through seemingly careless references dropped in the presence of Velma and Anouk, knowing they were the biggest gossips—that the Insect Tenders had foregone the shaved heads and white robes because she had a special task for them, a task that would require them to be able to blend in with the general populace. It was a weak excuse—the idea of those women with their eerie calm being able to blend in anywhere was ludicrous; they caused a stir whenever they went out into the city— but the other Tenders seemed to have accepted it. For now. Soon enough they would begin to wonder, and shortly after that her control would slip. Nalene did not think she would long retain her position if the Protector thought she could not control her own followers. How could she lead them against Melekath if they did not obey her instantly?

It was for this reason that she had not asked Lowellin for assistance in dealing with Ricarn, though she had seen him only last night. She'd been about to. In truth, she'd found herself spending a great deal of her waking hours thinking about the woman's insolence and trying to figure out how to deal with it. But when she opened her mouth to ask him for his help, she suddenly realized how it would sound and she'd kept it to herself.

Instead, she and the Protector had spoken of the Tenders' progress with their *sulbits*.

"The time draws very close," he'd said. "Kasai's army grows by the day. He will march on Qarath sooner rather than later. This is the only army that can seriously challenge him and it lies closer to the Gur al Krin than his own does. When he does, I want the Tenders ready to crush him. With his army out of the way, we will be free to concentrate on Melekath himself."

"There are perhaps a dozen women who can really control their *sulbits*," Nalene said. "Women that I would trust to back me up in battle. Beyond that, maybe another dozen who can be trusted not to kill themselves in a particularly stupid fashion. The rest would do us more good if they would join Kasai and help him." Nalene was pacing by then. It always upset her when she really thought about how small her "army" of Tenders was. "They are either weak or afraid, and the worst are both. The weak ones have to be helped every time they feed their *sulbits* because they can't stop the creatures by themselves." Controlling how much the *sulbits* fed wasn't just a matter of asserting control over them. They limited how much the *sulbits* consumed because of the concern that if allowed to feed freely, the creatures would grow too fast and become too strong for their Tenders to control them. "And the fearful ones won't let their guard down enough to fully meld with their *sulbits*." Tenders had to be able to meld with their *sulbits* in order to take hold of flows and manipulate them.

At her words Lowellin went to the edge of the balcony and stared out into the darkness. "We don't have time to be cautious. I want you to push them even harder, take even greater risks." He held up a hand to forestall her objections. "Soldiers are hurt and even killed while training all the time. A military commander understands that and sees it as an acceptable loss. You must learn to see it the same way."

Nalene bit back what she wanted to say and nodded her head.

"It's time for you to take the next step. I'm going to teach you how to work together, several Tenders diverting Song to another to make her attack stronger."

Nalene's eyes widened as he spoke and for the next hour or so as he explained to her how it would work she forgot her concerns in her excitement at trying out this new technique.

Nalene's thoughts returned to Ricarn. That woman was neither fearful nor weak. If Nalene could just bring her to heel, there was no limit to how powerful she and her *sulbit* would be.

The door to her chambers opened and Velma entered. Nalene sat still, listening, and was relieved to hear another set of footsteps besides Velma's. Inwardly she relaxed just a little. The first hurdle was crossed. Ricarn had answered the summons. Maybe this would go well after all.

The footsteps halted within the rooms. If Nalene turned she would be able to see them standing there, before her desk. But she did not turn. She was busy. They waited on her, not the other way around.

Finally, Velma said, "FirstMother?"

Nalene smiled inwardly. Velma had learned that she was not to disturb the FirstMother without an invitation. She waited several long seconds, then turned. "Come."

Velma walked onto the balcony, followed by Ricarn. For a moment Nalene thought she saw a hint of a smile on Ricarn's porcelain face—was she laughing at her?—but it was only her imagination. It was possible that Ricarn had never smiled in her life.

"Please, sit," Nalene said, gesturing at the wobbly chair. "Velma, you may go. If I need you later I will ring." Velma slept in one of the servants' quarters, where she was easily summoned by pulling the bell cord.

Ricarn sat down. Unfortunately, the irregular legs on the chair had no apparent effect at all. The problem was that Ricarn did not sit as a normal person would, but seemed almost to alight on the edge of the chair, where she watched Nalene with a steady intensity that was frankly unnerving. It was like having a giant praying mantis watching her.

Nalene reached for the words she had rehearsed for this moment and realized they were gone. Her mind was a blank. She cursed herself. She had planned to match Ricarn's calmness, flavoring it with magnanimity. She was loftily prepared to offer concessions to an unruly subordinate and be gracious in her treatment of the subordinate. Instead, she hadn't even started talking and she was already rattled. She took a deep breath and thought furiously. Then she remembered.

"I realize we started with the wrong hand the other day, and I wanted you to come up here so we could start over. I may have come down a bit harder than I should have. You are a leader. Surely you understand the demands of leadership. It is not an easy task and even the best of us can become cross and take it out on others." She paused. At this point a normal person would nod or frown. Do something. Anything. But still the praying mantis watched her.

"So I…I wanted to offer my…" She could not say 'apologies'. That sounded weak. "…my regrets. You no doubt came far and deserved a better welcome than I gave you, a woman of your standing." Still there was not the faintest flicker of emotion. Nalene wanted to scream.

"I am even willing to forgo my usual requirements regarding attire and…" She gestured toward her bald pate. "Since it is entirely possible that they go contrary to your Arc's beliefs." She was starting to feel desperate. Why wouldn't the woman say something? "It could even be argued that the reasons for these measures do not apply to your Arc and, as such, are unnecessary for you and your women." She sat back. Surely now Ricarn would say something. She was the FirstMother, after all. And she had just granted her a concession that any other woman on this entire estate would climb over her sisters to receive. They were not fond of being bald.

Silence.

"Have you nothing at all to say?" Nalene said, forcing a smile.

"We do not need such things."

Nalene started to come to her feet, then caught herself. "*What*?"

"We do not need your *sulbits*. Furthermore, we will not take them. That is what you were leading up to, isn't it?"

Nalene spluttered. She could feel her *sulbit*, fully awake. It had slid down her arm and waited in the shadows of her sleeve. She sensed its hunger. "I just offered you a serious concession!"

"So that you could pressure me to agree to take one of those things."

Now Nalene did come to her feet. She loomed over Ricarn, who still did not seem to have moved, except to tilt her head to meet Nalene's eyes. "You cannot fight Melekath with bugs!" she yelled.

"You cannot fight him by deluding yourself."

"And what is that supposed to mean?"

"Look at what you turned into. Little more than strays, begging for handouts, the smallest kindness."

Nalene drew herself up. She longed to set her *sulbit* free to feed on this insufferable woman before her. "You have no idea what we went through to survive. It was…" She struggled to find a word to express her feelings on this subject. "The humiliation was more than I could bear," she finished. "But there was nothing we could do about it. We were outlawed, the lowest of the low."

"Which made you perfect when Lowellin showed up and offered you a way out. He didn't even have to try."

"Now you speak ill of the one sent to us by the Mother? He is Lowellin, named Protector in the Book of Xochitl itself."

"The Book is very old."

"What do you mean by that?"

"Things change over thousands of years, sister. It would be foolish to assume otherwise."

"The Book is the word of the Mother, absolute."

"Perhaps it was. Perhaps it no longer is. Perhaps Lowellin is not what he seems."

"You are casting doubt on him?"

Ricarn shrugged. "Open your eyes. Look at him. I am not saying he is not the one spoken of as the Protector. Clearly he is far beyond an ordinary man. But I am saying that he uses you and our order for his own ends. He plays a game beyond the one he speaks of and I fear this game does not mean well for us."

Nalene's *sulbit* was in her hand. "I could make you suffer for that."

"Could you? Are you sure?"

Nalene drew herself up. "I am the FirstMother of the Tenders and I—" She broke off with a small cry and swatted at a bee on her arm. The insect avoided the blow and buzzed around her. "It stung me!"

"You were saying?"

"It is only a bee."

"Are you sure?" The bee landed on the table between them. There was an orange stripe around its middle and it was no kind of bee Nalene had ever seen. "Perhaps you are allergic to it?"

"That's ridiculous," Nalene said, but then the pain hit. She pushed her sleeve up and examined her forearm where she had been stung. There was a large red welt there, with some clear fluid leaking from it. "I don't…" she said, sitting back down. "I feel dizzy." Her voice sounded curiously small to her.

"But probably you aren't," Ricarn said, making a dismissive gesture with her hand. "After all, it's only a bee."

At that, the pain and swelling began to visibly recede. Nalene took a deep breath. Her *sulbit* had disappeared back into the depths of her robes.

"The difference between us is that we do not care if we die."

"What?" Nalene's brain felt fogged. "You're not afraid to die?"

"No. We do not *care* if we die." Ricarn pointed. The bee on the table lay dead.

"That…doesn't make any sense."

"It doesn't matter if our deaths make sense or not. We just don't care. It is something we learned from our friends. It helps us think more clearly." She waited, but Nalene had nothing to say. "I have told you what I won't do. But here is what I *will* do. I *will* use every power and trick at my disposal to help you in the war we face. I *will* give my life to defeat *our* enemies."

Now she moved, leaning forward across the table, and the look in her eyes was so utterly cold that Nalene shivered in spite of herself. "I will also watch Lowellin closely, and if there is a way out of his snares, I will find it. What I will *not* do is play your foolish power games, so leave them off and let us have no more of this."

She leaned back in her chair and studied Nalene the way a normal person might watch a beetle to see what it would do.

"What *are* you?" Nalene asked at last.

"A warning? An example? You choose." Ricarn stood in one fluid movement. "We will speak later." At the door leading back into Nalene's chambers she paused. "The young woman, Cara of Rane Haven." Nalene nodded. "Do not bully her. She is the only one of you who is thinking clearly at all."

TWELVE

Quyloc was utterly worn out by the time he headed for his quarters to sleep. Though there'd been no attempt to drag him into the *Pente Akka* since he killed the snakes, the strain of having to be constantly on guard was wearing him down. Added to that was the fact that he was sleeping hardly at all. He lay there for hours in the darkness, the *rendspear* gripped tightly in his hands, afraid that if he fell asleep he wouldn't be able to react in time when the next attempt came. Then, when he finally fell asleep out of pure exhaustion, he only slept fitfully, over and over dreaming that he heard the crackling noise that preceded each attack.

Or he dreamed that he was pulled through into the *Pente Akka* but he didn't have the spear because he'd let go of it while asleep. His fear of this happening was so great that he'd begun lashing the spear to his hand before bed.

He was so tired that when he got to his room that he just collapsed on the bed. Lying there, looking at the ceiling, he realized that he had forgotten to lash the spear to his hand. He was just going to lie there for a minute and rest first. It always took hours to fall asleep anyway.

Without meaning to, Quyloc fell asleep.

Somewhere in the depths of sleep he dreamed he was standing by a huge fire, trying futilely to warm his freezing hands. The fire crackled loudly and all of a sudden he became alarmed, certain that he was too close to the fire, that he was going to be burned. As he looked down at himself to see if any coals had landed on him, he suddenly realized what the crackling noise meant and he came instantly awake, his eyes opening.

Overhead he saw thick trees against a sulfur-yellow sky, but at the same time he could feel the softness under him that was his mattress. He was not fully over, still between worlds.

The spear was not in his hand.

Blindly, he lunged for it, his hand slapping at wadded blankets. His fingers found nothing. The blankets were fast becoming grassy soil when all at once his fingers met the spear shaft and closed around it.

Quyloc leapt to his feet. But he couldn't get his spear free. It was stuck halfway in the ground, halfway in his own world. He yanked at it as his head spun side to side, looking for the attack that he knew was about to happen.

There was a strange, gibbering cry and the sound of vines snapping. Panic rose in him and Quyloc jerked harder at the spear, trying desperately to free it.

Something crashed through a thick stand of ferns and charged at him. Though shaped like a man and not much taller than Quyloc, it was much broader and bulkier. Its arms were longer too, relative to its height, so that it ran using its knuckles as much as its feet. It was covered in dense, blue-black fur and long, yellow canines curved down from its upper jaw. When it reached him, it howled and swiped at him with one clawed hand.

Quyloc was forced to let go of the spear and duck under the swing, which whistled past his head, painfully close. At the same moment he sidestepped, just enough that the creature only clipped him in passing, instead of running full on into him.

The blow knocked him to the side, but he didn't go down. As the creature struggled to break its momentum and turn, he darted to the spear and pulled on it again.

It slid upwards a couple of inches and then the creature attacked again. At the same moment Quyloc could hear more crashing in the undergrowth and knew soon there would be at least two more of the things attacking him.

Quyloc temporarily gave up on trying to pull the *rendspear* free and snatched up a limb that lay on the ground.

As the creature ran at him, he swung the limb as hard as he could and hit it on the side of the head. It didn't seem to really hurt it, but it was knocked aside just enough that he was able to elude its claws once again.

Desperately, he tugged at the spear again and this time it came free. He barely had time to raise it before the furred creature was all over him in a frenzy of slashing claws. Movement in the corner of his eye warned him that another of the things was about to join the battle.

Quyloc threw himself to the side, away from the new attacker, rolling when he hit the ground and coming back to his feet.

But he was done fighting defensively. All that would do was delay the inevitable.

Before the one that had just attacked him could turn, Quyloc leapt forward and stabbed it in the side.

The blade easily pierced its flesh, sinking halfway into its chest, and it screamed, fighting to turn and shred him with its claws.

Quyloc ripped the spear free—relieved that the blade didn't catch on a bone—and spun to face the other attacker.

They were clearly more than dumb beasts because this one slowed when it saw what happened to its brother and feinted to one side, then attacked from the other.

Quyloc ignored the feint and slashed back across the creature's body, scoring it deeply across the lower chest. It howled and pulled back.

Two more entered the small clearing and spread out so that they had him surrounded. The one he'd stabbed first was still upright, but purplish blood poured from a wound in its chest and it was visibly slowed.

Quyloc stood in the middle, turning constantly, trying to keep them all in sight. He could summon the Veil. Even then, he could picture it in his mind. It needed only a touch of his will to bring it to him. But he knew that the moment he dropped his guard, they would swarm him. He wouldn't make it through before at least one got to him. Even if he did, one or more would probably make it through the opening before it sealed shut, like the snake did. He needed breathing room.

He feinted towards the one opposite the badly wounded one. It fell back a step and then he whirled and charged the other way. The badly wounded one threw up one arm and Quyloc chopped down through it. The tooth cut easily through its arm and slashed its face deeply.

It screamed and toppled sideways and he jumped over it and ran.

He tore through the jungle, the others in close pursuit. They were faster than he was, but he was smaller and more agile. He didn't run in a straight line, but ducked and dodged through trees and bushes.

He heard one right behind him, felt its attack before it came, and threw himself hard to the right, behind a tree trunk.

The thing swung, hit nothing and, before it could recover, he'd sheared most of its jaw away. It was amazing how well the spear blade cut, as if with a supernatural sharpness, but there was no time to wonder at it.

The other two were close behind. The trailing one altered its course to go around the tree the other way, as the first one swung wide to avoid his attack.

The smart thing to do then would have been to run and wait for his next opportunity to further cut the odds, but Quyloc could feel himself tiring and furthermore, he was suddenly sick of running, sick of being hunted down.

All this passed through his mind in an instant and then he charged the leading creature, the spear a blur in his hands. The thing swung at him and he shifted his weight to one side, leaning away from the blow, and cut its hand off.

Before it could really respond to the wound, he stabbed it through the throat, then ripped the spear to one side, tearing out most of its throat as he did so. It fell to the ground, dead instantly.

Quyloc spun and ran at the lone survivor. The thing tried to turn and run, but it was too late for that. Quyloc swung and its head fell from its shoulders.

Quyloc stood there panting, staring down at their bodies. He heard other noises in the distance and he summoned the Veil, and left.

THIRTEEN

Perganon took off his glasses and settled himself in the comfortable chair. In his lap was a book dating to the time of the Kaetrian Empire. He and Rome were in a small room of the palace for one of their informal history lessons. On the table was a large map of Atria. Rome had brought along a bottle of *tiare*, the peppery liquor made in Karthije. While Rome was pouring the liquor Perganon took the opportunity to look out the window. It had been a few days, but there was still a cloud hanging low over the Landsend Plateau. He wondered again what had happened up there. The city buzzed with wild rumors, but no one really knew. He accepted the glass of liquor from Rome and nodded his thanks.

"As you'll recall from our last meeting, after the siege of Durag'otal remnants of the army that had stood with Xochitl and the rest of the Eight founded a new city on the banks of a river less than a day's ride away. That city would become the capital of the Kaetrian Empire. At that time there was no hint of the desert that would become the Gur al Krin, only a broad scar on the earth that marked the place where Durag'otal had stood."

"I remember," Rome replied. "You said the first sand dune appeared hundreds of years after the founding of Kaetria and it was centuries more before the dunes grew to the point where they threatened to swallow the capital." He took a drink of the liquor and set his glass down. "But you said nothing about where the sand dunes came from."

"That's because I don't know. I don't think anyone does."

"Maybe you'll find the answer in those books the workmen found when they broke down that wall." Recently Perganon had asked for permission to expand the library into some adjoining, unused rooms. When the workers tore out the wall between the library and the rooms, they found a cache of books that had been hidden in the wall.

83

"I haven't had time to read any of them yet," Perganon said, aware that he was grinning like a child but seemingly unable to help himself. The idea of a whole treasure trove of new books excited him more than anything he could think of. Who knew what secrets they held? "But several of the ones I've looked at date to the time of the Empire and at least one appears to have been written by an early Tender."

"Look at you," Rome said, "grinning like a boy who's gotten a hold of his first teat. If I didn't know better, I'd say you were excited about those books."

"You could say that," Perganon said, sipping the liquor, "and you wouldn't be wrong."

"Any idea why those books were there? Who would go to all that trouble just to hide a bunch of books?"

"Someone who feared their destruction, I suppose. Often those in power are threatened by books."

"That's ridiculous. Who would be frightened by a book?"

"Rulers like to write their own history, Macht Rome, a history that paints them in a favorable light and their enemies in an unfavorable one. In essence, they want the only surviving narrative of events to be one that they approve. The existence of old books that refute that narrative can only be viewed as a threat."

"It seems to me any ruler who's afraid of a few pieces of paper with words on them isn't much of a ruler."

"And yet the annals of history are filled with such rulers." Perganon blinked and looked at the liquor in his hand. Had he drunk that much already, to be saying such things to the macht? He genuinely liked Wulf Rome, but he hadn't survived this long by being anything but circumspect.

"I'll never be one of those," Rome said, tossing back the rest of his glass and reaching for the bottle. "I want only the truth laid down."

"Truly, Macht?"

"I mean it. I've been meaning to talk to you about it so I guess now is as good a time as any. I want you to write a book about what's happening now."

"My Lord?" Perganon asked, shocked. He had considered the idea, of course, but discarded it. Surviving around kings required avoiding such unnecessary risks.

"Don't act dumb. I know you've thought about it. You're a historian at heart, just like the men who wrote those books you're always reading to me from. I bet you'd love putting this all down on paper and why not? The story of how Melekath escaped from his prison and the brave soldiers who defeated him? It's the greatest tale since the creation of the prison. Who wouldn't want to tell it?"

"Well, I must admit—"

"That's assuming anyone's still alive afterward to read it," Rome added. "If we lose, it's just a waste of what little time you have left."

"If you're serious, it's a risk I'm willing to take."

"Then do it. If you need more money for parchment or whatever, let me know."

"Thank you, Macht." Perganon could hardly believe his good luck. The thought of leaving his mark, of historians centuries from now reading his words, well, he could think of nothing he would rather have. He'd never married; he had no children. This would be his legacy. "If I'm not too bold, Macht, why?" As soon as he asked the question he kicked himself. It was best not to ask kings their reasons, all of which always came back to themselves.

"I know what you're thinking," Rome said. "You're thinking I want you to write some big story that will make me look good, like those songs of heroes they sing in the taverns."

Against his better judgment, Perganon nodded.

"But that's not it, not at all. I've been thinking. We've spent some time together by now, Perganon, you teaching me the old histories. And I'd like to think that it's helped me, made me better at this whole ruling thing. I've learned some things. Well, I'd like to pass it on. Maybe some of what we're going through here could help others someday. Probably not, but it could be. That's why I'm ordering you right here and now to write it all down as close to exactly as you can. The bad and the good both. The victories and the losses. It has to be the truth or it won't help anyone, don't you think?"

Perganon was stunned. At first he couldn't say anything. He realized he was going to have to completely reevaluate his estimation of Macht Rome. As much as he liked the man and respected his natural charisma, he'd always considered him a bit simple. But to hear this, right out of nowhere, well, clearly he'd underestimated Rome.

In that moment he realized that probably a good many of Rome's foes over the years had made the same mistake. Fortunately for him, it wouldn't cost him his life.

"I agree completely, Macht Rome," he said. "You have my word I will do just that."

"Great," Rome said, with a huge smile. He leaned forward with the bottle and refilled Perganon's glass. "Now let's get on with the lesson."

"In the beginning of the eighth century of its existence, the Empire was only peripherally aware of the Sertithian horsemen to the north. There was no reason for the Empire to turn its gaze that way. The Alon Mountains were a formidable barrier between the Empire and the Sertithian highlands, so the Empire did not much fear invasion from them, especially since there was only one decent pass through the mountains and it could be easily held by a small force of soldiers. Besides, the Sertithians were barbarians, with nothing actually resembling a city to their name. There was no reason to conquer them. Their lands were too cold and thin for proper agriculture. Throw in a decidedly hostile population showing no interest in trade and seemingly possessing nothing worth trading for, and there was no real reason to expand in that direction. Not when the west was so rich and fertile, bursting with diverse peoples and bustling cities. The fact that the Sertithians had never shown any interest in pursuing hostilities against their large southern neighbor further left the Kaetrians unprepared.

"But all that changed one day, and before you ask why, I don't know. No one does except the Sertithians. Perhaps they sought a challenge. Perhaps someone in the Empire offended them in some way. Whatever the reason, when the Sertithians came, they came in a wave, tens of thousands of horsemen that covered the land like locusts. The pitifully undermanned garrison at the pass through the Alon Mountains was quickly swept away. From there the invaders drove like a dagger into the Empire." Perganon bent over the table and pointed to Karthije on the map.

"There was a legion based in Karthije and had their commander had the sense to hole up behind their formidable walls, he likely could have held off the invaders until the Empire could relieve him. After all, horses the Sertithians had in plenty, but siege engines they had not at all and no force takes Karthije without siege engines." He coughed into his hand and smiled wryly. "Unless one has an axe like you do, of course. Which the Sertithians did not. Fortunately for them—and unfortunately for the Empire—the commander at Karthije was a vain man who resented being relegated to what he saw as a meaningless post and he sent his full strength into the field, confident that the Kaetrian army, better trained and equipped than any other, could crush the upstarts. Perhaps the promotion he felt he so richly deserved would result." Perganon shook his head, marveling at the foolishness of man.

"Instead the Sertithians swept through the legion like a scythe through wheat and barely paused on their charge south." He peered at the parchment. "No word on what became of the foolish commander, but the Emperor at the time, Cherlin, was not a man known for his patience. For the commander's sake we should probably hope he was killed in the battle. As I was saying, the legion barely slowed the Sertithian charge, and a charge it was. The Sertithian invaders were, one and all, mounted. They had no wagons, no foot soldiers, no camp followers to hold them back. Their horses were rangy, powerful beasts who could cover frightening distances every day without seeming to tire. They caught another legion at Managil, coming up on the city so fast that its commander was unprepared. He had received a warning from the commander of Karthije—indeed, most of the Empire was already aware of the threat—but he did not expect them so soon and his forces were also crushed."

"Wait," Rome interjected. "If this army was moving so fast, how did the commander at Managil know it was coming?"

Perganon nodded. "I'm glad you asked. This was due to the advanced system of signal towers used by the Kaetrians. They had a series of towers on top of mountain peaks throughout the Empire and a complex system of sending messages using mirrors in the daytime and fires at night. It really was quite an ingenious code they devised. I spent some time learning it when I was younger and..." He trailed off as he noticed the look on his macht's face. Rome wanted to learn history, but he didn't have much patience with details that didn't interest him.

"As I was saying, with the defeat of the legion at Managil the soft underbelly of the Empire was exposed. The legions normally based in Qarath were far in the west, battling an uprising beyond Fanethrin." He pointed to the western edge of the map. "Panic struck the Kaetrian emperor as he realized there were no sizable forces close enough to intercept the Sertithians before they got to the capital city." He leaned forward and took off his glasses. "No forces except for the Takare, that is." He gestured to the map again. "Not that the emperor thought they could do any good, as they were all at Ankha del'Ath, which you can see is far to the west. No way a force could cover that much ground quickly enough to intercept a mounted army moving fast. There weren't that many of them, either, probably not as many in their entire city as the Sertithians had in their invading army. On top of that, the emperor had no reason to believe they would even respond to his summons. They were part of the Empire, it was true, but in name only. None of their people fought in the endless struggles that the Empire engaged in. Only rarely did Takare even venture out of their territory. They were involved in the endless quest for personal perfection and self-control and not interested in wealth and power, the vices that drive so much of human behavior." He chuckled. "You can see why the emperor was panicking.

"But there was no one else and so the appeal went out. Save us."

"The Takare had a signal mirror too?" Rome asked.

Perganon shook his head. "No. As we talked about before, they just weren't interested in the goings-on of the Empire. But there was a garrison nearby, sort of an embassy—the Takare wouldn't let outsiders live in Ankha del'Ath, so the embassy was a few miles away—and they had a signal tower that the Takare had let them put up in the mountains.

"No one knows why, but for some reason the Takare responded. And that was when their legend was born." Perganon leaned over the map again. "They caught the Sertithians on the southern edge of the Plains of Dem, which is remarkable when you look at how far they had to go. Even with horses it would have been terribly difficult and the Takare were not horse warriors. According to the histories—which are often only slightly more accurate than rumors and tall tales—the Takare could run night and day for days on end without resting and with barely any food or water." He shrugged. "Evidently they were capable of that, because there's really no other way they could have gotten there in time. They caught the Sertithians in a broad flat valley that forms the outwash for a series of sharp hills. One of my contacts told me years ago that there are still the remains of a stone monument there, but I've never seen it. At first glance it was a terrible place to oppose a mounted force, in that the Sertithians would have unhampered mobility, a somewhat important factor when a foot army faces a mounted one."

Perganon opened the book in his lap, a cracked, leather-bound volume. "This is an account written by Selenus, an Empire historian, some decades later. He claims to have it from an eye witness, a boy who was herding goats in the area. It is probably somewhat exaggerated, but it is quite interesting."

It started out a day like any other for Culin, a boy just approaching his twelfth summer. He was herding the family goats just like he did every day. It was midday and he was sitting under a tree on a low hill west of the village where he'd lived his entire life. Culin liked this tree. Not because it was such a great tree, but because it was the only sizable tree for a couple miles. Which meant it was the only place to find shade on a hot day. Furthermore, it was on a low hill and hills were as hard to find as trees here on the plains. The hill was a good vantage point from which to watch the goats.

Culin was sitting under the tree, leaning against the trunk, day-dreaming, when he realized he was no longer alone. To the north, in the distance, some horsemen appeared out of the haze. That was unusual. Culin almost never saw anyone out here except other herders. Certainly not horsemen.

He got to his feet, rubbing his eyes, and to his surprise saw that it was more than a handful of horsemen. Far more. There were hundreds of them. Thousands. They just kept coming and coming, heading south at a fast trot. It looked like they would pass right by his little hill.

That's when Culin started to get worried. They were clearly warriors. Even from a distance he could see the long spears and bows they carried. He looked around nervously, thinking to flee.

But where could he go, really? The land was so flat. They were close now so there was no way they wouldn't see him. It would be simple for them to run him down and skewer him like a piglet with one of those long spears. They might even do it for sport.

Then he saw something even more surprising.

To his left, and directly in the horsemen's path, some people appeared out of nowhere. He rubbed his eyes again, briefly wondering if he'd fallen asleep and was dreaming.

Where did they come from? They must have been hiding in the tall grasses, but how did he not see them before?

There were quite a few of them, though not nearly as many as there were horsemen. He guessed about five hundred. They were dressed in simple, knee-length, belted shifts. They wore no armor and carried no weapons except for long sticks. Not only that, but a lot of them were *women*.

Culin was confused. What were they doing? The way they stood, in a long, spread-out line before the horsemen, it was almost like they were blocking the horsemen. But that was crazy. He looked to the right. The horsemen were wearing leather armor and since they were now closer he could see that they were carrying swords as well. Even if there weren't ten times as many of them, they'd easily win in a battle. Culin's father had fought for the Empire for ten years and he'd heard his stories. He knew enough about war to know that mounted soldiers were superior to foot soldiers, especially ones with no armor or real weapons.

The man leading the horsemen had a leather helmet with long feathers sticking up out of it and braided hair so long it lay on his horse's rump. All of the horsemen had braids, but his looked like the longest. It was dyed too, a bright red color. When the horsemen were about a hundred yards from the people on foot, the leader held up one hand and they came to a halt.

The leader sat his horse then, looking at the people standing in his way. Culin could see the leader's head turning side to side. He was probably thinking this was a trap, Culin thought. Da had told him a story about a time when the legion he was in set a trap for an enemy army, hiding most of their soldiers in the hills on either side and then crashing down on the enemy once the fight started.

But there was no way this was a trap. There were no hills, no nothing, to hide in. Culin started to feel afraid for the people on foot. They were going to get hurt bad. Maybe even all get killed.

The leader called out something in a foreign tongue and a large number of horsemen detached from the main body and moved forward, lining up facing the people on foot. Culin guessed there were twice as many horsemen in that line as there were people on foot. The horsemen all had short, curved bows in their hands.

A horn sounded and the horsemen charged. As they came, they unleashed a volley of arrows. Culin winced and put his hands over his eyes, afraid to see the death that was sure to come.

But he was curious too, and so he peeked between his fingers and what he saw seemed unbelievable.

It looked to Culin like the people on foot hardly moved. They kind of leaned to one side or the other and the arrows flew harmlessly by. A few slapped at the arrows instead, but the result was the same.

"That's impossible," Rome said. "*None* of the arrows hit?"

Perganon took a sip of the liquor, enjoying having an audience. "The thing about the Takare was that at an age when normal children are still mastering the art of running full speed without cracking their heads open, Takare children began learning to dodge missile weapons. The arrows and spears had padded ends for the young children, three to five years old. After that the missiles they faced were blunted, but of course they still flew hard enough to break ribs and tear flesh. By nine all the weapons they faced were real. Those who were not good enough died."

"They killed their own children?"

"You have to understand, Rome, that the Takare believed in rebirth. When one died, they believed he or she would return to them soon. They had special priests who attended births and supposedly had a way to look into the child and see who he'd been in his past life. These priests also helped the young children in the early years of their training to remember this past life so that the skills the warrior had had before could be reawakened."

Rome frowned. "You're telling me that they believed their kids could remember the skills they'd learned in their past lives? Is that possible?"

Perganon shrugged. "If true, it would give them quite an advantage. It would also explain what happened next.

Culin stared, openmouthed. How did they *do* that?

The horsemen tucked their bows away. Some drew swords, the others spears. An eerie war cry echoed over the battlefield.

He turned to look at the people on foot. They were just standing there motionlessly as the charging warriors bore down on them. Why didn't they run, or do *something*?

Only at the last moment did they do something. As the mass of charging horsemen struck their line, they acted, and what they did then was even more amazing than avoiding arrows.

Culin saw one woman dodge a sword blow, slide across in front of the charging horse and, before the rider could react and switch his weapon to the other side, she struck him with the end of her stick square in the ribs. He was knocked off his horse and as he hit the ground, she hit him in the temple with the butt of her stick, knocking him out.

One man stepped aside to dodge a spear thrust, then grabbed the spear and pulled. To avoid being pulled from his horse, the rider let go of the spear and leaned back. At which point the man struck him with the butt of his own spear and knocked him off his horse.

Another woman used her stick to flick aside a horseman's sword attack. Then she dropped the stick, leapt up in the air, and grabbed the man's wrist. A quick twist and he dropped the sword. Still in the air, she planted her feet against the horse's ribs, gave another twist that put his arm behind his back, then leaned back and pushed off the horse with her feet, tucking and rolling as she went over backwards, flinging the man over her head and sending him sprawling on the ground.

One man with gray hair bent his legs as a rider approached and dug the end of his stick into the ground. Leaning into it so that the stick bowed, he gave a tremendous push with his legs. Between the flex in the wood and the strength of his own leap, he rose into the air high enough so that the startled horseman found himself facing an opponent who was at his own level. The gray-haired man struck the horseman's wrist with a deft chop that caused him to drop the sword. With another chop he struck the man at the junction of shoulder and neck. For a moment the rider seemed okay, then he toppled to the ground.

One young man—he looked to Culin to be only a couple years older than him—slapped aside a spear thrust, then darted *underneath* the charging horse. As he went, a knife flashed in his hand and he slashed the cinch. Grabbing one end of the cinch, he continued on out the other side. Saddle and rider slid off the other side of the horse.

After dodging a sword blow, one woman grabbed her attacker's wrist, doing something to make him drop his sword. Then she swung around behind the horse's hindquarters and leaned away, allowing the horse's momentum to drag the rider from the saddle.

Two riders converged on a woman who stood frozen, seemingly uncertain how to react. Both riders raised swords, preparing to slash downwards. If she didn't move their horses would each strike one of her shoulders and she would go down under flailing hooves. But at the last moment she ran forward through the gap between the horses, just before they closed on her. As she went by them, her hands shot out, each one closing on a wrist. Momentum and gravity did the rest of the work as each rider was yanked from his seat and crashed to the ground.

Then the charge was over; the horsemen had passed through the line of people on foot. Culin saw that only one of the people on foot was bleeding. In contrast, over half of the horsemen were down. Many of them weren't moving. A few jumped up, waving swords, but they were quickly disarmed by the people on foot. To Culin it looked like it was no more difficult than taking toys away from misbehaving children. They easily dodged or slapped aside the attacks, then with a quick blow or a twisted wrist they took the weapons away.

Nor did the people on foot then use those weapons against the dismounted horsemen. They seemed satisfied with simply disarming them. Unless one of them broke his neck falling off his horse, they were all probably okay.

Those horsemen who were still mounted swung their horses about. They changed tactics this time, drawing together in a tight mass, concentrating their force instead of spreading out. The people on foot responded by drawing closer as well and raising their sticks. When the horsemen charged, the people on foot did as well.

When the two forces were about fifteen feet apart, the people on foot dug the ends of their sticks into the ground, the sticks flexed, and they vaulted into the air. The startled horsemen found themselves facing flying opponents.

While still in the air, they began striking with their sticks. Fists and feet followed and this time not a single horseman kept his seat.

Culin swung around to look at the rest of the horsemen, waiting with their leader, wondering if they would all attack now, wondering what amazing thing the people on foot would do this time. By then he felt like nothing they could do would surprise him.

But only the leader of the horsemen moved. He walked his horse forward until he was almost close enough to the people on foot to touch them with his spear. But instead of raising a spear or his sword, he drew a long, polished knife from his belt. He shouted something in his foreign tongue, then pulled his braid around in front of him and with a quick stroke cut it off and threw it on the ground before his horse.

When he did that, the horsemen on the ground—all of them that were conscious, that is—lowered their heads. They dropped to their knees and chopped off their braids as well. Soon the ground was covered with braids like colorful, dead snakes. Then they rose, gathering fallen weapons and whistling for their horses. Those who were unconscious had their braids cut for them and were lifted onto horseback and tied there. They mounted and rode silently back to join the rest.

A horn blew and the entire army of horsemen turned around and headed north without a backward look.

X X X

"Unbelievable," Rome said, shaking his head.

"It seems that way, doesn't it?" Perganon agreed. "And if this was an isolated account I'd agree with you. But this sort of thing was commonplace for the Takare. In the years after this the Takare fought on behalf of the Empire many times and many others witnessed the same sorts of feats."

"And then the Sertithians just went home?" Rome asked.

"They just went home," Perganon confirmed.

"But why come all that way and then just turn around? It doesn't make sense."

"Not to you or me. But there's probably things we do that don't make sense to the Sertithians."

Rome chuckled. "Yeah. I went to some party a while back for Protaxes, the god the nobility worship. That didn't make much sense to me."

"If I had to hazard a guess, from what little I know of the Sertithians, the whole thing was either a matter of some perceived insult or a challenge of some kind. Once the Takare answered that challenge, there was nothing left but to return home. I chose this story for today because with the Plateau's destruction the Takare might be a factor once again. I thought you should know."

"These people would be mighty allies against Melekath," Rome mused.

"So they would. From what I know of the Landsend Plateau, simply surviving up there might be the most impressive feat of all for these people."

"So after that the Takare became the Empire's elite troops?" Rome asked.

"It didn't happen overnight, but it was the turning point for the Takare. It marked the end of their isolationism. After they saved the Empire, the emperor lavished them with gifts. They were honored everywhere as heroes. Within a generation they were fighting in the Empire's wars. It was the beginning of the end, really. Prior to this they were ascetics, dedicated to their disciplines and fighting strictly on a personal level. After defeating the Sertithians they began the slide down the long slope that led eventually, maybe inevitably, to Wreckers Gate."

"What really happened at Wreckers Gate?"

"No one but the Takare really knows. The Empire fell soon afterwards and the only witnesses were the Takare themselves. But we do know that they slaughtered their own people there and that was apparently the last straw. They threw down their swords and walked away."

FOURTEEN

It was midafternoon and Cara was still scrubbing the stone walkways. Now that she'd done it for a few days, she'd more or less gotten used to it so that her back and knees didn't hurt so much and she'd come to realize that she didn't really mind the work. It was kind of peaceful in a tedious way. She could just forget herself, dipping the brush into the pail of water, scrubbing at the stones, dipping, and repeating.

The water in the pail was dark brown now, so Cara threw it out and carried the pail to a well that stood at the back of the property. Another woman—probably a servant, since she didn't have a shaved head or the white robes—was already at the well, turning the crank to bring up the bucket. She shot Cara a quick look, taking in the shaved head, and started to curtsy when she realized Cara wore neither the white robe nor the Reminder. Her look turned quizzical. Not wanting to answer any questions, Cara half turned away.

That was when she noticed the tree. She thought it was an elm, though she couldn't be sure. It was a large tree, with a thick trunk and lots of shade. She'd seen it before, but this was the first time she'd really looked at it. Most of the leaves were yellow and quite a few of them had fallen to the ground. That was odd. It was still too early for trees to be losing their leaves. Was it diseased? She walked part way around it, staring up into the leaves.

She noticed then that the shrubs nearby were also yellowing, and one appeared to be completely dead. As she started really looking around her, she saw that all the plants on the estate were suffering. Most of the grass on the wide lawns was turning yellow. Over the wall that separated the estate from the one next door she could see several trees and their leaves looked fine, though there was some yellowing in the nearest one.

The woman finished filling her pail and walked away. After filling hers, Cara walked back to where she'd been working. While she was gone, a group of Tenders led by the FirstMother had come out to train with their *sulbits*. Looking closer, she saw that the Tenders from Rane Haven were in the group, along with a few others who had recently gotten their *sulbits*. Cara surreptitiously moved closer so she could watch.

"You've learned how to control your *sulbit*'s feeding. Now I am going to teach you to meld with your *sulbit*. Melding with your *sulbit* is necessary if you want to exert finer control over the creature. It is also more dangerous, since it entails lowering the barriers between you and it."

Cara did not miss the way Donae's eyes widened when the FirstMother said that. Not for the first time she wondered if it was wise for her to receive a *sulbit*. She was not a very strong woman, and easily frightened.

Bronwyn, on the other hand, looked eager. Cara expected that she would be the strongest among them, maybe even as strong as the FirstMother someday.

"When you are melded with your *sulbit*, you will see what it sees. You will feel what it feels. You will be able to access its full abilities. Through it you will be able to take hold of flows of Song and bend them to your will."

That brought some excited murmurs from the women, and even Donae looked more hopeful. Cara had to admit that she was intrigued. Perhaps the greatest of the powers held by the Tenders of the Empire was their ability to manipulate raw LifeSong.

The FirstMother gave them a stern look and they all went quiet. "In order to meld with your *sulbit* you will have to lower your inner barriers and allow the creature into you. It will be difficult at first and you may find it frightening, but it is necessary if you are going to serve Xochitl and fight in her name. Bring forth your *sulbits* and hold them up. Concentrate on them. When you succeed in melding with them, you will be pulled *beyond*."

The Tenders took the creatures out of their robes and held them up. The FirstMother continued to give them instructions and one by one they managed to do it. Donae was last but all at once she gasped and said, "I feel it! I'm there! Oh." She put her hand to her mouth. "It's beautiful."

Cara had stopped working altogether and was staring at them. She had to admit that she was a little bit envious. Going *beyond* was something she'd always wanted to do, but doubted she'd ever have the ability. Now that they were doing it, she could not deny a certain amount of second-guessing about her decision.

"Time for the next step," the FirstMother said. She pointed at Bronwyn. "You first. Pick a nearby flow of LifeSong. Do you have one? Now, reach through your *sulbit*. You are one mind, one body. Focus on the flow and nothing else." She waited a few moments until Bronwyn nodded. "Now reach out and take hold of it. Only touch it briefly, then let it go. It is important that you let it go right away. If you wait too long, your *sulbit* will latch on too tightly, and you may have difficulty pulling away. It is young and does not know any better."

Bronwyn grimaced as she concentrated. She reached out with one hand. All the other Tenders were staring at her intently. Their eyes had a slightly unfocused look that told her they were *seeing*. She wished she could too. All at once a slight tingle went through her and at the same time Bronwyn's face lit up. "I did it! I touched it!" She pulled her arm back. "It was incredible. I could feel the power moving through it."

After her the FirstMother worked with the rest, coaching them to do the same. Some weren't able to manage it, but most did. Last to go was Donae.

The small woman was clearly afraid, but she squared her shoulders and reached out with one hand, her *sulbit* nestled in her other hand. As with the others, Cara felt the tingle inside her as Donae took hold of the flow, but it did not dissipate as the others had done. Instead it grew stronger. Cara quickly began to feel sick to her stomach. It felt like a hot wind was blowing across her skin and sweat beaded her brow. Suddenly Donae cried out.

"I can't let go! It won't let me!"

The hot wind grew stronger and now it felt like it blew off of a furnace. Cara's skin felt like it was blistering. The FirstMother shoved Donae hard. When she touched her Cara felt a soundless concussion and both the FirstMother and Donae were knocked down.

Cara realized that she was on her hands and knees, panting as she tried to draw breath. The hot wind was gone, but the world was blurry and she blinked to clear her vision. As if in from a far distance she could hear the FirstMother berating Donae. She felt a hand on her shoulder.

"You are too close. You must move away."

Cara looked up. Bent over her was the Insect Tender in the red robe. She tried to reply but it felt like her mouth wasn't working.

"You are vulnerable to what they do. It's not safe to be this close to them. Come away from here."

"But I'm supposed to be working," Cara protested.

In answer, Ricarn simply stared at her. She had the most piercing gaze of anyone Cara had ever seen. It struck Cara that she would hate to have this woman angry with her. It wasn't just her stare that was different about her either. Most people moved when they didn't have to, fidgeting or shifting their stance to a more comfortable one. This woman, on the other hand, held herself perfectly still while she waited for Cara to respond. She didn't seem impatient or angry either. Cara had the feeling that she was willing to stand there all day if necessary, simply waiting for her response.

Cara gave in and stood up. Ricarn started to walk away and she followed, first grabbing her brush and pail. From Tenders she'd overheard talking she knew who this woman was, but she had no idea what she wanted with her. There was something compelling about her. She seemed utterly sure of herself, but without being arrogant. She seemed like a woman who has reached her destination and now has all the time in the world.

Ricarn motioned to her to move up beside her. "Walk beside me." Cara obeyed. "You should stay away from them while they are training."

Cara remained silent. Was she supposed to respond? Finally, she said, "Are they dangerous then?"

"You know the answer to that."

"Do I?"

"Their true home is within pure LifeSong. Now they have been removed from it. How do you think they feel?"

Cara pondered that. It was something she'd never considered. "I would guess that they're hungry."

"It is only natural, is it not? What do creatures do when they are hungry?"

"They try to eat."

Ricarn gave Cara a sidelong glance. "All that lives is potential food to them."

Cara shuddered, suddenly realizing where this was going. "Do you think they will try to feed on those who hold them?"

"They already do. That is part of the reason the FirstMother has them spending so much time training the creatures. They are still small yet, and it is not so difficult to control them."

"But when they get bigger?" Cara ventured.

"Their appetites will grow as well."

"The FirstMother should be warned."

Something that might have been a laugh came from Ricarn. The sound made Cara's hair stand up. "Do you think she would listen?"

Cara shook her head.

"Why did the FirstMother take a *sulbit*?"

Cara shrugged. "Because she has no choice? Melekath is coming."

"Do you think it is true, that she has no choice?"

"Melekath has to be fought."

"Yet I see no *sulbit* on you. Clearly *you*, at least, have a choice."

"Well..."

"Is it the FirstMother then who has no choice?" They had reached a bench tucked behind a tree and Ricarn motioned to Cara to sit down, then sat beside her, turning to face her.

Cara didn't respond right away. Finally, she said, "We always have choices."

Ricarn gave her an appraising look and nodded. "Why did you refuse a *sulbit*?"

Her eyes hurt to look at, and yet it was hard to look away. It struck Cara that Ricarn had no shutters. When normal people opened their eyes on the world they were careful to always have the inner shutters closed. However they might appear, underneath they were hiding their innermost being behind those shutters. But Ricarn didn't do that. There was nothing guarded or hidden in her eyes. She looked out on the world clearly and frankly and did not care if the world saw inside her. But that did not mean Cara could read her. Ricarn had thrown open the shutters, but when Cara looked inside she could not make sense of what she saw. She was simultaneously the most frightening and the most compelling woman she had ever met. "I don't know."

"Yes, you do."

"No, really, I—" Another look into those cool, clear eyes and Cara dropped what she had planned to say. The look in those eyes said that Cara would not be able to get along the way she always had, staying quiet, hiding what she really thought, murmuring acceptance regardless of how she really felt. The look in those eyes said it was time to stop hiding and be true to what she really felt. Cara drew a deep breath and took the plunge.

"It hurts to be around them. I can't bear the thought of one on me."

"Why do you think that is?"

"I don't know. I truly don't. It's probably just because I'm afraid."

"Can you go *beyond*?" Ricarn asked her abruptly. "Can you *see*?"

"Not really," Cara admitted. "I think I *saw* once, but I'm not sure."

Ricarn stared at her, her head tilted slightly to one side. "A Tender who can't *see*."

"I'm sor—" Cara started to say, then stopped herself. Bronwyn was always telling her that she apologized too much.

Ricarn looked away. Across the lawns they could just see the women training. She stared at them as she spoke. "If you could *see*, you'd know there is a reason to be afraid of those things. They perch on the *akirmas* of the women who carry them and their roots go down inside, deeper every day. Surely they can *see* what is happening. But why do they pretend they cannot?" She sounded truly perplexed.

"Maybe they don't want to *see*," Cara said.

Ricarn's eyes snapped back to Cara and she nodded. "I believe you are exactly right. What do you think of the Protector?"

Cara hesitated. "I only met him once. I can't say—" Ricarn's look stopped her. She took a deep breath and looked around to make sure they were alone. "I don't trust him. I don't know why. I just don't." Her hand went to her mouth, surprised that she had said as much as she did. She scrambled for damage control. "Of course, I'm probably wrong. He is the Protector, after all, named by Xochitl. And I'm probably worried about nothing about the *sulbits*. I've always been that way, afraid of the smallest things."

Ricarn's mouth turned down in the slightest frown. "Don't do that."

"Do what?" But Cara already knew.

"Say what you think and then call yourself a liar."

The words struck Cara and she froze. She wanted to protest further, but she knew Ricarn was right.

"Maybe you don't trust the Protector because he is hiding something. Maybe you resist the *sulbits* because you are listening to your inner voice."

Now Cara found she could not look at Ricarn any longer. She turned her face away. "It could be," she admitted quietly. Just saying the words made her feel uncomfortable. Cara gradually became aware of how many bees there seemed to be nearby. Funny, she hadn't noticed any bees earlier. "But probably not. I've never been very good at that stuff. I was always behind in my exercises. I can hardly even hear LifeSong. And I never could find a *sonkrill*. I don't suppose I'll ever be much of a Tender at all."

"What does being a Tender mean to you?"

"I don't know," Cara said miserably, "but I think I'm probably not really one."

"It is clear that you do not know what it means to be a Tender, but you are not alone in that. Neither do any of them." She gestured at the Tenders who were training.

"You don't mean the FirstMother…"

"I mean especially the FirstMother."

"You're probably right." Cara lowered her head and waited for Ricarn to walk away. When she didn't, she looked up. "Why are you still here, talking to me?"

"That is the question, is it not?" Ricarn said. "In time you will find out." She stood up.

Cara saw a large, green bug land on the woman's neck and crawl into her hair. "There's something…something landed on you."

The woman reached into her hair and came out with a large green beetle. It walked across her hand unconcernedly. "Only an old friend," she said. "With news. I will need to talk to my sisters about this."

She put the beetle on her robe and it disappeared into a fold. She walked away without another word.

FIFTEEN

"There's a feral woman loose in the city."

"What?" Quyloc asked. Frink, the man in charge of his spy network, was giving him his daily report, but Quyloc realized he'd quit listening some time ago.

"There's a feral woman loose in the city."

Quyloc rubbed his eyes. Gods, but he was tired. How long since he'd had a good night's sleep? His exhaustion was getting worse. He looked up at Frink, forcing himself to concentrate. "With all the strange things happening in the city, how is one woman important?"

"I don't know that she is, but something about this struck me and I know how you like detailed reports."

Quyloc resisted the urge to tell him to forget about it. He really didn't feel good today. He was weak and just a little feverish. But he'd learned to trust Frink's instincts. He blinked to clear his vision and asked, "What struck you?"

"The word is she's killing people, but here's the thing. She's just a little thing, hardly more than a girl. She's mostly seen down by the Pits and she attacks people and kills them without a weapon. Accounts vary, but some say she has two creatures that she attacks with."

"What kind of creatures?"

Frink shrugged. "No one knows. No one who lives gets a good look at her. But I have an idea. I may be completely wrong…"

"Go on."

Frink continued talking but Quyloc didn't hear him because right then he saw something out of the corner of his eye, a flash of bright green. He turned quickly, but there was nothing there.

"Sir? Is there something wrong?"

Slowly Quyloc turned back to him. He'd been sure, just for a moment, that he saw the jungle, thick ferns and dripping vines right there in his office. His fever felt worse suddenly. "No…it's…I thought I saw something is all. Go on with what you were saying."

He didn't miss the look Frink gave the *rendspear*. Clearly he'd noticed the way Quyloc never let go of it, but he was smart enough not to ask and Quyloc wasn't about to offer information about it.

"Tess thinks the woman might be a Tender." Tess was a young woman in Quyloc's spy network.

That caught Quyloc's attention. "Why does she think that?"

"She's seen her once. It was from a distance and the light was bad, but she thinks it might be a Tender named Lenda, who she saw a few times when she was watching the Tenders at their old home."

"Maybe she's mistaken."

"Maybe. But consider this. Lenda is missing. Our eyes on the Tender estate haven't seen her in weeks."

Something finally penetrated Quyloc's fogged brain, something he would have caught normally. "You think the things she's killing with are *sulbits*."

"It makes sense. We know those things can drain a cow shatren in a few minutes." This wasn't news. The Tenders, while not advertising what they were doing to the general populace, were making no effort to hide their training from the workers on the estate. Quyloc had heard numerous detailed reports about what the Tenders were doing with their *sulbits*.

Frink left a few minutes later and Quyloc sat there for a bit, thinking. He was far too preoccupied with the *Pente Akka*. He was falling behind on what was happening in Qarath. He was falling behind everywhere, skipping meetings, losing his attention. If this kept up much longer he'd be completely useless.

He got up suddenly and left his office. He needed to go outside, to walk, to try and clear his head if he could.

He left the palace by one of the back doors. There was a large garden and a small orchard out here, between the palace and the cliffs overlooking the sea. Off to his left stood the tower. He walked to the low wall on the edge of the cliffs and looked out over the sea.

For a time he stood there with his eyes closed, the spear resting on the wall. The sea air felt good on his face, clearing his thoughts.

At one point he realized that he was not alone and he opened his eyes to see T'sim standing beside him. Quyloc turned to him.

"What do you want?"

"I thought I wanted to see the *rendspear* but now something else has caught my attention." He was looking at Quyloc's chest as he spoke.

Quyloc took a step back. "What are you talking about?"

"You have a…bite, don't you?"

Quyloc's hand went to where he'd been stung. "How did you know that?"

"I can *see* it. It does not look good."

Quyloc became alarmed. Quickly he tore open his shirt. The skin looked normal as always. "I don't see anything."

"Oh. I didn't realize. Here, let me help." So saying, the small man stepped forward surprisingly quickly and, before Quyloc could react, he tapped him on the forehead.

When his finger touched Quyloc he heard a loud concussion in his head and everything went dark for a second. He staggered back. "What did you do to me?"

"I merely helped you *see*," T'sim said calmly.

Gradually, Quyloc's vision returned, but there was a great pain in his head. "Next time tell me before you do something like that," he growled.

"Would you have let me do it if I'd told you?" T'sim asked calmly.

"No."

"What do you *see*?"

"Nothing. Everything looks the same."

"Are you sure? Look closer."

Quyloc rubbed his eyes and then he noticed the glowing, golden threads of light. They were all over the place. One of them seemed to be connected to him. "I *see* LifeSong," he whispered.

"You should be able to *see* even more than that. Look at that wall closely."

Quyloc did as he was told, but at first he saw nothing. He stared harder and all at once he realized that the stone appeared to be pulsing slowly. "What is it?"

"It is Stone force, the power that lies within all stone. The stone here was dug from the ground and cut away from the bedrock long ago, so there is not much within it, but stone never completely dies."

"It's incredible."

"There is energy within the Sky and the Sea as well, though you will have to push deeper to be able to perceive them and you may not be ready for that yet. Besides, there is still the matter of your little problem." He pointed one small finger at Quyloc's chest.

Quyloc looked down and what he *saw* made him gasp. There was an angry purple and black lump on his chest. Radiating from it were black veins several inches long.

"You got that in the *Pente Akka*, didn't you?"

"Something stung me."

T'sim looked at him curiously, his head cocked slightly to one side. "How do you feel?"

"Terrible." As he said it, Quyloc saw the jungle from the corner of his vision again and he turned his head suddenly.

"What is it?" T'sim asked.

"Nothing," Quyloc said, rubbing his forehead.

"What did you see?" T'sim persisted.

"I thought I saw the *Pente Akka*, but I didn't. Maybe I'm just hallucinating. I'm not sure what to believe anymore."

"It appears the venom is getting worse."

"I think you're probably right."

"Is there no antidote?"

"I don't know. I don't know anything. I didn't even know it was there until just now."

"What do you think will happen if you don't find an antidote?"

For a moment Quyloc just stared at him, wondering what to make of the question. But it was clear that T'sim was simply asking out of curiosity, maybe even childlike curiosity. He had a curiously smooth, unlined face, and he did look somewhat childlike.

What manner of person was he? Quyloc wondered. Was he a person at all? A sudden thought struck him. Could T'sim be one of the Shapers he'd read about?

"What are you?" he breathed.

"I am nothing," T'sim replied. "Just one who wants to know. I am harmless."

Quyloc nodded. The fact was, he *did* think T'sim was harmless. Despite the fact that Rome had found him in a city filled with dead people, where he was the only one living, Quyloc's gut told him T'sim was telling the truth.

"I don't know what will happen," Quyloc said.

"Will you die?" Again the innocent curiosity.

Quyloc hesitated before he replied. "I don't think so."

"And why is that?"

"Because the *Pente Akka* wants me alive."

T'sim nodded. "Ah, the *gromdin*. It has been busy then."

"What do you know about the *gromdin*?"

"Only that it seems to rule the *Pente Akka*. And that it seeks to be free in our world. I have not studied the place like Lowellin has."

"I'm starting to feel insubstantial," Quyloc said. He held out his arm and looked at it. "Sometimes, just for a moment, I feel like I can see right through myself. I think maybe I'm fading, losing my hold on this world.

"It is possible," T'sim agreed. "Do you have any idea how long this will take?"

"What? No, I don't! Why? Do you want to be there when it happens?"

"It would be something to see. I might learn something."

"Can't you help me?"

"I would if I could. You and Rome have proven to be very interesting. I would not like to lose you."

"But if something horrible is going to happen to me, you want to be there to see it."

T'sim nodded. "Does that upset you?"

Quyloc considered this, then, "No. I think I'm too tired to be upset."

"Well, perhaps you will think of something. You are the man who killed the *rend* after all."

Quyloc looked at the spear in his hand that he'd paid a too-high price for.

"I can help you with one thing," T'sim said. Quyloc looked up. "That weapon cuts flows."

Quyloc looked back at the spear, then at T'sim questioningly.

"It is a thing of the *Pente Akka*. No flows can enter there, for they are severed immediately."

"This cuts flows?" Quyloc said wonderingly.

"If you concentrate on them. But be careful."

"Why?"

"That world is anathema to us. You see how the poison affects you. If you use the spear to sever flows, there may be unpleasant side effects."

"What kind of side effects?"

"I don't know. I just thought you should know."

Quyloc went back to staring at the spear. When next he looked up, T'sim was gone.

Quyloc turned around and looked at the garden. There were golden flows all over it. He looked around. There was no one else out there.

He stepped closer. There was a patch of bean plants at the edge of the garden. He picked one at the edge of the patch and focused on the flow of Song connected to it.

He flicked the spearhead through the flow.

Nothing happened.

He moved closer and this time he stared at the flow for a minute, focusing all his attention on it.

This time the spear severed the flow cleanly.

The two ends flopped freely for a minute, then bumped into each other and stuck together. Soon he could see no sign it had been cut.

So maybe T'sim was wrong about side effects.

Jimith came out into the garden near the end of the day, to fetch some vegetables for the cooks. Jimith was young, no more than twelve years old. No one knew for sure. His mother was a maid in the palace, a young woman with no family. She died when he was but a toddler and he just sort of became the servants' mascot. There were a number of servants who had been around long enough to remember his birth, but they were sharply divided when it came to the year. Some said eleven years ago; others said twelve.

Jimith preferred to believe it was twelve years ago. He was just small for his age, that's all. Anyway, he might not be big, but he was strong and he was agile. Soft-footed too.

And cursed with an active curiosity. He'd been in every room in the palace, even the king's—macht's he reminded himself—chambers.

So when he went out to the garden to fetch vegetables, he didn't just get what he was told to and go right back in. Instead he loitered. He picked up a small stone that had escaped the gardener's eye, went to the low stone wall and threw it out into the sea. He watched it fall and make a tiny splash, then turned back to the garden.

That was odd. One of the bean plants didn't look right.

Jimith went over and crouched by it. The plant looked rotted, all spongy and brown. A weird smell was coming off it too. Drops of some kind of clear fluid were stuck on the stem of the plant, slowly flowing downward. He reached out one finger to touch one of the drops…

Then hesitated, and drew his hand back.

He stood up, wiped his hand on his pants and ran back inside.

SIXTEEN

"What's wrong with you!" the FirstMother yelled at Velma, slapping at her sleeve, which was blackened and smoking. "Are you trying to kill me?"

"No, FirstMother," Velma said miserably, hanging her head. It felt like even the FirstMother's *sulbit* was looking at her angrily. "I'm sorry, FirstMother."

Velma and three other Tenders—Loine, Serin and Uriel—were arranged in a semicircle facing the FirstMother. They were all tired. It was midafternoon and they'd been at this right since after the morning service. The looks the other Tenders sent Velma's way were anything but friendly; the FirstMother had made it clear there would be no stopping until they got this right, yet this was the second time Velma had lost control of the Song that she was diverting to the FirstMother.

It was the day after Velma had been sent to find the Insect Tender and bring her to the FirstMother. She didn't know what went on between them, but the FirstMother had been in an especially foul mood all day. At breakfast she just started yelling at them all, telling them they were worthless, that if they didn't work harder they wouldn't stand before Melekath any longer than a rabbit before a coyote. She might still be yelling at them except that out of nowhere the Insect Tenders, all three of them, showed up. Which was odd, because they hadn't come to any meals before. No one had even seen them eat. Maybe they ate bugs back in that strange shelter they were constructing in a little copse of trees that stood on a back corner of the estate.

At any rate, once they showed up the FirstMother went quiet. Just broke off in the middle of her tirade. Then she gave an odd sort of smile, a truly frightening smile actually, and said they should all strive to be like the Insect Tenders. Velma had no idea what she meant by that. Nor did any of the other women, as far as she could tell. Though she really didn't have all that clear of an idea what the other women thought, or spoke of. Ever since the FirstMother named Velma as her personal aide, things had been different. Now whenever Velma walked up on a group of Tenders talking, their conversation stopped, just died out. Now none of them ever came up and just talked to her, not even Arin and Serin, who she'd known since she was just a girl. Sometimes she thought being Nalene's aide wasn't such a great position at all. Sometimes she thought she'd like to just be herself again, even if it meant living back in the old, rundown place. It was a dump, and people hated them, but Melanine laughed a lot and she knew how to take it easy on a person. Not like the FirstMother, who wouldn't even let Velma use her name anymore, but made her call her FirstMother all the time, even when they were alone.

After that the Insect Tenders went with them to the morning service, something else they'd never done before. They stood in the crowd and just watched in that still, eerie way they had, while the FirstMother tried to pretend they didn't exist. Which she obviously couldn't, because she kept losing her words right in the middle of sentences and the service ended up being lots shorter than usual. Then she spent awhile yelling at the workmen who were building the temple with stones brought down from Old Qarath.

Sulbit training started as soon as they got back to the estate. Now it was afternoon and they'd had no lunch and hardly any breaks and Velma was so tired she thought she might collapse on the spot.

"Start again," the FirstMother growled, glaring at Velma. "And try to hold on this time!"

Velma sighed and nodded obediently. Being melded with her *sulbit* she could simultaneously *see* flows of LifeSong and the normal world, although it always made her feel a little dizzy to do so. Making it all harder was the fact that she'd never felt comfortable melding with her *sulbit*. She always felt faintly violated, having another awareness there in the innermost recesses of her mind.

Five cow shatren were securely tethered nearby, one for each of them working on this. She *saw* the flow of LifeSong connected to the cow she was using and tentatively reached for it. She hated doing this. She could see how much it hurt and upset the cow, who was no longer strong enough to stand, but had collapsed onto her side, as had the rest of them. On top of that, this was the first time she'd tried to take hold of any flow larger than what sustained a medium-sized shrub. There was a lot more power in the cow's flow than in a plant's.

When Velma touched the cow's flow the animal bawled weakly and she felt tears start in her eyes. She had to get it right this time. She didn't want to keep torturing the poor thing.

With the help of her *sulbit*, Velma was able to get a reasonably secure hold on the flow of Song. Then she began bleeding Song off it, but instead of trying to hold onto the power herself, she diverted it to the FirstMother, who had once again turned around and was staring at a pile of stacked stones some fifty paces away that they were using as a target.

She only bled a tiny stream of power at first, wanting to get it aimed just right before she went further. The streams from the other three Tenders were considerably thicker than hers was, all of them converging on the glowing spot on the FirstMother's *akirma* that marked her *sulbit*. The stream of Song had to be focused exactly on the FirstMother's *sulbit*. Otherwise, the FirstMother risked having her *akirma* gashed and possibly even shredded, depending on the quantity of Song.

Velma bit her lip and bled off more power. So far so good. Her stream got thicker, though it was still less than half the size of the others'. Cautiously she bled off still more power. Her stream was nearly the size of everyone else's now and she allowed herself a ray of hope that this time she was finally going to do it. She just needed to hold it a little longer, until the FirstMother reached the limit of what she and her *sulbit* could handle and released the pent-up power at the target.

One of the cows bawled extra loud and began thrashing wildly. Velma turned her head to see what was happening, just for a second—

And completely lost her hold on the stream.

The stream began to whipsaw wildly. Spewing raw power, the end of the stream snapped around and struck the stream controlled by Loine, the Tender next to Velma. The power fed back down her stream in a sudden, uncontrolled burst and Loine was lifted off her feet and thrown backwards.

Chaos erupted, Tenders trying to shut down the streams they were diverting, the FirstMother yelling angrily, cows bawling.

A few seconds later the last stream flickered and went out. Serin was on her knees, retching. Uriel was on her feet but wobbling badly. They had not completely escaped the backlash.

Horrified, Velma ran to Loine, crying her name over and over. She knelt beside her, babbling apologies.

Moments later the FirstMother arrived. She shoved Velma aside so hard that she fell on her side. "Get out of here! Haven't you done enough damage for one day?"

Tears streaming down her face, Velma stood up. More Tenders had arrived and were clustered around Loine.

"Is she okay?" Velma asked, but no one answered her. Adira turned and gave her a withering look.

With a wail, Velma whirled and ran off.

Velma ran blindly into the trees along the rear of the estate. She needed to get away from everyone. She needed to fall down and cry until there was nothing left. She was stumbling blindly down one of the stone footpaths when she came across the young Tender who had refused the *sulbit*. The girl—Velma couldn't remember her name—looked up from scrubbing the stones and came to her feet.

"Are you all right? Can I help you?"

For a moment Velma just stood there, staring at her stupidly. No, she wasn't all right. And she needed help, far more than this girl could give. She shook her head and pushed by her, leaving her behind.

She sat down in the dead weeds at the base of a tree that grew right up against the stone wall at the back of the estate. How long she cried she didn't know, but it seemed the tears would never end. It was not just sorrow over the women she had injured—her mind kept recalling how broken Loine looked lying on the ground—but everything. Fear of Melekath. The strain of fulfilling the role of the FirstMother's aide, a role she now knew she was horribly incapable of. Shame because she wasn't able to live up to the FirstMother's expectations of her. It was all too much and it all came pouring out of her in a flood.

Eventually the tears dried up and she sat there for a long time feeling completely drained and empty. She was a shell, hollow inside. There was nothing left. But she knew what she needed to do. What she would do. She would go to the FirstMother and resign her position. She would beg for forgiveness and ask for mercy. She would accept whatever punishment was forthcoming. If she was out here on the stone footpaths tomorrow scrubbing them with that girl, then it was only what she deserved.

Despite her resolution, however, she could not quite seem to make herself get up and go face the consequences. The sun slid to the horizon and still she sat there. Crazy ideas occurred to her. She would sneak off the estate and leave the city. She would live alone in the wilderness and pray to Xochitl without stopping, becoming like one of the legendary Tenders from long ago, women who withdrew completely from the world to live a life of prayer. Even as she thought these things she knew they were foolish. She was too weak and afraid. She would not last a week in the wilderness and she could not pray for more than a minute or so before her mind wandered onto something else.

She heard someone calling her name and started to respond but her throat was terribly dry and all that came out was a croak. But she didn't try again. Better to hide here awhile longer. The calling moved away, then started to come closer. Finally, it became clear to Velma that whoever it was would find her eventually and she pushed herself to her feet just as Perast walked up.

It was difficult, but Velma made herself look at Perast. They had been Tenders together here in Qarath for almost ten years, but Velma couldn't say she actually knew Perast. Maybe no one did. She expected to see condemnation on the woman's face, but whatever Perast felt was well hidden.

"The FirstMother wants to see you."

"Okay," Velma replied. Her voice seemed to come from the bottom of a well. She brushed leaves from her robe and her hands felt very far away from her. When she went to leave the spot at first she could not move and she had a sudden, panicked image of women coming out here to carry her in for her audience with the FirstMother. But then she found the key to her legs and followed Perast, somewhat unsteadily, back to the house.

The estate house seemed curiously deserted. The only person Velma saw was a Tender who stepped out of a room as they approached. She was carrying used bandages but Velma could not see more because she hurried away and the house was quite dark inside, no lamps or candles having been lit. Perast led her to the FirstMother's quarters, opened the door, then left.

Now Velma's legs betrayed her yet again and she stood, shaking, in the hall, until the FirstMother said, "Come in, Velma."

There was no choice but to obey. The FirstMother was sitting on the edge of her desk. She pointed to a chair before her. "Sit down." Again, Velma had no choice. When she was seated, she steeled herself and looked into the eyes of the woman she'd known longer than almost anyone alive and still knew hardly at all. She could not read what she saw there—though she was certain she saw rage—but then she had never been much good at knowing what other people were feeling. Her whole life she'd felt like everyone else operated by this secret handbook that explained what others were feeling and how to understand them. Only she'd never received a copy of the book so she'd just spent her life faking it.

"First, I want you to know that I am..." The FirstMother's words trailed off. Velma could see that she was struggling with something, but mostly she was just surprised that the woman wasn't yelling. "I am regretful." Now the FirstMother stood abruptly, went around her desk and sat down in her chair.

Velma was stunned. What was going on here? "FirstMother? I don't understand." Was she being cast out of the Tenders? Was that what the FirstMother was regretting? When the FirstMother didn't respond right away, didn't look up from staring at her hands, Velma continued. "I'm so, so sorry. It was all my fault. I failed you. I failed everyone. I know you're going to strip me of my position and it's okay. I know I don't deserve it. I will take any punishment you give me. Please don't make me leave, though. I don't have anywhere else to go."

Now the FirstMother did look up and Velma's confusion increased. Where was the rage that she had grown so used to seeing? Why did it look like the FirstMother had tears in her eyes?

"You're not going anywhere."

Velma stared in awe while the FirstMother rubbed her eyes. It looked like her hand was shaking, but surely that was just the bad lighting.

"This is not your fault, Velma. It's mine."

Velma's jaw dropped. "It's not...but I wasn't paying attention and then I...but, you..."

The FirstMother shook her head. "I have been pushing you, all of you, too hard."

"But...Melekath is coming."

"So he is. But we won't put up much of a fight if we've already killed ourselves off. I knew you were tired. I knew you were all tired. I could feel your control slipping. I should have let you stop before..."

"No," Velma said. "You're the FirstMother."

"Which means I don't make mistakes?" The FirstMother gave a rueful smile. "If only that were true." Now the FirstMother looked at her. "Go get some rest. I will need your help in the morning."

"You mean I'm...I'm not...I have my position? But I don't think I'm very good at it. I think you should choose someone else."

"Are you defying your FirstMother now?"

Velma winced reflexively, then was even more confused when she realized that although the FirstMother had rebuked her, she didn't actually *sound* angry. And with the FirstMother, when she was angry, she definitely sounded angry. With the FirstMother, Velma didn't need the handbook. She was easy to read.

"Loine has suffered some burns, and she doesn't remember anything of what happened. She doesn't remember the whole day, actually. But she's going to be all right. You can go see her in the morning." Still Velma sat there, struggling to come to grips with what had just happened, or not happened, in this case. "Go to bed, Velma."

Dazed, Velma stood and made her way to the door.

"Good night, Velma."

"Good night, FirstMother," Velma echoed dutifully.

"Velma."

"Yes?"

"Call me Nalene when we're alone. We've been friends a long time."

Velma nodded, then practically ran from the room. The only thing that made sense was that she was dreaming. She was probably still lying out there on the grass, nearly dead from her mistake. Certainly *that* hadn't just happened.

SEVENTEEN

Cara was sitting outside her hut that night, listening to the night sounds, when she heard someone approaching. She tensed, wondering who it was. It could be Adira. The young woman had already brought her food some time ago. When she did, she'd stared at Cara for a long minute, while Cara held her food and wished she'd go away. It seemed rude to eat while the other Tender was there, but she was feeling really hungry.

"I don't know what to think about you," Adira said finally. "I should hate you. I should spit in your food before I give it to you."

Cara looked at the bowl of thin soup warily.

"But I don't. Hate you, that is. Even though you rejected the Mother's gift. I should hate you, but I don't." Her strange, hungry stare traveled over Cara, taking everything in. "What is it about you?"

Cara didn't answer. Did this mean Adira hadn't spit in her food? She looked at the soup again. It looked fine and she realized then that it didn't really matter. She was hungry and she was eating this soup whatever it had in it. Scrubbing walkways tired a person.

Adira seemed to come to a decision. "I'll figure it out. I'm good at that."

Then she kept staring. Finally, Cara said, "Okay." Only then did Adira leave.

Now Cara sat there in the moonlight, dinner long since finished, and wondered if it was Adira who approached, if maybe she had figured out whatever she was trying to. Instead, she was surprised to see Donae walk up.

Donae had never been a very big woman, but she looked shrunken and positively tiny now.

"Donae!" Cara called out softly, hurrying to her. "What are you doing here? You could get into trouble." As she spoke she took the woman's arm and guided her to the rickety stool she'd been sitting on.

It wasn't much in the way of a chair, but it was all she had, scavenged from a pile of scrap wood behind the hut. Furniture had not been included in the exile deal.

"I'm already in trouble," Donae replied, in her soft, sad voice. Cara realized she was shivering and she hurried into the hut to get her blanket, about the only other thing she had. This she wrapped around Donae, though the night was warm.

"Oh, Cara," Donae said, then burst into tears.

Cara knelt beside her and took her into her arms, wishing, as always, that she knew what to say or do. But she didn't, so she just held her friend and waited.

"I should have done what you did," Donae said, when her sobs had subsided somewhat. "I shouldn't have taken the *sulbit*."

She cried some more and Cara held her, wishing for words.

"I wish I was brave like you are."

Now Cara did have words. "Brave? Like me? I'm not brave, Donae. I'm as scared as anybody."

Donae pulled back to look at her. Her tears were glistening tracks down her cheeks. "You *are* brave," she said fiercely, "and if I was brave like you I'd have said no too."

Cara squeezed her hands. "It will be all right."

"Will it? We're lost, all of us. The world is ending and I...I have this thing, stuck to me always." She leaned forward and lowered her voice. "I threw it away last night. I pretended like I had to go to the privy and I threw it down the hole. Then I ran." She sniffled some more. "This morning it was back on my chest, trying to feed on me. I almost screamed." She was squeezing Cara's hand so hard it hurt. "You saw what happened today. I can't control this thing. The same thing that happened to that Tender is going to happen to me. Or something worse. Oh, what am I supposed to do?"

Cara had no answers for her. She waited.

"I wish I was out here with you. I wish they'd take this thing away and make me a servant. I'm doomed."

"No, you're not," Cara said suddenly.

"But it's hopeless."

"It's not hopeless. There's always hope. You know what you need to do? Since you can't get rid of that thing, you have to learn to master it. You have to work extra hard at the training exercises. You have to make sure it can't get out of control."

"But I don't think I can."

"And I think you can. You just have to not give up."

"I don't know," Donae said, and gave herself over to crying more.

Cara stood up. "You have to get up now, Donae." She knew Donae, and the woman would cry all night if given the chance. "You have to get back to the others before someone realizes you're gone." She helped the woman up. "Listen to me. You can do this. Just don't give up. Keep trying, and when you're worn out, try some more. You'll be all right."

"You really think so?"

"Of course I do," Cara replied, hoping she sounded sincere. In truth, she was frightened for her friend, frightened of what would happen if her *sulbit* got away from her and there was no one there to help her out. "Just don't give up."

EIGHTEEN

"There it is again." Mulin stood with her eyes closed. "I think it's Lenda."

Mulin and Perast were hunting Lenda again, haunting the darkest corners and meanest alleys of Qarath in search of their lost sister. More than once they had caught a trace of her Selfsong, but every time it disappeared when they tried to follow it.

Perast turned her head this way and that as if she was sniffing the air. Both women were melded with their *sulbits*, needing the enhanced awareness melding gave them to have any chance of finding Lenda. "I feel it too. This way."

The women crept along the edge of the Cron River. They were beside the stretch of river that bordered the area known as the Pits, not far from the outside wall of the city. The river here was thick with filth and it stank. The Pits themselves smelled worse, full of rotting garbage, leaning remnants of buildings, and more than one dead body. Their footsteps seemed loud on the broken stones of the river's edge. Ahead was the dim shape of a section of wall, perhaps a leftover piece of a warehouse from the days when this area was still a functioning part of the city, before King Arminal Rix brutally suppressed an uprising here by walling the whole area off and ordering it burned down.

In response to her excitement and nerves, Mulin felt her *sulbit* slide across the back of her neck and down her arm, where its tail wrapped around her wrist, its head jutting out onto the back of her hand. It was half as long as her forearm now, almost as large as the FirstMother's. It moved like a snake, and it somewhat looked like one, except that the head was more rounded and it had tiny legs forming. Just yesterday eyes had appeared on top of its head, black and beady.

They made it to the section of wall and crouched behind it. "I think she's just on the other side," Perast whispered into Mulin's ear. Lenda's Song was fairly loud now, but the unique rhythm and melody that Mulin recognized as Lenda's was nearly lost in a much louder, cacophonous dissonance that was distorted and painful to her inner senses.

Mulin adjusted her focus so that the everyday world receded into the background and she could more clearly *see* flows of LifeSong. Then she peeked around the edge of the wall. She *saw* the glowing outline of a rat dart out and run behind a heap of garbage, that was itself filled with hundreds of tiny glowing shapes that had to be insects. Further off was the glow of what was probably a wild dog, and beyond it were two others. Attached to all of them were golden flows of LifeSong.

She leaned further out and then she could *see* Lenda. Her *akirma* was fragile and dim except for two bright patches on it about two-thirds of the way up. Those were her *sulbits*. From them thick tendrils extended deeply into Lenda, piercing the brightness that was her Heartglow. The sight made Mulin feel sick inside. Was her friend still in there at all? Did she know what was happening to her?

Lenda was crouched over someone who was lying on the ground, twitching feebly. There were two holes in the person's *akirma*. The *sulbits* were perched on the holes, sucking out the victim's Song. Whoever it was would not live much longer; already his Heartglow was flickering.

Mulin pulled back behind the wall. "It's her."

Nothing else needed to be said. They both knew what they needed to do. They would only get one chance.

Mulin looked around until she spotted one of the thicker flows of Song winding through the darkness of *beyond*. It was too far away for her to reach with her hand, but recently she and Perast had learned how to extend that reach, using the power of will, which grew stronger every day as their *sulbits* grew stronger. With her will she drew it close enough to take hold of it with her hand, while beside her Perast did the same thing.

She grunted softly as the extra power coursed through her. She held onto the power that she bled off the flow, letting it pool inside her, held back by the strength of her will. When she was nearly at the limit of what she could hold, she felt Perast tap her on the arm.

"I'll take the one on the left," Mulin whispered. "On three, we step out and release."

Mulin counted to three then, still maintaining her hold on the flow, she stepped around the end of the broken wall and raised her free hand. Perast did the same.

Just before she released, Mulin heard a change in Lenda's Song and knew the *sulbits* were aware of them.

The Song bolts, released nearly simultaneously, were blue-white flashes that lit up the surrounding area like lightning bolts. They struck Lenda's *sulbits* as she was standing up, and she was knocked to the ground in a spray of sparks of light.

"Don't let up!" Mulin yelled, striding forward. The initial Song bolt was expended, but she was still hitting her target with a steady stream of power that crackled and spat as it spent itself on the creature, and Perast was doing the same.

And it was working. The tendrils piercing Lenda's Heartglow had retracted and the creatures were sliding across her *akirma*, trying to find purchase but unable to under the onslaught of Song.

Just a few seconds more. If they could just keep it up for a few more seconds, they could knock the creatures off Lenda and drive them away. They could save her.

At that moment a tendril from the *sulbit* Perast was attacking writhed and lanced into the *akirma* of the dying man on the ground. It pierced his Heartglow and a flare of power raced back up it to the *sulbit*. Mulin started to call out a warning, but she was too late.

The *sulbit* pulsed suddenly, and a wave of power fed back up the stream coming off Perast. There was a concussion and she was lifted off her feet and thrown backwards, her scream cutting off when she hit the ground. The stream of power blinked out.

Even as Perast was flying through the air, Mulin *saw* the *sulbit* she was attacking start to do the same. She was already releasing the stream when the wave of power flashed back up it. It felt like a giant fist struck her and she was knocked backwards, but she got far less than Perast. She ended up on her knees, blood streaming from a cut on her lip and her ears ringing.

Through blurred vision she saw Lenda leap to her feet and whirl toward them. Despite the darkness, she felt she could see the savage snarl that twisted Lenda's features, the way her hands curled into claws as she took a step toward them as if to counterattack. Her robe was fouled and torn. The stubble that had regrown on her head was pure white. Her eyes were those of a wild animal.

Then she turned partway, stared off into the darkness, and stiffened, a predator that senses the approach of a larger predator. A moment later she bounded off and was lost in the night.

As she ran away, Mulin's *sulbit* slithered out onto her hand, its head raised as it stared after its fleeing brethren. For a moment she was sure it was going to go after them and she grabbed at it with her other hand, while at the same time commanding it mentally to stay. After a moment it slithered back up her sleeve, reluctantly it seemed.

Her pulse racing from the adrenalin, Mulin crawled over to her friend. Perast was lying on her back, motionless. Thankfully, she was still alive, though Mulin could tell from her Song that she was unconscious. Even her *sulbit* seemed to be unconscious.

The strangest thing happened then. Out of nowhere a soft wind began to blow. It blew past Mulin, carrying a cloud of dust that smelled of something she could not quite place. The dust seemed to coalesce around Lenda's victim and as the wind died away she saw a man standing there, looking down.

T'sim knelt beside the man. He rolled him onto his back, then opened his eyelids and stared into his unresponsive eyes.

"What did you see?" he asked softly.

The corpse's lips moved and something like a sigh escaped it, but no words.

"What did you see?" he asked again, leaning close to the cold lips.

But there was no answer. He was too late. Even if he wasn't, the man couldn't have told him what he wanted to know. The dead were useless. So many died at Veragin and not a single one of them had been useful either. Thousands of years and he was still no closer to answering the one question that truly interested him.

Sighing, he got to his feet. A sound from one of the Tenders made him turn. She was looking at him. It was time to go. Staying here would lead to uncomfortable questions, questions he did not want to answer. He looked around at the filth and decay of the Pits and his nose wrinkled in distaste. Looking down at his boots he saw that they were caked with the same filth.

He pursed his lips and began to blow, like a man whistling. But no whistle emerged. Instead, the wind came. It started around his ankles, circling him like an excited puppy. It rose, climbing higher, finally wrapping around his head.

When it died away, T'sim was gone.

NINETEEN

"Can I help you, Advisor?" Perganon asked, looking up from the book he was reading and taking off his glasses. Quyloc had just entered the library.

"I hope so."

Perganon closed the book and stood up from his desk. "I will do whatever I can."

"Have you read every book in this library?" Quyloc asked.

"Except for those," Perganon said, motioning toward a pile of dusty books on a table. "They were only recently unearthed when workers tore that wall out." One wall of the library had been torn out and a room beyond was visible.

Quyloc walked over to the table and looked at a couple of the books. One was in a language he didn't know. The others weren't in very good shape. There were hundreds of them. It would take months just to get an idea of what was here, and years to read them all. He turned back to Perganon.

"Have you ever heard of a place called the *Pente Akka?*"

"Some, but not much." Perganon glanced curiously at the *rendspear*, but did not ask about it.

"What do you know about it?"

"That it is a sort of shadow world existing beside our own. The book I read said it was connected to the sand dunes of the Gur al Krin."

"The Gur al Krin?"

"It was the writer's contention that the Gur al Krin is not a natural desert, but is instead a byproduct of the *Pente Akka.*"

"Why would he think that?"

"He had taken samples of the sand and subjected them to various tests, exposing them to weak acids. Then he compared the results to other sand exposed to the same things. I won't go into the details, but he claimed the sand from the Krin reacted differently from any other he'd found on this world."

Quyloc thought about the sands covering the borderland where he passed through the Veil. Could it be the same sand? Why had it never occurred to him before? He was starting to go when the librarian stopped him.

"Advisor, if I may be so bold," Perganon said. "Is the *Pente Akka* where you got the unusual spear you are carrying?"

Quyloc looked down at the spear, then back at the librarian. "Yes, it is."

Perganon's face lit up, though he tried to hide it and resume his professional mien. "I know you are a busy man, but it would mean a great deal to me if you would someday tell me more about your experiences there." He coughed into his hand. "It is not just for my own curiosity, mind, but Macht Rome has commissioned me to write a history of these times we are living in."

"A history?" Perganon nodded. "Okay. Someday I will tell you about it." *I just hope we're still alive to talk about it.* Quyloc opened the door to leave.

"Oh, one last thing," Perganon said. "One of these books was written by a Tender." He pointed to the pile of dusty books recovered from the wall. "According to my earlier source, it was a Tender who first discovered the *Pente Akka*. There may be something in there which sheds some light."

Quyloc felt hope dawn within him. "Which one is it? I will start on it myself."

"I'm afraid that won't be possible…unless you are familiar with ciphers?" Quyloc shook his head. "It is written in code, as if the author was putting down an account that was forbidden. It does not seem like a complicated code and I believe I can break it, but it will take me some time. I will start on it immediately if you wish."

"Do it," Quyloc told him. "Let me know anything you discover, regardless of the time."

Perganon inclined his head and Quyloc left the library. Could there be something in the book to help him? Maybe someone else had been stung like he had and had discovered an antidote. It seemed unlikely, but at this point he would grasp at any straw.

As he was walking the hallway suddenly disappeared and he found himself on the edge of a wide, bronze-tinged river. Something surged up out of the water in a spray of foam, teeth snapping.

Quyloc reacted without thinking, the spear whirling in his hands. Even as the jaws reached for him he struck the creature's great, leathery head. The blade sheared through its jaw and tore a large chunk of it away. It collapsed at his feet.

Turbulence in the water told him more of them were close behind, but Quyloc didn't wait to find out. He summoned the Veil to him, slashed it and dove through.

He was on his hands and knees on the sand under the purple-black sky. He scooped up a handful of the sand. He got to his feet, closed his eyes and visualized the spot in the palace where he'd been. A moment later he was there.

The sand was still in his hand. He looked at it. Was this the same sand he and Rome had trekked through in the Gur al Krin? It looked like it might be, but there was no way to tell for sure. Was Perganon's source right? Was the Gur al Krin a byproduct of the *Pente Akka*?

He dropped the sand on the floor. What difference did it make anyway? If he didn't find an antidote to the venom soon he was going to be trapped there. One of these times he was going to be too slow.

He left the palace, thinking that he needed to talk to Rome. The macht wasn't out in the exercise yard, so he went into the stables. The stablemaster and a handful of grooms were gathered around a horse they had down on the ground, its legs hobbled together so it couldn't get up. He walked over to them.

"Have any of you seen the macht recently?" he asked.

The stablemaster barely glanced at him, then turned his attention back to the horse. He was kneeling by the horse's front legs, a slender knife in his hand. There was a big swelling low down on the horse's leg. "No, sir," he said. "I will send someone to look for him if you want, but first we need to take care of this horse. If I don't get that snake venom out right now, the animal will die." So saying he made a quick cross cut on the animal's leg. "Hold him steady," he told the others, then he bent, sucked at the wound, spit on the ground, and repeated the action.

Quyloc turned away and left the stables.

TWENTY

Rome opened the door to the library and went in. He'd never actually been in the library before. The first thing he noticed was the wall that had been recently torn out. He looked through the opening and saw that the room beyond had been emptied of furniture and new shelves were being built. He didn't see Perganon anywhere. That struck Rome as odd. Where else would the librarian be, but in the library? In Rome's mind the man lived here, holed up with his books, maybe coming out after dark when everyone else was asleep.

He realized that there was a doorway in the back corner of the room that he hadn't seen at first. Through it was a second room, as full of books as the first one had been. Since there were no windows in the room it was pretty dark. He peered into the gloom. It looked like there was yet another doorway on the far wall. Curious, he crossed the room.

Just as he got there he saw Perganon backing out of the doorway, his arms loaded with books. He seemed to be talking to himself.

"Need a hand with those?" Rome asked in his normal voice, which could mildly be called booming and would have been almost yelling for most people.

Perganon jumped and gave a strangled cry. The tower of books started to topple and he backpedaled, trying to keep them from falling. Rome had to grab him to keep him from falling on his back. The books crashed to the floor.

"Why in Bereth's nine hells would you sneak up on a man like that?" Perganon yelled, thrashing in Rome's grip. "Were you born a lout or did it take practice?"

Rome started laughing and set Perganon back on his feet. Perganon whirled on him, his eyes flashing, ready to curse some more. He was a small man, with yellow whiskers turning to white and gnarled hands that seemed too big for his frame. Then he adjusted his spectacles and saw who it was. The color drained from his face and he started apologizing.

"Humblest apologies, Macht. I thought it was that servant boy with the crooked eye. He likes to sneak up on me. I am terribly sorry. I never dreamed—"

"Don't worry about it," Rome said, still chuckling. "You didn't know it was me." He bent to pick up one of the books.

"Leave those, Macht. I will pick them up later."

"Okay." Rome dropped the book back on the floor. "What's with the secret room?" He took a step toward the doorway.

"Nothing," Perganon said hurriedly, moving to get to the door first and swinging it shut. The door was faced with book-covered shelves and was nearly invisible when closed. "Just a place to keep the books that won't fit in the other rooms."

"You sneaky devil," Rome said, examining the door. "It *is* a secret room. How did you ever pull that off?"

"Oh, it was long ago. Some reconstruction was going on in this part of the palace. Somehow the plans were misplaced. Things were very hectic, what with the overseer on the project taking ill and having to be replaced by someone unfamiliar with the work already done. Then the plans reappeared and they may have been different from the original ones in some small ways that no one really noticed. Except for a young man whose uncle was a close friend of mine."

Rome shook his head. "I think you just told me this secret room is here because of you, but I'm not sure how you managed to pull it off. Can't say I'm surprised though." And he really wasn't. He hadn't known Perganon that long, but he'd spent enough time around the man to really respect his intelligence and cunning. Perganon had survived, and thrived, in a palace full of plots and machinations for almost two decades under the old king Rix. Anyone who could do that had his respect. He had also proven himself invaluable to Rome more than once with the wealth of information he had accumulated about the kingdoms near and far, everything from the number of soldiers each could field to how good their crops were this year.

"You sent word that you needed to speak with me right away?" Rome asked.

"I did, but Macht, you should not have come here. I would have been at your command. It is only seemly."

Rome shrugged. "I needed to move around. Too much time sitting on my backside was making me stiff. Besides, it gave me a chance to sneak up on you." He chuckled again.

"As you wish, Macht. Shall we go into the outer room and sit down?"

"Lead on." After taking one last look at the hidden door, Rome followed him to the next room. Perganon went to the desk and took a sheet of parchment out of a drawer. Then he went to a chair and sat down. Rome pulled up the other chair. There was a time when the old man would have remained standing, waiting for Rome to tell him he could sit, but Rome had told him plainly he didn't want that kind of subservience from him.

"I have received another report from Fanethrin." Perganon paused and it seemed the lines in his face deepened. All at once he looked much older. "I fear it is the last one."

Rome leaned forward, his hands on his knees, his attention fixed on the old man.

"My contact has fled Fanethrin and is in Karthije now, recovering from serious injuries. He says he barely escaped. There is a narrow pass called Guardians Watch between the Landsend Plateau and a high ridge that runs north from the Firkath Mountains. It was still open when he went through, but once Kasai's men seal that off, there won't be any way through there."

He paused while Rome digested this.

"Kasai has been busy. His blinded ones have conscripted thousands. He now controls everything to the west of the Firkath Mountains, from Fanethrin in the north, to the ruins of Ankha del'Ath."

"Ankha del'Ath? Isn't that the old city where the Takare used to live?"

"It is."

"Too bad the place isn't still full of Takare. Kasai would have a lot fewer men to trouble us with."

"They would be helpful," Perganon agreed. He took off his glasses. "Do you mind if I have a drink?"

Rome snorted. "Surely not. Pour me one while you're at it."

Perganon went to a shelf and removed a couple of books. From the back of the shelf he pulled out a dusty bottle of yellow liquor and two glasses. Carrying it back to the table, he poured two stout quantities of the liquor into glasses. Rome sniffed his and took a sip.

It smelled a little bit like sage with some other, unidentifiable odor. To his surprise, Perganon downed his in one pull. The old man sat back and fixed a glum look on Rome.

"His army is coming."

Rome sat forward, the liquor sloshing over his hand unnoticed. "How long until they get here?"

Perganon consulted the letter, silently reading to himself. He closed his eyes for a few moments. "My contact was in Fanethrin's army for many years and achieved some rank there." Never once had Perganon identified a contact by name, and it seemed he was not about to begin now. "He says the order came in to mobilize the army, but they still needed time. He estimated that they would need four weeks still before they could march, but that was about three weeks ago. My best guess is that Kasai will be moving in a week at most. After that..." He shrugged. "It depends on how much of a hurry they are in."

"This source is reliable?" Rome asked.

Perganon looked up, his spectacles resting on his nose. "Absolutely."

"Then we have a lot of work to do." Rome drained his glass and set it on the table, his head already full of plans. The south wall repairs needed to be hurried up. The weapon smiths needed to turn out a great deal more weapons and armor; many of the new soldiers from the conquered kingdoms were poorly equipped. There was still work to be done training the new recruits.

"A suggestion if I may, Macht?"

Rome turned back.

"If you could reach Guardians Watch first..."

For a moment Rome didn't understand what the old man was saying, then it hit him. "Where the mountains and the Plateau come together. Your man said it was narrow."

"It would be a strong position." Perganon spent a couple of minutes filling him in on what he knew about it.

Rome smiled grimly when he was done. "That sounds like a really strong position."

"If you get there fast enough."

"That's the question, isn't it?"

After Rome left, Perganon went to the shelves and looked through the books until he found the one he was looking for, a thick volume of legends and ancient tales. He removed it and took it to one of the tables, where he began to flip through the pages. He found the entry he was looking for, adjusted his spectacles and started to read.

Fearing the wrath of Melekath after the Banishment, the gods began to disappear. Tu Sinar fled to the Landsend Plateau. The people who lived there were forced to flee or were killed, for Tu Sinar would suffer no humans in his realm, blaming them for the War of the Eight.

In time a group of Tu Sinar's followers made their way to the Plateau and pled with the god for the chance to serve him. Grudgingly, Tu Sinar allowed this, but forbade them to set foot on the Plateau itself. They were given the task of watching for Melekath's return. Most of all, they were to watch for the Guardians, for when they were able to leave the Gur al Krin, where they had been trapped since the Banishment, Tu Sinar would know that Melekath's time was close.

These followers built a fortress on the southern edge of the Plateau, in the pass between the Plateau and the Firkath Mountains. It was a mighty edifice of stone, for in them lay some of Tu Sinar's power to Shape the stone. There they kept their watch for the Guardians for centuries.

But in time, Tu Sinar began to distrust his followers, and accused them of betraying him to Melekath. So it was that Tu Sinar brought down his fist on the edge of the Plateau and a massive piece of the cliff fell, crushing most of the fortress and killing his followers. Only one tower, on the southern edge of the pass, survived. The place became known as Guardians Watch, a grim reminder of the vagaries of the gods.

Perganon closed the book and poured himself some more of the liquor.

After leaving Perganon, Rome grabbed the first servant he saw and sent him running out to the barracks. A few minutes later a soldier left the palace on horseback, riding hard for the city's main gates, beyond which could be seen the dust rising from the new troops Tairus was drilling. Rome went to Quyloc's office and found him at his desk, staring blankly at a parchment, the spear gripped in one hand. He looked up when Rome entered.

"Gods, Quyloc, you look terrible," Rome said. Quyloc looked like he hadn't slept in a week. There were new lines in his face and dark circles under his eyes.

"I feel terrible."

"Still haven't figured out how to get rid of the hallucinations?"

"They're not hallucinations," Quyloc said irritably. "They're real."

Rome gave him a skeptical look. He'd heard some disturbing stories about Quyloc's behavior lately, shouting at nothing, swinging his spear at enemies only he could see. He'd nearly stabbed one of the servants with the spear.

"Are you sure?" When Rome said the words, Quyloc's head snapped up and there was rage in his eyes. Before he could respond, Rome spoke again. "Take it easy. I'm not calling you a liar—"

"No, you're calling me crazy." Quyloc was on his feet now, the spear held in both hands across his chest. Rome took a step back.

"I didn't say you're crazy."

"No, but that's what you're thinking."

"So you can hear my thoughts now?"

"I don't have to. It's written on your face," Quyloc said bitterly. "You've heard that I've been acting strangely and so you just assumed…"

"Look at it from my side, Quyloc. You tell me you had this dream and in the dream something stung you. But you've got no mark on you. Then you say something is dragging you into this weird place—"

"It's the hunter that's doing it. I know it."

"But every time you say it happens you're still here. People can *see* you."

"So the only conclusion is that I'm crazy."

"I don't think you're crazy."

"Then what are you saying?"

"I think going to that place has affected you. I think you've been through things that no one else can imagine. I think Lowellin has had something to do with this."

"I'm glad you have it all figured out so neatly," Quyloc said. The sudden anger drained from him and he dropped back into his chair. "Now it gets easier, what I have to do next."

"What are you talking about?" Rome asked, suddenly wary. He'd never heard Quyloc sound like this before, so bleak and doomed.

"I quit. You don't need me as your advisor anymore so I quit."

133

"Now you *do* sound crazy. You can't quit. I need you."

"You're the crazy one. Only a crazy person would want an advisor that he thought was crazy."

"I don't think you're crazy."

"No, you just think I can't tell hallucinations from reality."

He had Rome boxed in. He didn't know how to counter him. So he said the first thing that came to mind: "Don't quit. I can't do this without you."

Quyloc looked up, his eyes haunted. "You don't get it, do you? I *am* having trouble telling hallucinations from reality. I've been dragged into that place so many times and it's been so long since I had any real sleep that I no longer know what day it is. I don't know what I was doing before you got here. I could be imagining all this right now."

"Is it that bad?"

"It's worse. I don't know what I might do. Don't you see? I need to quit my position before I do real harm. I need to go away by myself and see if I can figure this out."

"You're talking about leaving?"

Quyloc nodded. "Tonight or tomorrow morning at the latest."

"Where will you go?"

Quyloc lowered his head and his next words were so soft Rome could barely hear them. "It doesn't matter."

A sudden, sick thought occurred to Rome. "You're going to kill yourself, aren't you?" When Quyloc didn't deny it he knew it was true. "Gods, Quyloc, it can't be that bad!"

"You really don't get it. I meant what I said about doing harm. I wasn't talking about accidentally killing someone with my spear. I'm talking about harming *everyone*."

"I don't understand."

"The *gromdin* wants *me*. Lowellin thinks if it traps me, it might be able to keep me alive long enough, draw enough Song through me, that it can shred the Veil once and for all. If that happens, that whole world gets into our own. Whatever happens then is going to be very bad."

"You don't know that for sure. Lowellin might have some reason for saying that—"

"I can't afford to take that chance. If I can't figure this out soon, I have to kill myself. It's the only way."

"I won't let you do it. I'll keep—"

134

"What would you do?" Rome broke off and stared at him, confused. "If you believed there was even a chance that your enemy could use you to kill everyone, what would you do?"

"I'd…"

"Exactly. You'd sacrifice yourself in a second. It's who you are."

"This is different," Rome said, but his words lacked conviction.

"You can't stop me, Rome." He shifted his grip on the spear and now the cutting edge of the tooth was at his own throat. "It would take only a moment. Even if you took away my spear you'd just be leaving me helpless and the *gromdin* would win."

"There has to be a way," Rome said.

"I haven't given up yet," Quyloc replied. "I may still think of something."

He seemed calmer now, resigned, but that just made Rome more worried. What was happening? Was it already too late?

"Why'd you come here?" Quyloc asked.

"What?" Rome asked stupidly, still lost in his thoughts.

"What are you doing here?"

"I came because we need to meet. Tairus is on his way to the tower room. I want you there too."

"Why?"

Rome told him what Perganon had said. "We need to decide what to do."

"No we don't. You've already decided. You just want us to tell you it's a good idea."

"You don't know that.'

"Rome, I know *you*. You are impatient. You hate sitting and waiting for your enemy to come to you. You want to take the battle to Kasai. It is at once your greatest strength…and your greatest weakness."

"Where's Quyloc?"

"He's not coming."

"Is he sick?"

"Maybe. You've heard how he's been acting?" Tairus nodded. Rome filled him in on what Quyloc had said was happening to him.

"Do you believe him?" Tairus asked when he was finished.

"I think I do. You didn't see the look in his eyes. He's scared."

"I'd bet a month's pay this is all Lowellin's doing," Tairus said dourly. "I've never trusted him. Ever since he got here he's had us chasing shadows this way and that."

"You may be right. I don't know. Right now I just want to figure out what to do about Quyloc."

"He'll figure it out on his own, Rome. He always does."

"He's never had to figure out something like this though."

"What can you do anyway? Have you ever seen this *Pente Akka* place? Do you have any idea how to get there?" Rome slumped in his chair. "This isn't something you can fight with steel," Tairus continued. "You can't do anything and neither can anyone else. I know you don't want to hear this, I know you two go back a long way, but it really comes down to this: either Quyloc will figure this out on his own, or he won't. Nothing you or I can do will change that."

Rome scrubbed his face with his hand. "I just feel so helpless. I hate this feeling."

"So get your mind off it. Focus on the things you can do something about. Why'd you call me up here? The messenger acted like it was something pretty important."

"It is." Rome told him Perganon's news. When he was done, Tairus shrugged.

"So? Kasai may have a bigger army, but we have walls. And time to prepare. When he gets here, we'll whip him and break his army."

"We're not going to wait for him." Tairus raised an eyebrow. Rome pointed to a spot on the map laid out on the table. "We're going to meet him here, at Guardians Watch."

Tairus peered at the map, then looked at Rome dubiously. "It's too far. There's no way we can get there before him."

"We could if we left tomorrow."

"That's impossible!" Tairus exploded. "Most of the new recruits are still useless. The soldiers from the other kingdoms still fight amongst themselves more than anything. And don't get me started on the supplies we don't have ready yet. It can't be done. It will take a week at least."

"We travel light and we travel fast," Rome said. "We load the soldiers with as much food as they can carry. We don't wait for the supply train but leave it behind and let it follow as best it can."

"We'll be out of food in four days."

"Not if we send riders ahead with coin. They buy up all the supplies they can find, cache them along our path."

"It's still suicide. Even if we make it to the pass before Kasai does the men will be exhausted and who knows how many we'll have lost along the way. We won't stand a chance."

"I think we will," Rome replied. "I talked it over with Perganon. He's been there before, when he was a young man. He says it's a narrow pass, and its spanned by an old stone wall, much of which is still standing. On top of that, he says the approach from the west is steep and rocky. Any army attacking up that slope will be vulnerable."

"When he was a young man? When was that, a hundred years ago? Things could have changed a lot since then. It makes no sense. Why would you leave the strength of these walls and risk everything out there in the open? You could lose everything in one day."

"Because if we sit here, we *will* lose everything. Kasai's army is five times the size of ours. What's to stop him from investing the city with half his force and then heading on down into the Gur al Krin with the other half?"

Tairus scowled and crossed his arms, but made no reply.

"We're not going to win this war by being cautious, Tairus. We have to take risks. If this works, we'll crush Kasai's army before it ever becomes a real force. Then we can focus our attention on the prison and be waiting for Melekath when he gets out."

"There's still the problem of Karthije," Tairus pointed out. "Do you think Perthen is just going to let you march across his land?"

"He surely knows about Kasai's army. I'm hoping he'll see where his best chance lies."

Tairus gave Rome an incredulous look. "You don't really believe that, do you?"

Rome sighed. "Not really. I guess we'll deal with him when we have to."

"What about the Tenders? Are you going to bring them?"

"I think we have to."

"I don't trust them any more than I do Lowellin."

"I'm not sure I do either, but we're going to be outnumbered. We need all the help we can get and you've heard what they can do."

"If they don't lose control. You know how it gets, once the screaming starts and people start dying. We don't know if they'll be able to handle it."

"I guess we'll find out." Rome realized then that they were not alone. T'sim was standing against the wall by the door, his hands folded over his stomach.

"T'sim!" Rome barked. "What are you doing in here? This is a secret meeting."

"My apologies, Macht," T'sim said, bowing slightly. "I believed you would need my services."

"I don't need your services! If I needed your services I'd let you know!"

"Of course," T'sim said smoothly. But he made no move to leave.

"Get out!"

T'sim bowed again and withdrew. Rome watched the door swing shut behind him. "How does he do that?"

"I don't know," Tairus replied. "I've given up trying to figure out anything anymore. I miss when things made sense." He stood up. "Since you've given me an impossible task, I better get started on it."

When he was gone, Rome leaned back in his chair and rubbed his temples. What he could use right now was a mug of ale.

There was a soft tap at the door. A moment later it opened and T'sim stood there, a silver serving tray balanced on one hand. On it stood a mug of ale. Rome sighed. Yet one more slice of weirdness in a world that was increasingly so.

But he was grateful for the ale.

TWENTY-ONE

Rome pushed open the heavy door into his royal quarters and went in, his mind filled with a thousand details that needed to be taken care of before they marched the next day. So absorbed was he that he didn't at first notice T'sim standing just inside the room. When he did he jumped slightly in surprise.

"What are you doing hiding in here?" he yelled.

"I'm not hiding," T'sim said mildly. "I came to offer you my services."

"Look, T'sim, the ale was good and I appreciate it, but I don't need your help right now."

"Perhaps not now, but are you not marching to battle tomorrow?"

"So you heard that. Well, everyone was going to find out soon anyway. Anyway, I won't be needing you."

"I'm sure you will."

"We'll be marching hard and fast. There's no place for you."

"I'll be no bother. You'll see."

"You're starting to anger me, T'sim."

"And I am very sorry for that, Macht," he replied, but remained where he was. "I don't wish to anger you."

"Then leave."

"But you will need my help packing." It was clear that someone had already begun packing for Rome. A large number of clothes were laid out on the bed, there were toiletries on the long table before the wall mirror, and at least a dozen pairs of shoes set out by one of the wardrobes. Two half-filled chests sat on the floor.

Rome looked at it all and groaned. "I should have never left the tower. Things were so much simpler there."

Opus bustled into the room right then, his arms loaded with fine clothes. Rome turned on him.

"What is all this stuff, Opus?"

"Your clothing for the march, Macht," Opus said, laying the clothes he was carrying on the bed. "You're leaving tomorrow. There's no time to waste."

"How do you know that? I only just made the decision an hour ago!"

"It is my job to know these things, Macht."

"Were you listening at the door?" Rome growled.

Opus shook his head emphatically. "I would never do such a thing, Macht, and if I did you could relieve me of my position immediately and it would be only just."

"Then how do you know?"

"When General Tairus left his meeting for you he gave orders to several of his aides, orders regarding the preparation of food, weapons, horses and other supplies armies require for marching. One of my staff overheard and informed me. I simply drew a conclusion from the available evidence."

"Huh," Rome said. "You're unbelievable, you know that?"

"I will take that as a compliment, Sire." He looked at T'sim. "May I ask who this man is?"

T'sim bowed. "I am Macht Rome's servant."

Opus shot Rome a flinty look. "You take on a servant and do not bother to inform your chief steward?" he said icily.

"I did not take on a servant!" Rome protested. "He just follows me around and now he's in my room. I don't need a servant. Maybe you can find something for him to do."

"I have been with the macht since Veragin," T'sim added. "My previous master no longer required my services."

"Do you have a letter from him recommending your services?" Opus asked.

T'sim shook his head. "Sadly, he was unable to provide one on account of his untimely demise."

"Isn't anyone listening to me?" Rome cried. "I don't need a servant! I can do things for myself."

"But I believe my services to the macht since then speak for themselves," T'sim added, ignoring Rome. "I am very good at what I do."

Opus appraised Rome with a critical eye. "There does seem to be rather less horse manure on his shirt than usual."

"That's just because I haven't been to the stables in the past couple days! T'sim has nothing to do with my clothes. He just brings me ale sometimes."

"Maybe you will have more success than I." T'sim raised an eyebrow questioningly. Opus gestured at the clothes he'd just put down. "Do you know what his latest thing is? He takes the clothes he doesn't like and he hides them. I found these behind a chest in a storeroom by the servants' quarters."

"This is unfortunate," T'sim agreed.

"I don't need a servant," Rome repeated, though more quietly this time. Neither Opus nor T'sim paid any attention to him.

"Perhaps you can help him to see that just because he is out running around with his soldiers there's no reason he cannot demonstrate the majesty of his office. With a bit of effort, he might actually inspire the common man to greater heights." As he spoke Opus was folding a black silk shirt from the pile.

"Inspire who to *what*?" Rome asked. "What are you talking about?"

"All that can be done, I shall endeavor to do," T'sim said solemnly.

"Then I would feel somewhat relieved," Opus said. "Knowing he is in good hands."

T'sim bowed. "The best."

"I don't need a servant." This time Rome said it to the table. "Look at that. Same response."

At the door Opus turned back. "Doubtless it is far too much to ask, even for one as capable as you..."

T'sim stopped in the process of folding a pair of pants.

"It is his beard. He has ever refused, but if you managed to trim the worst, I would be forever beholden to you. There are scissors on top of that table there."

"You're not touching my beard," Rome said.

"I will do my best," T'sim told Opus.

"That's all any of us can do," Opus replied, and left.

"He gets worse when you humor him like that," Rome told T'sim. "I know it doesn't seem possible, but he does."

"So you would not like me to trim your beard then?"

"Haven't you heard anything I said? I don't need a servant. I like that ale trick you do, but I don't need anything else."

"You might be surprised."

"But probably not. Look, whatever you think you know about wealthy people or nobility you can just forget. I'm not like that. I don't need people dressing me or feeding me or trimming my beard. In other words, I don't need a servant."

"At the very least I shall finish packing your clothes for the march." He picked up a pile of shirts and put them in a chest that was lying open on the floor.

"Still wrong. There's nothing to pack. A soldier only needs two of everything. Two pairs of pants, two shirts. That's so he can wear one while he washes the blood out of the other."

T'sim listened very seriously. "Is this true?"

"It is. So if you want to do something helpful, put all this stuff away. Or throw it away. I don't care. I don't have time for this. I have things to do." Rome walked over to the vanity table. He picked up a silver-handled hairbrush. "I won't need this," he announced, and tossed it back in the drawer. "Waste of space. I have to travel light." He poked through the razors, combs, scented hair oils, jars with powder in them, then settled for just opening a drawer and sweeping the lot of it in. "There," he said, satisfied. "That takes care of that." He saw a pair of dainty scissors that he'd missed and picked them up. "These are never to come near my face, do you hear?" he said to T'sim. "I like my beard the way it is."

Before one wardrobe sat a row of shoes, some shiny, others with large, brassy buckles or bows on them. "Won't need these either." Rome grabbed them up in an armload and tossed them in the wardrobe. He glanced at the shelf with the wigs on it and shuddered. Hooking a thumb at them he turned on T'sim. "You weren't thinking of bringing any of those, were you? It will be bad if you do."

T'sim shook his head. "It would not occur to me."

"Good." Rome clapped T'sim on the shoulder. "That should do it. Look how much easier I made your job."

After he had left, T'sim started whistling softly, an unusual tune that spoke of high peaks and lost places, unlike anything played by man. Then he opened the drawer on the table before the mirror, pulled everything out and swiftly and neatly placed it in a small chest, including not one, but two pairs of scissors. For a while after that he folded clothes and placed them in the two large chests, filling them to the top, then sealing them. After that he packed all the shoes into yet another chest. When he was done he stood back and surveyed his work. Then an impish smile spread across his soft cheeks and he went into the next room. When he emerged he was carrying two boxes. He set them on the bed, went to the wardrobe and removed two of the wigs.

Now Rome had everything he needed.

TWENTY-TWO

Bonnie made her way through the tavern, two mugs of ale clenched in one fist. It was early in the evening and the traffic was still light, but people were starting to trickle in. She didn't need to run drinks, not really, but she needed to do something. She couldn't sit in her room all the time, no matter what Rome said. She was a people person, and she liked being around people, even if they were drunk and stupid. Besides, she picked up a few coppers along the way doing this and a woman never knew when she'd need some coin, even if her lover was the macht, whatever that was.

As she pushed her way past a table crowded with six men, she felt a hand squeeze her backside, but she was ready for it. In the big pocket on her apron was a sewn leather bag, filled with lead shot and attached to a wooden handle. Without breaking stride, she seized it and gave the offender a quick slap on the side of his head.

"Ow! Bonnie, why'd you have ta go and hit me so hard for!" the man squalled, nearly falling off his chair.

"You know exactly why, Burk," she called back over her shoulder. "I'd thought you woulda learned by now."

The other men were laughing and slapping their knees. Burk scowled and came partway to his feet, looking like he wanted to push it a little further, but Gelbert coughed from his place behind the bar. He was a fat man, but there was still plenty of muscle under that fat and everyone who frequented the Grinning Pig Tavern knew that he could still club a man insensible with the best of them. Even if he couldn't, there were still Arls and Terk, the door guards, to back him up, and they were even meaner than he was.

So Burk sat back down, just as Bonnie knew he would, and even managed to force a smile onto his face. She also knew in an hour he'd have forgotten all about it.

"Coulda broke my nose, a bit to the right," he complained.

"On the up side, it might've helped fix your face," she retorted. She didn't even look at him, instead fishing out a damp rag and wiping an empty table. Her comment elicited a fresh round of raucous laughter.

"Nothing wrong with my face," he whined.

Bonnie stopped, put her hands on her ample hips, cocked her head and raised her eyebrows.

The men around Burk roared and his expression darkened. Bonnie figured she'd smacked him—verbally and physically—enough for right now. She didn't want him going off like a mad dog. "All in good fun, you know that, Burk. Just a little chivvying between old friends." He'd been coming into the Pig almost as long as she'd been working there, and he wasn't a bad sort, after all. Just lost his hold a bit when he drank too much.

"At least you ain't lost your touch," he said, rubbing the side of his head, where a red spot was already darkening toward purple.

"And I won't, you can set your hat on that," she replied, giving him a broad wink. He gave her a pretty sincere, if sheepish, grin and Bonnie went back to work. She knew how to handle these men. They were no more than big children, really. It wasn't just smacking them either. Part of it was knowing how to get down in the gutter and give and take with them, the casual insults and mockery that made up the foolish male world. Part of it was knowing when to stop before they got their precious pride bruised and had no choice but to do something stupid. Bonnie knew how and where to draw the line and she knew how to make them respect it.

She headed back to the bar, giving Lita a pat on the shoulder as she went by. Lita was at a table with a tattooed man with long, black hair. His accent marked him as from the south, likely Thrikyl. She was sitting on his lap practically pouring rum down his throat. Bonnie gave him a critical look. There was an art to what Lita was doing. You wanted them drunk enough so they spent money on you, got real generous and maybe even lost a bit of the stiff in their flagpole, but you didn't want them so drunk they got mean and started hitting.

Fortunately, Lita was a pro. The customer was pretty far along, but Bonnie wasn't picking up any bad feel off him. In fact, Bonnie had a gut feeling this one was a crier. Some men were that way. Wanted to tell you about their mothers or some girl who treated them wrong. It was all the same with her. Usually it was easier than tossing on the mattress, though not always. Not that it was an issue for her anymore. Not since Rome.

Then there was Sereh. Bonnie's eyes shifted to the thin, hollow-eyed woman dancing awkwardly with a man in the corner of the room. Sereh hated men. Hated them with a passion. There was a disturbing kind of crazy inside Sereh. Usually the girls who worked at the Pig got to know each other, got drunk, cried, got sick together. It kept them alive. It kept them mostly sane. But Sereh wouldn't have anything to do with the others. Bonnie's gut told her they'd find Sereh dead in an alley some morning.

But you never knew, she reflected. Sereh could change. She had only been here less than a year. Talind was proof that change could happen. She'd been hollow and bitter when she started here three years ago and she was a damn sight better now. She'd done a lot of crying on Bonnie's shoulder over those years. Bonnie knew she had good shoulders for crying on. It happened often enough.

The last woman in the room was Rowena. She was one of those women who seemed completely oblivious to the effect her body was having on the men she encountered, but who never missed the reaction of a single one of them. And she loved every bit of it. She was tall and exotic, with dark skin and almond-shaped eyes. Probably from Fanethrin, though no one knew for sure. One night she got drunk after the Pig closed and said something about escaping from her owners, but Bonnie never heard any more. She played dangerous games with the men, always stringing several on at a time, making them think they might be the one she'd let carry her away, but secretly laughing at them.

As bad as this life could be, Bonnie reflected, what the women who worked here were running from was usually worse. At least here there were men whose job was to pound into pulp anyone who tried to hurt the women. There were even friends. Out there, on your own—or stuck with a man who turned into a monster every time he drank—it could be a lot worse. She could speak to that experience herself.

Which had a lot to do with why she hadn't taken Rome up on his offer to move into the palace. Sure, he loved her now. But what about when he tired of her? Or worse, when someone finally hired the right assassin and killed him? Where would that leave her? How long would she last at the palace without him to protect her? She had no knowledge of the power games they played there. She'd be a kitten amongst the coyotes. At least down here she knew the score. She knew how to survive and do more than survive.

She surreptitiously touched her stomach and the bulge growing there. She was getting pretty far along in her pregnancy and would have to make some decisions soon. So far, no one had noticed, because she was a big woman and she wore loose dresses. But eventually she wasn't going to be able to hide it, not even from that blind fool she'd fallen in love with. Was she going to stay here and raise her child around thugs, drunks and prostitutes? How would Rome react when he found out? You never knew how a man was going to react to the news that he was a father. It might be the last time he ever spoke to her. Even if he didn't turn away, he wouldn't want her raising a child here, but he couldn't very well bring them up to the palace, could he? A king couldn't publicly live with a prostitute, no matter how popular he was. The people just wouldn't stand for it.

Probably he would put his foot down and move her into a small house somewhere closer to the palace. That way he could have her near but still pretend to his people that she wasn't important to him. She tried picturing the house. Nothing fancy, but with a bit of a yard. Maybe room for some flowers. It looked nice, and she admired it for a moment, then she slammed the door on it. She was a fool. Nothing like that was going to happen. What was going to happen was that he would forget about her, or he would die with a sword stuck in him, and she'd be back to living off her wits.

No, the only path open to her right now was to just keep this baby quiet, keep her eyes open and her guard up.

As if her thoughts summoned him, the door swung open then and Bonnie heard a familiar, booming voice. She waited quietly, standing at the end of the bar while he exchanged jibes with patrons and employees. He had two guards with him, quiet men who kept their hands on their swords and scanned the people in the room. With the Pig's no weapons policy, they should be the only ones in here with weapons other than the staff, but Bonnie was glad to see that Rome was finally taking some measures for his safety. The city was far too uneasy these days. Probably it was Tairus or Quyloc who insisted on it, because Rome was too stubborn. She'd have to thank them if she ever got a chance.

Then Rome's eyes fell on her and his face lit up in a smile that split his bearded face. The sudden, frank openness of his response caught her off guard and she felt her heart speed up and a blush spread across her cheeks. Astonishing that he could still have this effect on her, as guarded and wary as she was. Like a little girl she was.

"I would've been here sooner," he said, taking her in his arms. "I've been lost without my Bonnie. But there's so much to do. It never ends." There was a winsome, puppy look in his eyes that crushed the remainder of her defenses and made her want to slap him and kiss him at the same time. She settled for putting a finger against his lips.

"Can we just go upstairs where we can talk quietly?"

"Lead on, my lady," he said gallantly, bowing toward the stairs.

"Such a gentleman," she responded, pretending to titter behind her hand and fluttering her eyelashes at him.

"Only so I can take in the view on the way up," he whispered, giving her a smack on the butt as she passed.

She didn't reach for her sap this time.

Dreah, one of the young women who helped run drinks, knocked on the door to Bonnie's quarters a couple minutes later. She was carrying a tray with four mugs of ale on it. Bonnie took the mugs and pushed the door shut with her foot. Rome drank half the first mug in one draw and wiped at the foam on his mustache with the back of one meaty hand, then sighed. "That takes the dust off." He leaned back in his chair with another sigh and turned to her. "I've missed you."

Bonnie sat down, pulling her chair near his. She put her hand on his arm. "I have too."

He finished the mug of ale, set it down and scratched at his beard. "I've got bad news. I know you don't like it when I string it out so I'll just say it outright: We're marching tomorrow."

Bonnie's heart fell. For a moment she saw herself kneeling beside him on a battlefield, her tears mixing with his blood. She shook her head and the image fragmented and drifted away. She wanted to argue with him, to ask him why he had to go, but she didn't. That was not her and it would change nothing.

"Where are you going?" She tried to make her tone casual and light, but she didn't think she pulled it off.

"An army's gathering in Fanethrin. A big one. If we sit and wait for them, we'll lose. There's a place called Guardians Watch, where the Firkath Mountains and the Landsend Plateau come together. If we can get there first, could be we can beat them."

"That sounds like a long ways away."

He nodded wearily and she saw lines on his face that had not been there before. The burdens of rule were aging him. "It is. We're going to have to travel light and fast." He belched and reached for another ale. "I shouldn't be telling you this. You're probably a spy for Melekath."

"Sure I am," she agreed. "I've been waiting here at this tavern for you for years." She got up and sat in his lap. He smiled and squeezed her.

"I feel good right now. Like this is where I belong."

She said nothing, only stroked his hair.

"I want you moved into the palace before I go," he said. "The city's getting worse. You'll be safer there."

"I'm safe enough right here, Rome. The Grinning Pig has a strong door and only a fool would tangle with Terk and Arls."

"Still not as safe as the palace."

"Let's not spend what little time we have fighting. I'm not going and that's final."

He frowned at her. "You're a damned stubborn woman."

"I know. And if I wasn't you wouldn't love me."

"I just want you safe. You have no idea how important you are to me. If something happened to you, I don't think I could..." He choked up and his words tapered off.

"I'll make you a deal, Rome. Don't get yourself killed. Come back to me and I'll move into the palace with you."

"You mean it?"

"Yes...of course." Bonnie was surprised at herself. She hadn't meant to say those words. It was seeing his vulnerability appearing so unexpected like that. It caught her off guard.

"Well, I'm just going to have to come back alive then, aren't I?"

Bonnie held him close then and tried not to cry.

TWENTY-THREE

"Are you ready?"

Nalene jumped and her heart started pounding. It was late and she'd been frantically busy since word came earlier in the day that she and her Tenders—those who could handle their *sulbits*—were to be ready to march first thing in the morning. The hallway outside her quarters was dimly lit and she hadn't seen Ricarn standing against the wall. Lost in thought, worried about the upcoming march and the battle that would ensue, Nalene had been caught completely unprepared and she'd come awfully close to screaming.

"What are you talking about?" Nalene snapped.

"I asked if you were ready. Are you?"

"Why wouldn't we be ready? We will be traveling light. There isn't much to pack."

"That's not what I'm talking about. Are you *ready*?"

No, Nalene thought, they weren't ready. It was too soon. The Tenders had nowhere near the control that they needed. The *sulbits* were too small. She didn't have enough capable Tenders. "Of course we're ready." Could Ricarn hear the uncertainty in her voice? She peered at the woman, trying to discern an expression in the poor light, even though she knew it wouldn't help. It was impossible to tell what Ricarn was thinking even in the best light.

Ricarn stared at her and it seemed to Nalene that she could feel the weight of the woman's gaze on her skin. She wanted to say something, to break the weight of this unbearably long, silent moment, but she forced herself to stay quiet. She was sick of letting Ricarn get the better of her.

Finally, Ricarn said, "I believe you are. *You* don't believe it, but you are. And so are they. When the time comes they will do what they need to do. Some will die, of course. But it is war, is it not?"

Nalene's mouth dropped open. She had never expected to hear that. Oddly enough, she felt better. She really did.

"It's late. Is there anything else?" Nalene asked.

"Yes."

Then Ricarn just stood there, not speaking, not moving. Nalene realized that she was holding her breath. How did this woman stand so utterly still? How come she didn't fidget or shift her weight like an ordinary person? She wanted to shout at her. "Then what is it?"

"I came to tell you my sisters and I will not be accompanying you."

Nalene's first response was relief. This woman unnerved her. She couldn't think straight when she was around her. But she was the FirstMother. She was in charge. "I will consider your request. You should have brought this to me sooner. We leave in the morning."

"I know when you leave."

"You should have—"

"I did not come to ask permission," Ricarn said calmly. "I came to share information. We can best help here."

"Well," Nalene replied, thinking fast, "I was actually thinking that just yesterday. Without a *sulbit* you will be useless in battle anyway."

Nalene peered at Ricarn's face but could not see if there was any response to her words. She heard a buzzing then, as if a couple of bees had gotten into the estate house and swiveled her head, trying to see where the noise was coming from.

"So we would," Ricarn replied. "We are only simple women, after all." Then once again she just stood there, completely motionless, her eyes glittering in the weak light.

"Is there anything else you want?" Nalene cried at last. "I have many things to do."

"No," Ricarn answered. "I want nothing. I never do."

"Okay," Nalene said. "Good." She started to walk away, then paused and turned back as a sudden thought hit her. "One thing." Ricarn was still standing there motionless. "There is a Tender named Lenda. She…something went wrong when she went for her *sulbit*."

"She could not control her *sulbits* and now they control her."

"Yes," Nalene said, wondering how Ricarn knew. "If you find her… help her. She doesn't know what she is doing."

"We will," Ricarn said. "I do not believe she is forever lost."

"You think…you think there's still hope for her?"

Ricarn considered this. "There is. But perhaps not for much longer."

"I just…I just…I don't want her to get hurt."

Ricarn was silent for a long minute. Nalene had the feeling she was far away. "My sisters will look for her. They will find her. Our eyes are many."

Nalene hung there, beset by feelings she did not understand. Finally, Ricarn walked away and disappeared down the stairs. "Thank you," she whispered, soft enough so Ricarn could not possibly hear her.

TWENTY-FOUR

Quyloc was standing at the balustrade on the balcony outside his quarters in the darkness, looking down at the sea far below. Though there was only a sliver of moon, there was enough light to reveal the sharp rocks that jutted out of the water at the base of the cliff. It was several hundred feet down, more than enough. He could do it right now. Just climb onto the balustrade and jump off. It would be over in a few seconds. All the fear, all the confusion, all the suffering. The world would be safe then; the *gromdin* would have to find another person to use. Why should he keep fighting it?

A gust of wind blew across his face and when it died away he realized he was no longer alone. He turned wearily.

"What are you doing here?"

"I was curious to see if you were still alive," the little man said mildly, his hands folded in front of him.

"As you can see, I am. At least for now."

T'sim walked to the balustrade and looked over. "It is quite a long way down. I don't imagine you would survive the fall."

"That's the point, isn't it?"

"Do you think it would solve your problems? Dying?"

"All the ones I can think of."

"A final choice each person has, the option to end one's life. I have often wondered why more people do not choose it. It seems a logical choice, when nothing else seems to do."

"It's not so easy as that."

"But why not?" T'sim seemed genuinely puzzled. "You are frail creatures. It does not take much for you to die."

"I wasn't talking about that. I mean it's not so easy to make the choice."

"I confess I do not understand that either. When life has become unbearable, when there are no more solutions, why not choose to simply be done with it all? What could be more logical?"

"If you've come to talk me out of killing myself, you're doing a terrible job."

"But I didn't come for that."

"Then why are you here?"

"I came to ask you a question."

In spite of himself, Quyloc was intrigued. What question could he possibly answer for this...*being*?

"What do you think happens when you die?"

"What kind of question is that?"

The little man blinked. "An honest one, I assure you."

Quyloc stood there and stared at him. He looked utterly sincere. He considered the question. What *did* he believe? Then he shrugged. He was so tired. How long since he'd actually rested?

"You get to stop," he said finally. "You get to rest."

"That doesn't sound too bad," T'sim said.

"No, it doesn't." Thinking of Lowellin's words: *It wants you alive.* "There are worse alternatives."

"I think that more people don't choose death because they fear it. What I don't understand is *why* they fear it so much?" T'sim eyes seemed very bright, almost birdlike, as he stared at Quyloc, waiting for his answer.

"I don't know. We're afraid of the unknown I guess. Maybe we're afraid something worse is waiting for us."

"Worse? But I have seen many dead people and there is nothing. They are simply gone. How can that be worse than suffering?"

"Maybe it's because this life is all we have. It may not be much, but at least it's something. We're afraid to give it up because then we have nothing. Do we have to keep having this conversation? Don't you have somewhere else to be?"

T'sim continued as if he hadn't heard Quyloc. "I suppose since your time is so short you do not really have the chance to consider the alternative."

"What alternative is that?" Quyloc asked. He didn't really care. He wanted this conversation to be over, for everything to be over...one way or the other.

"The alternative to death is to live forever. People act as though they want to live forever without ever considering what it might actually be like to do so."

"You sound like you speak from experience," Quyloc said.

T'sim inclined his head slightly. "I do."

"So what is it like?"

"Dull. The world loses its flavor."

Quyloc considered this. "I guess I never thought about it that way." He turned to face him. "Who—or *what*—are you?"

"Only harmless T'sim, Advisor. I assure you."

Quyloc started to press him for more information, then gave it up. What difference did it make anyway? "For what it's worth, I believe you. But mostly I don't care. If you are done asking me questions, I have matters to attend to."

"Ah, your problem," T'sim said. "Have you decided which choice you will make then?"

Quyloc hesitated. "I think so."

"If you could drain the venom away, would you still choose death?"

"If I could…" Quyloc started, then it hit him. An idea. It wasn't much, but it was a possibility. It just might work. How did he not see it earlier? Had he completely lost his ability to reason?

"You have just had an idea."

"I did."

"Would you share it?"

"I'll tell you what. If I survive, I'll tell you. Now go."

"As you wish. I will see myself out."

Quyloc locked the door behind him, then went to his bed and lay down, the spear gripped tightly in both hands. He closed his eyes and concentrated. A moment later he was standing in the borderland before the Veil.

Where should he go? At least this time he was choosing the spot, so he should have some time and not be attacked right away. He visualized the ledge he'd stood on to kill the *rend*, then walked through the Veil.

He was standing on the ledge overlooking the jungle. Below him lay the huge carcass of the *rend*. Most of the flesh had been stripped from its bones, leaving only its huge skeleton. Its ribcage was large enough that he could have stood upright within it.

He unbuttoned his shirt. In the sulfur-yellow light of the *Pente Akka* the bite was a lump the size of his fist. The black lines coming from it went down to his waist and disappeared around his back. Reversing the spear, he held the blade against the lump, then cut a quick X in it, just like he'd seen the stablemaster do with the snake-bit horse.

When he squeezed the lump black ichor came out, thick and dark. He leaned over, careful not to get any of it on himself. He kept squeezing until there was nothing left, then stepped back. Most of the lump was gone, but the black lines looked no better.

Movement in his peripheral vision caught his attention and he looked down at the ground, was stunned by what he saw.

The black ichor was *moving*.

Quyloc started to summon the Veil, but it was too late.

Something rubbery and shapeless rose up from the spot and leapt at him. By luck more than anything he got the spear up and deflected the thing, ducking as it flew over his head.

It hit the ground and leapt at him again, but this time he was ready. He slashed with the spear, the thing squealed and fell to the ground in two pieces.

He backed away from it. Had that thing been living inside him?

Then he realized it was still moving, writhing on the ground, reforming. He stepped forward and stabbed it, once, twice. The thing went still.

He looked back at his wound. The source was gone, but the infection remained. He might have slowed the end, but he hadn't stopped it.

He summoned the Veil, cut it and stepped through. Once on the other side, he visualized the river, then stepped back through. Now he was on the banks of the river, the bronze water flowing slowly by.

He dipped the blade of the spear in the river, then pressed it against the wound.

The pain was so bad he screamed. The blade felt like it was red hot. He could feel burning fiery lines coursing down the black lines. He doubled over, biting back the screams, afraid he would summon the hunter.

But in time it passed. He straightened and looked down at his torso. The black lines were gone.

Hurriedly he summoned the Veil, slashed it, and jumped through. A moment in the borderland and then he went back to his quarters.

Quyloc sat up in bed, his heart still beating fast. Holding the spear, he went to the mirror and pulled his shirt collar down.

The enlarged veins were gone, as was the lump.

Quyloc went to a chair and sat down. After a moment he laid the spear down on the table and took his hand away. Nothing happened. Was it possible? Was he finally free?

He needed sleep. Tomorrow was going to be a long day, as were all of the ones to come. He started to go to his bed, then stopped and went back to the table and picked up the spear. Then he lay down, the spear resting on his chest.

It was best to be sure.

TWENTY-FIVE

The Landsend Plateau was tearing itself apart. The earth groaned and shrieked underfoot. Cracks crisscrossed the land. Smoke from the burning forests filled the air. Animals and birds fled the Plateau en masse, predator and prey alike ignoring the small band of Takare in their desperation to flee. The Takare, led by Rehobim, had been fighting their way north all morning, trying to make it back to Bent Tree Shelter, to find those they had left behind when they pursued the outsiders who attacked their village. Over and over again they had been forced to veer off their chosen path as their way was blocked by rents in the earth or burning forests.

Now they found their way blocked by a large barren. Barrens were areas of bare stone dotted with hot, sulfurous pools. Other than the tani and the occasional poisonwood, nothing lived on the barrens. Even during the best of times, crossing one was unpleasant, as if the very stone were leaching one's Life-energy away.

Rehobim hesitated for only a moment before setting foot on the barren.

"Wait!" Shakre called. "I don't think we should cross this."

"Why?" he asked, his head turning as he scanned the barren. "Do you see something?" Mist from the hot pools blanketed the barren, limiting vision.

"No, I don't."

"Then what is it?" Rehobim made no attempt to hide his dislike for Shakre.

"I don't know. It's just...I can sense something." As she spoke, she stepped onto the barren and the feeling of approaching wrongness suddenly grew stronger. She pulled her foot back. "We have to go around."

"We don't have time for your imaginings," Rehobim said. "Going around will cost us too much time."

So saying, he continued on, and the rest followed him. A few gave Shakre worried looks—over the years she had demonstrated her abilities a number of times—but they did not gainsay their leader.

Only Werthin stopped. "Can I help you, Windfollower?" Since leaving Bent Tree Shelter a couple days before Werthin had been keeping an eye on her, trying to help when he could.

"No, but thank you," she replied. She was truly grateful for his concern. More and more she felt like an outsider amongst her adopted people, a lone voice crying out warnings that none of the rest of them seemed to want to hear. Only Werthin seemed to actually hear what she was saying.

Not wanting to fall behind any more than she already was, Shakre hurried after the rest, Werthin right behind her. But every step she took deeper into the heart of the barren only increased her unease. There was something here, something that had recently awakened. It was like hearing heavy footsteps approaching, though she did not actually hear anything. She had no idea what it was, other than that it wasn't a living creature. She could hear no Song at all on the barren.

Whatever it was, it was getting closer quickly.

She scanned the sulfurous mist, trying in vain to see what it was, to figure out what direction it was coming from. But there was nothing moving except the water in the pools, which gurgled and bubbled, moved by currents from below. Ahead and to the left was a twisted rock formation that seemed to have grown straight out of the stone. Something could be hiding there, but, as hard as she tried, she couldn't determine if what she sensed was in that direction.

They walked for a few more minutes, sticking close together by unspoken agreement. Shakre's fear grew stronger with every step, but when she tried to call out to Rehobim to stop, he ignored her and hurried on.

Then, without warning, several of the sulfurous pools erupted at once. Steaming water shot high into the air. Out of the pools climbed creatures from a nightmare.

They were short and blocky and appeared to be made out of stone. They looked like creatures made by a small child. Their limbs were irregular lengths, their torsos squat and shapeless. They moved awkwardly, as if wearing bodies they were unfamiliar with.

In a terrible voice that was rough and difficult to understand, one of them cried out. "You failed! You didn't protect him and now he dies!"

The Takare fell back from them, weapons held up uneasily.

"I don't know what you're talking about!" Rehobim yelled back.

"You were supposed to keep the Plateau inviolate for your god." The creatures, arrayed in a semicircle before the Takare, began to move forward. "For your failure, you will die."

One of them ran at Rehobim and he swung his sword at it. When the weapon hit the thing it shattered. Rehobim barely managed to sidestep the thing.

"Go back!" he yelled, flinging the useless weapon down.

They ran. Fortunately, the stone creatures could not move fast enough to pursue them. A few minutes later they were off the barren. They paused and looked back. There was no sign of the creatures, but the mist was thicker now so it was impossible to see more than twenty paces.

"What are those things?" Rehobim growled at Shakre.

"I don't know for sure," she said tiredly. She thought back to when she went to the Godstooth, on the day she found Shorn. She remembered the creatures frozen in the stone along the river, and her sense that they were there to guard Tu Sinar, but had fallen asleep. "I think they are here to protect Tu Sinar."

"Well, it's clear we can't go that way now," Rehobim snapped. He seemed to blame her for this, as he did for so many things. "Come on. We have no choice now. We have to go around."

He spun on his heel and headed off to the west at a run. The rest fell in behind him, Shakre, with Werthin behind her, once again bringing up the rear. She was older than the rest of them and the truth was that she was finding the pace harder and harder to maintain. They had been running most of the day and she didn't know how long she could keep it up.

As they circled around the barren the land rose in a gentle slope that was only sparsely wooded. The fire had not spread this far yet and the air was clearer. Shakre allowed herself to hope that they would be able to find an open path. But when she got to the top of the slope, she saw the rest of them standing there, staring down the other side, and she knew it was an empty hope.

The slope dropped off more steeply on the other side and it afforded them a good view to the north and the west. Shakre could see that the barren ended just ahead, but that wasn't what everyone was looking at.

The forest that bordered the barren was burning fiercely. The fire extended west for as far as they could see. For a moment they all just stood there stunned. Shakre felt sick. They weren't going to make it in time. They had no idea which way to go. What was going to happen to the ones they'd left behind, who were mostly elderly or children? Without help, many of them would perish before they made it off the Plateau.

When Shakre turned to look at the others, she was surprised to see that all of them were looking at her. Even Rehobim. Their need struck her with an almost physical sensation. She could see in their eyes an almost childlike hope. She was the Windfollower. Couldn't she do something? The words came to her mouth unbidden.

"There may be a way that I can find us a clear path to them."

"How?" Rehobim asked roughly.

"Spirit-walking."

"What is that?"

"It's a way of leaving the body and traveling on in your spirit. But it takes a lot of strength to break the bond, to wrest the spirit away from the body, and I don't have it. I'm too tired. I don't have enough Selfsong."

"Then use mine," Werthin said. "Can you do that?"

"I could, but I would probably kill you." The Tenders of the Empire kept stables of young, healthy people to use as sources of accessible Song, bleeding off Life-energy when they needed to do something that required a lot of power. And those people often died. It was why those in their stables were slaves, and not free people. Since she'd never done this, she was almost certain to kill someone.

"Then why do you waste our time on this?" Rehobim sneered.

"Because I have done it before."

His eyes narrowed. "You just said it would kill."

"When I did it before, I used the wind." It was the night when she had first met the Takare, when she followed Elihu to the poisonwood. But the truth was that she didn't use the wind. It used her. It knocked her out of herself.

Would she be able to recreate that? She'd never tried. The idea of it frightened her. The wind was too wild, too uncontrollable.

Except that there were no other options. No matter how great the risk was, she had to take it.

"Do it," Rehobim said roughly. "Quickly."

"Can you do such a thing?" Youlin asked. The young Pastwalker fixed her with her intense gaze. A survivor of Mad River Shelter, she had only been with them for a few days, but already she had made a big impact on them, bringing memories of lost martial skills to the surface.

Shakre hesitated. "I think so. I hope so. It may just tear me apart though."

Werthin said, "If anyone can do it, Windfollower, it is you."

Shakre thought of how many years she had tried to shed that title, to be free of the wind, to go back to the time before she drew the wind's notice. Now she must do the opposite and embrace the wind. Now she would never be free. But all this she would do and so much more to save the lives of those who were dear to her.

"Okay," she said. "I'll try."

"Are you sure there is nothing I can do to help?" Werthin asked.

She started to say no, then reconsidered. The wind would supply the power to pull her from her body, but she also needed strength to help her hold onto it.

"Actually, there is. I will need help hanging onto the wind and I am already tired. But you should know that when I take LifeSong from you, it will leave you weakened."

"I do not care," the young man said stoutly. "There is no sacrifice if it helps our people."

Shakre sat down cross legged on the ground. The ground rumbled and smoke drifted around her. They were running out of time. Werthin sat beside her and she took his hand. "Just relax," she told him. "Don't fight me. Also, concentrate on me as much as you can. When I am finished, I will need your help to find my way back here." He nodded and she looked up at the Takare. "If I do not return soon, if I do not respond to whatever you say or do, leave me here." She looked at Rehobim as she said this and he nodded grimly. The others might protest, but he would do it. "It will mean I have lost myself in the wind. There won't be anything you can do and I will only hold you back."

All at once Youlin sat down on the other side of her and offered her hand. She had pulled her hood back, revealing her short-cropped black hair. "Draw from me as well," she said curtly. At that moment she looked very young. "I do not know exactly what it is you do now, but I am feeling that this is much more treacherous than you would have us believe. I am strong. I can help."

Shakre took her hand as well, then closed her eyes. She blocked everything from her mind, shutting out the roar of the nearby fire, the periodic cracking of the earth, the fear and desperation that kept rising within her. She shut it all out and allowed herself to fall into the mists of *beyond*.

There was no need to call the *aranti*, the creatures in the wind. They were everywhere, appearing as pale blue streaks that shot here and there, never still. At times they coalesced into something that looked like clouds, but clouds made up of amorphous masses of blue light, within which white light periodically flashed, like lightning within a thundercloud. There were faces within those clouds of light, appearing only briefly, then disappearing and reappearing elsewhere. The faces looked frightened.

One of the ethereal creatures seemed familiar, though Shakre could not have said how. Briefly she wondered if it had not been the wind bothering her all these years, but instead a single *aranti*. Why had the idea never occurred to her?

Shakre focused on it and lowered her inner walls.

Come.

The *aranti* raced to her, others crowding behind it. She kept the opening very small, knowing she would never be able to manage more than one of the creatures. Small as the opening was, the *aranti* noticed it immediately and crowded in.

As soon as it was within her she clamped down on it. It began fighting immediately. It was like clinging to a wild animal. Now was when she was glad for Werthin and Youlin. She drew heavily on them, hoping she was not hurting them, but knowing she had no real choice. They did not really know the risk, but they accepted it, as did she, to save those they loved.

The wind was slippery. It thrashed harder, trying to escape the very place it had so long tried to gain entrance to. Shakre clamped down harder, knowing she was losing her grip, but unwilling to give up. Mentally she shouted at it.

For so long I have done as you wished. I have followed your whims. Now you will serve my wishes!

It screamed back at her in its unintelligible, myriad voices, but she had no way of knowing if it understood her or cared.

It seemed not, because she felt her hold slipping and knew she was losing.

✗ ✗ ✗

All the Takare watched as Shakre closed her eyes and went *beyond*. A short time later she began to twitch. The twitching grew more pronounced. Her hands tightened on Werthin and Youlin and the shaking eased. Then it grew stronger again. Meanwhile, Werthin and Youlin's faces paled and they seemed to droop.

Shakre was tossing her head and moaning when Youlin said through gritted teeth, "We need help. She's losing."

Nilus moved first, dropping to his knees and placing his hands on Shakre's shoulders. The rest were right behind, kneeling around her and laying on hands. Last of all was Rehobim. His lip curled and he seemed about to refuse. Then with an oath he knelt and offered his strength up too. Hot wind and smoke swirled around the small band as they huddled there around the outsider woman who had come into their midst so many years ago. The ground screamed and stone melted, but they did not move. Gradually, Shakre's shaking eased.

Just before the wind got away, Shakre felt a new surge of energy race through her. It took her a moment to realize what had happened. More surges raced through her as the rest of the small band joined in. With her strength renewed she was able to take a firm grip on the wind. All at once she began to believe this might just work.

It was time to take the leap. She wasn't sure what would happen if this didn't work. She would be torn away from her body, that much she was sure of. Would her body die right away or linger on? She had no idea, but it didn't really matter. The time for caution had passed. There was time now only for action.

Take me to them. Take me to my people.

Still clinging to the wind, she released her hold on her body and, with a sudden, sharp shock the wind yanked her free and just like that she was spirit-walking. Briefly she saw her body from above, with the Takare gathered around her, and then she was racing upward at breathtaking speed, flying up above the smoke and chaos. Around her raced more *aranti*, crying out in their many voices, but she ignored them, focusing on keeping her grip on the one she rode. At the same time, she was trying to keep a hold on her body as well, but it was like trying to hold onto a thread while being swept away by a flood.

Higher and higher they rose and with the strength she borrowed from the Takare she began trying to bend the will of her ethereal mount, to make it go north, towards Bent Tree Shelter. At first her efforts seemed to have little effect as the *aranti* fought her with manic energy. Again and again she thought she had it under control, only to lose her hold and end up just hanging on. But she was not a woman who gave up easily and she kept trying, until finally the *aranti* slowed and turned to her command.

She looked down on the Plateau from a great height and at first she did not know where she was. Nothing looked familiar. The scene was apocalyptic. Huge cracks filled with lava rent the land and smoke billowed up from countless fires. It didn't look like anyone could possibly still be alive down there.

Then she saw something to one side and suddenly she knew where she was: the Godstooth. At least where the Godstooth used to be. The tall, white spire of rock that marked Tu Sinar's resting place was simply gone, as were the lake and the protective stone walls. In their place was a crater filled with lava.

From the crater great cracks radiated outwards in all directions, lava pouring down them, fires raging along their edges. As she watched, another explosion erupted from the depths of the crater, flinging stone and lava skyward. The wind bolted in fear and it was a few moments before she could get it under control once again.

But now she knew where she was and she could find Bent Tree Shelter. She drove her mount south and west, crossing nightmare terrain that bore no resemblance to the land she and Shorn had crossed months ago. Briefly she wondered what had become of Shorn, but she dismissed the thought. He was not her concern. Her family was. With the wind's speed it was only a short while before she reached her destination. She looked down and if she had had a voice she would have cried out in horror and pain.

A huge crack ran through the heart of the village. Most of the simple huts had fallen into it. She looked for and found Elihu's hut. It was perched right on the edge. The next tremor would topple it in.

Her shock and pain were so great that she lost control of the *aranti*. Seizing its opportunity, the creature bolted and she tumbled wildly through the air.

It was more difficult this time, but finally she was able to get the *aranti* under control once more. With a last look at the ruined village, she forced her mount southward, scanning every direction, telling herself they had to be out there somewhere, still alive.

It took too long and she was beginning to despair when she caught a glimpse of movement along the edge of a wooded area. She forced the *aranti* to take her lower and her heart suddenly lifted. There they were, strung out in a line and moving slowly south. They were approaching another crack in the earth, this one stretching east to west for miles in either direction. The sides of the crack were steep, but there was no lava in it. The villagers could still cross it.

Urging her mount higher, she scanned the southern horizon, trying to find familiar landmarks. Nothing looked familiar at first, but then she saw the low hills lying beside the broad barren and recognized the place where she and the others had stopped. Her heart lifted further. It was not far. The villagers were heading in the right direction. The forest between the two groups was burning, but the flames were dying down and she could see places where the fire, having used up all its fuel, had burned out altogether. It would be difficult, but they could make it through.

When she looked back at the villagers though, she saw that they were stopped at the crack. Then they started to move east, clearly hoping to circle around it or find a place where it was easier to cross.

When Shakre looked east, her heart fell. Molten rock was pouring down the crack.

X X X

I made a mistake. We left too late.

Over and over those thoughts came to Elihu as he led the survivors of Bent Tree Shelter across the Plateau. They should have left sooner and now it was probably too late. The Plateau had gone insane. The wildlife had fled. The ground was tearing itself to pieces. But for him, the worst was the plants. They thrashed, crying out in their strange voices of their fear and their pain, but they could not get away. They could only wait until fire or earth swallowed them.

The unease Elihu had been feeling for days had begun to increase shortly after Rehobim led the fighters after the fleeing outsiders after they attacked the Shelter. By the next morning Elihu knew it had been a bad idea to let them go. The whole village should have gone. If he was honest with himself, he'd known for days that it was time to leave the Plateau.

It had been in his heart a number of times to tell the others, but he'd ignored it. He'd said nothing, even as the moans and whispers of the plants grew ever louder. Even as he felt the poison that seeped up into the plants from below seeping into his own limbs, he'd told himself it couldn't be that bad. He'd used the fact that he was still weak from his encounter with the poisonwood—when he would have died had not Shakre pulled him free of its grasp—to put off making the decision. He kept hoping that there was an answer, that they could save their land. But he should have known better. When the gods fought among themselves, people became insects whose only hope was to get out of the way.

The outsiders' attack had caught him by surprise. If not for the the huge, forbidding outsider, the one many called Taka-slin, he and everyone he called friend and family would have been killed. Maybe that was why he had stood by and said nothing when Rehobim gathered the young and the strong to chase down the outsiders. Maybe he wanted vengeance too.

Near the end of the day yesterday, unable to continue ignoring the feeling of impending doom, Elihu sought out the other Walkers. Their numbers were sadly depleted. With Meholah's death at the hands of the first band of outsiders—the day Jehu received the mark of Kasai on his forehead—the village had no Huntwalker. Sick and unable to rise off his bed, Asoken, the Firewalker, was killed by the outsiders in his home. That left only two Walkers besides Elihu. He found Intyr, the Dreamwalker, sitting on the ground near the edge of the village, staring into nothing. Her blue-dyed hair floated around her head in the wind. But no matter what he said to her, she did not respond. He did not know whether she walked her dreams, or if the shock of what had happened had bent her mind.

That left Rekus. The Pastwalker started to shake when Elihu asked him what he thought they should do.

"Why do you ask me?" His face twisted and his hands moved over his clothing, touching his face, pulling at his hair. He was a tall, thin man with long, gray hair. There was a haunted look in his eyes.

"You are Pastwalker."

"There are no answers in the past." Rekus tried to walk away, but Elihu would not allow him.

"You are Pastwalker. It is your duty."

"And I belong in the past. I have nothing to offer my people." Rekus was nearly yelling. Around them Takare were studiously trying to look away.

"That is not true. You have guided us well for many years."

"Yet it was I who shouted that we should do nothing. I said the outsiders would not return. I was wrong and Takare died."

"We were all wrong. But that is the past."

"The past is all I know. I have no place in leading our people into the future."

So Elihu gave up on Rekus, left him pacing by the fire, talking to himself. He looked at the sky, felt the vibrations in the soles of his feet, listened to the plants.

And decided to wait until morning.

In the morning, strange clouds blew overhead. Animals raced by them, heading south. The plants tossed violently even though there was no wind. It was clear to Elihu that he had waited too long. Which was why the survivors, a ragged band of several dozen—mostly children, the sick and the elderly—now hurried through a worsening nightmare of smoke, fire and chaos.

They followed the main trail south when they left the village. Not only was it the shortest route off the Plateau, but it was the way the warriors had gone and Elihu knew they would need to find them if they were to have any real hope of making it off the Plateau alive. They simply could not move fast enough. There were children and old people who would need to be carried. Without the other members of the village it was likely they would not make it halfway.

They had not been walking long when the earth started to move under their feet. There were cries of fear and Malachy, the oldest man in the village, fell down. They stopped and Elihu helped Malachy up, daring to hope that there would be no more tremors, at least not that day. But shortly afterwards there was one even more violent. A tree toppled nearby, nearly striking Rekus, who hung near the back of the group, walking with his head down.

Then came the boom of a mighty explosion to the north. Rekus looked up and into Elihu's eyes; both knew where the explosion had come from. The Godstooth.

"Faster!" Elihu cried. Lize and Ekna—two bent, elderly women, inseparable friends since their husbands had died during recent winters—were right behind him and he pointed them down the trail. Neither could see very well and they peered into the distance uncertainly, but they went willingly. He moved on back down the line of villagers, urging them to hurry as they passed. Yelis hurried by, clutching her newborn infant who was only three days old. At the end of the line was Rekus. He kept looking back over his shoulder at a growing cloud of ash and dust that was rising into the sky. His face had gone white and there was something in his eyes that told Elihu he was close to breaking. Rekus started to open his mouth to speak, but Elihu cut him off.

"I don't care!" he snapped, pushing in close to the taller man. "Right now I need your help getting these people out of here. Later you can blame yourself—if we're still alive."

Rekus closed his mouth and hurried on after the others. Elihu was just turning to follow him when he saw movement back up the trail, in amongst some saplings. It was Jehu, the mark of Kasai dark on his forehead. Elihu had not seen him since the outsiders attacked the village and he had thought that maybe he'd followed the warriors when they left. Jehu was stick thin, his long hair hanging unbound and unwashed, his clothing in tatters. Since that fateful day when he was marked, the Takare generally left Jehu alone, lowering their voices when he was around. He was a wound that none knew how to heal, too painful to touch. More than once he had awakened the village during the night with his screams. Elihu turned back.

"Hurry, Jehu!"

Jehu froze, like a deer caught in the open. He seemed moments from fleeing, but Elihu didn't give him a chance. He ran to Jehu, stumbling once as another tremor shook the ground, and grabbed his arm. Jehu tried to pull free, but Elihu tightened his grip.

"Listen to me!" he cried. "I need you. Your people need you!"

"You don't understand," the young man said. His eyes were very large in his face and he was trembling like a leaf. The burn on his forehead was red and inflamed. It looked like he had been clawing at it.

"No, I don't. But I understand that you are the only young man here. Get up there and help Malachy."

"But I can't—"

"Yes, you can. You've known that man your entire life. Look at him." Malachy had paused and was leaning against a tree, breathing hard. "He won't make it another hour without your help. Put down your self-pity and help him!"

Jehu sagged all at once and quit trying to get free. "Okay," he whispered.

They stumbled on through a growing nightmare. Twice they had to leave the trail they were on and veer west, forced aside by sudden rents in the earth. As the day progressed it became harder and harder to make any headway. Some of the cracks they came across were filled with molten rock and the burning forests filled the air with choking smoke.

It was afternoon when they came upon yet another crack in the earth, this one stretching east to west right across their path. There was no molten rock in it, but the sides were steep and the rock loose. Elihu hesitated and the ragged band of survivors came to a stop around him. There was no talking. Exhaustion was evident on their faces. Intyr had a burn on her arm and Ekna was bleeding from a cut on her leg. Rekus was limping badly. Elihu himself was having trouble. He had not fully recovered from the poisonwood venom and he had nausea and chills. He looked at them, and then down into the crack, where he saw broken bones waiting for them. He made a decision.

"We will go around," he announced. "It looks shallower to the east. There may be a better place to cross that way." It did seem like the crack was smaller in that direction and it would be good to swing east for once, since it would send them more in the direction the warriors had gone.

He took two steps east—

And was struck by a gust of wind so hard he nearly fell down. Surprised, he peered about him, but saw nothing. He tried again.

Again the wind struck him. But this time the pressure was sustained. It was like he was being pushed.

"Maybe the other way," he said, and turned around. He made his way past the group and started to follow the crack west.

Again the wind came out of nowhere, throwing dirt in his eyes, pushing him back.

All at once the realization hit him and he wondered at his own denseness. He smiled. "Shakre," he said softly.

He turned back. Closest to him were Lize and Ekna. Their faces were calm and trusting as they steadily returned his gaze.

"Can you make it down there?" he asked, gesturing into the crack.

They peered down through the smoke and Ekna coughed and rubbed her eyes. As one they shrugged. "We can only try."

To the others he said, "We will cross here. Yelis, you lead." Though she carried a baby, she was young and strong. She would know how to pick a good route. Behind her followed Ekna and Lize and Elihu held each one's arm in turn, guiding them over the edge and down.

The wind gusted around him once more and he thought he heard voices, but the words were completely alien. "I know, I know," he said. "We're going." The voices rose in pitch and intensity and he straightened, looking around. Then his eyes widened. "Hurry!" he yelled to the others. "We must go faster!"

To the east the crack was filling with molten rock and it was coming their way.

The sides were steep, the stone loose. Yelis had not gone three steps before she dislodged a stone the size of her head that bounced crazily toward the bottom, taking others with it. This was crazy. It was impossible that they would be able to make it across without half of them getting injured. But they had no real choice.

Slowly the survivors made their way across the crack. There were some falls, but somehow no one was injured badly. Last to cross were Jehu and Malachy, the young man providing a steady hand to help the old man over the worst spots. The molten rock had reached them by the time they arrived at the bottom. Jehu helped Malachy over the lava and the old man started up the far side. But then Jehu stopped, standing on a large rock and staring down as the lava began to spill around him. The villagers called his name but he ignored them, his face turned away. The lava grew deeper. It was near his feet now. He looked up and his eyes met Elihu's.

"Don't do it," Elihu whispered. "Don't do it."

The lava rose higher. It was almost lapping against Jehu's feet. One moccasin was starting to smolder.

Finally, almost reluctantly, he jumped the rest of the way across and climbed up to join the others.

Controlling the wind had taken its toll. The final straw was the effort and emotion expended to push Elihu to lead the villagers across the crack. As she pulled back from him, Shakre felt her hold slipping. It was not just her control of the wind that was slipping, either. It was her hold on herself. She felt frayed, tattered, like smoke drifting apart in a breeze. Her thoughts were increasingly fuzzy and disorganized. She retained enough of herself to realize that it was the wind. Humans were not meant to be so close to it for so long. It was blowing away the boundaries of who she was. If she spent much more time with it she would lose herself forever. But a terrible lassitude was drifting over her. As she rose into the air she looked down on the villagers and for a moment she could not think who they were or why they had seemed so important to her. They seemed so small and insignificant. The wind was carrying her away. Why fight it? Why not just give in and be free? The wind was free. She could be free with it. She could fly past everything, never dragged down by her burdens again.

She let go of her hold and abandoned herself to the wind.

Youlin opened her eyes suddenly. Something had gone wrong. Something had changed. Through her connection to Shakre she'd been able to see, as if through a thick fog, what Shakre saw. She'd even shared some of the woman's thoughts and feelings, though only distantly. As a result, she knew that the villagers were close by and she'd seen the way through the burning forest to intersect with them.

She also knew that Shakre had let go. If they did not act fast, they would lose her. Her breathing had stopped and she looked curiously insubstantial.

"Help me," she ordered the other Takare. "Focus your strength. The wind is taking her away." As they did so she felt her hold on the Windfollower strengthen and then she began to pull. At first nothing seemed to be happening and she wondered if they would lose the outsider woman now. But she was not a woman who liked failure and so she gritted her teeth and poured herself into the effort. The wind was like a dog that would not let go of a bone, but now Youlin had a good grip and she was not going to let go either. Every time she pulled Shakre toward her people, the wind pulled her back the other way. How long this went on she did not know, but all at once the wind let go and Shakre came back to them.

Youlin opened her eyes. Shakre's face was gray, but she was breathing again, albeit shallowly.

"She's back."

One by one the Takare released their hold on Shakre and stood. Some grimaced. Others held their heads. All of them were weakened by what they had just been through.

"Was it only more time lost?" Rehobim demanded roughly. He was breathing hard. "Did she find them?"

"I know where they are," Youlin said. "I can lead you to them." She looked down. Of all of them, only Werthin still remained crouched beside Shakre.

"Go," he said. "I will take care of her."

Following Youlin, the Takare left at a trot.

TWENTY-SIX

Werthin leaned in close to Shakre and called her name. He rubbed her hands between his and called again. Her eyelids fluttered, and then her eyes opened. But she did not look on him. Her eyes were unfocused and it seemed he saw clouds floating in their depths.

Werthin stood, unsure what to do, and looked after his kinsmen, disappearing into the smoke. "I do not believe Rehobim will return this way. I believe he will find a reason to miss us." He looked down at the still form of Shakre. "He hates you. More than makes sense for what you have done. The way he looks at you...it is as if you bear a secret about him, something he cannot have others knowing. I believe he would kill you if he could." He looked to the south, through the smoke, past the scarred land and the toppled trees. "I think we must make our own way down."

Stooping, he lifted her in his arms. Her body felt strangely light and he had a sudden, irrational thought that she would dissipate in his hands, that she was smoke rather than flesh and blood and she would drift away from him. It was as if the wind had blown something out of her and now there was only this shell left. He began walking, trying to ignore the tremble in his limbs that attested to his own weariness.

Was part of her still with the wind? he wondered as he walked. Was she still trying to find her way back? Not knowing what else to do, but desperate to help her, he began talking. Maybe the sound of his voice would guide her.

"You must return to us, Windfollower." He frowned. "That name no longer fits. You no longer follow the wind. You mastered it, made it serve you. I name you Windrider." He stumbled, but managed not to fall. How weak he was now, and yet how strong was his resolve. This woman had saved his people; he would not fail her. "Your people need you more than ever before, Windrider. Rehobim is right. We must fight the outsiders. To do otherwise is to become like Jehu.

173

But you are right too. If we fight only with hatred, we will lose ourselves. Just as we did before. This is not just a battle for our lives. It is a battle for our spirits. We can lose one. The other is too precious."

After that he spoke to her of other things. He spoke to her of her home and the people she knew as family. He spoke of the endearing things they did and the annoying. He spoke in their voices, imitating them. It was something he had always been good at and often around the fire at night he had entertained the children with his ability.

And, over and over, he called her name. "Shakre. Windrider. Come back to us. Your people need you."

Most of the time she lay still in his arms, but at times she fought him, though there was no strength in her struggles. Her head snapped side to side and her eyelids fluttered, and he saw nothing of her in her eyes. Several times she cried out and even spoke, but the voice was not her own and the words were in a language he had never heard, a language he did not think was human. At times she wept, and a wordless begging came from her as she sought to convince him of something he could not understand. Once her eyes opened and fixed on him. They were a milky gray and clouds drifted across them. Her mouth opened and she began to curse him in what he guessed was the language of the wind.

But he did not let go. He held on to her, and he talked. He carried her through the close of the day and into the night, through fire and smoke, upheaval and explosion. Then he carried her in the darkness, through a nightmare landscape of flame and breaking rock. Many times he had his way blocked and had to back up and go around, try a different way. He lost his sense of where he was, only that he must keep going. Somehow, though he stumbled often, he did not fall down. Somehow he found the way through the destruction and at last the edge of the Plateau stood before him.

Dawn was just breaking off to the east, visible through a break in the clouds of smoke. Fires burned fiercely behind them and to the west a massive lava flow poured off the edge, spreading destruction in the valley far below.

Shakre drifted in the clouds. They were thick and gray and unending. They wrapped around her and filled her being and she could no longer remember who she was. There was no time. There was no self.

Voices called to her from the clouds. They sang and whispered and laughed. They drew her and she longed to join them. They were free. Nothing weighed them down. They went everywhere, saw everything, and none of it mattered. No more fear or pain. No more worrying about the fragile lives of those she loved. She could be with the voices in the wind. It was the only logical choice.

She reached out to them.

But something was wrong. She could not go to them. Something held her. It angered her and she tried to push it away. When it would not go she fought it like a mindless wild thing. Still it would not release her. She cried and begged it, explaining that she had a new home now and she must go to it.

None of it worked. Her bonds remained and at last she ceased struggling against them and fell limp. Gradually it occurred to her the nature of her bonds.

They were words. The words were carried on a voice. The voice spoke her name.

Shakre.

It was heavy, that name. It was a burden she did not want. But now that she had heard it, she could no longer avoid it. It settled over her like a weighted net and she could not get free of it. Trapped, she stopped trying to flee and turned towards the voice that spoke her name.

Windrider.

All at once her world came crashing back. With a cry, she fell from the heights and slammed back into the earth. Lost and afraid, she opened her eyes and a soft, distant glow greeted her. It was the sunrise and her family needed her. She began to cry.

Werthin became aware that something had changed. He looked down on Shakre. Her eyes were open and she was looking at the sunrise. The clouds were gone.

"Is it you?" he asked.

She nodded.

"Welcome back." All at once she felt a great deal heavier, as if some essential part of her had only just then returned. He realized how tired he really was and set her down.

"Thank you," she said.

He inclined his head.

"Did it work? Are our people safe?"

He pointed. To the east a line of people could be seen making their way down the side of the Plateau.

"I believe that is them."

Shakre stared at them for a while and felt something lift in her heart. She realized something else then: the Plateau had stopped moving. Tu Sinar's death throes had stopped. "What is next for us, I wonder?" she said.

"I don't know," Werthin said, sitting down with a sigh. "But I need to sit here for a while."

It was the middle of the day before Shakre and Werthin stumbled into the Takare camp. The camp was in the forest at the edge of a broad meadow that sloped down and away to the south and the east. Rehobim was the first one to see them. Tired as she was, Shakre did not miss the look in his eyes, a look that was quickly hidden. Disappointment? Anger? She couldn't be sure, but she did know he was not happy to see her, not that it was a surprise.

The survivors—and she was pleased to see that most had made it—crowded around her, many speaking at once, patting her arms, shoulders, touching her hair. It was as if they needed to reassure themselves she was real. Tears filled her eyes and she thought that she had never realized how completely she had become a part of them.

When finally they let her go and stepped away, all that remained was Elihu, standing an arm's length away from her, his eyes sparkling with unshed tears.

"It is good to see you again, old friend," he said softly. Then he came to her and hugged her.

Shakre breathed in the warm smell of him and suddenly she was crying and shaking uncontrollably. "I thought I'd lost you," she said.

He pulled back so he could look into her eyes. "I heard you were the one who was lost, in the wind."

She took a deep breath. Even then she still did not feel wholly herself. "It was the only way I knew to find you. And then you started to go the wrong way."

"I never knew you could be so pushy," he said with a slight smile.

"And I never knew you could be so obstinate."

For a long moment he looked deeply into her eyes in the piercing way he had. "Have you truly returned to us?"

She shook her head. "Not completely. I feel...hollow." She looked up at the sky. The wind was moving the tree tops. "I cannot close it away from me. Not the whole way. It echoes inside me. It doesn't like that I have eluded it. It still wants something from me, though I do not have any idea what."

"It is alien to us," he replied. "We cannot truly understand what drives it, what it hungers for."

Shakre leaned against him, savoring the feel of his solidity. "It does not feel as hungry down here as it did on the Plateau. But I still feel its fear."

He laid his head against hers. "The plants are different down here as well. They are not as aware of themselves. They are sunk deeper. But they fear as well."

"The poison is not as strong, but it is still here."

"It is a beautiful land," Elihu said, gesturing.

Ash drifted around them like black snow, coating the ground and the plants, and there was smoke in the air, but it was still beautiful country. The trees were tall, thick and luxurious in their foliage, mostly pine and fir, but generously mixed with oak, beech and cedar. The grass in the meadow was thick and long. Nearby a small stream flowed and in the distance, across a small valley, was a large stone cliff face wrapped in ivy.

"Life here does not fight so hard for survival," Shakre said.

"The hunters have already found game and we won't lack for food tonight," Elihu added. It was then Shakre noticed the large fire burning and smelled the meat roasting over it. Her stomach growled and Elihu chuckled. "Riding the wind makes you hungry I see."

"So does going for a day without eating," she added. She stopped him when he started moving toward the fire. "Stay for a moment yet with me," she asked. "Much is coming and I wish to hold onto the moment for a while longer." She did not have to explain further. Elihu understood her. He always understood. So he leaned into her and they stood close together, closer than they ever had before, and merely looked on their people.

The children ran and played in the stream, exclaiming over how warm the water was. People talked about the abundance, the wood that was so plentiful, the game that was so fat and slow. This was truly a different world.

Only a few took no part in it. Youlin, the Pastwalker, sat under a tree cross legged, huddled under her hood, speaking to no one. Pinlir sat sharpening his captured weapons on a stone. He was a stout man moving past middle age, his gray beard braided. The outsiders had killed his father, Asoken, the Firewalker, while he lay sick in his hut. Driven by rage, he had been the oldest to go with the war party while his wife, Birna, had remained at Bent Tree Shelter. Now she sat near him, watching him with a worried look on her face, but he seemed oblivious to her.

Rekus sat near the fire, staring blankly into the flames, his long arms wrapped around his skinny legs. Jehu stood off to one side under a tree, his arms folded around himself, looking like he was shivering. Rehobim stood at the edge of the camp, staring to the west, his sword gripped in his fist, as if ready to fling himself into battle at that very moment.

They were sitting around the fire that evening after eating when Shakre spoke up. "There must be other survivors." There were nods. She was not the only person thinking of it. "Tomorrow we must begin searching for them."

Her words seemed to anger Rehobim because he said, "Why don't you ride the wind again and find them?"

Shakre hesitated, thinking about it. In truth, she still felt thin and insubstantial. She didn't think she could go through that again right now and keep herself, but they were her people and if they needed her, she would do it. Before she could respond, Werthin jumped up.

"No!" he said. "You ask too much. It is too soon. She almost died. We cannot ask this of her."

Rehobim stood as well. His face was dark. "*I* lead here. You do not speak to me this way."

"Your hate has fouled your vision," Werthin replied, not backing down.

Rehobim's hands curled into fists and he started towards Werthin. But before he could close the distance between them, Elihu rose and moved between the two men.

"In the morning we will look for our people," he said calmly. "You will see. We are a hardy people. There will be many others who made it off the Plateau."

The two men stared at each other for a moment longer, then Werthin nodded and walked back to his seat. Rehobim stared down at Elihu. He was a full head taller and decades younger, but Elihu spoke with calm authority and Rehobim knew he could not ride over him. Not yet.

"In the morning we will go," he said, and sat back down.

Then Pinlir stood up. Birna made as if to hold onto him, but he shook her off. He was holding an axe in both hands and his bearded face was fierce. "I will go west," he said. "And any who wish to come with me. I will search for our people." All present knew he meant to hunt the outsiders, but none said it.

"I will go west too," Rehobim said. He looked at Nilus, sitting to his right. "You will lead a party east. We will find our people."

"In the morning, then," Elihu said, returning to his seat.

Who will lead our people? Shakre wondered. The Walkers were few and their authority diminished. Rekus had not even looked up during the exchange and Intyr sat beyond the firelight with her eyes closed. She looked at Youlin. The young Pastwalker sat to Rehobim's left, but her dark eyes gave nothing away. They had lost their home and their ties to the past. Much was unsettled. There was war coming, and in war her people would likely turn to those who led the fight, which meant Rehobim. But he was rash and impulsive. His insistence on chasing after the outsiders who had attacked the village had left them divided when they most needed to stick together. Tragedy had only narrowly been avoided. Would they be so lucky next time?

Shakre slept poorly that night, troubled by a recurring dream in which she was floating away while the Takare went about their daily lives, completely oblivious to her cries. Each time Elihu awakened her, holding her hand, reassuring her that she was okay. Now, standing in the predawn light watching the search parties prepare to leave, she felt exhausted, more tired than when she went to bed. The wind was no more than a light breeze, but it seemed to scratch at the windows of her mind and her skin crawled at its touch.

"Still you carry the night with you," Elihu said. He was standing next to her, his hand on her arm.

"It's the wind," she admitted. "It frightens me. It is…inside me, and I am afraid it will never leave. I will always be at its mercy."

"It is very soon," he said gently, raising his hand to stroke her hair. "You are still weak. In time, maybe you will feel different."

"I hope so. I don't know how much of this I can take. It has always carried on, but it's worse now. It never stops talking. I still don't understand what it says, but I have this feeling, as if I'm about to, or that I did and just hid it from myself."

"You do not want to hear what it has to say."

She shook her head. "No. I don't. You know, there was an old man who lived outside the town near where I grew up. He spent most of his time talking to something that wasn't there, arguing with thin air, slapping at nothing. Sometimes he would weep for no reason or rave and throw himself down. People whispered that he was a Caller—one of those who can summon the wind—and said that it was the wind that drove him insane. They said it happens to all who listen to the wind eventually." Shakre leaned her head on Elihu's shoulder. He was so warm, so solid, so…there. "I am afraid that is how I will end up."

"I have seen you talking to yourself before," Elihu mused.

Shakre straightened and looked at him. Then she saw the faint smile on his face. "Not helpful, old man."

"Not everyone can handle the other voices," Elihu said. "Their worlds are not like ours. To those who are already cracked slightly, the voices can shatter them completely, like a clay pot that is not made correctly will crack when put on the fire. But if the clay pot is made correctly, it will not crack, even if the fire is fierce."

"Are you calling my head a clay pot?" Shakre asked with mock severity.

"But not a cracked one," he responded with a smile.

"Keep it up and you may end up with a cracked pot," she said, leaning against him once more.

The two parties had formed up and were about to leave the camp. Nilus started to walk off, then turned and looked at Elihu, who raised his hand in silent approval. Nilus nodded and led his group into the woods to the east. In contrast, Rehobim studiously avoided looking at Elihu or any of the Walkers, even Youlin. Shakre sighed. Not long ago it would have been unthinkable for a group to set off on a major undertaking such as this without some sign of approval from one or more of the Walkers.

Elihu heard her sigh and interpreted it correctly. "He burns with a secret shame. In his mind, only war will wash it away."

Shakre straightened. "He led our people to vengeance when they needed him to stay and guide them. I fear we won't be so lucky next time."

"When have the Takare ever been lucky?" Elihu asked.

"But now, more than ever, we will need the guidance of the Walkers," Shakre said. "He is hotheaded and impulsive and I don't like where he wants us to go."

"Maybe the time of the Walkers has passed," Elihu said, gesturing with his chin at Rekus, who was hunched over himself, staring at his hands. "We were born of the Plateau, but we live there no longer."

"Maybe Youlin can make him see sense," Shakre said, though not very hopefully. Rehobim had ignored her as well. Still, she carried a great deal of authority amongst the warriors, who had not forgotten the time she spent helping them relive past identities and how important that had been in reawakening long-dormant skills.

"Perhaps," Elihu agreed. "But will her leadership be better? I cannot see anything about that one. She is a moonless night under the trees."

"Weren't you trying to make me feel better?" Shakre asked, giving him a sidelong glance. "Because it's not working."

"I'm just trying to hold onto you so you don't fly away again. At least not without taking me with you," Elihu said with a chuckle.

TWENTY-SEVEN

When Netra awakened from nightmares of being chased by Bloodhound the first morning after fleeing the plateau, she looked at a world that had turned gray. At first she thought she was still trapped in the nightmare. Ash had drifted down during the night and covered everything. Trees sagged under it, bushes and boulders were buried under it. In the distance she could hear a low, grinding hiss. She stood, wincing at the pains in her muscles, and moved out from under the trees where she had slept. What she saw when she looked up made her gasp. The plateau looked as though a giant's fist had struck it. Huge rents snaked down its face, filled with sluggish rivers of molten rock. Wild masses of black clouds hung heavy over it.

For a while Netra just stared at it in disbelief. She wasn't going to find her mother. If her mother had been on the plateau, she was most likely dead. A terrible sorrow drifted over her and she wrapped her arms around herself, the pain nearly causing her to cry out. She had come so far for nothing. What was left for her now? Her mother was dead. She was in lands controlled by Kasai and she might be found by its followers at any time, whereupon she would be burned. Even if she survived, what difference did it make? She and everything she loved was going to be destroyed in the cataclysm to come.

She heard a noise and raised her head. A squirrel was running down the trunk of a nearby tree, leaving tracks in the ash. It reached the ground and darted over to a boulder, then began digging at its base. A few moments later it came up with a pine cone and it raced back up the tree. Watching her with its bright little eyes, it began to strip out and devour the seeds from the cone. Netra watched it for a minute, then took a deep breath and wiped the tears that had gathered on her cheeks.

She dug around in her pack and found her meager rations. She ate what she could and came wearily to her feet. So long as she still lived, she would not quit. She stuffed her blanket in her pack and put it on her back, then straightened and considered her options. To the west Kasai was gathering an army. Obviously she wasn't going that way. Qarath was east and south, and it was a logical choice, since the FirstMother was there, but she knew she wouldn't be going that way. Not yet. There was only one place she wanted to go right then.

She looked south toward Rane Haven. Where else could she go? She had to know if her sisters were safe. Then she would have to convince them to come with her to Qarath. The Haven was too dangerous. She would tell them what she had seen and together they would figure out what to do. Her mood brightened somewhat as she took her first steps. She still had family left. She wasn't entirely alone.

She hadn't gone far when she heard heavy footsteps behind her. Wearily she turned and eyed the huge, copper-skinned warrior who had saved her from the tree-thing.

"What do *you* want?" she asked him, not trying to keep the irritation from her voice. She had not forgotten his first words to her. *Why did you not leave me to die?*

"I...follow you." His voice had an unusual accent.

"What? Why?"

He stood there for long moments, his face impassive. His features were coarse, his nose broad and flat, his eyes deep set and burning amber below a thick brow. He was hairless. Scars crisscrossed his face, too regular to be accidental. Something his people did to themselves, then. She thought he wasn't going to answer, but at last he said, "I owe you a—" He paused, searching for the word and then settled for some of his own. "*Tenken ya.*"

"Whatever this *tenken ya* is, you don't owe it to me."

His heavy brows drew together and something like a snarl lifted one lip. The next words cost him dearly. "You saved my life. I owe you."

"No, you don't." She strode up to him and poked him in the chest, which was about eye level for her. "You saved me, I saved you. We're even." She gave him her fiercest stare, daring him to contradict her.

"No." He crossed his arms and stared down at her. He was a rock, a mountain. His tone and his posture said he had decided and he would never budge.

"Can't you count?" She held up her right forefinger. "I save you." She held up her left forefinger. "You save me." She held them next to each other. "Even."

"No," he said again.

"Explain it to me."

For just a moment he looked startled, then his face settled back into its normal impenetrable frown.

Netra turned and resumed walking.

Again the ponderous tread followed her. She whirled on him. "Look, I release you from your debt. You don't owe me anything."

He just stood there staring at her.

"Go on." She waved her hands as if he were an irritating insect. When he still didn't move she snapped suddenly, the strain of too many terrifying days breaking loose. "I *killed* to save you, but you don't remember because you were unconscious and *dying*. I trapped a deer and dragged it over to you so I could drain its Song, which I then used to keep you alive." She wiped away an unbidden tear. "Do you have any idea what it felt like to do that, to kill an innocent animal like that? Do you have any feelings inside you at all?"

He flinched before her words and she felt a twinge of guilt, but she was angry now. Her voice was hoarse and she was almost growling when she continued.

"And then I find out you *want* to die! Why, if you'd just told me that in the beginning, I could have saved everyone a whole lot of trouble." She stopped, breathing hard, wiping angrily at tears she couldn't control. "I don't want anything to do with you, do you hear me? Go kill yourself somewhere that I can't see."

His face visibly twisted and something vulnerable peeked through just for a moment. In a voice so low she almost didn't hear it, he said, "Allow me this. I have nothing else."

His words shocked her to silence. Now she looked away, suddenly shamed by her outburst. Weariness overwhelmed her once again. She wanted to lie down and just give up. It felt like she had been tired and afraid forever. "Okay," she mumbled. "You can come with me. But just know that you can go any time. You don't owe me anything."

She started walking again, but after a short distance she stopped and turned around. "I'm sorry I yelled at you. Things have been...difficult lately. I'm a little tired." Which was a huge understatement. "Anyway, my name is Netra. Who are you?"

"I am Shorn."

"That's an unusual name."

His heavy brows drew together, considering her words.

"But I suppose that makes sense, since you are clearly an unusual person. If you *are* a person. Where are you from anyway?"

His lips tightened, but he did not respond.

"Not a big talker, are you?" He just stared at her, his expression unreadable. Netra shrugged. "Have it your way."

She continued walking. Strangely, she realized that she was glad he was coming with her. How long had she been on her own? Why had she ever left her home? It all seemed so silly and childish now, the way she'd acted toward the women who were her family. When she got home, the first thing she'd do was apologize. At least she hadn't been exiled like her mother. At least she could return home.

She paused and looked back at the plateau. She'd lost her mother, but she still had her family. That counted for a lot.

For the next few hours she and Shorn walked through a world as gray as Melekath's dreams. The sun was a barely visible glow in the sky, hidden behind clouds of ash and smoke. The ash on the ground was deep enough that it was hard to find and follow a trail, so they spent a lot of time fighting their way through bushes and slipping on hidden loose stones.

Several times she tried to engage Shorn in conversation—all the time alone had made her desperate for someone to talk to—and when that failed she found herself thinking back over the last few months. It was unbelievable how much had happened and how fast. It was only a short time ago that she had just been a foolish, hard-headed girl battling Brelisha over her lessons, trying to get out of her chores, sneaking out to follow wildlife through the hills. Then came the nightmare in Treeside, when Tharn killed Gerath. After that she and Siena went to Nelton and there she'd been attacked by Gulagh. She couldn't even remember the name of the Tender she'd killed to escape Gulagh.

Consumed by guilt, she'd fled the Haven, going to find her mother. She hadn't been able to help the ancient tree in that nameless town, nor had she been able to help the girl shot with an arrow while she fled the monsters that burned her family alive. Then the same monsters caught her and nearly burned her to death, before she'd miraculously escaped and then spent a few days being chased by Bloodhound, only escaping when he fell down the side of the plateau.

Then she finally made it up onto the plateau, only to be attacked by some kind of creature living within a tree, then saved by whatever it was that was following her now.

It was beyond crazy. It was unbelievable. She gazed around her at an ash-covered world and knew she was far too small for it. Nothing she did made any difference. She was so worried about whether she was doing the right thing, but the truth was it didn't matter. Forces were in motion that were so much bigger than she was.

It was late afternoon when the sun finally broke through the ash clouds for a few minutes. By then the ash covering the ground had begun to thin and there were bare patches here and there. They hadn't made it very far, partly because of Netra's exhaustion, and partly because she was not dropping down into the valley she had traversed on her approach to the Plateau. Instead she stayed up on the long ridge of broken stone that jutted north from the Firkath Mountains. She couldn't bear the thought of running into Bloodhound and his ilk again. Though he appeared to have been badly injured by his fall off the cliff, she wouldn't be surprised to hear his cry in the distance. As far as she knew, he was completely healed by now. Who was to say what was possible anymore? Staying up on the ridge slowed them down, but it was worth it if she could avoid Kasai's minions.

They stopped beside a small stream to camp. The water was fouled with ash, but not so badly they couldn't drink it. Netra knew it would be better if she didn't light a fire. Bloodhound could be right over the next hill. But the truth was that she didn't care. Not right then. The truth was that she needed the comfort that the fire would provide and she was willing to risk everything for it.

As she coaxed the small flames into life, movement caught her eye and she saw Shorn approaching. She sat up, ready to argue with him if he told her to put it out, but to her relief he simply sat down across from her with a grunt. He had a dead shatren, probably a yearling, in one big fist and he proceeded to clean it with what was probably a short sword, though it looked like nothing more than a large knife in his massive hand. Once Netra would have been sickened by the sight, but now she only watched numbly.

The meat was sizzling, fat dripping into the flames, when guests arrived.

"You'll be letting the whole world know where you are with that fire," a woman's voice said.

Netra jumped and came to her feet, ready to flee. Shorn stood in one smooth motion and took one huge step. Before the woman could move his hand was around her throat and she was lifted onto her toes.

"We mean no harm," she said, choking out the words, raising both hands to show they were empty. "Just drawn to the light, like moths we are." She was dressed in a worn traveling cloak. Behind her stood a man, shorter than she, his face pale and smudged with ash. The man said nothing, made no move to help or to flee. "We're not the enemy, I promise you that." The woman pulled the hood back on her cloak. One eye was swollen shut and surrounded by blue-black flesh. Her hair was long and gray.

Shorn looked to Netra and after a moment she shook her head. She sensed no malice in the couple, just weariness and fear. He let the woman go. If she had not been so tired, so filled with her own thoughts and fears, she would have sensed their approach. Carelessness would get them killed.

"You can stay," Netra said. "I'll share the fire. I can't say for him and his food, though." Shorn had picked up the skewer where he'd dropped it in the fire and was brushing dirt and ash from the meat. He seemed to have completely forgotten anyone else was there. No, that wasn't right. He looked like someone who didn't care that there was anyone else there. They were nothing to him.

"Beacon or no, we could use the time by a fire. The days have been hard and we're about worn through," the woman said, dropping a rough pack she carried and sinking to the ground with a sigh. She gave Shorn a sidelong glance and rubbed her throat. "Just when I think there's nothing left to surprise me."

All at once Netra realized why the woman had pulled her hood back. She was letting them know that they weren't marked with the burn on the forehead. She noticed that the man had pulled his hood back also. "How did you escape them?"

"They didn't see us. Boys went into town that day. Good boys, ours were. Not tall, but strong. In the day's work, they could *help*. An' they respected their ma, that's me." Her voice trailed off as she faded into the past. But then something flickered in her eyes, a returning sadness, and she picked up again, though softer than before.

"They were gone not long when we decided to follow, thinking about going to town, getting a tall glass of Jemin's rum to take the dust off. But the small cart was broken, and we cut across on foot." She gestured vaguely, as if Netra could see the place she was talking about. "Came through the hills and up to town from the woods. Saw the questioners, the black spot most took rather than burn." Her voice went tight. "They had our boys and was nothing we could do but run."

"And keep running," the man put in softly. The woman turned and patted him on the shoulder.

Out of nowhere the woman said, "We'd take it as a kindness if you'd give us your blessing."

Netra's eyes widened. "You want *my* blessing? Why?"

"You're one of Xochitl's aren't you, a Tender?"

Netra hesitated before replying.

"I understand your reluctance. You don't know us. You think we might turn you in. But you saw we're not marked. We couldn't hand you in even if we were setting to. They'd lay hold of us, too."

"I still don't understand why you want my blessing."

"Why not? Who else is going to save us? Wasn't it Xochitl who did for Melekath before?"

"It was."

"Then maybe she'll come back and fix him again. What else do we have?"

"I don't know," Netra said. Did they have anything? she wondered. Was it all just foolish hope?

"Might not be Xochitl who does the saving," the woman confided to the man as she levered herself onto her knees and bent her neck to receive Netra's benediction. "Could be one of the others, but it's best to keep all the gods happy. Whatever gets the job done." The man nodded and followed her lead, then hobbled closer on his knees until he could have reached out and taken hold of Netra's feet.

Netra stared down at the backs of their necks and it was all she could do to swallow. The waiting began to grow long and she knew she had to do something. Bending over, she laid a hand on each of them and breathed, "Go then, with the Mother's eyes upon you."

The woman sat back and her eyes flickered to Shorn, still cooking the haunch over the fire. "Once I would have feared such a creature. Now I think you have Xochitl already helping you. I'm thinking no blinded man would easily question him." Her smile was feral. "If I had anything left, I'd give it to see that."

⚔ ⚔ ⚔

In the morning the two people stood with their meager belongings and faced east. "You sure you won't come with us, Tender?" the woman said. Neither she nor the man had offered names and Netra had not offered hers either. "Qarath is the only safety. Stories say her king topples walls with a glance and eats fire for breakfast." The smile she gave was humorless. "Half true would be good."

"We will," Netra assured her. "But first I have to gather my

188

family."

"Might be they're already there. That's the smart walking."

"We shouldn't have stayed this long," the man said abruptly.

She spun on him. "I know. I know! But we had to know for sure about our boys, didn't we? Had to know for sure." Her shoulders dropped. "We stayed too long."

Without another word she and the man walked out of the tiny clearing and disappeared into the shreds of gray.

When they were gone, Netra turned to Shorn. "Still planning on following me? Or have you changed your mind?"

He simply stared at her impassively, giving no indication of how he felt either way. But neither did it appear that he'd changed his mind.

Netra was surprised at how relieved she felt about that. The thought of being alone again was unbearable. Though he barely talked and showed about as much emotion as a stone, she'd already come to depend on his presence. There was something very solid and reassuring about him. Despite knowing almost nothing about him, she realized she was starting to trust him.

"I'll take that as a yes," she said. "I guess you'd like to know where we're going though, right?"

No response. Netra shrugged and continued.

"We're going south, around the eastern side of those mountains there. My family lives there, the women who raised me. We'll meet up with them and then head to Qarath." He didn't turn to see where she pointed, nor did his expression betray the slightest interest. His amber eyes remained fixed steadily on her. She realized that he really didn't care where they went. It was all the same to him. She remembered what he said: *I have nothing else*, and felt a pang of sympathy for him.

What manner of creature was he? Where did he come from? How did he end up here?

All these questions she wanted to ask and more, but she knew he wouldn't answer her. Not yet, anyway. Perhaps in time.

Even the Song coming off him was different, unlike any person she'd ever met. From it she could pick up very little about his emotions other than a bright, hot rage that overshadowed everything else. But she had a feeling that the rage was only a cover, that underneath it was a terrible pain, one he could not risk touching. She guessed that pain was connected to his being here, isolated from his people.

Had he been exiled? Had his people been destroyed?

Too many questions and no answers.

TWENTY-EIGHT

It was late afternoon a few days later when Netra realized they were not alone. She was paying attention this time, and she heard their Songs before she could see any sign of them.

She held up one hand and came to a stop in the trail. Shorn paused behind her. Closing her eyes, she concentrated, trying to learn more. It was not hard to figure out that these were people she did not want to deal with. Their Songs had that same burned feel that she remembered all too well from her encounter at the burned farmhouse, and the days of flight from Bloodhound and the others. The four men who approached had been marked by Kasai.

"Four of them," she said softly to Shorn. "Just over that low ridge there." She looked around. "We need to hide."

They were on a small game trail, still hugging the side of the high ridge leading off the Firkath Mountains, which were beginning to rear up toward their full height. Pines and firs dominated the slopes, with patches of aspen here and there. They were in a wide, grassy meadow. The best thing to do would be to backtrack, hide in the trees until the men had gone by. She was hurrying back the way they had come when she realized that Shorn wasn't following and she turned.

Shorn was still on the trail, and he was walking toward the men. They appeared over the top of the ridge and started down. Because of the trees, it didn't look like they had seen him yet, but they would soon. She ran back towards him, calling as loudly as she dared, her heart hammering. Catching up to him, she grabbed his arm, trying to pull him off the trail. But he simply ignored her and continued striding forward.

She froze there, uncertain whether to run or stay. As if she was no more than a ghost, she could do nothing but watch as events unfolded.

The men broke out of the trees and saw Shorn. They stopped, uncertain what it was they were seeing, not realizing that it was already too late for them.

As soon as they saw him, Shorn broke into a run. His speed was stunning, much greater than anything his size should have been able to achieve. The men were still drawing their weapons when he hit them. He had two swords and a long dagger hanging from his belt, but he didn't draw them. He just waded into the men, swinging.

His first punch caught the lead man square in the face. There was a loud crack as the man's neck broke and he was flung backwards, knocking one of the other men down.

The next man got his sword out and raised it before his face, trying to stop Shorn's next hammer blow. Shorn's fist smashed through the blade like it was a twig, driving it back into the man's face. As the man started to crumple, Shorn drove his other fist into his body, shattering his ribs and driving the pieces into his heart and lungs.

Shorn grabbed the third man's neck with one hand, his leg with the other. Lifting him into the air, he snapped him across his knee, like someone breaking kindling for a fire.

The last man, the one who had been knocked down, scrambled to his feet and started to run. Shorn caught him with two long strides, then swung him in one fist and smashed him into a tree, the impact cracking his skull open.

Just like that it was over. It all happened so fast that Netra almost couldn't believe what she'd seen. The sheer violence of it was horrifying, beyond anything she'd ever imagined. Not only that, but Shorn did it so methodically, so impersonally. He didn't look angry. He didn't look upset. He showed less emotion than a butcher would after slaughtering chickens.

Netra was suddenly furious. "You didn't have to do that!" she yelled, running over to him. "We could have hidden, waited until they were gone."

In answer, Shorn knelt and rolled the closest one onto his back, then pointed at the black mark on his forehead.

"I know what they are," Netra snapped. How could he be so calm? Her heart was racing and her hands were shaking uncontrollably. "I still don't think you had to kill them."

"They would bring more," he said simply. He made it sound like the most obvious thing in the world. In war, one killed one's enemies. What else was there? What else could there be?

She stood there staring at him, her chest heaving as the adrenaline slowly faded. Why couldn't he at least show *something*? Was he that inhuman? Was he as much a monster as the things she was fighting against?

Then she slumped, and wiped one hand weakly across her face. "Maybe you're right. I just wish…I used to think there was another way." Maybe there wasn't. What else could one do against an enemy that offered no mercy, that burned children alive? She looked down on the bodies, thinking that she should offer a prayer for them or bury them or something. But she found no prayer inside her, only a relief to be alive while they were dead.

If only they were all dead.

Two at a time Shorn picked up the bodies and tossed them into the undergrowth, making sure he removed their dropped weapons as well, though not before examining them, presumably to see if they were worth keeping. When he was done there was no trace of the brief, deadly battle, except for some crushed grass. Any others passing this way would probably not know anything had happened here.

As they walked away Netra looked inside herself and wondered if there was anything left of the woman she had thought she was. She'd been so confident, so sure of her beliefs, of what was right and wrong. Now she no longer knew. Death crowded her on every side and more and more it seemed pointless to resist. Maybe she would have to be harder to survive in this new world she found herself in. Maybe there was no place left for softness or compassion.

TWENTY-NINE

Several days later Netra climbed up on a rocky outcropping to look around. From there she could see over the thick trees and down into the valley below. Not too far away was a town. She stared at it awhile. It looked like the abandoned town where she tried to save the little girl and had been captured by the old woman. She wondered what had happened to the girl. Did the burned man catch her and force the question on her? Did the crazy old woman catch her?

She decided on the spot that they were going to go down to the town. She told herself it was the sensible thing to do. Once again she was nearly out of food and she should be able to scavenge some there. But the truth was more than that. She wanted to know about the girl. If she was still there, if she was still unmarked, she would make the girl come with them. By now she should realize that her father was never returning.

In a world of death, Netra could save at least one life. She would have this one small victory.

Climbing down off the rocks, she told Shorn, "There's a town down below us. We're going to go see if we can find some food." She hesitated, then decided she needed to tell him her whole reason for going. "There might also be a little girl down there who can use our help. If there's any way we can save her, I want to do it."

Shorn's face betrayed nothing. Whether he thought her plan noble or foolish he gave no sign. Perhaps he simply didn't care either way. Probably he saw his debt to her as no more than a task his honor required him to fulfill. His complete impassivity frustrated her suddenly.

"You could say something once in a while, you know. Like, 'I think that's a great plan, Netra!' Or how about, 'That's the dumbest thing I ever heard. You're going to get us both killed.'"

Her sarcasm had no effect on him either. He just stood there, waiting.

"Fine. Have it your way. I'll just keep talking to myself. You cut in whenever you feel like it."

She stomped off down the slope and he followed. Pretty soon her fears started to rear up and she began to question her decision. The thought of encountering Bloodhound and the others again terrified her. She should stay as far from them as possible. She tried to remind herself that a little girl's life could be at stake, but that didn't really help. She told herself that she no longer needed to fear Bloodhound because of Shorn, but that didn't help much either. With every step she became more frightened.

Because of her fear, she stuck to the thickest parts of the forest and stayed as quiet as she could. But it was pointless because Shorn stomped through the forest like an enraged bull shatren, breaking off limbs as he went. Over and over she whispered at him to be quiet, but her pleas made no difference. He either could not or would not move quietly and there was nothing she could do about it. She thought about telling him to wait while she went on ahead, but decided she felt safer this way and finally gave up saying anything to him.

Every few minutes she stopped and tested the currents of Song, listening for any trace of Kasai's men. Each time she found nothing and gradually some of the tension left her.

At the last of the cover she stopped and peeked out. The ground was flatter here and just a bowshot away stood the wall surrounding the town. For a long time she crouched there, listening to her inner senses, but she could find nothing.

"I think it's safe. Let's go."

They circled around the town until they came to the gate she'd left through. Taking a deep breath, she walked up to the gate, Shorn beside her, his head turning as he scanned the town for danger. But nothing moved within the town. There was no sign of life at all.

She stopped inside the gate and looked around, getting her bearings. The partially-burned house where she'd seen the girl wasn't too far from there. She led Shorn down a street, then turned onto another one. A few minutes later they came to the house. It was a sprawling one-story building of stone and wood, with a large, fenced-in garden. Part of it had collapsed in the fire.

She opened the gate and walked up to the front door, Shorn close behind. The front door had burned completely away and she stuck her head inside the house. She could hear no Selfsong, but maybe the girl had grown weak from hunger or was injured and dying. She had to rack her brain for a moment before she could remember the girl's name.

"Alissa!" she called out in a loud whisper. When there was no answer she called louder. Then she looked at Shorn. "What do you think?" To her surprise, he answered.

"I think there is no one here."

"She might be out back." She entered the house and he followed.

But there was no sign of the girl anywhere, even out back. She and Shorn returned to the street.

"I want to look around some more. She might be in another part of town, searching for food."

The two of them walked down several streets. Every now and then Netra called out the girl's name, but there was only silence.

After a half hour of this, Netra suddenly sensed another Song for the first time. Woven into it was the ancient, burning hatred that she'd become all too familiar with. Motioning Shorn to be quiet, she moved to the next corner and peeked around it.

Standing a few feet away, looking like she was waiting for Netra, was the old woman who had captured her. She had a rope in her hand. Netra's hand went involuntarily to her neck. The abrasions had healed, but she still remembered how it felt, choking on that rope.

"You're back!" the old woman cackled. "You won't get away so easy this time, you'll see!"

She was raising the rope when Shorn came around the corner. Her eyes grew very large and she stopped. "Oh," she said, "you're a big one."

She tried to run, but Shorn caught her easily. Before he could do anything to her, Netra yelled, "Don't hurt her! I want to talk to her!"

Shorn turned around and dragged the old woman back to Netra. She tried to fight him, but nothing she did made the slightest difference. He was holding her by the upper arm, lifting her up enough that her toes just barely touched the ground, and she couldn't do much besides spit at him in impotent rage, which he completely ignored.

"Tell me where the girl is and I'll tell him to let you go," Netra said. "You won't be harmed."

"You mean Alissa?" The woman's eyes lit up as she spoke and a dark smile came onto her face. "That's what you came back for?" The old woman began laughing. "Oh, that's too funny, really it is."

"Just tell me where she is," Netra snapped. "I won't ask you again."

"In the bellies of the buzzards, that's where she is!" the old woman crowed. "I finally caught the little brat, snared her with this rope right here. She'll never throw rocks at me again."

"You...*killed* her?" Even though it shouldn't have been a surprise, still the news staggered Netra.

"Wrung her neck like a rat, I did! You should have seen her eyes bulge out!"

Horror and grief battled with rage inside her. "Why? She was just a little girl. How could you do that to her?"

"What do you care? You didn't know her." She turned her head to look at Shorn, then back to Netra. "Tell him to let me go now. I kept up my end. You gave me your word."

Shorn gave Netra a questioning look. More than anything she wanted to tell him to snap the old crone's neck. She hated this woman. She wanted to see her dead, to repay her for her evil. The words were on her lips.

But would it bring Alissa back? Would it change anything? There was no one else here for the old woman to harm.

With great difficulty she said, "Let her go, Shorn."

Shorn released the old woman and she stood there, rubbing her arm where he'd held her. "I hope the burned man catches you soon," she spat. "I hope you scream for hours before you die."

"Come on, Shorn," Netra said, turning away.

She'd only taken two steps when she heard a sickening crunch behind her. She spun in time to see the woman collapse on the street, her head flopping bonelessly. Shorn was looking at her expressionlessly.

"Did you...? Why did you do that? What's wrong with you?"

Then she spun and hurried away from him, unable to look at him any longer.

$$X \quad X \quad X$$

Netra set a fast pace back up the slopes of the Firkath Mountains, almost as if she were running away from Shorn. Her thoughts were confused and she wanted to get away from them as much as him. She was torn in her feelings about him. On the one hand she was beginning to trust him. She felt safer around him. She was starting to depend on him and his solid presence.

But at the same time he horrified her. The brutal, callous way he killed frightened her. Not because she was afraid he would harm her. No, what frightened her was the fact that despite what she said to the contrary, she was grateful for his ruthlessness. Those four men in the clearing would have chased her if it wasn't for Shorn. They would have dragged her back to be burned. The old woman had killed a helpless child and laughed about it. She could not deny that she was glad they were all dead.

And what did that say about her? Was she becoming a monster too? What had become of the young woman who'd sworn to nurture and protect all life?

It wasn't until it was almost dark that she stopped. Shorn had fallen behind and she could hear him crashing around in the bushes below her. It sounded like he was going the wrong way. She felt guilty for leaving him behind like that. What had he done to deserve such treatment except try to help her? Why was she always so hard on those who reached out to her?

"I'm up here!" she called.

The crashing sounds changed direction, veering toward her. When he caught up to her she proceeded more slowly. They continued on until she found a spot deep in a thicket of trees where the ground underfoot was carpeted with pine needles and dead leaves. No one would be able to sneak up on them here. She didn't light a fire. She wanted to be alone in the darkness with her thoughts.

Shorn sat down nearby, his bulk just dimly visible in the blackness. His amber eyes seemed to glow slightly. It seemed to Netra that he was looking at her, but it was a long while before he spoke.

"I do not understand. What is happening?"

"Only the end of the world," Netra replied, surprised at his question. She thought it was the first question he'd asked her.

Shorn made no response. Netra thought about it and realized she hadn't given him much of an answer. He was following her around in the midst of a war without having any idea what the fighting was about. Surely he at least deserved to know more.

"Should I give you the short answer or the long answer?" she asked. He did not reply. After a minute she said, "We really need to work on your conversation skills."

"I do not think so."

Something about the way he said it, so solemn and serious, struck her as funny and she started laughing.

"What is funny?" he asked, and she laughed harder.

When she finished laughing, she wiped her eyes. "Thanks. I needed that. I almost forgot I *could* still laugh. I've been through so much lately, seen so many awful things."

She grew sober, trying to figure out where to start. "Thousands of years ago Xochitl led seven other gods in a great war against Melekath and his Children." She paused, thinking. "You probably don't know who Xochitl or Melekath are, do you?"

Shorn said nothing.

"Okay, let's go further back, then. Long ago, Xochitl, greatest of the gods, created life, including her greatest creation, humans. But one of the other gods, Melekath, hated and envied Xochitl and so he began to plot against her. In time, he was able to subvert a number of her people and lead them away from her. Xochitl summoned the other gods and raised an army to march against Melekath, all the time hoping he would repent. But he chose to fight and so she had no choice but to raise a prison from the earth, and seal Melekath and his Children away forever."

She remembered that day she and Siena left the Haven for Nelton, when she'd first thought about how terrifying it must have been for the Children as the prison sealed shut over them, blotting out the sky forever. Siena had claimed that they had chosen evil and so deserved what happened to them, but that explanation hadn't sit well with Netra then and it didn't sit well now. Maybe the choice those people had been given was the same choice the burned man gave her. Join or die. What kind of choice was that? Why couldn't Xochitl have found some way to only imprison Melekath?

"Now that prison is breaking. Kasai and the other Guardians are already free. Those people with the burned mark on their foreheads are part of the army Kasai is raising. Melekath will soon be free and when he is he will destroy everything, maybe break the Circle of Life itself."

Silence descended once again. Netra was thinking about going to sleep when Shorn finally spoke again. "What kind of beings are these, who can live for thousands of years?"

"They're gods."

"Your gods walk among you?"

"They used to. Xochitl has been gone for a very long time. None of the other gods have been seen for a long time either."

"Are you sure they are gods?"

"What? Of course I'm sure they're gods." But then she wondered.

Dorn, the Windcaller she and Siena met on the way to Nelton, the man she thought might be her father, had said that "god" was only a word for something beyond human understanding.

"How will you fight this god Melekath?"

Netra sighed. "I don't know. Our only real hope is that Xochitl returns and once again defeats Melekath."

"It is not much to fight a war on," he said.

"I know." She touched the *sonkrill*—the rock lion claw she'd found at the end of her Songquest—hanging around her neck, remembering how her spirit guide appeared to her when she was held prisoner by the burned man, how it felt like it helped her see how to drain Song from those men and use it to free herself. That was the third time her spirit guide had helped her against a Guardian and afterwards she'd believed that maybe the reason Xochitl hadn't appeared yet was because she was trapped or imprisoned somehow and was just waiting for the right person to free her. She'd even had the audacity to think that maybe that person was her, that she was the chosen one.

Now all that felt foolish and far away. She was only one tiny piece in a vast puzzle. She just wanted to go home and see her family.

"I don't know what's going on. I wish I did. It would make everything a lot easier."

She sat there in silence for a while, her arms wrapped around her legs, trying to see the stars through the branches of the trees overhead. Finally, in a small voice, she said, "It's hopeless, isn't it?"

Shorn spoke bluntly. "Probably."

"Well, thanks for that," she said, her tone as cutting as she could make it. "I feel a lot better now."

"You still breathe. Your enemy has not won yet."

She stared at his still form for a long time, but he did not move or say anything else. "I guess that's something," she said at last.

"It is the only thing."

THIRTY

They were awake early the next morning. Netra went through the food they had scavenged in the town before they left. There wasn't much for her. A few potatoes, some carrots and a bag of beans. The beans were rock hard, completely inedible unless she could cook them for several hours, something she couldn't imagine having the time to do.

Shorn was slicing pieces from a smoked ham with his dagger. Wordlessly, he offered one to her.

Netra recoiled, shaking her head.

"You will not last long, eating…" He frowned at the food she held in her hand. "Leaves? Is this the word?"

"Vegetables. They are vegetables."

"Why do you not eat this?" he asked, holding out the meat again.

Why, indeed? she wondered. Her stomach growled suddenly and she was aware of how weak she was. She had been getting by on so little for so long. She was always hungry. If only she could take the time to cook properly.

"I don't eat meat," she said at last. "I am…uh, I *was* a Tender of the Arc of Animals. We…they don't eat animals. Tenders value life above all else. They vow never to kill, not for any reason."

His heavy brows drew together. "You are no longer this…Tender?"

"No. Maybe. I don't know. I broke my vows when I…when I killed." She thought of the Tender in Nelton that she'd pushed in front of Gulagh's attack.

"Then you have no reason to eat only those." He pointed at the vegetables.

"No. I guess I don't," she admitted. "But I still don't want any."

He looked at her curiously, unspoken questions in his eyes. Then he shrugged and went back to eating.

"Tell me more of these Tenders," Shorn said later, when they had stopped to rest. "There is nothing like this on…where I am from."

She shot him a look, surprised. He had said the words casually, but she sensed this was something very important to him. Despite his distant demeanor, he seemed poised on the edge, waiting for her answer.

"The Tenders are dedicated to Xochitl, the Mother of Life. Their job is to protect and nurture life. There are Tenders for all the Arcs of the Circle of Life: Man, animals, plants, and so on. At one time there were Tenders of the Arcs of Birds and Insects also, though there have been none for centuries, as far as anyone knows. The Tenders of each Arc are dedicated to preserving the life within their Arc. When the Mother created the Tenders, Xochitl gave them power, the power to control LifeSong, which is the energy that runs through all life. They were to use this power to help the life under their care, healing it when sick or injured."

"Tenders are respected among your people?"

Netra snorted. "At one time, yes. The Tenders were revered for their healing. There were Havens everywhere. But during the time of the Empire the Tenders grew too powerful and lost their way. They abused their power and Xochitl turned away from them and took their power away. After the Empire fell…well, people don't like us…them too much anymore."

Shorn asked no more questions, but she could see him thinking. She had a feeling that the things she had said were alien to him and found herself wondering about his people.

"Your people have no such beliefs?" she asked him.

His massive head swiveled toward her, then turned away. He did not speak for several minutes and she thought their brief conversation had come to an end when he said, "We believe in war. There is nothing else." There was such doom in his voice that it frightened Netra. His words were choked in ashes and her heart went out to him.

"Is that why you left?" she asked impulsively.

"I did not leave," he said harshly.

Netra felt the pain in his words and she wanted to reach out to him, but already he was standing and walking away, the doors around him slamming shut. "I'm sorry," she said, and the words felt small and pathetic in her mouth so that she wished she had never said them.

"It's taking too long, walking up here," Netra said a few hours later. "It will be easier walking down in the valley." Shorn said nothing, merely looking in the direction she pointed with his flat, impassive gaze. "It's riskier down there, but we can move faster and hopefully we'll get out of the area controlled by Kasai's followers before they find us."

Then she stood there, unable to take that first step down. The memory of being chased by the burned man and Bloodhound was still raw and painful. She shot a sideways glance at Shorn, seeking reassurance. It was different now, she told herself. She was no longer alone.

"They chased me for days after I escaped them. It didn't matter how fast I ran. They were always there." She realized her hands were shaking and she tried to stop them but couldn't. "The worst of all was Bloodhound. He never lost my trail, no matter what I did. If he hadn't fallen on the slopes of the plateau, he would have caught me. I have nightmares about him every night. I know it's silly. I know he's not waiting for me down there and even if he was, well, you're here now. I guess you'd just kill him like you kill everyone else. But I can't shake the feeling."

Shorn gave her a quizzical look, unsure what she was talking about, but he said nothing. Netra clenched her fists and forced herself to start walking down the slope. She was sick of running, sick of being afraid. She had to face her fear or she would never overcome it.

The first day was easy. They saw no more refugees, encountered no bands of killers wearing the mark of Kasai on their foreheads. Netra found a trail that snaked through the rolling, grassy hills and they made good time. Game scurried through the grass and the water whispered sleepily to itself in numerous small streams. Here and there stands of trees, some kind of oak she wasn't familiar with, dotted the hills. The trail wound more west than south, but she thought it would turn south before too long. If it didn't, it would be easy enough to cut across the hills.

By the next morning she was beginning to relax. Probably they had already traveled far enough south to be free of Kasai. There was no way Bloodhound would be out in this area. The trail began to head south and the weather was nice. She was actually feeling pretty good when far to the north, just for a moment, she heard a howl. She knew instantly what it was.

Bloodhound.

Netra spun toward the north and stopped dead. Suddenly the air was too thick. It was hard to breathe. Her heart was pounding. She pulled her hair back away from her ears, straining to hear every sound.

There it was again. It was unmistakably Bloodhound. She heard that howl every night in her nightmares.

Netra stared off into the distance, her eyes blurring with tears. "Not again," she moaned, the days of running suddenly washing over her, drowning her. She turned to Shorn, clutching his arm like a drowning woman. "He was...he fell and he was injured. Badly. He should need months to heal." She seemed to be imploring him to believe her, as if then he could convince her that she was imagining things. "It *can't* be him."

The howl came again and it was closer.

Netra started to tighten the straps on her pack. "We're going to have to run," she whispered, as if Bloodhound might already be close enough to hear her.

But Shorn was already moving. Not south, the way she wanted to go, but north. Straight towards the howl. Netra stood and watched as he crested the next rolling hill, then dropped down the other side, disappearing from sight. She looked around, suddenly feeling very vulnerable and exposed.

With a small cry, Netra ran after him. He was moving swiftly and by the time she got to the top of the rolling hill, he had already crested the next one. She paused there for a moment, unsure what to do, then took off after him again.

Over the next half hour Bloodhound's howl became much louder and closer. From the top of one small hill Netra thought she saw bunched figures in the distance, one figure leading them. She knew him immediately. Knew him by the odd, hunched over way he ran, nose down as if sniffing the earth for clues.

Then she could go no further. She found a small copse of trees and hid in them, waiting. Was there a burned man with them? she wondered. Would Shorn be able to defeat him? What if there were too many of them and they killed him? He wasn't invincible, no matter how powerful he was. Should she just run, put as much distance as possible between herself and them?

But she didn't run. She told herself over and over that Shorn would defeat them and he would return. Bloodhound would be dead and she would finally be free of him. It occurred to her at one point that she hadn't heard Bloodhound's howl for some time. Maybe that meant that Shorn had already killed him. If she tried hard, she thought she could hear shouts and cries in the distance, which meant that Shorn had—

"Caught you."

An arm closed around her neck, squeezing hard. Netra knew instantly that it was Bloodhound, though it seemed impossible that he had snuck up on her. Choking, she clawed at his arm, trying to free herself, but he was cruelly strong and she could do nothing against him.

His hold tightened and now she couldn't breathe at all. For a few more panicked moments she fought wildly, with no more thought than a wild animal. Already her vision was growing dark. Bloodhound was saying something, but she couldn't tell what it was over the roaring in her ears.

She was dying. She knew this now. Her fingers fell nervelessly away from his arm. Oddly, she felt herself slipping *beyond*.

She seemed to slip sideways and all at once she was outside herself, looking back at her own *akirma*. Pressed up close behind her was Bloodhound's *akirma*, which was covered with what looked like a gray cobweb. The web shifted and something like red sparks erupted from inside him.

Superimposed over the scene was the normal world. She could see herself hanging limply in Bloodhound's arms. His lips were pulled back, baring his teeth, and it looked like he was laughing.

Laughing.

Suddenly, she was enraged. This creature, this *monster*, had chased her for days. He'd tormented her and why? She'd done nothing to him.

She would tear him to pieces. She would make sure he never came after her again.

Summoned by her rage, a half dozen tendrils of will sprouted from her *akirma* simultaneously and stabbed into Bloodhound's *akirma*. As if from a great distance she heard him scream, but it only drove her to a greater frenzy.

In a heartbeat, his Song rushed into her. Swollen with power, she grabbed the arm wrapped around her neck and snapped it like kindling. He screamed again and she laughed. Still holding onto his broken arm, she jerked him over her shoulder and slammed him to the ground. She heard bones breaking and welcomed the sound.

"Never again!" she screamed, throwing herself on him and pounding him with her fists.

She knew he was dead then, but still she kept beating on him, all her fear and desperation pouring out of her in a flood she couldn't control.

How long she kept it up she didn't know, but at one point she felt a hand on her shoulder, pulling her away and lifting her to her feet. Shorn was there, his eyes wide with concern.

"I killed him," she gasped, her words as raw as her throat. "He's dead. He'll never chase me again."

She almost started crying then but her own weakness disgusted her and she pulled herself away from him and stalked away without a glance at the broken form of Bloodhound lying on the ground, his blood seeping into the dirt.

After that Netra thought only of flight, running from what she had just done, what she felt within her. But at length she slowed her pace and allowed Shorn to catch up with her.

She expected guilt, but when she looked inside, she found none. She tried to summon it, but it was not there. What she did find was anger and a savage joy that was troubling and wonderful at the same time. A man was dead. Some part of her cried out that she should feel sorrow for this, but it was very far away and she would not listen to it.

She faced Shorn as he caught up to her, crossing her arms over her chest. "He deserved it. He chased me and he would have given me to that thing to be burned. I am glad he is dead."

Shorn looked at her and she thought she saw something in his eyes that she didn't like. He looked troubled. It made her unsure and she wanted more than anything else to be sure.

"You were right, you know," she said. "This is war and mercy is only weakness."

Shorn seemed almost to wince as she flung the words at him.

"What's wrong?" she asked. "Isn't this what you wanted?"

"I did not…" he began, then stopped.

"You didn't what?"

But Shorn would say nothing more.

As the day went by, Netra's hard resolve faded and then disappeared.

It seemed unbelievable to her what she had done. The memory was there, but it was as if another person had done it.

"I'm sorry," she said to Shorn as the sun began to set. He gave her a curious look, but said nothing. "I don't know what happened to me."

They walked in silence for a few minutes. "I can't describe what it was like, those days and nights of running from that man. It was horrible, like a nightmare I couldn't wake up from. I felt so alone. Nothing I did made any difference. I couldn't get away from him no matter how I tried. Today, when he grabbed me, I just went crazy. Everything poured out at once. But that's not me. I don't want to be that kind of person. I'm not a killer." As she said the words she pictured the Tender she'd pushed in front of Gulagh's attack in Nelton and her own words sounded like a lie.

"I'm not a killer," she repeated, but could summon no conviction. *What am I becoming?*

She started to cry then and couldn't stop. She stopped walking and just stood there, her whole body shaking. She wrapped her arms around herself and cried for everything that had happened, from Gerath's death to Alissa's. It all poured out at once and swept her away.

For several minutes Shorn stood there looking at her. Then he moved closer and awkwardly put his hand on her shoulder, just for a moment, and then he pulled away.

THIRTY-ONE

That morning when she woke up, Shakre felt more or less normal for the first time since riding the wind. The wind blowing over her felt like sand rubbed in a raw wound, but she no longer feared losing herself to it. Though she still felt weak, she decided she would go for a walk. She wanted to see some of the land the Takare now found themselves in, land so different from the Plateau. It was a nice morning, chilly but nothing compared to the weather she was used to, and the rain that had fallen overnight had washed away much of the ash coating the land. When she turned to waken Elihu she saw that he was already awake, his bright eyes fixed on her. He rose silently, seeming to know what she planned even without words. They crept through the sleeping camp and out into the forest, heading toward the ivy-covered cliff, just visible in the distance downhill from the camp. They had barely entered the forest when a sound made Shakre turn. It was Werthin, a worried look on his face. Shakre shook her head and waved him back. His concern was touching, but right now she wanted to be alone with Elihu.

Werthin had left with the first search party that went east and he'd returned within a day of leaving, escorting almost a score of survivors from Splinterhorn Shelter. A day after that another group came in from the east, escorted by two more of the searchers. There had also been a group of survivors from the west. They spoke of meeting Rehobim's group, but Rehobim sent no escorts with them, telling them he needed his warriors for fighting.

He had also sent word with them that they were to go to Youlin to learn of their past lives and begin practicing with some of the weapons taken from the outsiders. Almost all who were of fighting age did so. They were awkward at first, but they were improving quickly. All of them had lost loved ones—apparently more than one group of outsiders had invaded the Plateau—and the intensity with which they approached their training was unsettling. Yesterday they had trained until it was dark, some by themselves, others sparring with a partner. Those who did not have weapons trained with clubs or practiced hand-to-hand fighting. They were nearly silent as they trained, with none of the mocking and jeering that so often accompanied warrior training, each one completely focused on the task at hand. Those who sparred went at each other with a silent ferocity that made Shakre fear her skills as a healer would be put to the test, but somehow when they stepped apart there was never any blood or broken bones. Finally, Shakre could watch no longer and went to find Elihu, who was helping a group of Takare—mostly older men and women, who looked askance at the activities of the younger ones—with a rough shelter.

"I'm beginning to wonder if I know my adopted family at all," Shakre said.

Elihu's expression revealed nothing as he turned to look at those who were training, but she could feel his concern all the same.

"It is as though I have been living with people who were only wearing costumes all these years and now I wake up one day to find that they have thrown the costumes away and I don't recognize the people underneath at all."

"Not all of us," he said. "Others feel as you do."

"Yes, but not very many."

"We were warriors for far longer than not," he said.

She took his hand. "Is it just me? Is the problem mine?"

"We are caught in a war between the gods," Elihu said.

"Tu Sinar is dead. I wish I could believe that Melekath will stop there."

"But you don't," Elihu said, drawing her close.

"No," she said miserably. "I don't. And now I have to stand by and watch while people I have come to love change into something else."

"Yes, you do," he said softly. "But what they will change into is not yet set. You may still have a say."

But that was yesterday. Now it was a new day and the sun was rising. She needed to put away her fears and be grateful for what she did have.

They had circled around so they could get on top of the cliff and were nearing the edge when Elihu stopped suddenly and pointed. Jehu was standing on the edge of the cliff. As they watched, he wrapped his arms around himself and shook his head vigorously, as if refusing someone insistent. "No!" he yelled. "Get out of my head!" Then he stuck his fingers in his ears and hunched over. When he straightened, he seemed to have come to some sort of resolution. He squared his shoulders and started to step off.

"Jehu, don't!" Shakre yelled, startling him so that he turned.

Tears were running down his face. "I have to," he cried.

"No. You don't," Shakre said.

"Yes I do. It's my fault so many of our people have died." He wore his long black hair unbound. The wind gusted and his hair blew aside, revealing the black thumb print, stark against his pale skin. His features were very fine, almost delicate, and the pain that gnawed at him from within accentuated his fragility.

"It's not your fault, Jehu. You have to know that."

"It is. Don't you *see*?" He clawed at the mark on his forehead so that blood ran and his expression was anguished. "I wear Kasai's mark and that means it can see through me. It knows where we are because of me. Kasai's men will come again and this time they will kill us all. I have to kill myself before that happens."

"It sees through you?" Elihu asked. "Why did you not say anything before this?"

"Because up there I could hide from it sometimes. It wasn't always inside my head."

"And now you can't anymore?"

"No," he moaned. "I can't hide anymore. It is watching always, watching from inside my head, and now it talks to me too, tells me terrible things. I can't...I don't know how long I can hold on. Sometimes it is as though my hands do not belong to me anymore." He buried his face in his hands. "I should have died when the others did, with Meholah. I have stained everything with my cowardice. It's the only thing left that I can do."

Elihu and Shakre exchanged looks. If what Jehu said was true, then they had a big problem. Shakre turned to Jehu. "You're right, Jehu. This has to end."

Jehu's eyes widened. "You...you agree with me?"

"Yes. But killing yourself isn't the only answer."

"It's not?"

"No. It is time to heal you, to erase that mark from you."

Now he was really staring. "You...no one can do that," he breathed. "Kasai is too powerful."

"But not all powerful. Listen to me, Jehu. I can heal you. I have ridden the wind and I can do this."

The look in his eyes changed. He was thinking about what she said, looking at it inside.

"You will have to trust me," she continued. Her voice took on a deeper, more authoritative tone. "Have I not always done what I said I would do? Did I not lead our people to safety?"

He hesitated, then nodded.

"Then come away from the edge and we will do this. I will heal you."

Like a half-wild animal he crept toward her, suspicion and hope warring within him. "If this does not work, you must let me kill myself."

"It will work," Shakre said sternly, hoping she sounded more confident than she felt. She had no real idea what to do. But she had to try. She couldn't just let him kill himself. *And if it doesn't work?* she asked herself. *What will you do then? Will you let him carry out his threat?* She would think about that later.

"I will have to give you something to sleep first," she said.

He eyed her suspiciously. "I don't think it will work. I don't...I don't really sleep anymore. It keeps me awake."

"One thing at a time, Jehu. Trust me."

He hesitated, and then nodded.

Shakre opened the small pouch of healing supplies that she carried with her everywhere. If life on the Plateau had taught her anything, it was that danger waited everywhere and it was best to be prepared for it always. She breathed a sigh of relief when she saw that she was carrying hemsroot powder. A pinch of it dissolved in water made a person dizzy. Three pinches and the same person would sleep deeply through the night. Telling Jehu to tilt his head back, she dropped the powder in his mouth.

A short time later Jehu's eyes started to close. Mumbling something unintelligible, he staggered sideways. Shakre and Elihu caught him and gently lowered him to the ground.

"How will you do this?" Elihu asked.

Shakre shrugged. "I don't know. I just know I couldn't let him kill himself."

"Perhaps if you knew more about what Kasai has done to him..."

"I tried several times to examine him, but he would never let me." Shakre crouched beside Jehu. Closing her eyes, she breathed deeply, calming herself, then slipped *beyond*. His *akirma* had a large black spot near the top, corresponding to the burn on his forehead. This much she had *seen* before, from a distance. It didn't really tell her anything. She needed to *see* deeper inside him. She steadied herself, shutting away all distractions, and narrowed her concentration until it was a fine point, like a needle she could push through the surface of his *akirma*. She felt pressure in her head, and then she was through.

A network of black lines branched out from the black spot, crisscrossing the interior of his *akirma* like a spider web. They were stretched taut. What in the world *were* those things? Would it be possible to rip them out of him? Ever so gently, she touched one with her will.

Jehu gasped and writhed on the ground. Pain blossomed across the expanse of his *akirma*.

Withdrawing from *beyond*, Shakre felt Jehu's forehead and checked his pulse. His heart was racing and his skin was hot to the touch.

"What happened?" Elihu asked.

"The burn goes beyond his skin," she said, frowning. "It is anchored to the very core of his being. It is almost as if the burn is a seed that was planted on him and then sprouted roots that spread throughout his *akirma*. I thought maybe I could tear them free and release him." She turned her face up to him. "I don't know what to do. All I did was *touch* one of them. You saw how he reacted."

Elihu looked thoughtful. "Whatever it is, it serves as a connection between those who bear the mark and Kasai, allowing Kasai to see through their eyes, and apparently even exert a certain amount of control over them. Jehu said that on the Plateau he could hide sometimes, so maybe there was something up there serving to protect him."

"Tu Sinar," Shakre said. "But now the god is dead and Jehu has no defense."

"No wonder he wants to kill himself. Who of us could stand what he has already been through?"

"Maybe it is the only solution," Shakre said. "Maybe death is the only way to free him from Kasai."

Elihu looked at her with wide eyes, clearly astonished. "Is this the woman I know? The woman who never gives up?"

"I know, I know," Shakre replied. "It's just, he's suffering so much and there's nothing I can do. I can't bear to see him like this."

"He is not the only one. There are many more who bear the mark. Is death the only answer for them as well? Rehobim clearly thinks so."

Shakre sighed. "I'm still so tired. My thoughts haven't been right since riding the wind—" Suddenly she broke off and put her hand to her mouth. "The *wind*," she said wonderingly.

"What is it?"

"I never told you, but when you were caught by the poisonwood it had done something like this to you."

"What did you do?"

"I used the wind. I forced it to blow *through* you, and the poisonwood lost its hold."

"So you might be able to do the same with Jehu?"

"I might. It is risky, terribly risky. It could be that removing the roots will kill him. Or, if I cannot control the wind, it may shred his *akirma*. The wind's power is not like the power that flows through living things. It can destroy more easily than heal."

"And yet, a moment ago you spoke of allowing him to kill himself as the only way to be free," Elihu said gently.

She stared at him. "I have to try, don't I?"

"What can I do?"

"Hold my hand. I may need to borrow strength from you."

Shakre knelt beside Jehu. The look on his sleeping face was almost peaceful. He was more slightly built than most Takare, who tended to be rangy and large-boned. He'd always seemed too fragile for the harsh life on the Plateau. She remembered his birth, how he came into the world so quietly, something studious and intense in his eyes right from the beginning. Intyr, the Dreamwalker, had taken him into her arms as she took all newborns, but then she'd been unable to name his past life for several days. Shakre had always wondered if the woman had finally just picked a name out of pity for his parents. Maybe Jehu wasn't Takare reborn. Maybe his was another spirit that simply wandered in.

Jehu shuddered in his sleep and his face twisted. One hand rose off the ground and the fingers curled into a claw. Even in a dead sleep he couldn't hide from the Guardian known as the Eye of Melekath.

Shakre looked up at Elihu, crouched beside her with the sun over his shoulder. His eyes told her everything she needed to know. She couldn't wait any longer. For good or bad, this had to be done.

"If this doesn't work, Jehu," she whispered in his ear, "may the peace of Xochitl greet you at the end of your journey." The old prayers were still comforting, even if she no longer believed them.

Xochitl is gone.

It is only us now. We make this what it is.

She wasn't sure if they were her thoughts or not. It didn't matter. She crossed her legs and slowed her breathing, focused her concentration so that the rest of the world slid away, then caught an exhalation and let it pull her *beyond*. For a while she just looked at Jehu, studying the black smudge affixed to his *akirma*, the thin black roots that radiated from it. She really had no idea how she would do this. When she'd used the wind to cleanse Elihu of the poisonwood's taint she'd been desperate, nearly out of her mind with fear of losing him, and she'd simply reacted. She'd pushed the wind into him, but she wasn't sure how she'd done it or if it would even work in this case. Jehu's *akirma* looked so fragile, like the touch of the wind would scatter it like a cobweb. It was unlikely this would work. What was more likely was that she would simply kill him.

But what choice did she—did he—have? There were some things worse than death.

When she looked for the wind, it wasn't there. It was then she realized that she had not felt the wind all day. That was irritating. The wind bothered her for years, making her dance to every nonsensical tune it came up with, and when she needed it, it was gone.

Without thinking, she called it angrily, like summoning a petulant child. The words that came out of her were not human language, nor did she consciously choose them; they came from the depths of her subconscious mind.

All at once the *aranti* was there, an amorphous cloud shot through with blue light that flashed and streaked erratically, faces appearing and disappearing in its depths. It was the same one she had ridden and it approached reluctantly, drawn in by the force of her command. When it was close enough, she took hold of it, using the strength of her will. She was surprised at how much easier it was this time.

Not sure what else to do, she pressed the *aranti* up against the black smudge.

Nothing happened.

She pushed harder and all at once broke through the outer layer of Jehu's *akirma*. Eagerly the *aranti* rushed into Jehu, and the change from reluctance to eagerness was so abrupt that she lost hold of the creature and it charged wildly around inside him. Desperately, Shakre sought to grab it, but at first it eluded her. Finally, she corralled it and then found she didn't have the strength to drag it from him. She had to draw on Elihu, but finally she was able to pull the *aranti* from Jehu. The *aranti* wriggled out of her grasp and raced away.

Turning her attention back to Jehu she saw that the black smudge and the lines that radiated from it were gone, every trace of them washed away like mud in a stream. But Jehu's *akirma* was in tatters, perforated with holes. Selfsong was leaking from him and she could *see* the intense, gathering glow of his Heart, preparing itself for the rush as it escaped his dying body.

Shakre threw herself on him, pouring her own Selfsong into him, weakening herself until consciousness left her.

Elihu watched as Shakre closed her eyes and went *beyond.* For a time she was motionless and then her head swiveled side to side as if she was looking for something, though her eyes were still closed. All at once her mouth opened and strange words issued from her. In response, a gust of wind blew across the meadow, raising little clouds of ash as it went. It swirled around her and then seemed to disappear.

Jehu twitched and his mouth stretched open in a silent scream. The twitching grew stronger and his head snapped side to side. Elihu felt some of the strength leave him and knew Shakre had drawn on him. Then Jehu cried out and what looked like a puff of black smoke came out of his mouth and blew away. After that he went still, his face deathly pale.

Shakre seemed to be wrestling with something and Elihu gripped her hand tightly, wishing she would draw more from him. All at once the wind returned, swirling around Shakre, tossing her hair. It died away and Shakre leaned over Jehu. Her eyes opened but she was not looking on the world. She tore her hands from Elihu's grasp and put them on Jehu's chest, a moan coming from her. A few seconds later a sigh came from her and she collapsed across Jehu.

When Shakre woke up she had no idea where she was at first. She could see sunlight coming through the trees overhead, the limbs still bearing a dusting of ash. It looked peaceful and for a moment she simply lay there, comfortable in the emptiness. But then it came rushing back to her and she rolled onto her side. Jehu lay nearby. There were hands on her then and Elihu helped her sit up.

"Are you okay?" he asked.

"I'm...I will be fine." In truth just sitting up was enough to make the day spin around her.

"Again you push yourself too far," Elihu said sternly. Shakre started to protest but he interrupted her. "You asked me to hold your hand in case you needed my strength, but when you did need it you used your own instead. You are too weak to do that. It was foolish of you."

Shakre leaned against him, knowing he was right. It had been a long time since she'd heard him so serious. It struck her that it came from the depths of his concern for her and she felt warmed inside. "I acted without thinking. I'm sorry."

Elihu tilted her head up and stared into her eyes for a long moment. Then he nodded. "I believe you." He turned to Jehu. "He is weak, but his pulse is steady."

Shakre placed her fingers on Jehu's throat. It was as Elihu said. He was pale and drawn, but the burn was gone from his forehead, leaving only an angry red blotch. Going *beyond*, she *saw* that his *akirma*, while brittle, seemed intact. She listened to his Song and relief filled her at the new purity of it. It was weak, but it was clean. "I think he will be all right," she said.

"Is it all gone?"

Shakre focused, looking deeper, then nodded.

"Then you have done it again, Windrider." The smile she loved so much was back on his face. "Is there anything you can't do?"

Shakre groaned. "I can't walk back up the hill to the camp." By the look of the sun, evening was coming on fast. She must have been out for hours.

"I will go and get help..." Elihu paused. "...if you will try to not kill yourself while I am gone."

"I promise."

Elihu stood and looked down on Jehu. "If one can be healed, then there is hope for all who have taken the mark."

"Yes, I guess there is."

"This is a powerful thing you have done."

"Yes," she agreed. She watched him disappear up the hill and she felt good, really good. It was only a small victory, no more than an ant bite to a bull shatren, but it seemed like much more. One life had been saved from the darkness. For now, that was enough.

Jehu stirred and his eyes opened.

"How do you feel?" she asked him, placing her hand on his arm.

At first it seemed he did not hear her or he did not understand. His eyes focused on nothing and it seemed his breath stopped. He blinked twice. Then he started to cry soundlessly, the tears spilling down the sides of his face.

Shakre gripped his arm more tightly, saying nothing. He turned his head and looked into her eyes. Wordlessly, she helped him sit up, though the effort started her world spinning again.

He looked around him. "I forgot what it looks like. I forgot color." He took a deep breath. "I forgot odor. I forgot everything."

Now Shakre felt the tears as well.

"When Kasai was in my mind it was like there was a barrier between me and...and who I thought I was. I could feel some things, but they were not real. I can't explain it. Who I had been was only a distant memory, and always the voice was there, telling me I never existed, that only it was real." He put his head in his hands, pained by the memory. "You can't imagine," he whispered. "Everything was shrouded. I was so alone."

He turned on her suddenly and gripped her arm with both hands. "Thank you. You have no idea what you have done."

She could hardly see through the blur of tears.

"I was alone behind that wall...except for *it*. Kasai was always there, whispering to me, speaking of death and killing. I had to stay away from everyone as much as I could. I didn't know what I would do."

Shakre hugged him to her, a great weight falling off her. Melekath had not won yet. There was still hope.

THIRTY-TWO

Rehobim's party returned several days later, spilling into the meadow in a rush near the end of the day. Two had bandages, and Pinlir walked with a limp, but none were missing, for which Shakre breathed a sigh of relief. Rehobim had a fierce look on his face and over his shoulder he carried a rough sack that clanked as he walked. He swaggered over to the fire pit as the Takare looked on. Word had spread quickly when Rehobim's party was sighted and most of the Takare had gathered before he set foot in the meadow. The camp held nearly a hundred of them by now, as more refugees trickled in every day.

Rehobim dumped the contents of the sack on the ground and a variety of weapons—swords, axes, maces, daggers—spilled out. Then he turned to face his people. He was shirtless and a necklace of animal teeth was clearly visible around his neck, the long, curved tani canine prominent in the center. Sweat glistened on his chest. He looked strong, primeval, and fierce.

"We have brought the war to our enemies," he said, baring his teeth, a sword gripped in one hand. "Pinlir."

That was when Shakre noticed that Pinlir was also carrying a sack. There was a savage light in his eyes as the broad-shouldered man stumped forward to stand beside his leader. Wordlessly, he upended the sack and a dozen or so heads fell out. There were gasps from some of those gathered and Shakre felt her stomach turn. She felt eyes on her and tore her gaze from the grisly scene to see Rehobim staring at her, a predatory look in his eyes.

"We found them two nights ago," Rehobim said, his stare not leaving Shakre. "None of them survived."

Shakre reached out and found Elihu's hand. She squeezed it tight, trying to right a world that was tilting crazily.

218

"This is only the beginning," Rehobim continued, freeing Shakre from his gaze to look out over his people. "We will go after them again tomorrow, and every day. We will not rest until we have killed them all. They will learn that killing the Takare leads only to death." He raised his sword. "The world will once again fear our name."

A roar answered his words as the people gathered there gave voice to the fear and grief and exhaustion of the past days, as they cried out their rage at the violence and death that had found their loved ones. There were some who did not cry out, but they were few and mostly the old and the very young. Shakre gripped Elihu's hand so hard she thought his bones must break.

"Who will stand with me?" Rehobim cried, thrusting his sword into the air.

They roared again and there was a general rush forward. Severed heads were kicked aside as those without weapons jostled to grab from those on the ground. Shakre thought she was going to be ill but she was cognizant of Rehobim's gaze on her once again so she fought to appear outwardly calm. She waited for the uproar to die down, then let go of Elihu's hand and made her way forward.

It was hard to do. She didn't want to do it. She wanted to stay with Elihu and say nothing. She knew what awaited her, how her words would be taken by most of those present, and inwardly she quailed. The easy thing, the thing she most wanted to do, was nothing. But she also knew she could not do that.

"I would like to speak."

Voice stilled and faces turned toward her.

"You have nothing to say, Outsider," Rehobim sneered. Some of those who had gone with him added their voices to his. "She would have us bow to the invaders!" he yelled. "She is not to be trusted. She speaks for them."

Many of the Takare stared at Shakre with hard, suspicious eyes and she was suddenly aware of the fact that she did not know most of them. The Takare from the other Shelters had heard of her, surely, but they did not know her. They saw her only as an outsider, and after what they had been through they would have no reason to trust her.

All at once Elihu was by her side, his eyes fixed on Rehobim. He did not raise his voice and his posture remained completely nonthreatening, but when he spoke every eye went to him. "*You* do not decide who speaks and who does not. That right is reserved for the Walkers and *I* am Elihu, Plantwalker for Bent Tree Shelter." He barely came up to Rehobim's shoulder, but all at once he seemed the taller of the two. Rehobim's face darkened but he could not hold Elihu's gaze for very long before he looked away.

Elihu's gaze passed over the Takare and when his next words came it seemed to every person there as if he was speaking to them.

"It is not true that she is an outsider. She *was* an outsider. Nearly twenty years she has lived among us and for all those years she has never been anything but one of us. She is Shakre Windrider and I am proud to call her friend, not just to me, but to all Takare. Hear her and judge her words for yourself, but never doubt that she is one of us."

Shakre had never loved Elihu as much as she loved him then. She wanted to hold him as tightly as she could and never let him go. Swallowing, she drew a breath to speak, conscious of the way her hands were shaking. She looked at the Takare. Despite Elihu's words, most stared at her stonily.

"I am not standing here to speak against this war. Violence and death grieve me, but it seems we have no choice." Now some of them looked confused. This was not what they expected. Shakre looked down at the heads on the ground at her feet and let the sadness in her heart envelop her. Not long ago such a scene would have been unthinkable. She took another deep breath and briefly touched Elihu's shoulder before continuing on.

"I stand here because I love the warm, kind-hearted people who adopted me when I had nowhere else to go. I love those people and I don't want to lose them." There was some shuffling now and many exchanged looks, wondering where she was going with this. "There is more than one kind of death. There is the death that comes for the body and I know the Takare do not fear this death because I have seen you face it bravely for many years. It is the other kind of death I fear, the kind that happens in here." She put her hand on her heart. "When that happens the body may still live, but the person is dead." For some reason her eyes fell on Birna, Pinlir's mate. She was staring at Pinlir with a look of anguish, tears streaming down her face. Shakre felt the sorrow rise up again inside her and had to fight through it before she could go on.

"It is hate that causes this kind of death, as the person we were is destroyed and something ugly left in its place." She resisted the urge to look at Rehobim. "I stand here because I want to ask you to fight this war without hate in your hearts. Fight the burned ones, but remember that underneath the mark they wear, underneath the terrible things they do, lives a person who was born as you were, raised by family who loved them." Now there was some muttering and she sensed that she did not have much longer. She needed to say what she was there to say quickly. "Fight not with hatred or savagery in your hearts, but with sorrow that you are forced to kill those who are your brothers."

Rehobim barked out a sharp, bitter laugh. "They are not our brothers," he spat. "They are vermin, lower than the divels that eat our stores of food in the winter. They are to be killed without remorse."

Many voices rose in support of him.

"They are only people," Shakre insisted, knowing it would do no good but determined to speak as long as they let her. "People who were frightened and in their fear made a decision they have to suffer with for the rest of their lives. They deserve our compassion, not our hatred. They have made a mistake, but that does not make them monsters. They chose as they did out of fear. They are not evil. They are only afraid. Any of us could fall prey to the same fear."

As she said these last words Rehobim stiffened as if struck and his eyes blazed. All at once the truth of it struck her, what must have happened to him that day when Meholah and the other hunters were burned by the outsiders. *He saw it happen, but he was too afraid to do anything. That is why he torments himself so.* Her anger at Rehobim disappeared then and her heart went out to him, empathizing with the guilt and shame he must have carried since then. All his actions had been a futile attempt to wash that shame away.

"I will not listen to this!" Rehobim shouted. "They are outsiders and they have murdered our people! No death is too painful for them!" Yells greeted his words and weapons were shaken in the air. There was madness in Rehobim's eyes and Shakre actually wondered if he would attack her.

"Come," Elihu said in her ear, taking her arm. "You can do no more now."

Shakre let herself be led away. She had not gone far before the strength leached from her legs and she had to cling to Elihu to remain upright. He led her to a place of quiet and helped her sit down, then sat beside her. They looked back at the gathered Takare. Rehobim was saying something to them but Shakre, thankfully, could not hear what it was.

Elihu looked at Shakre with pride. "Just when I think you will not surprise me again, you do. In one moment you appealed to our pride and our courage, while at the same time using them to nudge us toward compassion."

"I don't know that it made any difference though," she said gloomily.

"Do not judge how your message was received. You delivered it. That is all that counts. When they are ready, they will hear it."

X X X

It was near dark and people were gathering around the fire that evening when Rehobim first noticed Jehu, who was standing near the fire with his back to Rehobim. Rehobim had been in a foul mood since Shakre spoke and he was clearly looking for someone to take out his anger on.

"You have no standing here, burned one," Rehobim growled. "Leave before I kill you myself."

Slowly Jehu turned. His hair was tied back. The red blotch where the burn had been was mostly gone. He looked slight next to Rehobim's broad build, and his eyes were wide, but his words were steady enough. "I am Jehu, of the Takare. This is my home."

Rehobim's eyes narrowed and he walked over to Jehu, then leaned in for a closer look. "Your mark. Where did it go?"

Jehu looked like a deer ready to flee, but he held his ground. "Windrider healed me."

Rehobim spun, his eyes searching until he found Shakre, seated against a nearby tree. Elihu was seated next to her. "How did you do this?" he demanded.

Shakre started to stand up, then decided she was too tired. "It was the wind. It blew the mark away. I only guided it."

Rehobim looked from her to Jehu and back again, clearly suspicious.

"It is gone," Shakre said. "You can see for yourself."

Rehobim swung back to Jehu. "It may be gone, but its mark is still on you. You betrayed your people and we will not forget."

Now Elihu stood and walked up to Rehobim. "How did he betray his people?" he said softly. "By being afraid? Is that what his crime is?"

Shakre held her breath. She had told Elihu her suspicions about Rehobim, what she thought he had done on that day when Meholah and the other learners were burned. Now he was all but telling Rehobim that he knew too.

Rehobim scowled. "We are at war. The weak and the cowardly threaten us all."

"You didn't answer me, Rehobim," Elihu persisted. "I asked you if being afraid is now a crime."

"When it endangers our people it is," Rehobim said sullenly.

"And you have never been afraid?"

Rehobim's face grew very dark. "You walk on broken ground, old man."

"You were not afraid when the outsiders burned Meholah and the learners?"

Rehobim froze. Those Takare who were nearby quit their conversations, sensing the tension in the air. "What are you saying?" he said between clenched teeth.

"But you were not there, were you? You said you had been sent by Meholah to follow a splinterhorn trail and when you came back they were already dead."

"You doubt me on this?" Rehobim said. Violence coiled in his muscles and Shakre wanted to call out, to do something to stop this before it was too late. "I, who have killed more outsiders than any of our people?"

Elihu stared steadily at Rehobim without speaking. Finally, he said, "Being afraid is part of being alive."

"Fear leads to death," Rehobim replied. "I say the traitor is not welcome here."

"Such is not for you to decide," Elihu said. "You do not lead here."

And there it was, Shakre thought. Finally, it was out in the open. More and more Rehobim had been acting as if the Takare were his to command.

Rehobim sneered down at the older man. "Yes, Plantwalker, you are right. How dare I step forward when it is you and the other Walkers' place to do so? We know your heart. Let us hear from the Huntwalker." He made a show of looking around. "Except we have no Huntwalker. He was murdered by the outsiders. It is lucky," he said, looking at the meat already cooking over the fire, "that we have not starved yet.

"Or maybe we can turn to our Firewalker." Again he looked around. "If only he had not been murdered by the burned ones when they attacked our village." Pinlir, who was Firewalker Asoken's son, glowered at Rehobim and laid his hands on the axe at his side. Shakre had a feeling that Rehobim had gone too far with that comment. Her feeling was strengthened a moment later when Rehobim bent over, picked up another piece of wood from the pile, and threw it on the fire. Traditionally, it was the Firewalker who tended the fire, or the one apprenticed to him. Rehobim was pointing out that such a person was no longer needed.

"What about our Dreamwalker? Maybe she can guide us." Rehobim turned his hot gaze on Intyr, who was sitting off to the side, staring into nothing. She had not spoken in days and had to be fed or she would not eat. Shakre found herself wondering what nightmares she saw in her dreams.

"Pastwalker," Rehobim continued, "What would you say?" All eyes turned to Rekus, who paled.

"I do not..." the tall, thin man stammered. "I cannot find..." His voice trailed off and he looked at the ground. He hardly ate anymore either.

"But you had many words before, Pastwalker. Tell us, shall we cling to the old ways? Shall we look to the past for answers and wait meekly for Kasai to find us yet again? How well did that go for us?" Rekus would not meet his eyes. Shakre remembered that he offered himself first for the question when the burned ones surrounded their village. At the time she had thought he did this from a desire to set an example for his people. Now she wondered if he had done it out of guilt, when everything he said would not happen did.

"See?" Rehobim said to Elihu. "Our Walkers have nothing." Several Walkers had come in with the refugees and his gesture encompassed them. None of them spoke. "Yet we have food in our bellies. Our fire burns strong and fuel for it is plentiful. No guidance comes from the past. Down here our dreams are our own. Down here the plants do not strike at us at every turn. The game does not turn on us. There is no threat from the Mistress, Azrael. She is gone, or dead. Tu Sinar is dead. The gods that enslaved us are dead. Without them we are once again our own masters. We do not need those who guided us when the gods' venom waited for us at every turn. We do not *need* them." He shot a contemptuous look at Elihu. "Even if you do not like this new truth that makes you irrelevant, it does not change things. We no longer need you."

To Shakre's surprise, Elihu said, "Your words are true. The dangers we faced on the Plateau are not the same as those here. But this does not mean that there are not other dangers, traps we would be wise to avoid setting foot to, nooses we want to keep our necks from. Nor does it mean that now you shall be our leader and tell us what to do." He stared steadily at Rehobim, his posture relaxed, his voice calm. There was nothing in his demeanor or voice that could be construed as a challenge. But neither was he backing down.

Rehobim was readying a reply when Youlin came forward. Her slight form was swathed in furs, though it was warm enough down here that most Takare were wearing simple tanned leather, and her face was hidden in her hood. "Do not discount the past as a source for answers, Rehobim," she said. He looked startled, which was not surprising as Youlin generally supported him. She turned to face the gathered Takare and her eyes glittered from the darkness of her hood. "But the problem is we have not been looking far enough into the past. For too long we have focused too much on the tragedy of Wreckers Gate, when we were deceived into fighting against our own kin. "I say we look further back, to the time before that. To the time when we were feared and respected by all the outsiders. A time when nations trembled at the sight of us. It is time to stop abasing ourselves before the mistakes of the past.

"There is a lesson in Wreckers Gate. A valuable lesson that we should never forget. But it is not the lesson our Pastwalkers have been feeding to us for centuries. Raising our weapons against our own people was a grievous mistake, but that mistake pales before the much larger one." She waited then, letting that sink in for them. Those Takare who had been engaged in other tasks around the camp had ceased them as she spoke and walked up to hear what she had to say. Now every ear waited in anticipation of what she would say next.

"Our mistake was casting our weapons aside."

Though Shakre was expecting the words, still she was stunned, and she was not the only one. What she said contradicted the very foundation of what the Takare had made themselves into since the tragedy of Wreckers Gate. And while it was clear they were moving away from that foundation, still it was a shock to hear it said aloud so bluntly. There was almost a gasp from the Takare.

"Our mistake goes back to when we allowed the Kaetrian Empire to enslave us. It was we who should have been the masters. The Empire should have been ours. Instead of throwing our swords down we should have turned on the Empire and drenched it in blood until the life of each Takare we had been tricked into killing was repaid a hundredfold."

For a long moment every Takare was still as they struggled to absorb this idea which had perhaps never been voiced by one of theirs before. Shakre and Elihu exchanged looks. This was the culmination of all she had feared ever since the first appearance of the outsiders and Shorn, when the kind, gentle folk she had lived among for two decades awakened and became something else. The ripples of change that had washed against the Takare in the past months had morphed into a flood. What would be left when the water receded? Shakre wondered.

"Let me lead you to a different time in our past," Youlin said. "Let me show you a time when all feared us and none raised a hand against us without paying the highest price, that you may see how far we have fallen…and how high we will rise."

She began to chant then, taking them with her on a journey to the past, a journey that would define their future…

The bodies were frozen when the Takare warriors rode up to them. Snow had fallen overnight and the bodies—six of them—were partially covered in a white, gauzy drift. They lay in a short canyon, a spot where the trail dropped down to follow a stream as it wound between two low cliffs. The ambush had been brutally efficient. The victims had not even had a chance to run or defend themselves. They lay in the snow in single file, each pierced by several arrows that had clearly been fired from above. Three were elderly, two men and a woman, and the other three were barely into their second decade, their faces carrying the smoothness of adolescence.

The leader of the warriors—a broad-shouldered man with his hair tied into multiple braids and a scar that ran across his forehead—held up his hand and his followers came to a halt, their horses' breath steaming in the frigid air. The warriors numbered ten, both men and women. Their mounts were of excellent breeding, their saddles finely tooled and their cloaks rich with gold thread. They wore hardness like armor and anyone observing them would be quick to see the contradiction between their finery and the cold look in their eyes. Their weapons were plain but of the highest quality and worn from countless hours of use. They sat their horses with the coiled grace of cats, compressed lethality that could explode in any direction at a moment's notice. They stared at the bodies on the ground dispassionately. Those on the ground, though dressed more simply, still had something in their features that spoke of kinship with the warriors who looked down on them.

"This must be answered," said one of the warriors, a tall, lean woman with graying hair and twin swords strapped to her back.

"As it will," said the leader, touching the sword at his side. His horse snorted and stamped its foot. "Skeler!" he called. At his call a woman appeared at the other end of the short canyon. She was dressed all in red and a strung longbow was in her hand. When they had first spotted the bodies she had peeled off from the rest, disappearing into the surrounding forest.

"They went south," she called. "The trail is easy to follow."

The leader nodded, then returned his gaze to the frozen corpses. "The answer will come soon, my brothers and sisters," he said to them, then spurred his horses through them, the rest following.

They reached their destination in the mid-afternoon, a sleepy village sitting in a clearing at the base of a small hill. The village had a stout palisade around it and probably three dozen homes, including several of brick that were more than one story. The warriors made no effort to conceal their approach and long before they reached the village the alarm bell tolled. Men ran from fields around the village and soon the palisade bristled with bows, swords, axes and pikes. Men in mismatched armor hurried back and forth.

The Takare warriors stopped a bowshot away from the village and arranged themselves in a line facing the main gate. For a time, they just stood there, staring at the village while its defenders shifted nervously. Then the leader lifted his hand and opened the clasp that held his rich cloak in place, letting it fall to the ground behind his horse. The rest of his warriors followed suit. A sound of dismay rose from the defenders as they saw the red sashes each man and woman wore. Every citizen of the Empire knew those sashes: the Takare. The most feared warriors in the known world.

A handful of defenders broke then, jumping down off the rampart and fleeing into the village. A while later they could be seen climbing up to the ramparts at the rear of the village and dropping over the palisade to run away.

"Answer them," the leader said to the graying woman with the twin swords strapped to her back. She nodded and trotted around the side of the village. She moved almost leisurely, as if she had no concern that they would escape.

"It wasn't us!" one man yelled. He had a shock of red hair and the thick forearms of a smith. "The ones you want ran off this morning!"

The Takare did not reply, sitting on their horses and watching.

More cries arose from the village and there seemed to be an argument going on. Then the main gate creaked open. A rotund, nearly bald man stuck his head out. He withdrew and more voices were raised. Moments later he reappeared, arms pinwheeling as he sought to keep his balance. Once he did, he stood there, his eyes fixed on the frozen warriors, wiping his hands over and over on his clothes. Straightening his shoulders, he walked toward the silent warriors.

"Uh...Lords and Ladies," he stammered. "I am Trel, the mayor of this town and I have come to..." His voice trailed off as a scream came from the forest on the other side of the village, quickly stilled. His face turned pale and sweat ran down his face.

"Our brothers and sisters have been killed," the leader of the Takare said. "The killers came here."

"Yes, they came last night...but they left." The mayor's eyes darted up and down the line of silent killers, seeking something that he could not find. "We told them—"

He was still speaking when the leader's sword flashed into his hand and took his head from his body. Slowly he toppled to the ground.

At a gesture from the leader the warriors began to walk their horses forward. Cries rose from the defenders on the wall and a handful of arrows flew out. Most of the warriors simply slapped the missiles aside as if they were flies, but the leader grabbed the one aimed at him out of the air. Then he snapped it in half and threw it on the ground.

The defenders held their positions for a few more seconds, then broke and scattered.

The leader stopped before the gate. One of the warriors, a young man, slid down off his horse and ran to the wall. He climbed it easily and dropped out of sight on the other side. Moments later the gate swung open and the warriors entered the village.

Eight of the warriors entered. One stayed outside and circled the walls to watch for those who escaped the net. By the time it was dark the village was in flames and the warriors were riding away. Their people had died, and they had given answer.

Youlin brought them out of the vision and looked down on them. "*This* is the past we must remember," she said hoarsely. "When we were truly great. When those who spilled Takare blood repaid the debt ten times over."

As she finished speaking a great shout went up from the Takare and weapons were thrust into the air.

Shakre and Elihu exchanged looks and then made their way through the cheering throng and into the darkness. "They belong to him now," she said to him when they were away.

Elihu sighed. "I tried. I did not think I could stop him, but I had to try. He may not carry it so lightly in the future. Leadership is a heavy burden, heavier than he knows."

"What do we do now?"

"What we have always done," he told her lightly. "We live. We wait. We do not know what tomorrow may bring."

She shook her head in admiration. Always Elihu had been like this. No matter how dire the situation, he always seemed to bob to the top. Nothing held him down.

Later, as Shakre was preparing to sleep, Werthin appeared out of the shadows and stood there. She did not see him come, and was only aware of his presence by the nuances of his Song whispering inside her. Elihu was already lying inside the rough shelter they had built up against one of the tall trees.

"I will go with them in the morning," Werthin said. His eyes were cast down and something in the way he held himself made him seem very young. It struck Shakre then that he was not even as old as her own daughter, Netra. If the world was normal, if so many things were different, he might be standing before her shyly asking her permission to court her daughter.

"I know you do not approve," he said hastily, "but I must go. I heard your words and I will guard my heart, but I must fight or give up who I am." He hung his head miserably.

Shakre put her hands on his shoulders and waited until he looked into her eyes. "I understand," she said softly.

"You are not displeased with me?" He sounded incredulous.

"Not at all. You have heard my words. It is all I could ask." She smiled at him. "Return safely, Werthin. Your people need you."

He nodded vigorously. "Thank you. I will hold your words inside."

She watched him disappear into the darkness and the heaviness inside her lifted somewhat. One, at least, heard her. Perhaps there would be others.

Shakre watched the next morning as Rehobim prepared to lead his warriors against Kasai's forces once again. There were nearly fifty warriors with him now, grim faced men and women strapping their weapons close, and packing away food and water.

"I would like to say only one thing," she said, walking up to him. She would not change any hearts, she knew that. But the words were there and she must say them or live with the regret.

Rehobim spun on her. "More words to weaken us?" he hissed. "Mercy for those who seek our blood?" Youlin stood nearby, lost in the depths of her hood, but Shakre felt her eyes on her.

"No. I offer only a reminder, to go with what Youlin showed us last night." Rehobim hesitated, but the others were watching and Youlin made a gesture that seemed to indicate her approval. Finally, he nodded and she turned to the warriors and raised her voice.

"Youlin Pastwalker is right. We cannot cling to the past. That past is gone. It died with our reluctant god." She motioned to the shattered remains of the Plateau that loomed over them. Smoke still rose from it in a few places and the wounds on its face were raw and new.

"I ask only that you remember your history. Remember who you are. *All* of it." Some frowned. The rest looked confused. "What made the Takare great was your mastery. Your struggle was always to master yourselves, not others, to rise to greater and greater heights through defeating the greatest enemy of all—the enemy inside each one of us. You were great because this was your focus and you could not be swayed.

"Now it is time to fight again and I wish only to remind you of this. You fight an external enemy, but your greatest enemy is still within." Her eyes flicked to Rehobim, who stiffened. "Those you fight do not have the courage of the Takare. It will be up to you to show them what true courage looks like.

"It will be up to you to show them what it means to be Takare."

She turned toward Rehobim and Youlin. "May the spirit of Taka-slin go with you."

There was silence when she finished. Here and there were knitted brows as people absorbed the import of her words. Rehobim glared at her, but there was nothing he could really say. He turned away and began issuing orders for their departure.

THIRTY-THREE

Late one afternoon Shorn and Netra stopped on a small hill dotted with cedar and scrub pine and looked at a house tucked in the hollow below them. It was made of gnarled cedar logs and packed earth and a rough barn stood nearby. No one seemed to be about.

"I've been here before," she said. "I spent the night here on my way north."

Shorn simply stood there, watching. The sun glinted off his copper skin and his eyes were in deep shadow.

Netra closed her eyes and slipped inside herself, listening to the currents of Song that eddied around them, hoping for any sign of Grila, Ilan or their sons. Fearing that instead she would find the dark, burned feel of those marked by Kasai. A moment later she opened her eyes. "It's empty. They're gone."

There was no wagon. Had they ever returned from the town? Did a burned man come on the town while they were there? Were they charred corpses now, or did they carry Kasai's mark on their foreheads?

She started warily down the hill toward the house. Even though she sensed no Selfsong here, that didn't mean there was no one here. The fact that Bloodhound had been able to sneak up on her like that worried her. Somehow he had been able to mask his presence; maybe others could too.

There was a charred spot near the barn, some blackened bones poking up through the ashes, marking the spot where they had burned the calf with the thing growing inside it.

The front door was closed but it yielded to her and they went into the shadowed interior. The place was neat, the rough mattresses stacked against the wall, plates and bowls on the shelf, cookpot hanging over the dead fire. On the table was the brush Grila had used to brush Netra's hair. She picked it up, feeling her throat close, and turned to Shorn.

He looked bigger than ever in that tiny room, bent over to keep from hitting his head. He seemed to fill half the space. Some sacks hung from the walls and there were several wooden boxes. He began to go through these, looking for food. It felt like stealing and she started to protest, but then said nothing. Clearly Grila and her family didn't need it anymore. He found some dried meat and stuffed it in his pack.

Netra went to the door and stood there. There was still at least an hour of daylight left. They should be moving on, making as much distance as they could before dark. She came to a sudden decision.

"We're staying here tonight. It will give me a chance to cook some real food."

An hour later Netra had a pot of beans mixed with carrots and onions cooking over the hearth. It was soothing to her somehow, the familiar rituals of preparing food. As she went through the motions of chopping and seasoning and stirring she felt herself beginning to relax. Some of the craziness of her life began to chip away and she even found herself humming a song she hadn't thought of since childhood.

When the food was ready she went to the door and called Shorn in. "I made some for you, too," she told him when he came in. "Sit down and I'll serve you."

Shorn went over to the table, pulled out one of the chairs and looked at it doubtfully. Though it was sturdily built, when he put his hand on the seat to test it—a hand that was nearly the size of the seat—it looked like a child's toy.

"Maybe not," Netra said surprising herself with a chuckle as she pictured him sitting on the floor, a splintered chair beneath him. "I guess there's always the floor. Here." She handed him his food.

Holding the bowl carefully between his thumb and forefinger, Shorn maneuvered his bulk over against the wall and sat down. Then he looked at Netra questioningly.

"Go ahead," she said. "It won't hurt you. It might even be good for you."

He sniffed the food, then nodded. He took the spoon, holding it like it was a toothpick, and spooned some into his mouth. Then he nodded again. "This is good," he rumbled, sounding surprised.

"Of course it's good," Netra chided him, taking a big bite herself. She watched Shorn with the too-small spoon and laughed again. "Oh forget it. Just drink straight out of the bowl. It'll be easier for you."

Looking relieved, Shorn did so. Netra settled down to eating, and was surprised at how a feeling of comfort and warmth just seemed to spread outward from her stomach as she ate. With each bite the world outside seemed to shrink just a bit, becoming almost manageable. With each bite she felt more and more herself and she found herself feeling very grateful to Grila and her family. Once again, when she needed it most, they had sheltered her and comforted her. She said a prayer for them, wherever they were.

When the food was gone the two of them just sat there, Shorn leaning against the wall, Netra with her chair turned so she could gaze into the embers of the cook fire.

Netra slept in the next morning, not waking up until the sun had been up for more than an hour. Lying there, she felt truly rested for the first time since she could remember. No nightmares had plagued her. She felt hopeful, ready for whatever the day would bring.

Netra packed up the extra food she had cooked and they set out, making their way south once again.

"You've probably been wondering what I was doing up there on the plateau, by myself," she said after they'd been walking for a while. She looked over her shoulder at him. He was wearing his usual stone face. "Or not," she said. "You might be wondering why I talk so much and hoping I'll stop." She paused. Still no response. "But since you're not going to say anything, I'm just going to tell you anyway."

They were in an area where the going was easy and she slowed her pace until he was walking beside her. "I was looking for my mother. I thought she might be up there. I'm not sure why I thought that. It sounds kind of crazy when I say it out loud, doesn't it?"

She glanced over and saw Shorn looking at her with what might have been a puzzled look on his face. She wondered why, then mentally shrugged and moved on.

"I never knew my mother. She left when I was a baby. She was exiled from the Tenders and left me with them to be raised. I always thought she was dead, and when I found out she was alive, I left the Haven to go find her." She shook her head ruefully. "It seems pretty silly now, looking back. She left nearly twenty years ago. How in the world was I supposed to find her?"

They walked in silence for a while, then she continued. "But finding my mother was only part of the reason I left. I think you should know the other reason, if you're going to keep traveling with me. When you hear, you might change your mind." That thought was terrifying. She didn't want to be alone again. But she also had to tell him. She couldn't carry it alone anymore. "I left my home because…" She swallowed hard. It was difficult to say the words. "I left because I killed a woman." She looked at Shorn to see what his reaction was, but he was once again staring straight ahead, revealing nothing. For some reason that irritated her. "So? Don't you want to know *why* I killed her? Or does killing no longer mean anything to you?"

Slowly he turned his head to look at her. "You will tell me if you want to. Or you will not. It is your choice."

Netra felt bad then, for what she'd accused him of. Why did she keep attacking him?

"I will tell you. I don't know if you want to hear it or not, but I need to say it. I killed her to save myself. Oh, everyone said I shouldn't feel guilty about it, that she was going to stab me or that she was going to turn us over to Gulagh, but none of it helped. None of it changes the fact that I took another person's life." She thought of Bloodhound then. "And now I've done it again."

He turned his head to look at her again. "I do not understand. They would have killed you. Why are you guilty?"

She stared at him for a long moment, then looked away. "I don't know. I thought I was better than that."

They camped in a ravine that night and built a small fire. They had finished eating and Netra was sitting on the ground looking up at the stars when she announced, "I've figured it out."

Shorn gave her an inquiring look, but said nothing.

"I know where you're from."

Shorn raised a heavy eyebrow.

"You must be from across the sea. It's the only thing that makes sense." She smiled, waiting for his reaction, feeling smart for having figured it out.

"The sea?" he said.

"Yes, the sea. The one to the east, by Qarath. I've never seen it, of course, but I learned about it and saw it on maps. Karyn said it's huge, though no one knows how big it really is, because no one's crossed it in thousands of years, since before the Empire, before even the Banishment."

"No one crosses the sea? Why?" Shorn seemed genuinely

surprised by this.

"Because it's too dangerous. It didn't use to be. People used to sail on it in big ships, but then there was the war between the gods of the sea and the gods of the land and anyone who went out on it was killed. For a long time no one would even live by the sea because monsters would crawl out of it and kill everyone."

"This does not still happen?"

"Not in a long time. Anyway, I thought that maybe your people lived across the sea and that somehow you found a way to cross it but your ship sank and that's why you're trapped here."

Shorn seemed unsure what to say. Finally, he scratched his neck and said, "I have never seen this sea you speak of."

She stared at him for a while. "Never?"

He shook his head.

"So...no ship?"

Another shake.

"Where are you from then?"

He didn't answer for a long time and she was sure he wouldn't answer. But then he pointed to the sky and said, "Up there." He pointed to a different area. "Or maybe over there. I do not know these stars."

For a moment Netra just sat there, stunned. Then she said, "That's not possible. Nothing lives up there."

Shorn shrugged and said nothing.

"But they're just dots of light. How could you live there?"

"They are suns. All of them. Like yours."

"Those are *suns*?" The thought staggered her. How could there be more than one sun? "And there...and there are people living on lands by those suns?"

He nodded.

"And you come from one of them? What is it called?"

"Themor."

"Oh," Netra said faintly. "That's why you never heard of Xochitl or Melekath. You probably never heard of Atria either."

He shook his head.

She stared up at the stars. Her whole world suddenly felt very small and insignificant. He came from a place where nothing that went on here mattered. At all.

"But...how did you get *here*?"

"You do not have a word for it. Like a ship, but metal and made to fly between the stars."

Netra thought about this for a while, but she could make no sense of it. A giant metal ship that flew between the stars? It seemed impossible, but then she looked at her copper-skinned companion and he was impossible too. She sighed and leaned back against a rock. Who was to say what was possible and what wasn't anymore? She voiced the only other question she could think of.

"Why?"

The look he turned on her was filled with pain. The wall he hid behind slipped fractionally and she could *feel* the anguish that filled his soul. Twice he opened his mouth but no words came out. Then he stood and walked away. At the edge of the firelight he paused, his back to her. The words that finally made it out came from between gritted teeth. In a barely audible voice he said, "I failed. I am...*krenth-an*, one who is seen no longer by his people." Then he disappeared into the darkness.

Netra felt sick inside. There was so much pain in those words. No wonder he wanted to die. She feared losing her world and he had already lost his. And she had been so harsh, so critical of him. "I'm sorry," she whispered.

Netra blinked at the tears in her eyes, trying to swallow the lump in her throat. This, then, was what drove him. This was what crushed him. He did not return and finally she lay down on her blanket, staring at the embers of the fire as it slowly died.

THIRTY-FOUR

They were walking the next morning when Netra suddenly stopped. Sitting on a boulder beside a large ravine was a man with his back to them, bent over something he held in his hands. Shorn started forward, but Netra put her hand out and held him back. Then she closed her eyes, listening to his Selfsong. It was hard to hear, as if he was very far away, but she heard nothing hostile in it, none of the scorched wrongness of those marked by Kasai.

She led them in a short arc that took them around to one side, hoping to see what it was he was doing. As they got closer, she could see that he held a piece of wood in his hands, like a short club, but too thin to be one. He was humming as he ran his fingers along the wood, over and over again. Under his fingers the wood slowly changed shape, as if it was clay instead of wood. The neck stretched and grew thin, the body rounded and bowl-like.

He looked up and his eyes fixed on her as if he'd known she was there all along.

"You're a Tender, then," he said. He was an ordinary looking man, slightly built, with thinning brown hair and a wispy mustache. It was hard to tell his age. He could have been anywhere from thirty to sixty.

"What? How do you know that?"

"Song bends around you." His eyebrows drew together. "Interesting, though, since you don't have a *sulbit*."

"What's a *sulbit*?"

His eyes shifted to Shorn. "He's a big one. Where did you find him?"

She wasn't sure what to say. "He's not from here."

"No, he's not." His eyes took on a distant, unfocused look. "Not from anywhere on this world. He's an interesting one."

"Who are you?"

238

"Don't you know?" When she shook her head he set down the piece of wood he was working on and picked up what she'd thought was a flask sitting beside him. But now she could see that it was a small harp. He plucked a few strings and immediately she knew what he was.

"You're a Musician."

He doffed an imaginary hat. "The very same."

"What are you doing here?"

"The question is what are *you* doing here?"

"I'm going home."

He cocked his head to one side. "Not to Qarath? To join the fight?"

"Afterwards."

He nodded as if it was what he'd expected. "There's a god there now, you know. Maybe more than one. They think we don't notice, but we do."

"There's a god in Qarath? Who? Is it Xochitl?"

"No, not Xochitl. But one who was close to her. Lowellin."

"The Protector?"

"The same."

"And he's helping the Tenders?"

"In a way. But you can't really trust him. You can't really trust any of them. The gods only want to win. They don't care what they break along the way."

"This is still good news. If Lowellin is helping us, that means Xochitl will too."

He shrugged and went back to shaping the wood. It was eerie how the wood changed shape under his hands. "Maybe, maybe not. She's been gone a long time. Could be she *can't* help." He held up the wood and looked at it sadly. "I've ruined this with my clumsy hands." He tossed the wood away. "You're very passionate, aren't you?"

"If by that you mean I care, you're right. I care a great deal."

"Be careful with that. Passion has a way of being blind."

"I want to stop Melekath. I'll do whatever it takes."

"Like I said. In Qarath, you'll fit right in." He stood. "There's nowhere to go, but I'm leaving. Maybe I can find an empty mountaintop for my last song. If none of my brothers have gotten there first." He looked down at her. "Don't look for any of my brethren in Qarath. Except Tinn, of course. He may still be around. Tinn was always wrong in the head."

Then he jumped off the rock and walked off. As he was leaving, he walked behind a bush. It was just a little bush, but he never came out the other side. He was just gone.

Shorn gave Netra a questioning glance and she shrugged. "They can do that, disappear when they want to. It's part of their power. If they don't want to be found, they aren't." She realized then that he'd never answered her first question. "I wonder what a *sulbit* is. He seemed surprised that I didn't have one. It must be something that the Protector gave the Tenders to help fight Melekath. Do you realize what this means?"

Shorn just looked at her blankly and she laughed at his expression.

"The Protector was appointed by Xochitl long ago to watch over the Tenders. He hasn't been seen since before the Empire, shortly after Xochitl disappeared for the last time."

She paused, but Shorn only shrugged.

"This changes everything. If the Protector is here, then that means Xochitl sent him to help us fight Melekath. Which means she has forgiven us and is returning our power to us so we can fight. This is our chance to finally redeem ourselves." She was getting excited now. This was tremendous news.

"He said not to trust the gods."

Netra frowned. "He did. I wonder why he said that." Then she shook her head. "It doesn't matter. We can trust the Protector. He is Xochitl's right hand. Probably he's just worried because of what the Tenders did the last time we had power."

"You told me you are not a Tender. Not anymore."

That brought her up short. "I don't know, Shorn. I broke our most sacred vow. But in war, people die. And this *is* war. When we get to Qarath I'll confess to the FirstMother and let her decide. If she wants to cast me out, then I'll accept that. But if she says I can join the fight, then I'll do whatever it takes. No matter what the cost is to me." Shorn looked troubled at her words and she asked him, "What's wrong?"

But he only shook his head and wouldn't respond.

"Well, you be as gloomy and as worried as you want to be. I'm taking this like the good news that it is. Melekath's coming, but we're no longer helpless. What could be better than that?"

THIRTY-FIVE

The high valley Netra and Shorn had been walking through petered out over the next few days and a gradual, but steady, descent began. They were coming around the edge of the Firkaths now, only a few days away from the Haven. The bushes, trees and tall grasses of the high valley began to give way to the more familiar plants of Netra's home. Cactus began to appear here and there, bristling with thorns. The land became rockier, the hills steeper. The sight lifted Netra's heart more than she would have expected. After so many days away, running, afraid, it was all so normal and familiar that she found her eyes misting up and a lump in her throat. On a rock outcropping Netra saw a type of lizard she recognized and stopped.

"Look," she said. "See that?" The lizard puffed itself up, then began to raise and lower itself, as if it was doing pushups.

Shorn fixed his amber gaze on the small creature. "What is it doing?"

"I'm not certain, but I think he's warning us."

Shorn's head turned and he studied the terrain around them. "Of what?"

"That this is his land. He claims this spot and we had better stay clear."

"He is too small."

"Tell him that."

The expression on Shorn's face was such that Netra abruptly broke out in a laugh. He shot her a stern look, clearly unhappy that she was laughing at him, and that made her laugh harder.

"I do not see what is so funny," he said stiffly.

As her laughter died down, she responded, "Neither do I. I just know it feels good."

They continued to lose elevation and the desert Netra loved so much completely took over. She pointed out things to Shorn as they

241

went along, naming the joshua tree, with its long stiff spines in place of leaves, and the catclaw tree, with its thorns sharp and curved like a cat's claws. She saw no sign of blight down here and she found herself feeling hopeful for the first time in many days. Melekath had not won yet. He had not even completely freed himself from his prison. In the bright warmth of the day, everything seemed possible. She floated along in these happy dreams, chattering to Shorn about whatever crossed her mind.

"I fell into a cholla cactus once," she said, pointing at a waist-high cactus with its stiff, thorn-covered segments. "When I was a little girl. I was trying to climb this big boulder out behind the Haven and I slipped and fell right into it. It took hours for Siena to pull all the thorns out of me. She said I snuck out the very next day and she found me out at the boulder trying to climb it again. I was so determined. I made it too." She chuckled. "I guess I've always been a little hardheaded."

Later, they were picking their way across a dry wash that was choked with mesquite and catclaw. Netra pointed to one of the catclaw trees.

"You want to be careful with this plant, Shorn. The thorns bite deep and they'll shred you. The trick is, once it catches you, stop. Don't bull through like you always do. Back up and pick them free. Otherwise, you're going to tear yourself up."

One thing Netra had noticed the first day of traveling with Shorn was how he walked. He didn't walk so much as *stomp*. It was as though every plant and rock was a personal affront. He kicked over rocks, ripped off branches with the temerity to accost his passage and simply stepped on whatever was small enough to fall under his feet. He left a trail of destruction a blind man could follow.

She ducked under a low-hanging branch and skirted around a catclaw tree that seemed to reach for her. Right behind her was Shorn. It didn't sound like he was being careful at all. She started to warn him again, then stopped. If he didn't want to listen, that was his choice. She heard a grunt and knew he'd caught himself on the catclaw. She turned just as he growled and tried to force his way through, but only succeeded in driving the thorns deeper.

"Stop," Netra said. "You're only making it worse." He gave her a baleful glare, but he stopped. "Now, back up. I told you, you can't fight through this bush. Once it's caught you, you have to stop and go back. Most of the thorns will let go then, and the others you can unhook as you go." Reluctantly, Shorn stepped back, uttering some words in his strange language, words she was certain were not compliments. He got most of them unhooked from his skin, but grew angry at the last branch, a small one that had gone through his pants and embedded its thorns in his leg. That one he grabbed and just ripped from the tree, then yanked it from his leg and threw it from him. Of course, his pants ended up with a tear and his leg started dripping blood.

Netra just shook her head as he came up to her. "I'm guessing you've never been anyplace quite like this. But out here, everything's got thorns. Lots of them. You can't just charge straight through everything. Here, look at me. This is what I mean."

Shorn gave her an irritated look, then shifted his gaze over her shoulder, pointedly ignoring her. "Look at me. C'mon, look." Slowly, he did. "How many scratches do you see on me? How many tears in my clothing? Thorns?" There were none. "Now look at you." She pointed out half a dozen scratches, some still bleeding. "Your clothes will be ruined in a day at this rate. You've got to give a little. Learn to go around instead of fighting through."

He frowned at her, but made no reply.

"Now, this isn't so bad, but you're going to see worse. Let me tell you about cactus. It's a kind of plant covered in thorns. No, not like those on the mesquite or the catclaw. I said *covered* in thorns. You're really going to have to pay attention to them." He had stopped looking at her again and she became a little aggravated. "This is important. Listen to me. See, there's one now," she said, pointing to a cactus by their feet. It was a small cactus with relatively minor thorns. "Now, it may not look like much but…"

While she was talking he very deliberately stomped on the cactus, which flattened under the impact. Then he lifted his foot and made a show of looking at the bottom of his boot. No thorns were stuck there.

"You win," Netra said, throwing up her hands and turning away. "Throw yourself on every cactus we see." Just wait, she thought. Just wait.

It was only a couple of hours later that Netra saw the first jumping cholla. "Now *that* is a cactus," she said, pointing. "It's called jumping cholla. See how it looks soft and fuzzy? It isn't. Those are thorns. Thousands of them, covering every inch of the plant. The spines are sharper than any needle, sharp enough to easily pierce the thickest leather boots." She looked at his feet. "Best of all, the jumping cholla likes to come with you. That's how it spreads seeds. You know how when you bump up against a mesquite or a catclaw the thorns stick you, but unless you rip them free they stay behind when you move on?" Shorn was looking at the horizon, giving away nothing of what he did or didn't know. "Well, these don't. When the jumping cholla sticks you, it stays with you. A whole chunk of cactus—just covered on all sides with thorns—simply breaks off and continues on with you. Seriously, these pieces are the size of your fist..." She paused at looked at his enormous hands. "Well, not *your* fist, but a normal-sized one.

"But that's not all. Remember the thorns you got in your hand earlier? How you just pulled them out? Well, that doesn't work with the jumping cholla. The spines have tiny barbs all up and down them, so small you can't see them. But you'll know they're there when you try and pull them out. Because they don't want to. Come out, that is. What you end up with is a big old chunk of spines stuck in you that you can't pull out and no way to grab onto the thing to pull it out." She lowered her voice and leaned closer. "Know what's even better? When you're trying to get that one chunk out, the one that's sticking thirty or forty needles in you that hurt like the devil, you'll end up with a few more chunks of the cactus stuck in your feet and legs. Because there's always a bunch of them lying on the ground around the main plant, like thorny traps. Just waiting for you to blunder into them. Which you will, because it seems to be what you do best.

"Oh, and one more thing. It's funny how those furry little critters that are just lying harmlessly on the ground seem to find a way to get stuck way up on your calf or your shin somewhere. That's because they, you know, *jump*."

Shorn met her eye during the last part of her speech, his expression clearly saying he thought she was exaggerating.

Sure enough, that afternoon the jumping cholla increased in number. They topped a ridge and she saw that the far side was covered with the stuff. It would have been easy enough to stay along the top of the ridge and skirt the patch, but she was feeling annoyed by Shorn's attitude and instead followed the slim game trail they were on right into the heart of it.

They had not gone far when she heard a muffled oath behind her. Shorn had a chunk of jumping cholla stuck in his foot. He bent to pull it out, got too close to a cactus, and got one stuck in his forehead. With an outraged cry, he straightened and grabbed the piece stuck in his head. The thorns bit deep into his fingers, but he snarled and tore the piece free, leaving a scattering of thorns behind in his head. Now the piece was stuck thoroughly to his hand. He shook his hand, hard, but nothing happened.

"Shorn, look out!" Netra called, but it was already too late.

Shorn's face clouded with rage. He swore again and stepped back. Like magic, three more bristling chunks appeared on him, one on the back of his calf, almost up to his knee. "What is this plant?" he bellowed. With his free hand he drew a sword and struck the offending cactus, whereupon several more came free and stuck in him. He looked like a pincushion.

And that was finally too much for Netra. She gave herself over to the laughter, laughing so hard she had to sit down. When she recovered enough to look up, Shorn was prying ineffectively at one on his leg with a sword. She went to him, still wiping her eyes. "I'm sorry, Shorn. I didn't mean to laugh. I just couldn't help it. You looked so funny there and I..." She chuckled again, then restrained herself. "I'm sorry. I know it hurts. Here, let me help you. I think you've gotten off to a bad start here," she said. "I take it you don't have cactus where you come from?"

He shook his head and winced as she pried a chunk off him.

"Maybe this can be a learning experience for you." He gave her a baleful look and she laughed. "I'm serious. You know, you deal with everything by just charging right at it. It doesn't really matter what it is. Maybe you need to learn that sometimes you have to go around an obstacle. Not everything can just be bull rushed."

"I do not need a lesson from a plant."

"Are you sure?"

Sometime later, when all of the cactus was out of him, Shorn looked at a single thorn he held in his fingers. He held it up to the light, squinting to see it better. Then he looked at her.

"I do not like this plant."

That night they camped in a wash. Netra built a fire and they sat there in silence. From the darkness came a rustling sound and Shorn's hand went to a weapon, but Netra stopped him.

"It's okay," she whispered. "Just wait, and watch."

Sometime later she saw a pair of eyes glittering in the darkness and she pointed them out to him. They stayed still and finally a tiny face topped with a pair of huge ears popped into sight over the top of her pack, regarding them curiously. It crawled over her pack, then paused, and they could see its bushy, striped tail.

"Ring tail," she whispered. "Terrible thieves."

A while later they heard coyotes in the distance, first one, then two, and finally a whole chorus of them. Bats swooped overhead and an owl hooted from the top of a saguaro.

Later, Netra asked Shorn something that had been on her mind for some time. "Can't you get in your metal ship and fly home? Even if you were exiled, there must be some who would welcome you."

He was quiet for some time and she began to think he wouldn't answer her. "My *kelani* crashed. It is…broken. It was made that it would do so. "*Krenth-an* can never return." He looked down at his hands.

"I'm sorry, Shorn," she said softly. "I truly am. I know it can be no replacement, but I want you to know that you are always welcome anywhere I have a home. With me you are not *krenth-an*. With me you are family."

The look he gave her was surprised, but he said nothing. Once again they sat in silence, while the moon rose and climbed into the sky. Shorn was almost completely motionless during that time, staring into the flames silently. Netra was getting ready for bed when he surprised her by starting to talk.

"I am a Themorian. We war with the Sedrians. It is *velen'aa*, a war which does not end. My fathers have fought them always."

"A war that doesn't end? What's the point of that?"

He gave her a baleful look, then shrugged. "It is the way it is." He sat in thought for a while. "*Velen'aa* is not just war. It is any fight which fills a warrior's life. To embrace it is the beginning of *unserti*…what your old ones would call…wise?"

"Oh, you mean wisdom." Netra shook her head. "That doesn't seem very wise to me."

"Do you wish to hear my words or not?"

"Okay. Sorry."

"*Velen'aa* leads to *terin'ai*."

"What is *terin'ai*?"

"It is the…what do you call that which cannot be found?"

"Hidden?"

He nodded. "Yes. It is the hidden, the shadow of a self. To face it is to face one's self honestly, without excuses or regrets. It is the greatest battle a Themorian can fight—all Themorians, not just the *naak'kii*, what you call warriors." He cleared his throat. "*Terin'ai* is the reason for *velen'aa*. Do you understand?"

Netra started to say she didn't—what kind of crazy belief required a person to fight an unending battle in order to reach some kind of wisdom that was hidden inside?—then saw the look on Shorn's face and instead nodded. "Sure."

"To face the one inside is not easy. A Themorian must not flinch. Even if what he faces goes against what he feels in here," he touched his chest, "he cannot turn away. He must be strong and sure. Only then can *terin'ai* be found. Only then can he earn the right to stand before the Has Trium'an, the Keepers of the Blessed Land, after his death. Only then will they allow him entrance."

"I think I understand," Netra said. "It is a spiritual path. If you follow it, your gods will reward you after death."

"We do not believe in gods," Shorn rumbled. "Only the Keepers, who were once like us but stood tall and earned more."

Netra nodded, confused again, but not wanting Shorn to stop. It was clear the words were difficult for him to say. Over and over he started to speak, then hesitated, while he seemed to wrestle with something inside himself.

"It is important that you understand this, or you will not understand the rest. You must know that I led many warriors, but I was never *snek* or *cla'sich*. Such are beneath notice."

"What are those?"

Shorn's lip curled, showing many teeth. "*Snek* are leaders who waste their men in foolish battles, calling it *terin'ai*, instead of stupidity. *Cla'sich* are cowards, who hide behind others, then hide it from themselves." He lifted his chin. "I am less than the *vessernees*, small bugs that bite under here." He motioned to his arm pit and Netra suppressed a smile. It was hard to imagine this fearsome warrior plagued by something as simple as a bug. "But I am not *snek* or *cla'sich*."

He drew a deep breath. "I have fought Sedrians many times and I have killed many. I never refused my orders and I never doubted when I killed." He stared fiercely at her, willing her to believe. And the thing was, she did. She'd seen him kill and walk away without a backward glance.

"We were ordered to attack a Sedrian colony on the first moon of Quantus. I commanded the *kelani* Hil Mek and five more besides. The colony had been left undefended. It was an easy opportunity." Now it got really difficult for him. Twice he started to speak and almost choked on the words. The third time he succeeded. "There were only young there. No warriors. It was a school for those who only recently left their homes, who were just beginning their training. They were brave. They were not afraid to die. They did not ask for mercy."

Netra sat forward, already fearing, dreading what he would say.

"But I could not give the order. I called the *kelani* back before they could fire." He lowered his head, his great fists clenching and unclenching.

For a moment Netra was stunned, speechless. "But...I don't understand. That was a *good* thing you did. Killing helpless children isn't something to be proud of."

When he fixed his eyes on her, a deep rage burned in them. "You understand *nothing*," he hissed. "I refused my duty. I threw away everything."

"But surely when your leaders learned it was only children—"

He cut her off with a curt gesture. "You do not *listen*. It mattered not their age. The young of today become the warriors of tomorrow. To let them live is only to let them kill your own people someday."

"But you saved so many lives!"

He shook his head, still glaring at her. "I saved nothing. My officers..." He searched for the word. "They took my command. Then they destroyed the school and killed them all. On Themor I went before the Grave and they spoke my guilt and my punishment. Exile for me. My family, all of them, became unnamed. The house of Mak'morn is no more." He lowered his head and with his next words she understood that his anger was not for her at all, but for himself. He poured out the barbs he had been lashing himself with every moment since that day. "There is something wrong with me." He looked at his hands helplessly, as if they belonged to someone else. "I do not know what it is. I cannot make it go away. You must know," and here his self-loathing reached new heights, "that it is still in me. If I was there again, still I could not give the order. I am no *naak'kii*. I will never face Koni Anat, who comes for true warriors at the time of their death. I will never face him in the only real battle of a warrior's life. I am broken. There is nothing left of me."

Netra didn't know what to say. She wanted to rail against his people, the sickness in them that made them live so brutally. She wanted to recoil from him, this alien being who had reacted with mercy and compassion and now hated himself for it. She wanted to rage at him until he saw how wrong he was. But all that came out was, "In my world, mercy is to be valued. We believe that to stay your hand is more difficult than is attack. What you feel in you should be cherished and nurtured."

He stared at her, and she could see that he wanted to believe her, but his self-hatred was too strong. Finally, he stood. "This is why I must repay my debt to you. It is all I have left." Then he walked off into the darkness.

THIRTY-SIX

The ache in her heart had not subsided the next morning, but Netra knew there was nothing more she could say to Shorn right then. He was wrapped tight around himself, walled off with loathing and self-contempt. Her words would be pebbles thrown at a fortress. But neither could she stand aside and do nothing. So she did the only thing she could: she talked to him. Not about what he had done, but about her world, about the life around them. She shared with him her love of the land and all its denizens. She named plants—the towering saguaros standing stately on the hillsides, the tough grasses that eked out a living between blazing sun and arid soil, the spindly, wax-leafed creosote that smelled so good after a rain—and pointed out the birds, a badger den, coyote tracks and the discarded skin of a snake that had molted.

She showed these things to him and she told him stories, whatever came to her: the time she'd trapped a gopher and caught it with her bare hands, only to drop it when it bit her. The time when she was little and came across her first velvet ant. It looked like a brightly colored tuft of fur blowing across the ground, but when she picked it up it stung her and she cried for an hour.

She spoke of the women she'd grown up with, how cross Brelisha always seemed to be, the opposite of Siena who always had a soft lap and softer words for a little girl who was always getting into trouble. Of the time when she talked Cara into sneaking out of the Haven after dark to watch a lightning storm and they both ran home screaming when lightning struck so close they were knocked down.

She told him of her Songquest, how she had fasted for days and then stumbled into the cave where her spirit guide appeared to her. In a faraway voice she told him about finding the claw that was her *sonkrill*, how the beams of light came out of the depths of the cave and joined with the light that was within her. It was something she

250

had never told another, but it seemed right and she did not hesitate. When she was done she showed him the scar on her arm, where the rock lion clawed her, though he did not look.

She talked and the day passed, but Shorn never replied. He seemed to pay no attention and did not look when she presented her *sonkrill* to him or showed him the scar, but she had a feeling that he heard more than he let on, that he was in fact clinging to her words. And why wouldn't he? He had lost everything. The bedrock he had built his life on had shifted and he had no idea what to believe anymore. It hit her then—

The two of them were not so different.

At that moment she made her own vow to him, to match what he had made to her. *I will not fail you, Shorn. I will stay with you, whatever happens, and together we will find the light again.*

He gave her a sharp look then, as if he had heard and she found herself wondering if she'd said the words aloud accidentally. But when he saw her looking at him he turned his face away and after that she kept her words inside, leaving what she had said to sink in, hoping they could bring some nourishment to the parched recesses of his heart.

THIRTY-SEVEN

Rome and Tairus stood on the wall above the main gates, watching as Qarath's army marched out of the city. Though it was before dawn, it looked like most of the city had turned out to watch the army's departure. The large square just inside the city gates was packed. The city watch had their hands full keeping the crowd back so that the soldiers could pass through. The crowd was oddly silent. There was an anxious feel in the air. Men stood with dour looks on their faces. Women clutched their children close. The threat was growing by the day and their army was leaving. Who would protect them now? Were they being abandoned?

"Don't leave!" a woman yelled suddenly.

As if her words broke an invisible wall, other voices rose as well.

A man climbed up on the statue that stood in the middle of the square. "They're running away!" he yelled. "Leaving us to be slaughtered!"

The ripple of voices became a flood, more people crying out in fear and anger. Scuffles broke out in the crowd.

"You better say something to them," Tairus said. "This is going to get ugly fast."

Rome began yelling for silence, but it did no good. His voice was lost in the din. The roar of the crowd grew louder. Rocks flew through the air, struck the column of soldiers. Nervously, the soldiers' hands went to their weapons.

It might have all fallen apart right then in a frenzy of fear and blood had not the Tenders at that moment emerged from the narrow street that led into the square from the rest of the city. At the sight of them the crowd grew still, every eye fixing on the FirstMother, who rode in the lead.

She rode out into the center of the square, followed by two dozen Tenders, all on horseback. Behind them came their guards, one for each Tender, all of them mounted as well, their white cloaks billowing behind them.

Halfway across the square the FirstMother stopped and surveyed the crowd.

"Do not be afraid," she said. Her voice was loud and clear in the stillness. "It is not the way of Xochitl to wait passively for the enemy. We are carrying the fight to him. We march to face Kasai, the greatest of the evil one's minions. We will destroy him and his army and then we will return and do the same to Melekath!"

She threw up her fist and the crowd began to cheer. Just like that the ugly tension bled away.

"That was close," Tairus said. "I thought…"

"I did too. I should have known they would be afraid. I should have told them what it is we are doing…" Rome's words trailed off and his thoughts went to Quyloc. Quyloc would have known this would happen.

Where was Quyloc now? Had he left the city? Was he even still alive?

At that moment the future looked very bleak. Always in the past he had overcome every obstacle the world threw at him. He'd survived Rix's attempt to have him killed. He'd survived the Gur al Krin. He'd taken the crown.

But that was with Quyloc at his back. Now his old friend was gone and he felt lost. What madness was this, that he march his army so far on the slimmest of hopes? Why not stay here and wait for Kasai instead?

"Well, look who's here," Tairus said.

Rome turned. Quyloc was mounting the stairs, the *rendspear* in his hand. He hurried over and had to resist the urge to grab his old friend in a hug when he got to the top. Quyloc hated being touched.

"You made it!"

Quyloc's smile was faint, but it was there. "Is there room for one more on this march?"

"Of course there is." Rome realized he had a huge, silly grin on his face but he couldn't seem to stop it. Lowering his voice so no one else could hear he added, "I can't tell you how glad I am to see you." He eyed his friend. Quyloc still looked wan, thinner than he should have been, but the blackness he'd been carrying the day before seemed to have dissipated. "You look different. What happened?"

"I purged the venom. I broke the hunter's hold on me."

"How did you… Forget it. There will be time for that later. I'm just glad you're here."

"Not as glad as I am." Quyloc looked down at the crowd. It looked quieter now, calmer. The Tenders were just passing through the gates. "It never occurred to you to speak to them, did it?"

Rome shook his head. "I had too many things on my mind. It just slipped away from me."

They stood in silence for a while, watching the soldiers pass through the gates and down the road to the west. Finally, the last company appeared, several hundred strong, their armor flashing in the sun. Feathers and plumes and flags flew everywhere. Their horses were proud, expensive animals, their weapons the finest quality. Behind them groaned a wagon train bulging with the accouterments of wealth and accompanied by a small army of servants.

"So you let the nobility come?" Quyloc asked.

"Atalafes caught up to me last night. He was angry at being excluded. I told him they could send whoever they wanted but since they have no official rank they'd be subject to the orders of even the corporals."

"I bet he loved that."

Rome smiled. "It was the best part of my day. I also told him if they didn't keep up, they'd be left behind."

"Most of that crap won't make it through the first day," Tairus observed. "What do they think this is, a picnic?"

"I assume you put them in the rear on purpose?" Quyloc asked.

Rome chuckled. He couldn't believe how much better he felt, now that Quyloc was here. "I thought eating a little dust would help them learn some humility. You should have seen Atalafes when I told him that. I didn't know a person could actually turn purple."

"Are you okay now? Is the venom gone?" Rome and Quyloc were riding side by side, Qarath several miles behind them.

"Yeah."

"How?"

"I saw the stablemaster bleed snake venom out of a horse. It gave me an idea. I went back to the *Pente Akka* last night." Quyloc told him the rest of what happened.

"It attacked you?" Rome said in disbelief. "The more I hear about that place the worse it sounds. Are you sure you got it all?"

"I cauterized the wound with water from the river. I think that took care of it all."

"I thought you said touching the water there nearly killed you last time."

"It did."

"So how come you were able to touch it this time?"

"I don't know. Maybe I'm stronger now."

"But now you're done, right? You never have to go back there again?"

"I wish that were true." Quyloc swatted at a horsefly that was buzzing around his horse. "But I think I have to go back."

"Why?"

"The hunter has already almost trapped me twice. This last time it got me when I was sleeping. What's it going to try next?"

"Maybe it'll give up now."

Quyloc gave him a dark look. "It'll never give up. It will just try again and again and eventually it'll get me."

"So you're going back and try and kill it."

"What else can I do?"

"Do you have a plan?"

"Not yet. But I'm working on it."

"Is there anything I can do?"

"There is. But you're not going to like it."

"Name it. I'll do anything."

"If it traps me there, and I can't get back, kill me."

"Quyloc—"

"Promise me, Rome. You don't know what it's like there. I don't want to be trapped there. Who knows how long that thing could keep me alive? Beyond that, I don't want to be the one responsible for shredding the Veil."

Rome took a deep breath. "I wish you'd never gone to that place."

"I know how you feel, believe me. But we need this spear. I'm not sure yet if it will work, but I have an idea how I can use it on Kasai."

"What is it?"

Quyloc shook his head. "Not yet. Let me think about it some more. I will tell you what I think we can do about King Perthen." Quickly he outlined his plan.

Rome whistled when he was done. "Your spear will do *that*?"

Quyloc nodded. "I think it's a great plan. I have to confess, I've been worrying about what I was going to do about that old bastard. There's no way he's going to be reasonable."

THIRTY-EIGHT

"I'm starving," Donae said. It was afternoon and she and the other Tenders were riding with the army.

"You can't be. You just ate."

"It doesn't feel that way. It feels like I haven't eaten in days."

Owina sighed. She knew how Donae felt. "It's not you, it's your *sulbit*. You know that, right? You've spent so much time lately melded with it that you're having trouble distinguishing between what you are feeling and what it is feeling. Remember, the FirstMother warned us of this."

"I know," Donae said sullenly, "but I still feel hungry. When do you think we will be able to feed them?"

"Probably not until the end of the day. The macht wants to move fast."

"I hope I can control it that long. It keeps trying to feed on my horse."

"Be strong. You can do this. You're in charge, not it." Owina tried to sound confident, but the truth was that she was having the same difficulty and, looking around at the other Tenders, she could see that she was not the only one. Karyn's face was screwed tight with concentration. Bronwyn was riding along with her eyes half closed and hadn't said a word for hours.

"Maybe I should let it have just a little from my horse," Donae said. "Just to settle it down a little."

"No," Owina said sharply. "You know that's a bad idea. You must never give in. The sulbit must always know you are in control."

"Donae!"

The little woman looked up guiltily. "What?"

257

"I felt that!" Owina hissed. Just ahead, Bronwyn had come out of her contemplative state and was looking back. "I know what you're doing!"

"I only took a little. I'm…I mean it's so hungry."

"It doesn't matter how much you took. You can't give in to it at all." Owina was starting to wonder if the FirstMother had made a mistake, allowing Donae to accompany them on this march. She knew the FirstMother was desperate for as many Tenders as she could bring to the war, but Donae just wasn't all that strong.

"I'm sorry," Donae said mournfully. "It won't happen again."

Bronwyn reined her horse in close. "Did you do what I think you did?" Donae nodded. "If you do it again, I will report you to the FirstMother."

"You wouldn't really do that, would you?"

"I would and I will."

Donae lowered her head.

By the time they stopped, a couple hours after dark, Owina was engaged in a constant battle with her *sulbit*. The creature was hungry and it never stopped trying to get her to feed it. By early afternoon it had attached itself to her wrist. Over and over her arm muscles twitched with the desire to lower her hand and press it to the horse's neck. Eventually she had to give up holding the reins and ask the guard assigned to her to take them and lead her horse. Then she could focus completely on controlling her *sulbit*.

By late afternoon all the Tenders except Bronwyn and the FirstMother were having their horses led by the guards so they could focus on their *sulbits*. The horses grew increasingly skittish and one of the Tenders nearly fell off when her mount snorted and jumped suddenly. The guards were almost as nervous as the horses. Haris, the one leading Owina's horse, rode as far from her as he could, holding onto the very end of the reins.

When the macht called a halt, Owina was so grateful she thought she would cry. Donae actually was crying, both arms clamped tightly across her chest.

The FirstMother turned her horse around to face them. She looked tired and her bald scalp was sunburned. "Let's go feed them. Leave your horses with the guards. We don't want the animals any more nervous than they already are."

Wearily the Tenders dismounted, careful to keep their *sulbits* away from the horses. The guards led the horses away, the men just as eager as the animals to get away from the *sulbits*.

The Tenders followed the FirstMother back along the road toward the small herd of shatren the herders had driven along behind the army all day. All along both sides of the road the soldiers were making camp. Only a few were building fires. Most were just throwing their blankets down and lying down. The shatren were at the very rear of the army, already spread out and grazing beside the road.

"Bring us one," the FirstMother told one of the herders. The man bowed and ran off, shouting to the others.

Soon he was back leading one of the shatren. He tried to hand the lead rope to the FirstMother, but she told him to keep hold of it. His eyes grew large and he stood back as far as he could while still holding onto the rope.

The Tenders crowded around the animal and put their hands on it. Their *sulbits* scurried down their arms and clamped onto the beast, which gave one startled bawl as they began to feed, then went quiet. The animal's eyes glazed over and it began to shake. Once it went to its knees, the frightened herder let go of the lead rope and backed away, rubbing his arms.

In less than a minute the shatren was dead. Owina stood up slowly. Some of the stolen Song tingled within her and she felt surprisingly better. Most of her aches and all of her exhaustion were gone. She felt like she could get back on her horse and ride for hours more. It was clear the other Tenders felt the same. Donae was actually smiling.

Then she looked down at the dead shatren and a sense of guilt settled over her. Was this what she had become, killing in order to sustain herself? What had she come to, that killing could make her feel so good? How was she to reconcile this with the Tender oath to preserve all living things, especially since she was of the Arc of Animals?

As they walked back to where their guards were preparing their camp, she spoke of her guilt to Karyn.

"I feel the same way," Karyn said, "but I think we need to look at it this way: people kill animals to eat them all the time so they can survive. How is what we did any different? At least the shatren did not suffer. It was less painful for the creature than a knife across its throat."

Owina could not argue with her reasoning, but still she lay awake for some time that night, unable to completely shake the sense of guilt she felt.

⚔ ⚔ ⚔

"That was a rough day," Rome said. "I haven't felt this old in a long time." He stretched and his back cracked. He and Tairus were sitting by a small fire on a flat spot on top of a small rise in the middle of the camp.

"You're telling me," Tairus replied with a groan. "I thought the horse was supposed to do all the work."

"At least we made it almost as far as I thought we would. We'll have to keep up this pace if we want to reach that first food cache in three days."

"Let's just hope it's there," Tairus said sourly, pulling off one of his boots and rubbing his foot. "If it's not this is going to get a whole lot harder."

"It'll be there," Rome said, more confidently than he felt. "There are enough villages and farms in the area and the men I sent out have enough coin to buy whatever they need."

"You're probably right. It's the caches in Karthije territory that I should be worrying about."

"That's your problem, Tairus. You worry too much. We'll cross that river when we get to it."

"And you don't worry enough. You know what a miserable bastard King Perthen is."

"I know. But surely he has word of what Kasai is doing. Karthije is lots closer to Kasai's army. That has to make some difference."

"Keep telling yourself that. And while you're at it, remind me what happened to the two emissaries you sent to him, you know, the ones that didn't return?"

Rome sighed. "I know."

"How are we going to handle him?"

"Quyloc and I have been talking. He has an idea."

"You mind sharing it with me?"

"Not yet. We're still working on it."

"I hope it's a good one. My money says we're going to show up outside Karthije tired and awful hungry. There won't be a lot of room for error."

"At least we'll have a little extra food from the shatren brought along to feed the Tenders' *sulbits*."

"Aye, there is that," Tairus said sourly. Right after the Tenders fed their *sulbits* the dead shatren had been butchered and cooked. "I heard some of the men talking. They said the meat tasted foul."

"I'm sure they're just imagining it."

"Are they? I know what I'm imagining, and it isn't good. That's no natural way for an animal to die."

"We've been on short rations before. Everything tastes good then. They'll be fighting to chew on the bones soon enough."

"Reckon you're right," Tairus replied. A commotion down the hill made him turn his head and squint into the darkness. "I wonder what that's all about."

It was hard to see in the dim light, but someone was approaching. Whoever it was, he was angry. A few seconds later two men walked up to the fire. The one in the lead was dressed in dusty finery.

When he saw who it was, Tairus stood up. "I'm glad I'm not you right now. Enjoy your company." He walked off in the opposite direction.

Rome stood up, wishing he didn't have to deal with this right now.

Dargent was a big man, though his size was mostly softness and fat. The blond hair plastered to his head from a day of sweating was thin and disappearing fast. He'd removed his armor but he was still wearing the same clothes that he'd been wearing underneath it and they were dirty and sweat stained. The nobles' supply train was far in the rear so he probably had nothing to change into. His face was coated with a thick layer of dust. He started to talk and then had to stop and cough.

"I will not tolerate this! It is an outrage!" he fairly yelled

"What is?" Rome asked mildly.

Dargent was so angry his mustache was quivering. "I will not march in the rear again tomorrow. It is dishonorable, despicable and...I won't take it. Tomorrow my men and I will be in the lead, as we should."

Rome lifted his water skin and took a long drink. When he was done he wiped his mouth and recorked the skin, still without replying. His lack of response clearly increased Dargent's anger, for he swore under his breath and clenched his fists.

"Is this your final word on the subject?" Rome said, his voice still calm.

"What?" Dargent's bull head swung this way and that, sure he was being mocked. "Of course it is!"

"Okay, then," Rome said. He turned to look over his shoulder for someone he could use as a messenger and was only mildly surprised to see T'sim standing there, though he'd swear the small man wasn't there just moments before. Nor did he remember seeing him the whole day. "Go get Nicandro, would you, T'sim? Tell him to bring a couple of men with him too." As T'sim started away, Rome casually added, "And have him bring chains." T'sim nodded and disappeared into the darkness.

It took a moment, but what he'd said finally got through Dargent's head. Having the man with him tug anxiously on his sleeve probably helped. "Chains?" he said finally. "What are the chains for?"

"Didn't Atalafes tell you?"

"You mean *Lord* Atalafes?"

Rome simply waited.

"What was he supposed to tell me?"

Now Rome let some heat into his voice, though he still kept his voice low. Men were sleeping and they needed that sleep. "I told Atalafes that he could send whoever he wanted, but I also said that if any of them gave me any difficulty, any difficulty at all, I would put them in chains and leave them."

"What...?" Dargent spluttered. "You can't be..." Much of his anger seemed to evaporate, replaced by genuine confusion. It was as if a lifetime of privilege had conditioned him to believe that he was above such things, and now he couldn't fathom a different reality.

Just then Nicandro arrived. He was a short, bald, sinewy man, dark skinned and muscular. He had a big smile on his face and two hulking soldiers with him. They didn't seem as cheerful as he was. They looked like they were angry at having to move after a long day of marching. Nicandro carried chains slung over his shoulder. "Is this the one, Macht?" Nicandro asked, indicating Dargent. Dargent's companion had shrunk back at their approach and he seemed to be trying to melt into the darkness.

Rome nodded. "Chain him up. Drag him down to the road. Leave him in the middle so that those who come after can't miss him."

"You can't mean to go through with this," Dargent said. He was still having trouble believing what was happening.

When Nicandro approached him with the chain he slapped at the little man, which only made Nicandro grin wider. Nicandro spoke to the two who accompanied him and they clapped huge hands on Dargent's arms. He struggled, but was no match for their strength. Nicandro began to wrap the chain around him. He fought harder, but to no avail. In a remarkably short period of time he was trussed up like a hog for market. Nicandro looked to Rome, who nodded. Then the two burly men started to drag him away.

"Mercy, Lord!" Dargent yelled.

Rome motioned for them to stop. "Do you have something to say?"

"This is most unseemly..." Dargent began and Rome again motioned them to drag him away. Suddenly, the big man broke. Actual tears came from his eyes. "My apologies, Macht!" he cried. "Please don't do this."

Rome considered this for a moment, then he said, "You have no problem with marching at the rear?"

"None. None at all," Dargent babbled. "Wherever you want me."

Rome thought about this for a minute. Finally, he said to Nicandro, "What do you think?"

Nicandro's smile grew larger. "I'd slit his throat." Dargent paled visibly at these words.

"That's always your solution." Rome thought a bit longer. "I'm probably going to regret this, but...let him go, Nicandro."

In a minute Dargent was free. As he started to scurry away, Rome stopped him. "I've heard word that you've been calling yourself *General* Dargent." Dargent swallowed visibly. "But that can't be right, is it? Because that would be impersonating an officer and that's a hanging offense."

Dargent bowed his head, then walked away quickly.

THIRTY-NINE

It was a hungry army that finally made it to Karthije. The last two food caches had been gone, the soldiers in charge of gathering and protecting them slaughtered and left to rot in the sun. They'd been able to scrounge a little bit of food as they marched, but not very much. The farms they'd passed had been stripped bare of any crops ripe enough to eat, the livestock driven away, the farmers staring at them sullenly.

Clearly Perthen, the king of Karthije, was not planning on being reasonable.

Tairus was in a glum mood as they approached the city, which sat perched on a low range of hills. Its walls were high and thick, made of huge blocks of granite. More and more he was thinking they'd come all this way for nothing. They couldn't just pass the city by; they'd starve long before they made it to Guardians Watch. Which meant they had to take the city.

Even with the help of Rome's axe, this was going to be difficult. Perthen was a wily old bastard. Doubtless he had plans to keep Rome from getting close enough to his walls to use the axe. Then, once they made it inside—which they would, eventually—it was going to be a bloody business, taking the city street by street. Karthije's soldiers were well-trained and equipped. They wouldn't roll over and lie down like the other cities they'd conquered. A lot of men on both sides were going to die.

Worst of all was the time they'd lose. There was no way they'd take the city in less than a week. By then Kasai would be through the pass. They might as well give up and march back to Qarath right now.

Tairus swore under his breath, cursing every stiff-necked monarch that ever lived. Might they all rot in Gorim's blackest hell.

Rome heard him swearing and clapped him on the back. "Cheer up, Tairus. It's not as bad as you think. We've a few tricks left to play still."

Tairus glared at him. "Since you won't share those tricks with me, I've no reason to cheer up. I find my foul mood suits me just fine."

In the past couple of days Rome and Quyloc had spent quite a bit of time together, talking in low voices. Tairus knew they were planning something and it angered him that they didn't involve him. But every time he brought it up, Rome just told him they were still working on it, they hadn't figured it out yet, and he'd know in good time. All of which improved Tairus' mood not at all.

But if Tairus was in a foul mood about being left out of the planning, it was nothing compared to how angry the FirstMother was. She'd all but threatened to take her Tenders and go back to Qarath. Even now it felt to Tairus like he could feel her angry gaze on his back. That woman did not like being ignored.

"You wouldn't like it if I told you, believe me," Rome assured him.

"How about you tell me this much? What orders should I give? Do we prepare for a siege or should I just tell them all to take a nice long nap?" They were only a half mile or so away now. The top of the wall bristled with soldiers watching them.

Rome looked up at the sun. It was late afternoon. "Give the order to make camp."

"You don't want them to form up at least? What if Perthen decides to sally forth and attack?"

"He's not going to do that," Rome said confidently. "He'll want to talk first."

"I hope you're right. If you're not, this whole march could be over by sundown."

"I hope I'm right too."

The FirstMother came riding up then. She and her Tenders had been riding near the front of the army the last few days so she was never far from Rome.

"I demand to know what the plan of action is. If we are going to attack the city I need to prepare my Tenders."

"Not so fast, FirstMother," Rome told her mildly. "We're going to see if we can reason with him first."

"The man who destroyed the food caches and killed your soldiers is not going to listen to reason," she snapped.

"Well, he hasn't heard our best argument yet."

"Which is?"

"Just wait. You'll see."

The frown on her face expressed how she felt about waiting.

"Let's go see if he's ready to talk," Rome said. "FirstMother, General Tairus, if you would come with us?" When Tairus started to order a company of soldiers to accompany them, Rome stopped him. "That won't be necessary. We'll be under a white flag."

Which didn't necessarily mean Perthen would honor it, Tairus thought, but he knew he'd get nowhere arguing with Rome. Not when he was like this. He was in one of those moods and Tairus had seen enough of them to recognize the signs. When he got like this he was disgustingly positive and confident, no matter how unreasonable he was being or how risky his decision was. He wouldn't listen, no matter how Tairus tried. At times like this it was like he was listening to something no one else could hear.

The fact that Rome had always been proven right in the past was no consolation to Tairus. Sooner or later Rome was bound to be wrong. It could be today just as easy as any other day.

They approached the city, Tairus waving the white flag over his head. At the edge of bowshot they stopped.

"We might be here awhile," Rome said. "Perthen wants to make sure we know who's waiting on who."

A good hour passed before the gates swung open. From out of the shadowed opening a block of heavily armored men marched, shields flashing, swords out. In their midst was a palanquin bearing the king. They covered about half the distance to the Qarathians, then stopped and waited.

"I'm starting to really hate this guy," Tairus growled. Gods, but he was hungry. He'd had no more food than the soldiers, nothing but a handful of dried meat and a piece of stale bread in two days.

They rode forward, but before they had gone very far one of the soldiers detached from the rest and ran up to them. "You will not enter the presence of King Perthen on horseback. He orders you to dismount and walk."

That brought another curse from Tairus. He felt certain the soldier had been told to use those exact words. Perthen was doing everything he could to humiliate them.

The FirstMother's scowl deepened and Quyloc's jaw tightened, but Rome just dismounted as if it was the most natural request in the world. He actually looked cheerful, which only soured Tairus' mood further.

They followed the soldier back to his king and Tairus noticed for the first time that Quyloc had taken the leather covering off the *rendspear*. It was the first time he'd seen the covering off since they left Qarath and he wondered at it. Was Quyloc thinking of using it on the king? His gaze shifted to Rome. The black axe was still slung across his back. What was going on here?

To Tairus' experienced eye it was clear that Perthen's men were seasoned soldiers who had seen action. Their armor was clean and well cared for, but it had seen hard use, as had the soldiers that wore it. Nor did he sense any wavering in them that would indicate that loyalty to their king was half-hearted. This would not be Rahn Loriten, conquered this summer. They would not turn their king over to Rome and welcome the Qarathians with open arms.

The soldiers parted and the palanquin came to the forefront and then stopped. Perthen stepped off it and approached them, flanked by four heavily-armed soldiers. He was a short, wiry man probably in his sixties, with short-cropped, iron-gray hair and a belligerent squint in his eye. His manner of dress was simple, with only a heavy gold chain around his neck and a large gold ring to designate his status. His face was tight with barely-controlled anger.

"Hungry, are you?" Perthen said without preamble. "Not as much fat on Karthije as you expected."

"There was no need to kill my men," Rome said. "They had orders not to fight you."

Perthen shrugged. "They were enemy soldiers on my lands. I need no other reason than that."

"And the emissaries I sent you?"

"Spies." Perthen gestured vaguely behind him. "Their heads are stuck on pikes somewhere. They learned the price of spying."

"They came openly, carrying letters from me. How does that make them spies?"

"Details." Perthen waved his words off as if they were flies. "They should have known what would happen. I've never pretended to be what I'm not." He threw the last words at Rome, clearly intending them to be insulting to Rome.

But Rome did not rise to the bait. "What do you want, Perthen?" he asked mildly, hooking his thumbs in his broad belt.

"For you to turn around and scurry back to your rathole. That's what I want," Perthen snapped.

"You know I'm not going to do that."

Perthen shrugged again. "Then I want you to die."

"It might not be so easy as that."

"No? Are you starting to believe your own legends, then? The mighty Wulf Rome, who breaks walls with a thought, beloved by all, savior of the world." Perthen spat on the ground at Rome's feet and Tairus tensed, his hand moving closer to his weapon. The soldiers accompanying Perthen tensed also, but Rome stayed calm. He put his hand on Tairus' shoulder.

"You're no legend," Perthen sneered. "You're just a man with a toy and you will bleed and die just like any other man. You see, I'm ready for you. My archers have orders to only target you. If you get past them, there's boiling oil in those big pots up there. You'll never get close enough to touch my wall."

"I was hoping to avoid a fight." There was no threat in Rome's manner, but no surrender either. He was utterly calm, as if the outcome was a forgone conclusion and he was just playing along to humor Perthen. His attitude seemed to just anger Perthen further.

"Even if you do get through my wall, it will cost you dearly. You'll lose men, more than you can afford, I'll wager. It will take weeks to conquer us and you'll miss getting to Guardians Watch before Kasai." Perthen was grinning now, a dark, ugly expression. "Yes, I know what you're up to. I have my spies too."

"Then you know how important this is, why we should work together."

Perthen's face twisted with rage. "I'll die before I do that."

"It won't be just you dying. Lots of innocents will too."

"I don't care."

Rome just stared at him and waited.

"I'll grant you one other option: Pass on by. Go around. I won't trouble you, if you don't trouble me. It will be hard going for you, with nothing to eat. But you're a living legend, so maybe you'll make it. You have your little battle and I'll wait here and laugh as Kasai crushes you. Could be Kasai will welcome new allies."

Calmly, Rome said, "You are a fool."

"What did you say?" Perthen hissed.

"If you think you can ally with Kasai and escape what's coming, you're a fool. You'll die and so will all your people."

"No," Perthen said, his hands balling into fists. "A fool would fall at your feet as you demand. A fool would hand his kingdom over to you."

"Kasai destroyed an entire plateau to take revenge on one of the gods who built the prison. Every last person in Veragin is dead. Even the flies and the rats are dead. But that's nothing. It's going to get much worse. Be a real king and do what's right for your people, for all people, before it's too late."

"Oh no!" Perthen said mockingly. He waved his arms. "Save us, mighty Wulf Rome. Save us from the darkness."

"Enough of this," Rome said, showing anger for the first time. "We have far to travel yet and we've wasted too much time here already. I ask you again: What do you want?"

"Good," Perthen replied. "Finally we get down to it. I thought you would never stop talking. It's simple, really. I want you to submit."

"What?" Tairus said, unable to contain himself any longer.

"Submit. Turn your army over to me. We'll march to the pass and defeat Kasai. Simple as that."

Tairus spluttered, his hand dropping to his sword, but Rome stayed him. "Easy," said softly. "I have this."

Rome turned back to Perthen.

"What will it be?" said Perthen. "I grow tired of waiting out here listening to peasants."

"Just so we're straight," Rome said. "You would sacrifice everyone, not just your people, but everyone, in order to hold onto your power?"

"Don't be ridiculous," Perthen replied. "That is what you're doing, not me. I just gave you the same option you gave me."

"You've lost your mind," Tairus said. Again Rome stayed him.

Perthen came forward a step. There was something in his eyes that did not look quite sane. "The thing that scares you is—" He leaned close and lowered his voice. "—that I *am* willing to sacrifice them all to keep power. The question is, are you? So I ask you again. Will you submit to me? Hand over your power? Or will you sacrifice it all?"

Rome said nothing, but Tairus could see he was thinking about it. Suddenly he was afraid. Rome valued his men too much. He would hand over power to this madman. But to his vast relief Rome said, "No."

"Yet this is what you ask me to do! You are a child. You know nothing of what it means to rule. You are no true king, *Usurper*. What will it be? Will you give in, or will you sacrifice them all?" He sneered at Rome. "You are no ruler. You do not have the balls," he punctuated this with a gesture, "to do whatever it takes to hold power. That's how I know you are not a true king. You are only a pretender."

It was then Tairus noticed that Quyloc had moved off to the side a few steps and was staring at something. But there was nothing there that Tairus could see. What was he doing?

"I will give you one more chance," Rome said quietly.

"Don't threaten *me!*" Perthen snapped, spittle flying from his mouth. "I have a hundred men who will fall on you like that if I give the order. I could have you killed right now."

Rome ignored the threat. "I was not threatening you. I was only trying to avoid trouble. Join me. Just for this. Once the battle is over your army, your rule, is yours once again. I will depart this place and go back to Qarath. You will have lost nothing."

"Of course you would," Perthen said. "Because you are the great and good Wulf Rome, a king who keeps his word. And I am a trusting idiot." He crossed his arms. "You know my terms. Submit to me. Or fight. Your choice."

Tairus saw Rome glance at Quyloc, who was holding the spear at a downward angle, and give him the merest nod. Then Rome looked back at Perthen. "Have it your way, then."

Quyloc made a quick, short slash at nothing.

"It will be my—" Perthen started, then broke off. His face went pale and his eyes bulged. His knees buckled and he fought to stay upright. A soldier stepped forward and took his elbow but he shook the man off.

"What did you do?" he choked. His face had turned gray and he swayed. He stared wildly around him and his eyes fell on the FirstMother. "Was it you, Tender witch?" But she was not looking at him. She was staring at Quyloc.

Perthen fell to his knees with a groan. His men hurried forward and lifted him between them.

"One more chance," Rome said. "The next will be worse. You may not survive."

The man who looked up at Rome was a different man. Fear filled his eyes and all at once Tairus knew he was beaten. He looked shrunken, old. "You...you win," he gasped. "I...submit."

"It is a wise decision," Rome said.

The block of men withdrew to the city and Rome looked at Tairus. "I told you diplomacy would work. You just needed to have a little faith."

"What did you do to him?" Tairus asked Quyloc.

"I convinced him he was wrong," Quyloc replied.

As they were riding back to rejoin the army, Nalene rode up next to Quyloc. He was just rewrapping the spear in its leather cover.

"What did you do to him?" She sounded frightened, which surprised him.

"Didn't you *see*?"

She swallowed and nodded. "But how is such a thing possible? What *is* that thing?"

"It is a *rendspear*."

"Where did you get it?"

"In a place Lowellin showed me, a place called the *Pente Akka*."

"I've never heard of this place."

"I often wish I hadn't," Quyloc said, thinking of all he'd been through.

"Where is this place?"

"I don't really know. I don't actually go there in my body."

She gave him a startled look. "You know how to *spirit-walk*?"

"Not in the sense you are thinking. I only know how to go to this one place, a borderland between our world and the *Pente Akka*." As he said this though, he began to wonder. Could he go other places?

"And while there you just found this weapon?"

Quyloc gave her a grim smile. "If only it were that easy. I killed something very large and from one of its teeth I made the spear."

She was looking at him suspiciously now. "If I had not seen what you just did I would call you a liar."

"If I hadn't been through all I've been through, I'd call me a liar too," he said wearily. "Even now I doubt much of it."

"How will such a weapon help us against Melekath? He will not have a flow you can cut."

"I don't know for sure." He thought of what he had learned about Shapers and the power within the three Spheres of Stone, Sea, and Sky. Lowellin had said that the *Pente Akka* was anathema not just to LifeSong, but to the power within the Spheres as well. "But I think if I stick him with it, he won't like it."

271

Lowellin stood in Ilsith's shadow and watched as Rome faced off against Perthen. No one saw him. Nor would they, if he did not choose.

"They are both very interesting," a voice said.

Lowellin turned and regarded the small man who stood there, hands folded neatly over his stomach, his long coat as clean and neatly brushed as ever, the silver buttons well-polished.

"How did you find me here?"

T'sim shrugged. "Shadows do not mean much to the wind."

"Why are you here? What is it you want?"

"I don't know," T'sim admitted. "But it has been missing for a very long time."

They watched as Quyloc slashed a flow of Song like cutting the strings on a puppet. Lowellin turned on the small man, suddenly angry.

"Where did he learn how to do that?"

T'sim shrugged. "He is a very resourceful man."

"I warned you not to interfere."

"But this is as you wished, is it not? For a human to carry a *rendspear* against Melekath? What good if he does not know how to use it?" A small look of surprise crossed his face. "You did not know the weapon could do that, did you? That is what angers you."

"It is…unexpected," Lowellin grudgingly admitted. "How did you know?"

"I only guessed. I was not sure."

"Why did you tell him? I thought the *aranti* did not take sides."

"We don't. He was frightened. I only wanted to help."

"You've actually started to *care* about them?"

T'sim blinked. "Perhaps. I am not certain I know what this means. But I am pleased he did not kill himself as he thought to do."

"You've been among them too long."

"Perhaps. Yet you spent longer among them than I have, and it has not affected you. Why is that?"

"They irritate me."

"Oh, I see. You hate them for their place in Xochitl's affections."

"I cannot hate something so inconsequential. They are simply nothing to me."

"I did not realize you were given to self-delusion."

Lowellin scowled at T'sim. He moved closer and jabbed the small man in the chest with his finger. "Be careful you do not anger me."

"The longevity of your wrath is well known." T'sim did not seem upset by Lowellin's threat. "Have you still not found Xochitl's location?" When Lowellin did not reply he continued, "All this is for her. What good if she does not witness it?"

"Why don't you go somewhere else? Bring Rome a beer or something."

"He does not need me right now. I have time."

"I tire of you."

"I tire of everything. But this interests me. The humans can go to the place we cannot. There is some depth to them I never suspected. They each carry a shadow of themselves, like a dream of one's own self. Without substance, requiring no flow to sustain it, that shadow self can enter the *Pente Akka*. How clever of you to figure this out. But you were always the clever one, the great Lowellin."

Lowellin ignored him.

"How many did you send there who never returned, I wonder? What is different about Quyloc? What will happen if you cannot control him?"

"You know far less then you think."

"Probably. But I have time. I have no plans so I can see clearly. Unlike you." The little man stroked the buttons on his jacket. "I wonder: What will you do if the fight with Kasai goes ill? You have only one army. Poor strategy to lose it, with no time to find another."

"Why don't you go plague the king?"

"He doesn't need me right now. When he does, I'll be there," T'sim said placidly.

FORTY

"This really hurts," Gelbert complained. "Can you look at it again?"

"I just looked at it, Gelbert," Bonnie replied. "Not five minutes ago. It's the same."

"Just look at it. It feels worse," the big man moaned.

Bonnie was sitting at one of the tables in the tavern, drinking a cup of tea and enjoying the quiet. The first regulars wouldn't wander in for an hour or so and with the shutters open and the sun coming in the windows the tavern wasn't a bad place to be.

"Can't it wait?" Bonnie asked, but it was too late; he was already pulling up his shirt. What she saw made her drop her cup of tea. It hit the table with a loud thunk, then rolled and fell to the floor.

"What's that?" Gelbert asked, twisting to look behind him. "You're breaking my mugs! You'll pay for that."

"Sure, Gelbert. I'll pay," Bonnie said quietly.

"What's it look like? Is it bad?" Gelbert cried, still trying to look at his own back.

"It's fine, Gelbert. Just a little worse." It was hard to keep her voice steady. There were streaks of black spreading out around the edges of the bandage. She began to unwrap the bandage. This morning Gelbert was wiping tables when a spider dropped down on him from the ceiling and bit him on the back. That was only a few hours ago. Then the odor hit her and she stiffened. She knew that smell. The rot was setting in. But how could it be? It was too fast.

The answer was that anything could happen these days. Everyone knew that. There was crazy in the air. People were cracking. Just last night old Tern, a patron of the Grinning Pig for years now, had stood up from his chair, started screaming bloody murder, then stabbed himself. Right in the heart. He was dead before he hit the floor.

Bonnie knew she should seriously consider taking Rome up on his offer to move into the palace. A body just wasn't safe down here anymore. But she also knew that she wasn't running, not yet. Rough and crude and disgusting these people might be, but they were the closest thing she had to family. Not the patrons of the tavern, many of whom would rob or rape or kill her if they had a chance. But the people who worked at the tavern. The two door guards, Arls and Terk. There was Tomy, the kid who worked as a gofer, the barmaids, kitchen help, the other whores. They fought, schemed, argued, made up, got drunk and cried on each other's shoulders. In short, they were a family. She couldn't just leave them here. It wouldn't feel right.

She touched her stomach softly. Course, there was another coming, who was also family, and closer than all of them. She had to think about her. Or him. Though she thought of the baby as a her, it could be a him.

Gelbert gave an odd little cry. "It's bad, ain't it? I knew it was gonna be the end of me."

"No, Gelbert. You're not going to die." It was hard to look at the wound, the flesh turned green and black, dark fluid leaking from it. The skin was beginning to slough off around the edges.

"I knew that healer was a hack," Gelbert moaned, dropping suddenly into a chair as if all his muscles had given out at once. "He had that look about him. Didn't charge enough, neither. You can't trust them if they're too cheap."

"You argued with him for half an hour about the price, Gelbert," Bonnie reminded him. "The poor man had no choice but to go down. It was either that or die of old age while waiting for his coin."

"Nay, he was a fake. I knew it all along and now I'm dying," Gelbert moaned, leaning forward to rest his head on the table.

Bonnie patted his shoulder while trying to think of something to say. Arls caught her eye with a questioning look, but she just shook her head. This was beyond her. There was nothing she could do for Gelbert. Behind Arls, Tomy paused in his sweeping and looked from Bonnie to Arls, confusion on his face. Then the door swung open.

A woman in a red robe stood there, the sun at her back. Her bearing was regal, her eyes cold. Almost as one, the men in the room drew back from her, though she was beautiful in a cold way and their normal response should have been a hungry leaning forward. But Bonnie, for some reason, found hope lighting in her heart.

"There has been trouble here," the woman said, striding into the room, the door swinging shut behind her. Her path led her toward Tomy and he scrambled to get out of the way.

"Aye," Bonnie said.

"Let me see." Gelbert had started to get up, but Bonnie held him in place with an elbow and a strong grip. With only the smallest of moans, he submitted and lay back across the table.

"I am Ricarn," the woman said as she bent over the wound.

"Bonnie."

"What was he bitten by?"

"A spider."

"How long?"

"Less than three hours."

"Then perhaps there is still time. First, we must remove the dead flesh."

"Dead flesh?" Gelbert cried, flopping on the table as he tried to see.

Ricarn gave Bonnie a look and Bonnie said, "Hold your tongue and keep your fat arse still, Gelbert. Or find someone else who cares." The man whimpered and lay still.

"These will help," Ricarn said softly. She made a pass over the affected area with her forearm, the red fabric of her robe trailing behind. In its wake she left a mass of white grubs that swarmed over the infected and dying flesh.

Bonnie felt her gorge rise and almost stepped back, but she mastered herself. They were only bugs. They weren't touching her. This woman was here to help.

"What is it? What's happening?" Gelbert whined.

"It's healing, that's what's happening," Bonnie replied. "Now be still."

For long minutes the two women watched silently while the grubs swarmed over the wound and the dead flesh disappeared. Then Ricarn nodded. "That is done." She swept her arm over the area yet again and the creatures disappeared. Bonnie saw no sign of them on her robes or on her skin.

"This will take care of the infection," Ricarn said, producing a small stoppered vial from her robe. "Spread this on the area and he should recover."

"*Should?*" Gelbert said.

"Be still," both women said at once.

Ricarn started toward the door.

"Thank you," Bonnie called after her.

Ricarn stopped and turned around, fixing Bonnie with that level, somewhat cold stare. "It's going to get worse. I will do what I can."

Cara was passing through Tel's Market Square when she felt him. Well, really, what she felt was something disturbing the flow of Song in this area. There were unusual fluctuations in the currents. Her first thought was that this was another bizarre outbreak, some kind of new disease maybe, or a plague of deranged rats flooding through the streets. She stopped and surveyed the crowd, using what she had learned from Ricarn to slip *beyond*.

After speaking to the Insect Tender the first time she'd figured she would never hear from the woman again. Surely Ricarn had too much to do to bother with one disgraced Tender. But Ricarn had come to talk to her a number of times and she had showed Cara some of the techniques her Arc used to go *beyond*. It was much easier than the way Cara had learned from Brelisha and she practiced it every day.

That wasn't the only thing Ricarn had done for her either. The Insect Tender must have spoken to the FirstMother about her because in the days after their first encounter Cara noticed that the attitude of the other Tenders changed. They still avoided her, but they did not glare or treat her badly. Her food had noticeably improved in quality. Donae came by to talk to her regularly and she'd spoken with the other Tenders from Rane Haven as well. Even Adira had softened toward her. She still seemed perplexed by Cara, but she was much friendlier and even brought her a battered old chair one night.

Cara still spent a lot of her time scrubbing the walkways. No one told her to, and she guessed she could probably stop and no one would say anything, but she actually found it easier to concentrate on the exercises Ricarn had taught her if she did them while scrubbing and besides, she needed something to do. She couldn't sit around all the time. But now and then when she tired of it, she would go explore. After about her fifth tour of the estate she had grown tired of it and one day she just walked right out the main gate. No one tried to stop her or even say anything to her. Now she had begun to explore Qarath. Which was how she had ended up in Tel's Market Square.

Her vision cleared and all at once she could *see* the flows of LifeSong. They seemed to all bend toward the center of the square. Taking her time, she made her way through the crowd. It was not easy because she was still getting used to handling normal perception and *beyond* at the same time. It could be very disorienting. It was as though the surreal world of *beyond* was superimposed on the normal world, or like one eye was seeing one world, while the other saw a different one. But Ricarn had told her she would get used to it. Until she did, she usually avoided moving around while trying to deal with both worlds at once.

Near the center of the square was a statue of some long-dead man peering at the horizon. At its base was the source of the disturbance. He was a little man of indeterminate age, with a plain, forgettable face. Cara shook her head. It was kind of hard to look at him. Perhaps he had a small mustache; perhaps he didn't. He had brown hair. Or he might have been bald. His clothes were those of a common workman and he carried a small bundle, maybe a loaf of bread he was taking home to his family or some small tools for his trade. There was something about the bundle. When she tried to look at it more closely it seemed to slip away from her. Over and over she tried, then discovered she was looking at the statue instead, or studying a building across the square.

He removed the cloth from the bundle and raised something to his lips. All at once Cara knew what it was and what he was.

The man was a Musician.

Cara smiled. All her life she'd wanted to see a Musician, but they didn't make it as far into the hinterlands as Rane Haven. Several of the Tenders there had seen them and she'd asked them over and over to describe the experience to her. At which point they'd always shake their heads and say something about how it just couldn't be described. What did their instruments look like then? What did they look like? The answer was always the same: I can't remember. They couldn't remember, but the experience was one they'd never forget.

Now she was going to get to see one herself. This was good, not just for her, but for everyone. The people of Qarath could use a break from the madness that assailed them. Music, real Music, could make a real difference.

It looked as though his instrument was a flute, though it was difficult to tell as he was still cloaking it while he prepared himself. Musicians were masters at hiding in plain sight, bending Song around them to disguise what they were and to disguise their instruments as something they were not, an ordinary item perhaps, or a tool.

Then the Musician began to *play* and Cara was transported. He drew LifeSong to him, through his instrument, and then passed it back to the people. His Music was sunshine on green leaves. It was fields heavy with crops and trees laden with fruit. It was children playing in the rain and fresh-baked bread.

People lit up. Smiles spread across their faces as every one of them stopped what they were doing. They drifted closer to him, their expressions distant. Two boys that were fighting stopped and one put his hand on the other's shoulder as they faced the Musician.

A bent, gray-haired woman was yelling at a young man, shaking an arthritic finger at him. When the Music started she stopped in the middle of a sentence, her finger still suspended in mid-air. A smile spread across her face and she turned toward the Musician.

Cara moved closer. The crowd was starting to get thicker, closing in about the man and cutting him off from her.

Suddenly Cara's peacefulness shifted to alarm. A new flow had appeared, as if drawn by his Music. Where the other flows were like thin streams of clear, golden water, this was yellow and cancerous.

Cara shouted, but her voice was lost in the power of his Music. She tried to get to him, but there were too many people in the way. Horrified, she watched as the yellow flow entered his flute. His eyes bulged and strangled noises came from him, but he kept playing.

But now the Music which emerged was harsh and grating, filled with madness and death. Whole forests dead and gray. People driven mad by some disease. Entire cities burned and the land turned black while the rivers were clogged with corpses. The effect on the listeners was immediate. Their faces stretched in horror. People screamed. Some fell to the ground. The Musician's back arched and his face contorted, but he could not bring the flute away from his lips. He writhed and capered in a mad dance, his eyes red, spittle flying from his mouth.

And through it all the insane music climbed ever higher. Cara fell over on her side, screaming but unable to hear herself. Wild, disjointed scenes danced behind her eyes while worms crawled under her skin. She was dimly aware of people around her on the ground as well, thrashing and kicking. It seemed to go on forever and all she wanted in the world was to throw herself from a cliff, from any place high, and make the music end with a thud and a snap of breaking bone.

Darkness pressed in on her vision and the ground seemed to be pitching underneath her, but she could *see* the Musician and how he fought the poisoned flow. He went to his knees, muscles standing out in a futile effort to tear the flute from his lips. Blood poured from his nose and ears.

Then the music rose in a final shriek and the flute exploded. The Musician pitched over on his side and blessed silence returned.

It was several minutes before Cara could sit up. A terrible headache pounded behind her eyes; she tasted blood in her mouth and knew she'd bitten her own tongue. Around her people were crying and a few were struggling to rise. Some lay motionless, blood pooling under them. A few people had entered the square and were walking through the crowd, looking for loved ones or helping people to their feet.

Weakly, Cara crawled over to the Musician. He lay forgotten, a crumpled, shrunken shape. His whole face was bruised, his eyes wild and staring. The flute was splinters, some of which had lodged in his face. She closed his eyes and rolled him onto his back.

There was a hand on her shoulder.

"We will take him now," said a voice.

She turned her head to see two men standing over her. They were nondescript, utterly ordinary in every way and she knew they were Musicians as well. One had a bow slung over his shoulder and the other had what looked like a pouch such as messengers carried. The air around each blurred somewhat when she rubbed her eyes and she knew those were their instruments.

Gently they lifted the broken form of their comrade and carried him away. Cara watched them go, realizing a moment later that she already was unable to picture the faces of any of them.

FORTY-ONE

TWO days after Rehobim left with the war party Shakre had her first vision. It was not the kind of vision that some called prophecy, born of a fever dream, bizarre glimpses of things that might or might not come true someday. No, this was more as if she was all of a sudden seeing through someone, or some*thing*, else's eyes.

She was walking through the forest, looking for plants she could use to replenish her healing supplies. Quite a few of the refugees showed up with burns or other wounds and she had gone through most of what she'd brought with her. The problem was that the plants down here were very different from what lived on the Plateau, so nearly two decades of knowledge gained up there was useless. She had tried to call on older knowledge—from her days when she was still living at the Haven—but the land around here was much different from that too. Where the Haven sat in a desert, all rocks and cactus and thorns, the land here was thick forest, ferns and rushing streams. With Elihu's help—he could not speak with the plants down here the way he'd been able to on the Plateau, but he still had a deep connection with them—she had been able to identify a moss that worked well for packing wounds and a small bush whose root could be brewed to make a tea that was effective against fevers, but it was a far cry from the wealth of options she was used to.

She stopped and looked around, wondering if Jehu was nearby. He had been a great help so far, tirelessly searching for the plants she asked for. He was a man reborn and he seemed determined to do anything he could for his people. He was often the first to greet new refugees, helping them build shelters of lashed-together limbs packed tight with leaves and mud. He was usually up early gathering firewood or carrying water.

Shakre did not see Jehu, but her eye fell on an unusual pale flower growing from a dead stump and she turned to look at it closer. As she did, all at once she was no longer looking at the forest.

She was looking at a great city from above and some distance away. Then she was hurtling towards it. Its walls were made of a stone so dark they were almost black. On a plain outside the city stood a mass of soldiers, all staring at something on top of the wall. It was a figure, but she couldn't see it clearly.

Now she turned away and raced in the other direction. It was then she realized she was seeing through the wind's eyes.

The wind changed direction yet again, speeding back towards the city, then turning away just when she thought she would get a good look at the figure. It did this several more times and she came to understand that the wind feared the figure, but at the same time it was consumed with curiosity and was drawn to it as a moth to flame.

Finally, it turned toward the city once again, going closer than before and she saw the figure clearly. It was tall and skeletally lean, its skin white and smooth and hairless. Its face was completely featureless except for two holes where a nose should be, and a short, vertical slash underneath.

It turned its face toward her and Shakre felt a sick lurch in the pit of her stomach, coupled with a sudden, desperate desire to get away from it. It raised its hands, the palms facing outwards, and her fear turned into terror. An eye opened in the center of its forehead and fixed on her. In that instant she knew she had drawn its attention, that it knew her now and had marked her.

Shakre blinked and she was back in the forest once more, on her hands and knees, struggling to breathe past the icy hand that gripped her heart. She heard footsteps approaching at a run and then Jehu was there, helping her up.

"What happened? Are you okay?" His fine features were marked with worry. With Werthin gone, Jehu seemed to have appointed himself her guardian.

"I don't know," she admitted.

"I should not have gone so far," he said. "I should have stayed close."

Shakre shook her head. "I am okay. I'm not sure what happened, but it wasn't anything you could have helped with."

"You should sit down," he said earnestly. "Do you want me to fetch Elihu?"

"No," she said. "I'll be fine." Seeing the look on his face she patted him on the shoulder. "You can escort me to find Elihu, though. I want to talk to him."

Later, after they had found Elihu and Jehu had gone on his way, Shakre sat down on a fallen log, rubbing her temples. "I think I *saw* through the wind," she said. She went on to describe the experience. "It is more accurate to say that I saw through the perception of an *aranti*, a being that lives in the wind. I think it is the same one I used to heal Jehu and to find you and the rest of the villagers on the Plateau. I think maybe I'm connected to this creature somehow now and that is why I saw through it."

"Why not?" Elihu replied. "We have seen stranger. Plants have only a dim awareness, but now and then there is one who is much more. Though I have not found any down here yet," he added. "Why not the wind as well? Perhaps the stones and the water also are home to creatures that we have not learned how to listen to."

Shakre nodded. Who was she to say what was possible anymore?

"Do you know the city you saw?"

Shakre shook her head. "No, but I believe it was Fanethrin."

"There were thousands of soldiers, you said. Could they have been Kasai's army? Did you see if they were marked with the burn?"

"No. The *aranti* was not interested in them and so I could not see. But I feel in my heart that they were."

"Which means the figure you saw on the wall..."

"Must have been Kasai," Shakre said reluctantly. "That's what I was thinking." She stood up and started pacing. "It *saw* me, Elihu. It saw *me*."

"You don't know that," Elihu said gently.

"But I do. It knows of me now. It knows of *us*. We are not a problem for it yet, but our numbers are growing. Rehobim will lead the Takare deeper and deeper into the western lands and eventually Kasai will respond." She turned frightened eyes on Elihu. "You don't understand. The Takare may very well be the greatest fighters ever, but Kasai has tens of thousands of soldiers. We will never defeat them."

Elihu took hold of her arm and stopped her pacing. "You guess and worry about things that may never be."

"Do I? Think about it, Elihu." She pulled away from him, picked up a stick and started to draw on the ground. "Here's Fanethrin in the northwest of Atria, west from where we are. South of us is the city of

283

Karthije. Beyond it are a handful of smaller cities, and further south and a little east is Qarath. Down here, in the south, is the Gur al Krin. That's where the Banishment happened, where Melekath's city, Durag'otal, was sunk under the ground. Kasai is raising an army, right? It must be to support Melekath when he finally frees himself. Now look at how it is all laid out." She waited while Elihu studied the crude map. "When Kasai gets ready to take its army to the Gur al Krin there are two choices. The shortest route is to go due south, then swing southeast once past the Firkath Mountains." *Which will take Kasai directly by Rane Haven*, Shakre thought sickly. *Oh, Netra.* "But why would he go that way and leave the armies of Karthije and Qarath at the army's back? I don't know much about war, but if it was me I'd want to go this way, swinging around the Firkaths on the east side, and crush those cities while I was at it. That way there's no one left to threaten Melekath."

Elihu was silent for a time, digesting what she had said. Finally, he nodded. "Your thinking is sound."

"If that happens, Kasai's army will pass right by us. We need to be ready to move."

"*If* that is Fanethrin you saw," Elihu added. "It may have been somewhere else."

"True," she conceded. "But it makes sense. It is a big city and there are a lot of people nearby to swell his ranks. We can assume Kasai is not too far away, since it was sending soldiers up onto the Plateau. The only other cities it could be would be on the other side of the mountains, and I'd think those would be too far away. Why raise an army so far from your master?"

"What do you want to do?"

"I don't know what I *can* do," she admitted, sinking down onto the fallen tree again. "Rehobim isn't going to listen to me."

"Perhaps Youlin."

"I doubt it."

"Kasai will not be able to bring such a force against us without our knowing it far ahead of time."

"I know," Shakre said. "They can't sneak up on us and they can't keep up if we run. But it's more than that. This is bigger than just the Takare. This is about all the people of Atria and the lands beyond. It may be about the future of Life itself. We are all in this together. We should be telling Karthije and Qarath what we know. We should be fighting with them!"

"I cannot see Rehobim agreeing to that," Elihu said with a wry smile.

"No. Me either. I feel like we should do something but I don't know what."

"Watch for more chances to see through the wind's eyes," Elihu suggested. "We should know all we can."

Shakre nodded.

"I will talk to Youlin," he added. "As a Walker, she may listen to me. If I can convince her, she may be able to convince Rehobim. But we will need to know more. We do not have much yet."

That night Shakre awakened from a sound sleep with a sense that something was wrong. She opened her eyes, but instead of seeing the roof of the little shelter she shared with Elihu, she saw a very different scene.

The skeletal, white-skinned figure stood in a cobblestone plaza on top of a huge block of crudely cut stone. It was motionless, its arms hanging by its sides, its head tilted back as if it studied the sky. Tall, iron braziers ringed the square, flickering in the wind. Arrayed before the figure were several dozen figures clad in gray robes. All were kneeling, their faces pressed to the ground.

Kasai raised its hands and held them out, palms outward. The eye in the center of its forehead opened suddenly. From its palms came a wave of gray fire that engulfed the kneeling figures. They began to writhe. Some came to their feet, only to fall back down, while others thrashed on the ground. Their mouths stretched wide in screams that made no sound. The entire scene was silent, surreal. They clawed at their eyes as they thrashed, while gray flames flickered around their heads. Kasai watched impassively.

In moments it was over. Kasai closed its hands and the gray flames died out. Its lipless mouth opened and it seemed to speak, though again Shakre could hear nothing. But when it was done, the robed figures rose to their feet unsteadily and stood before it. They turned their faces toward their master. Where their eyes had been were only blackened holes.

Shakre gasped and sat up. A moment later Elihu sat up and she grabbed his arm.

"What is it?" Elihu asked.

"Another vision."

"Was it bad?"

"What do you think?"

"My arm hurts."

"Do you remember the blinded man who led the attack on the shelter?" Shakre asked.

"One does not forget such things."

"I think I know what happened to him." Shakre described what she had seen.

"Kasai controls its army through them, then," Elihu said.

"I think so." She leaned her head on his shoulder and forced herself to loosen her grip on his arm. "Oh, Elihu. The suffering of those who went through that. I could *feel* it. I couldn't hear anything that went on, but I could see and I could feel. At least, I imagine that I could feel it. Such pain." She shivered.

"It helps to know anything we can," he said. "If you could control the *aranti*, learn more, maybe Youlin would listen to me." He had approached Youlin around the fire that night, but she had sat lost in her hood, not even acknowledging his words. She did not move until later, when she went to some of the new refugees and led them down the paths that led to their past lives, awakening the forgotten skills within them.

"I will try," Shakre said. "But I don't like it. These are not things I want to see."

Elihu patted her on the back gently. "All these years among the Takare and you have not yet learned that what you want counts for nothing in the whims of the gods."

The warriors returned several days later, in the middle of the afternoon on a day when the wind blew scudding clouds across the sun and rain fell periodically. They pulled behind them a small cart loaded high with weapons.

"More of them died," Rehobim said to the Takare who gathered in the meadow. He pulled a sword from the pile and tossed it to a young woman, another refugee who had come in during his absence. "Nearly fifty more who will never bleed our people again." He tossed an axe to a middle-aged Takare, his long hair showing streaks of gray. He looked startled but caught the weapon with practiced ease. Youlin's past walks and the ceaseless training were paying off.

"They had surrounded a farmhouse," Jakal said. He was a young man, a refugee from Fallen Rock Shelter. He had only been in camp for a few days before heading out with Rehobim's warriors on this latest mission. "They never saw us coming. We killed most of them before they even turned around. They never thought to look behind them." He joined Rehobim in handing out the weapons.

Youlin walked up as the last weapons were distributed and looked into the cart. "What are these?" she asked, pulling a clay jug from the bottom of the cart. It was one of six, heavily wrapped in blankets to protect it from breaking.

"Something the farmer was happy to share," Jakal said with a laugh. From the tone of the laugh, Shakre had a feeling that the farmer had not been entirely happy with the transaction.

Youlin opened the jug and pulled the cork. Taking a sniff, she wrinkled her nose and frowned. "Spirits," she said, turning the jug upside down and beginning to pour it out.

In flash, Rehobim had snatched it away. He loomed over her. "This is not yours."

"It is not our way," she replied, not backing down. "It is a demon that destroys us from within."

"It is a harmless escape, and one our fighters deserve," Rehobim said, putting the cork back in.

Youlin looked as if she would retort, but then turned away, pulling her hood up to hide her face as she walked away.

Later, after it was dark, Shakre and Elihu were sitting near the fire. Rehobim and a handful of his closest followers were in a knot on the other side of the fire, passing one of the clay jugs around. Their faces were flushed, their eyes bright. They laughed often, and laughed harder when one of them, a young woman named Hareed, stood up to go relieve herself and fell flat on her face.

Youlin sat back from the fire on a log that had been dragged up for a seat. She had her hood up, obscuring her face, but Shakre was certain she was watching the warriors as they got steadily drunker. She had a feeling that, in this area at least, she and Youlin agreed. Youlin sought to return the Takare to their martial past, and that past was at odds with the loss of control that drinking brought with it.

Elihu came up and sat beside her. She watched him as he stared at the warriors and noticed that the cheerful gleam did not leave his eyes. No shadow crossed his face at all.

"How do you do that?" she asked finally.

He turned his gaze on her. "Do what?" he asked innocently, though there was a glint in his eyes that said he knew exactly what she was talking about.

"Watch that and stay cheerful," she said, gesturing at the warriors. "Not just that, but all of this. Your people have lost their homeland. They teeter on the edge of destruction and you still smile."

"Why not stay cheerful?" he asked. "If I rage and cry it will change nothing. My tears will not stop Melekath or cause Kasai to disband its army. They will not feed my people or guide them through the forest they are lost in. So I choose differently. Since it makes no difference, I choose the path that makes me feel better."

Shakre sighed. "I wish that didn't make sense, but it does."

Elihu shifted his gaze back to the drinking warriors. "How do I know anyway? I see this path they take and it appears to lead to a cliff. But does it really? I cannot yet see the cliff. Perhaps there is a branch in the path that will lead them away from the cliff to safety. No. I have spoken my piece. I have tried to divert them and they choose to continue on. Now I choose to walk with them. I respect their choice and I recognize that I do not know all the answers."

"That's it? You'll just do nothing?"

"I didn't say that. I will wait, and I will watch. It may be that tomorrow or the next day a fork in the path will appear and a nudge will start them down it. But until then, I choose to smile."

Shakre laid her head on his shoulder. "You did it again," she whispered. "And don't say 'Do what?'"

In answer he touched her hair and she sat and watched her adopted people. Really watched them, turning off the inner judgment that cried out, and just observing. What she saw were people running from the darkness inside them. They hid it from each other and from themselves, but there were quiet moments when they grew still, when they thought no one was watching and then the darkness slipped out. Times when the laughter died and the emptiness stole in in its place. Something slipped inside her then and she understood all at once. They had lost their homes. Their entire world was turned upside down. And now they had killed. However justified they might feel, all could feel one hard cold fact in their hearts: they had taken life. Killing took its toll. The alcohol helped blunt the memories and make them tolerable.

Shakre sat up, turning her head to tell Elihu of her realization, and all at once the scene shifted and she was once again seeing through the wind.

She looked down on a sprawling camp, dozens of fires spread over a small valley, soldiers gathered around each one. She saw the glint of weapons being oiled and sharpened. In the center of the camp stood a cluster of figures dressed in gray robes. She knew in a heartbeat they were eyeless ones. They stood before a central figure, taller than the rest, his body lean as a blade. Achsiel. She would know him anywhere, even from far above. As she watched they went to their knees, hands outstretched to him. The air shimmered and glowed above him and he held his hands out to them in benediction, spreading the glow to them. Then she lost her hold and tumbled back to earth.

Shakre opened her eyes and realized she was lying on the ground, Elihu bent over her. Others loomed over his shoulder. "I'm okay," she said. "Help me sit up."

"What happened?" Rehobim said, pushing his way through the people who had gathered around Shakre and glaring down at her suspiciously.

"She saw through the wind," Elihu said. "It has happened several times now."

"Why was I not told of this?" he demanded. Shakre noticed that he was weaving slightly.

"It began while you were gone," Elihu replied mildly. "And you seemed busy tonight." He gestured toward the clay jug, sitting on the far side of the fire.

Rehobim crouched. Shakre could smell the liquor on his breath. "What did you see?"

"I saw an army. They were camped in a valley. With them were maybe half a dozen of the eyeless ones, including the one who led the attack on our village. Achsiel."

Rehobim hissed and stood up, wobbling for a second until he caught his balance. "I want that one," he said. "I will have his head on a stake." His words were slurred ever so slightly. "Where is this army?"

"I don't know," Shakre said.

Rehobim stared angrily into her eyes. "Yes, you do. The moon is full. You must have seen something. Think."

Shakre started to refuse him once again, but then closed her mouth. What *did* she see? She replayed the vision in her mind. There it was, just a flash before the connection was broken, outlined against the distant horizon.

"I saw the Plateau," she said. "There was a long, high ridge of broken rock, coming from the mountains. It reached almost to the edge of the Plateau. Oh," she said. "I know it now. It's a pass. I think it's called Guardians Watch." She had looked on it from above years before, when the wind drove her mindlessly across the Plateau.

"Were they on this side of the pass, or the other side?"

Shakre closed her eyes, concentrating. "On the other side."

"How close are they to it?"

"It is distant still. They have not begun the climb into the foothills."

"Then we still have time," Rehobim said, climbing to his feet. "We can catch them before they reach the pass if we leave in the morning and move fast."

"No!" Shakre cried, struggling to her feet. Rehobim turned back on her with a hard glint in his eyes. "There are too many."

Silence met her words and then eyes swung to Rehobim for his response.

"Kasai knows of us," she blurted out, hoping to say something, anything to get through to him.

"Kasai's soldiers are little more than children lost in the woods," Rehobim sneered. "They cannot hide from us. They cannot beat us, though they outnumber us ten to one. We are Takare."

"Kasai is a creature countless centuries old," Shakre insisted. "It has powers we cannot dream of. Do not take it lightly. Even the wind fears it."

"The wind is mindless and foolish," he scoffed. "Kasai is a relic. We are thunder and lightning."

"This may be a trap."

"You think I haven't considered this? You think I am a fool as well as a coward?" His face went red and his hand dropped to the hilt of the sword on his hip.

Shakre spoke quickly to defuse the situation. "You are neither. Everything you have done has proven that."

"What would you have me do?" he asked. "Shall we cower here and wait for Kasai to destroy us?"

She shook her head. "I only ask that you be careful. You have led our people on successful raids. Surely Kasai has noticed you. Eventually it will try and destroy you."

"*Our* people?" he scoffed. "*You* are not Takare." Shakre said nothing to this. There was nothing to say. "Go away. I am finished with you."

Yet Shakre held her ground and played her last card. "I would like to go with you tomorrow. I am thinking you can use an extra healer with Linir injured." Linir was a young man from Close Barren Shelter, and already an accomplished healer. He was an enthusiastic supporter of Rehobim who trained as hard as anyone and fought side by side with the rest. He favored the quarterstaff and was blindingly fast. But in the last battle he had slipped on a loose stone and took a deep wound in the abdomen. He would not go anywhere for some days.

"We still have Unin," he said brusquely.

"Yes, but Unin is only one and you plan to take all who can fight with you. It might be you will need another healer."

He stared at her suspiciously, but did not answer at first. The tani tooth around his neck glinted in the firelight and his hair was unbound, still wet from washing it in the stream. He wore only his tanned leggings, his chest and feet bare. His face was covered with several fine cuts in various stages of healing. Though they had not seen Shorn again, still he kept up the practice of marking himself after each victory and several of his lieutenants did as well. "We travel very fast and you are not young."

"You may leave me behind if I am too slow."

"You will not hinder us? You will not try and save burned ones or heal them as you did Jehu?"

Shakre lowered her head. "I will not."

"Swear on your outsider god."

"I swear by Xochitl."

"Then you may follow. We leave before the sun." He walked over to the clay jug and took a long drink, clearly done with her.

Shakre backed down then, and let Elihu guide her off to the shelter they shared. "It is a trap; I can feel it," she said to him. "Kasai marked me somehow when I saw it at the city. Now it's feeding me the information it wants us to have. It is aware of us and this is its plan to crush us."

"What are you going to do about it?"

Shakre sighed. "I don't know."

"Are you well enough to do this?"

"I have to be. What else can I do?"

FORTY-TWO

They set out early the next morning and they moved at a steady run, nearly a hundred and fifty Takare men and women. By mid-morning Shakre was beginning to worry that she would not be able to keep up. Fortunately for her, Werthin ran along beside her. When her steps began to falter he stuck out his hand.

"Give me your pack."

Shakre started to refuse, then shrugged out of the straps and handed it over. This was no time for pride. Losing the extra weight helped, but within an hour her legs were once again like lead, her breath burning in her chest. She had not seen Rehobim, who led them, in hours, and only intermittently did she glimpse the tail end of the line of warriors. Behind her she could hear Werthin, his steps steady and sure. When did she get so old? she wondered.

Werthin put his hand on her shoulder. "We will walk for a while," he said.

"But we'll be left behind."

"It is no matter. We know where they are going. We will catch up."

It felt good to walk. They had been steadily climbing for much of the day and this stretch was especially steep, with huge boulders that had fallen from the slopes of the Plateau scattered across the slope. Some had clearly fallen recently, carving a path through the trees as they went. The trees were thinner here but still huge, with moss coating their trunks and streamers of it hanging from the lower limbs. To her left the slope fell away down to a nameless valley floor far below. To her right loomed the bulk of the Plateau, much of its face unclimbable cliffs hundreds of feet high, like some primeval fortress.

The face was broken in places, where the lava had poured down. Twice that day they had been forced to climb over hardened flows that stretched far down into the valley. Those crossings had not been pleasant, the rock pocked with cracks and sharp edges. There were places where the stone had hardened and left air pockets just below the surface, the skin of rock covering them thin enough that anyone stepping on one would plunge through. Worst of all was the sensation she'd felt when she touched the rock with her bare hands. Pain like a dwindling scream lanced up into her arms when she did and she had jerked away, bizarre images dancing behind her eyes. There were things in the stone that did not die easily. It made her think of what Elihu had said about beings maybe living in the stone and water.

They reached the top of yet another slope and Shakre paused for a moment to catch her breath. Ahead the path dipped, crossed a flattened area, then began to climb again. On the far side she could just see the last of the warriors disappearing from sight. But that was not what held her attention.

Far ahead and off to her left was a mountain range, undoubtedly the Firkath Mountains. From the mountains a long ridge of broken stone led north, pointing straight at the Landsend Plateau like a finger. Up there, where that ridge met the Plateau, would be Guardians Watch. If she could get there fast enough, before Rehobim led them through it and down the other side, she might still be able to talk him into caution. The pass would be a strong location, and not a place where they could be easily snuck up on or trapped. Perhaps he would listen to her, just this once.

She forced herself to start running again. To take her mind off the pain, she turned her thoughts to the *aranti*. She wondered if it really was the same *aranti* whose eyes she saw through each time. If it was, then it stood to reason it was the one she had ridden when she searched for the survivors of the Takare. Perhaps they had become linked to each other during that time. If only she could learn to reliably call it and make it obey her. To be able to see through its eyes whenever she needed to, and make it look at what she needed to see, would be a powerful help. She remembered Kasai fixing its gaze on her the first time she saw through the wind and shuddered. Perhaps the creature was in its thrall. If that was the case, then trying to control it would be a terrible mistake. There was no way to know for sure, but she decided that it was a risk she would take if she got the chance. There were no safe or easy paths left to her or her adopted people.

She was concentrating so hard that she missed the dead limb on the ground and tripped over it. She fell to her knees heavily and in a flash Werthin was beside her, helping her up.

"Thank you," she said, grateful once more for his help. She stopped and leaned against a boulder to rub her knees. "Will you always be carrying me?" she asked lightly.

"If I am needed."

"How did you carry me all that way, when we fled the Plateau?" she asked.

"You were not yourself," he replied. "You weighed no more than a child when I first picked you up. I think part of you was still with the wind."

Shakre had only vague memories of that time. "I was. I still do not know how I found my way back."

Werthin looked away. "I spoke to you."

"You did?"

"I did not know what else to do. So I spoke to you of our home and our people. I had nothing else."

"It worked. I really think your voice was how I found my way back," she said.

"You spoke also, but the words were strange. I thought then you were speaking to the wind."

"You heard me speaking to the wind?" Shakre asked.

Werthin shrugged. "I do not know for sure."

"Can you remember any of it?"

He shook his head. "I do not think I could even make the sounds." He gestured at the sun. "The day runs to its end. If we are to make the pass by dark, we have to go."

They started off again and now Shakre had something new to think on. Was it possible she had spoken in the *aranti*'s language? She had allowed it inside her that day. Who knew what had really happened? She thought back to the day when she had used the *aranti* to heal Jehu. The wind had been absent when she started, and in her irritation and worry she had simply snapped at it without thinking and it had come to her. She tried to remember what she'd said, but nothing came to her. She'd simply reacted. Which meant the knowledge was buried within her, and the stress of the moment dropped whatever barriers she held up against it.

It was almost dark by the time they reached the pass. It was only a few hundred paces wide, with a ruined tower on the south end and the crumbled remains of a stone wall stretching across it. The north side of the pass was littered with huge blocks of black stone that had fallen from the Plateau long ago. Shakre stared at them, wondering if the tower on the south side had a twin on the north, buried now under rubble. Were the people who manned it able to escape in time?

"So you are still with us," Rehobim said as they approached. "I thought you had given up and turned back."

"Will you wait here for Kasai's men?" Shakre asked, ignoring his comment. "It is a strong position." The land on the far side of the pass sloped steeply down a rock-strewn slope, then plunged into thick trees.

"You know nothing of war," he said dismissively. "We would not hold it for long. Our only hope is to catch them sleeping and kill so many they do not threaten us again." He did not seem as angry as he usually did, so that his barbs were flung more out of habit than malice. "See there," he said, pointing. Far down in the valley below dozens of campfires burned, their smoke snaking lazily skyward. "We can be there in only a few hours and catch them while they sleep. We are lightning and thunder. We arrive like the storm and we leave as fast."

Shakre felt doom on her heart and wanted to argue with him further but she knew it would do no good. It was as Elihu said. She would have to follow along and hope there would be a moment when she would have an opportunity to divert them before they went over the cliff.

They left the pass once the darkness was complete and Shakre marveled at how quietly the Takare could move. They made no more sound than shadows as they slipped between the trees and the rocks. Up ahead the flicker of the enemy's campfires drew steadily closer. She walked at the very rear, close enough to avoid losing the Takare forces, but far enough back that she could not give them away. She had refused Werthin's offer to stay with her and sent him on ahead. He had done enough for her already and she did not want Rehobim to turn against him.

Scouts sent out by Rehobim when they first reached the pass had returned, confirming that the camp held at least a thousand of the burned ones. They had set up their camp in a large, flat meadow beside a stream. Their sentries were careless and noisy. They could approach without being noticed, slip in and kill the enemy before they could react. If they made a mistake, they could melt into the forest and disappear. It was perfect. The only unusual thing, the scouts reported, was that the meadow Kasai's forces were camped in was dotted with tall, stone columns that looked to be manmade, probably some structure built during the Empire that had crumbled away, leaving only columns as tall as trees.

Now they were nearly to the enemy camp. Through the trees Shakre could glimpse campfires that had burned down, blanketed shapes lying around them, and some rough tents here and there. It was not a very orderly camp. Shakre paused and quested ahead with her inner senses, as she had done a number of times already. Had it been a normal army she would have been able to learn quite a bit this way: a good idea of their numbers, whether they were asleep or awake, a sense of the overall mood of the camp. But the Song flowing from the camp was raw and confused, as it always was from those who bore Kasai's mark. Muddying it further was the fact that at least a handful of blinded ones accompanied them. They were completely opaque to her inner senses, like dark spots at the edge of vision. She could neither determine their location nor their number. Everything looked quiet, but her gut told her that something was terribly amiss. Unfortunately, she couldn't figure out what it was.

Shakre came upon a pile of huge stones that were too regular to be natural, probably part of whatever structure had yielded the columns in the meadow. She climbed up onto the pile and from there she could see much of the meadow and the camp. The stone columns encircled most of the meadow and one, taller than the rest, stood in the center. They showed white in the faint light and seemed to be flat on top. Something about them made her uneasy, though she was not sure why and there was no time to ponder it now, for the Takare had reached the edge of the camp and were spread out around it, waiting. She could not see them, but she could sense them, vital flows of clean Song amidst the muddiness that spread outward from the camp.

Then the Takare charged into the camp, their racing forms visible in the light of the flickering campfires. Blades stabbed into sleeping forms and screams rang out. The Takare were swift and implacable. The enemy had no chance.

But something was wrong. Shakre crouched on the stones, trying to figure it out. All at once she understood and a moment later the warriors did too.

The screams were too few. A warrior flipped back the edge of a blanket with his sword. Underneath was piled dirt. The Takare slowed their onslaught, looking around in alarm, weapons raised to meet the enemy they could not see.

And then the trap sprang shut.

On each of the columns around the perimeter of the camp a cloaked figure rose. Shakre knew in an instant what they were.

Blinded ones.

They raised their hands and coronas of gray flame sprang from them. As one they slammed their fists together.

Sheets of gray flame shot from one column to the next, wrapping around the meadow in an instant, cutting off escape. Several Takare were in the path of the flames as they spread and they screamed horribly as the flames engulfed them from head to toe.

Then new flames shot out from each column, lancing toward the center column on which stood a waiting figure, a sharp blade of a man.

Achsiel.

The gray flames struck him and instantly doubled, then doubled again, the flames coalescing into a writhing, burning web that began to settle earthward.

With a wild cry, Rehobim flung his spear at Achsiel, but it caught on fire as it passed through the burning web and turned to ash before reaching its target. Arrows flew at the other blinded ones but they were just as useless.

One Takare raced to the central column, his knife clenched in his teeth, and started to climb. He hit the flaming web and lit on fire. Somehow, with a superhuman effort, he fought his way through the flame and actually made it to the top of the column. But he was a burned husk of a man and as he raised his knife weakly Achsiel merely kicked him in the face and he tumbled backward and down.

A few Takare charged the wall of flames around the edge of the camp, but those that managed to make it through fell dead before they'd taken a half dozen steps and lay there burning. The rest could only watch helplessly as the flaming web settled down onto them. In less than a minute they would all be dead.

Shakre watched in horror. What the destruction of Tu Sinar and Landsend Plateau had failed to accomplish was happening here, right now. It was the end of the Takare as a people.

And then she snapped.

Her hands curled into fists at her sides and she flung her head back, a bizarre, unearthly cry breaking from her.

But this was no ordinary cry. It was the sound of a storm breaking, of winds that could level forests. It was the sound of the hurricane.

More than that, though it was a summons, a *demand*, delivered in a language never meant for human lips.

She did not consciously choose the words. They came from deep inside her, left over there from her time lost in the wind. They came pouring out of her, driven by her need and her fear.

And the *aranti* answered.

In a heartbeat it howled around her, its cry matching her own. With a strength born of despair and fear Shakre took hold of the *aranti* with an iron grip.

Obey me, she shouted at it in its own language.

Then she flung it at Achsiel.

The *aranti* shrieked across the meadow and struck Achsiel with gale force. He was thrown from the top of the column. With a cry he plunged into the fiery web.

There was a concussion as energy fed back on itself and exploded. The shockwave knocked the blinded ones off their columns and tossed the Takare like leaves. The flames went out.

Silence descended over the meadow, broken only by the moans of the dying. Slowly the Takare got to their feet. The first to act was Pinlir. He walked to the nearest blinded one who was still moving and methodically chopped off his head. Then he proceeded to make his way to the others who were still living and do the same.

By then Shakre had climbed down off the tumble of stones and made her way into the clearing. She felt dizzy and lightheaded. Worst of all, her vision kept switching between her own eyes and the *aranti*'s perception. She had to keep looking down at her own feet to see if she was still walking on the ground.

"What happened?" Jakal asked.

"He just fell," someone answered. "The one on the middle column fell and then the whole thing exploded."

There were other voices raised then, a confusion of theories and explanations. Shakre said nothing, but she felt Werthin's gaze on her, though she did not look at him. Her relief was overwhelming. Her people were still alive. Only moments ago she had been sure they would all die. Shakily, she sat down.

"It was the wind!" cried someone else, his voice rising above the din. "I saw the trees shake!"

For many of them, newcomers who had barely heard of the Windrider, that meant nothing and they continued talking. But those from Bent Tree Shelter knew and they turned to look at Shakre, who avoided their eyes.

"It's time to go," Werthin said, bending over and placing his hand on Shakre's shoulder. She did not resist while he helped her up. "There may be more of them nearby."

He was speaking to Shakre, but others heard. Some went to their fallen comrades, who were burned beyond recognition, and they were wrapped in blankets and picked up. Others gathered what weapons they could find. Awareness of where they were had returned and there was no more talking.

As Werthin helped her out of the clearing, Shakre looked up and saw Rehobim. He was standing by himself, his head down, his arms hanging at his sides. He had not spoken or moved since the attack ended. Once again his rashness had nearly doomed his people. What would become of him now? she wondered.

They slept in the pass that night. When Shakre awoke the next morning the camp was stirring, preparing to move out. Her sleep had been deep and she had heard nothing during the night, barely remembered even walking back up the ridge. But clearly the Takare had been talking, those who knew her sharing information with the newcomers. She knew it was so by the way they treated her. A day before she had been someone to be tolerated, perhaps even overlooked. A skilled healer, but an outsider and therefore not quite trustworthy. Now they looked on her with awe that bordered on fear, but only when she was not looking. When she turned to face them, they turned away or looked down. They were not obvious about it, but they moved out of her way and were careful to make sure she did not touch them.

The exception was Werthin. He stayed by her elbow, anticipating her needs. Before she could pick up her pack he darted in and snatched it up. She shrugged and did not argue with him. The fact was that she still did not feel like herself. On the first downhill she tripped twice and nearly fell down. Her legs seemed to belong to someone else.

Rehobim didn't speak at all on the walk back to the main camp. When Jakal approached him and tried to speak he snarled at him and the young man didn't try again.

Youlin was ready for them when they walked into the meadow the next day. She was standing with her arms crossed, her hood thrown back to reveal the fire in her eyes. On the ground around her feet were the broken shards of the clay jugs that had once held liquor.

FORTY-THREE

"We should make it to the Haven tomorrow," Netra said one evening after they'd stopped and made camp. "You'll finally get to meet the people I've been talking about so much."

Shorn looked at her, then down at himself.

Netra nodded. "You're wondering how they will react to you. I've been wondering the same thing. When we get close, it will probably be best if you let me go on ahead and prepare them. I imagine they're a little nervous with everything that's going on and seeing you at the front door might send them stampeding out the back." She grinned at the mental image this produced. "Just give me a few minutes with them and then I'll come outside and call you."

Shorn pondered this for a while. "And then?"

"I'm not sure what you mean."

"You will go to Qarath? Where your order prepares to fight?"

"I think so. I mean, that's what I think we should do. I can't make them go there, of course, and Brelisha can be pretty stubborn."

"And if they do not go? You will stay with them? Or go to Qarath?"

"Well, naturally I'll..." She frowned. "I don't know. Honestly." She sighed. "Do you have to do this? I just want to be excited about seeing them again. I don't want to figure out what's next."

"But you will not hide from this fight?"

She shook her head. "I can't see myself doing that. I don't think I *could* do that. No, I think if they don't want to go to Qarath, then you and I will go on alone. I mean, if you want to come with me. If you haven't changed your mind."

The look he gave her told her exactly how unlikely that was. Netra was relieved. She'd had a tiny fear in the back of her mind that he would leave her once they reached the Haven, and truth be told, she wasn't ready for it. She'd grown accustomed to having him there, as solid and steady as a mountain. Somehow, with him around, the world just didn't seem so big and scary.

She leaned across their tiny fire and patted his arm. "I'm glad," she said softly. "I don't want to do this without your help."

He looked at her hand—small on his thick arm—then back at her. She pulled her hand back. Once again her heart went out to him, wishing there was something she could do or say to ease the massive burden he carried.

"You know, since you showed up, I don't feel nearly as afraid. I don't feel as hopeless either. I still don't have any idea what to do, but I feel like if we just keep moving forward, sooner or later we'll know. What do you think?"

Shorn looked at the stars overhead, then nodded, the movement barely visible in the firelight.

Netra didn't spend much time stopping or resting that last day as the two approached the Haven. In her mind she pictured the reunion with her family over and over. She apologized to them all, even Brelisha. She hugged them. She cried with them. She sat up late with Cara, sharing everything that happened. She would be back with her family and everything would work out somehow. She would never turn her back on them again.

It was mid-afternoon when the first faint sense of unease intruded on her happy fantasies. It was there and gone quickly, like catching a whiff of a dead animal rotting in the distance. She paused, a frown on her face. Then it was gone and she shrugged. The taint was here, too. That's all it was. At least it wasn't as bad as it was to the north.

However, she sensed the wrongness several more times during the next couple hours as she and Shorn made their way around the edge of the Firkath Mountains and approached the Haven. Something was definitely wrong. Something had passed through here.

It was nearly sunset and Netra was practically running when she topped the last high ridge separating her from her home. From here she could see the stone buildings of her home nestled at the edge of the broad valley below. What she saw stopped her cold, a small cry escaping her.

"No!"

Her home was a heap of rubble. It looked like a giant fist had come out of the sky and smashed it flat.

She took off running.

Gasping, tears running down her face, Netra stood before the wreckage of her life. The massive stones that had formed her home lay in a shattered tangle. Not a single wall still stood. Even the trees that surrounded the place had been torn down, their trunks snapped.

Tharn. Nothing else could have done this. The Guardian had followed her back to the Haven after all. There was the sound of heavy footsteps and Shorn came up beside her, but when he touched her shoulder she moaned and pulled away, folding in on herself. She would not allow herself to be comforted. *She* had led the monster here. *She* had left her family alone to face it. Her family was dead and it was all her fault.

She saw something then, in the midst of the ruins, something that was not stone. On unsteady legs she climbed up onto the ruins, fearing what she would see, but knowing she *had* to see.

It was a hand, sticking out between two broken stones. Most of the flesh was gone, picked off by the carrion eaters.

With a cry, she fell to her knees. She couldn't breathe. The world tilted crazily around her.

Then she started clawing at the stones in a frenzy, as if whoever was buried under there might still be alive. She moved one stone, rolling it off to the side. The next one was too large for her. Her fingers slipped and part of her fingernail tore away. She welcomed the pain—it was only what she deserved—and shifted her grip, trying to get leverage.

Then Shorn was there. With his help the stone moved easily. Wordlessly, the two worked side by side and the pile of rubble slowly shifted. Some of the stones were too big even for Shorn to move with his inhuman strength. He had to pull timbers out of the wreckage and use them as levers to shift those stones.

There were two bodies underneath. Netra stood trembling in the darkness looking down on them. They had been rotting for some time, but Netra knew instantly who they were.

Siena and Brelisha.

"Why didn't you run?" Netra asked. The cold stones had no answer. The night sky didn't care. The women who had raised Netra lay broken and staring at nothing. The sky pressed down on her everywhere and she could not breathe; she was choking on guilt and sorrow. She had done this. She'd left them to this fate.

Shorn acted first. The two women lay sprawled on the old rug that had long covered the floor of Sienna's quarters. Drawing a blade, Shorn cut the rug in half, then swiftly rolled each body into a square of rug. More gently than Netra would have thought possible, he picked them up one at a time and carried them out of the rubble. Nearby were the remains of what had once been the Haven's garden, the plants shriveled and dead now. An ancient spade was stuck in the ground at the end of one of the rows and Shorn took this and began to dig.

Netra watched numbly, knowing she should help but somehow unable to do so. These women had been like two sides of the same mother to her. She had fought them, laughed with them, cried with them. And now she would never be able to speak to either again. She would never be able to tell them how sorry she was.

The tears were pouring down her face when Shorn finished the graves. Silently he laid the two bodies into the hole, then scrambled out. With the spade in his hand, he stood by the pile of dirt from the hole and looked expectantly at Netra.

No words would come. Netra slumped to her knees and her tears fell into the hole. Shorn began to fill the grave.

Netra rose early in the morning and stared at the gray sky. What had happened here? Where were the rest of her sisters? Were they safe? And over and over, pushing through the questions, was the ugly knowledge that this was her fault, that she had drawn Tharn here and then abandoned her family to deal with the Guardian.

Shorn rose a short time later and came to stand beside her. For a long time, as the sun rose, he said nothing. Then he said, "What will you do now?"

She turned on him. The tears were gone for now, and something else was settling in their place. "This was my fault," she said brokenly. "I should have been here."

"You could have saved them from what did this?" he asked. His face was impassive, his words flat, but still they stung.

"No. I couldn't have. But that doesn't change anything. I *should have been here*."

"So that you could have died with them?" Now his words were sharper. "Is this what they would have wanted?"

She withered under his words and hung her head. "You don't understand."

"I understand that you are still alive. You can still do something. So I ask: What will you do now?"

She shook her head. "I don't know."

"The other women did not die here."

Netra shook her head. "I think they were gone when Tharn arrived."

"Where did they go?"

She shrugged. "I don't know. Probably Qarath."

"Then that is where we go."

Netra shook her head again. "I don't know. I can't...it's hopeless."

"This was not your fault. You could not have stopped this." His words were implacable. "But there is much you can do now. If you give up now, then you have failed your family."

Netra rocked under the impact of his words. She wanted to lie down and cry. She wanted to scream and beat on the ground until her hands bled. But she could not deny the truth of what he said. Her shoulders sagged. "You are right."

"Use their deaths to make you stronger," he said. "Use them to fight back."

Netra stared at him for a long time, then she nodded. "Okay. Let's go."

But before gathering her things together she went to the new graves and knelt beside them. "I'm sorry," she said softly. "I'm sorry I didn't listen to you. I'm sorry I left. I'm sorry I wasn't here."

A beetle trundled across the fresh dirt. Ants wandered here and there looking for food. A woodpecker landed in a nearby tree and squawked at her, annoyed by her presence. Nothing had changed. Everything had changed.

Netra stood slowly, feeling brittle, as if one more shock would shatter her. Slowly she paced around the ruined Haven, stopping when she came to the place where the room she'd shared with Cara had stood. For a few minutes she dug through the broken stones and bits of wood, looking for something she could take away. The only thing she found was a simple clay bowl that Cara had made a few years before and given her for her birthday, but it was smashed into tiny pieces. She let the pieces trickle through her fingers and then turned away.

"I'm ready to go now," she told Shorn, hefting her pack. She felt the graves at her back, the shattered pieces of her life before. She'd wanted to be free, but she'd never expected it to happen like this.

She told herself that she would be strong, that she would not look back, but of course she did, over and over until her childhood disappeared forever behind her.

FORTY-FOUR

The army was three days past Karthije. It was night time and Rome was wandering through the camp. It was something he'd been doing most nights since they left Qarath, talking to the men, sharing drinks from the flask of rum he carried, assessing their mood. There were only a few fires. The soldiers were worn out from the fast pace and the long hours and most turned in as soon as they ate. The fact that the land was becoming hillier and steeper was taking its toll on them as well. However, there were still a few up, staring into the fires, talking quietly. They were subdued, and Rome didn't blame them. So much had gone on in the past months that they didn't know what to expect. Every one of them had seen bizarre things, things that couldn't be fought with a blade. Now they were marching hard and fast to face an army whose capabilities they couldn't really know or prepare for. If they lost, the survivors would be a long way from home, and that home would have precious little protection. It was enough to make anyone somber.

Rome stopped at a small fire with only one man sitting by it. The man looked up as he approached and gave him a nod, then went back to staring at the fire. Rome handed him the rum and sat down on the ground beside him.

The man drank and wiped his mouth with the back of his hand, but did not hand the flask back. "You know I been down many a road with you, Macht," he said, taking another long drink off the rum. He sighed appreciatively and handed the rum back reluctantly. Long ago he'd lost an eye to a sword, and when the stitcher sewed the socket shut he'd pulled too much down from the top. The result was that what was left of his eyebrow was pulled down on the outside, giving his face a perpetually angry look. But the truth was that Felint was a gentle man outside of battle. "I'd march along with you and hold the nail while you tack Gorim's tail to the ground, I would."

"I know," Rome agreed. He'd sat around many a fire with Felint. The man had seemed old even when Rome was just starting out. He kept his hair shaved almost to the scalp, and it was the same iron gray it had always been. Maybe the man didn't age at all.

"But this one's got me cold inside, it has."

Rome sighed. He felt the same way. He just wasn't allowed to say it.

"I hear stories of crazy monsters what can tear a man's limbs off and use 'em for toothpicks. I hear their general burns people with a look." The old veteran shrugged and reached for the flask. Rome handed it to him again. He drank, then gave it back. "But I don't mind that too much, mostly. Being a soldier's about marching in the dark and fighting in a blindfold. It's just the way it is." He rubbed the missing eye. "But it ain't the same this time, is it?"

Rome said nothing, just waited.

Felint looked about him to see there was no one nearby before speaking again. "Usually, the cost of losing ain't too bad. Git yourself killed, okay, but that's the regular price of admission. Git your city sacked and burned. There's rape and murder, all kinds of unpleasantness, especially the burning part. Takes a while to rebuild." He leaned back and his back cracked. "But that's the point. You can rebuild and life goes on." He coughed and gave a rough laugh. "Didn't know I was such a thinker, did you, Rome?"

Rome shook his head.

"Won't be no rebuilding this time will there? If we lose?"

Rome hesitated, torn between what he wanted to say and what it was his duty to say.

Felint waved off his words before he said them. "Don't need to answer. It's what the Tenders say, every day in the city. It's always, 'Melekath's gonna kill everything livin'. Melekath's gonna break the Circle of Life.' Whatever that damn thing is. Is it true?"

Rome looked at the flask in his hand. He looked up at the stars, pressing close overhead. Then he stared into Felint's one good eye. "I believe it is," he said softly.

"Then we better damn well fight!" Felint said with fierce intensity, clapping his macht on the shoulder. "An' we better damn well win!"

For a moment Rome just stared at him, then he nodded. "If it can be done, we'll do it."

"We're following the Black Wolf," Felint said. "Course we'll win!"

"Of course," Rome agreed, standing. "Get some sleep, Felint."

"Sure. Maybe later. Don't need sleep as much as I used to. Ain't got much time left. Don't want to waste it sleeping."

After he walked away, Rome wandered out toward the picket lines on the north side of camp, planning to talk to the sentries before turning in. "It's Rome," he called out as he got close to where he guessed the sentry line must be. He heard a call back and walked in the direction of the voice. "All quiet?" he asked, when a shape loomed out of the dark.

"Nothing but bats and bugmice."

"Any sign of our scouts?" Rome wanted no unnecessary surprises and he wanted to do whatever he could to make sure Kasai didn't know he was coming, though, since he didn't know what Kasai was capable of, that might be hopeless. Kasai might be watching the army right this moment. Still, he had to try, so two days ago he had put the word out amongst the Karthijinian troops that he wanted the most experienced trackers and hunters in their squads sent to him. He'd ended up with ten weathered men in rawhide and heavy beards. While staring at them, thinking they all looked somewhat alike, one of the Karthijinian sergeants approached him nervously.

"What is it, sergeant?"

"Macht...uh, these are the Telinar brothers."

"That's why they look alike."

The man nodded uncomfortably. He was clearly sweating, though it was cool. He looked like the kind of man who sweated a lot.

"Are they my scouts?"

The man nodded again.

"I don't think they were in my army this morning. Where'd you find them?"

"They're not in the army. They live out in the Fells, Sire," the man explained, keeping his eyes fixed firmly on Rome's shoulder. He said it as though Rome should know what that meant.

"I don't know what that is," Rome said.

"It's west and north of here. Next to the Plateau. Hard country. Lions, bears and...things you don't normally see. They know this country. None know it better. I figured they'd be your men."

Rome looked them over. They looked hard enough.

"Only one problem," the man said quietly.

"What is it? Speak up, man. I'm not going to bite you."

"They don't think much of authority." He leaned closer and lowered his voice. "I had to offer them liquor to even come talk to you. It doesn't matter what kind," he added hastily. "So long as it's strong."

Rome gave the men another look. "Are they as good as you say?"

The man's head bobbed. "Certain they are. Certain. None better."

"Then they're who I want," Rome said. He turned to the brothers.

"I'm not a man who likes surprises," he said. "That's what I need you for."

If the men were impressed to have the famous Wulf Rome addressing them personally, they didn't show it. Most of them were squatting or sitting on the ground cross-legged. If there was any real group response at all, it was a collective shrug. One of the brothers looked like he'd fallen asleep.

"I don't want the enemy to know we're here until it's too late. I want you to scout ahead. If you find anyone who looks like he's in Kasai's army—"

"You mean those with a burn on their foreheads?" one asked. He was a tall, young man with his hair tied into two braids and some teeth strung on a necklace.

"Yes. And—"

"So we can cut their throats?" Seemingly from nowhere the young man had produced a knife as long as his forearm and he was stroking the sharp edge.

"Yes. The important thing is that—"

"I've a mind to cut some throats," one of the other brothers said. He was scarred from some childhood illness, with a beard that stretched almost to his waist. He was the one Rome had thought was asleep.

"Cut all the throats you want," Rome said, starting to get annoyed. "The important thing is that—"

"The nervous guy said we'd get liquor," another brother chimed in. Like the rest, he was tall and lean, but his beard was gray.

Rome took a deep breath, trying not to lose his temper. "You'll get liquor."

"Soon, though," another brother said. "The dust is bad today."

"Shut up while I'm talking to you!" Rome finally yelled.

"Okay. Jes' trying to help," the first brother said. He barely looked up. Most of his attention seemed focused on the knife.

"Kill any scouts you find. If there's too many of them, make your way back to the army without being seen and report to me. Above all, don't let them see you."

As one, they managed to look offended that such a thing could even be possible. There were mutters and shaking heads.

"We don't get seen," said the brother with the gray beard. "Less'n we want to."

"Do you want horses?" Rome asked. He was determined to stay cool, whatever it took.

"Naw," said the scarred one. "Already ate yesterday."

"No," Rome said. "For riding. So you can go faster."

"Stranger," said another brother who was picking at his fingernails with a knife, "horses don't go faster where we go. Horses just taste good."

Rome took another deep breath. "Okay, don't take a horse, then. Go on foot. The important thing is—"

"Yeah, kill the ones with the burns, don't let them see us, go fast. We got it," another brother said laconically. "If that liquor don't show up soon I got somewhere else to be."

There were nods and sounds of assent from the others.

"You'll get your liquor," Rome said wearily.

"Soon, right?"

"Yes, soon."

Since then Rome had seen only one of the brothers, and the man refused to tell him anything until he got a flask. The man's report was barely two words long and basically conveyed that the way ahead was still clear. Rome had called out the Karthijinian sergeant who recommended the brothers, but the man, though clearly frightened, stubbornly insisted that the brothers were the best men for the job.

Rome stared into the darkness for a while, wondering where the brothers were right then, then headed back to the small fire that T'sim had built for him. As he approached, he saw that someone was sitting by the fire. It was one of the brothers, the one with the gray beard.

"Your report," Rome said, handing him the nearly-empty flask.

The man shook the flask and frowned. He downed the liquor quickly, but said nothing.

"What did you see?" Rome pressed.

The man looked up at him—Rome thought he might be the one named Tem—and held up his hand as if indicating he should stop talking. Rome was speechless. He found himself wondering if maybe

311

this brother was mute and tried to recall if he'd heard him speak when he'd met them the first time. What good would a mute scout be? Could his brothers understand him?

Just then another brother materialized out of the darkness. It was the one who looked the youngest, with the twin braids. He sat down without a word and pointed at the flask. The gray-haired one—Rome was pretty sure it was Tem and this one was Rem—shook his head and flipped him the empty flask. As if on cue, both brothers gave Rome a wounded look. But now Rome was starting to feel stubborn. He wasn't producing any liquor until these guys talked. Who was in charge here, anyway?

"Soldiers, I need your report," he said formally. He sounded foolish even to himself. "Tell me what you saw."

The brothers exchanged looks and hidden smiles passed between them. Rome could feel his face getting hotter. Then all at once the young one spoke.

"Tem don't like talking without the others here." Tem gave him a meaningful look. "And he ain't happy about the liquor problem."

"Forget about the liquor," Rome said. They both looked upset by that and sat up in consternation. "Tell me what you learned. We have no idea how long it'll be before the other brothers get here and I can't wait forever."

"Oh, they'll be here soon enough," the braided one said. "Then you'll hear."

"You don't—" Rome started, then broke off as another brother materialized out of the darkness. He was surprised. He'd heard nothing. Clearly the sentries hadn't heard anything. Not even the dogs that were trailing the army and raised a fuss at everything had heard anything. These men were good.

In quick succession three more appeared out of the darkness and arranged themselves around the fire. There were many exchanged looks and subtle hand gestures that Rome could not interpret. Then the young one said casually, while fingering the edge of his long knife, "They're back. Could be trouble."

The others leaned forward at this news and more hand gestures flew.

"Who's back?" Rome demanded.

The scarred brother looked up as if just noticing Rome was there for the first time and said, "Warn't we promised liquor? Don't tell me Tem drank it all."

Rome started to argue with him, then thought better of it. He didn't want to be here all night and threatening them didn't seem like it would do any good. "Okay," Rome said. "T'sim, will you..." He trailed off. T'sim was already there, a flask in each hand. He handed them out to the brothers who settled themselves more comfortably, looking for all the world as if they were there for the long haul.

"Now will you tell me?" Rome asked through gritted teeth. He was thinking he could kick the closest one before the man could move.

"I found some of them, the enemy, what with the burns on 'em," the young braided one replied. "Ten of them."

Rome dropped down into a squat. "Did they see you?"

The young man gave Rome a flat look that clearly said what he thought of being asked such a dim question. "If I don't want to be seen, I ain't seen. That's all." He took a long drink from a flask and passed it on. "They weren't seeing any too good anyway. Dead, every one of them."

"Dead? Who killed them?"

"Getting to that part," was the laconic reply. The young man stretched out by the fire with a sigh, leaning on one elbow and staring into the flames. "They were ambushed, and ambushed clean. None of them burned ones got away. None of them drew blood. But they spilled plenty."

"They were ambushed?" Rome was puzzled by that. Who else was out here, especially in a large enough group to kill ten men? "Did you track them?"

The brothers exchanged looks and a few heads were shaken. Their looks wondered: Was this man who led them a stone-faced simpleton? "Naturally. That's what I do, isn't it?" He wiped the knife on his leggings and sheathed it. "I tracked them back towards the Landsend Plateau. There was five of them. They moved fast and I couldn't catch up." More looks were exchanged, serious ones this time. The brothers already knew what Rome was about to find out.

"Well, who were they?"

The young man shrugged. "Only ones they could be, I reckon." A few of the brothers shook their heads. "There was a broken arrow at the ambush, of a design we don't normally see around here. And they headed north toward the Plateau, which being ruined and all prob'ly ain't such a good home no more. From what I seen, I'd say the Takare have returned."

"The Takare? But they've…" Rome trailed off. Of course they'd reappeared, now that the Landsend Plateau was devastated. There was still smoke rising from it and the occasional rumble.

The young man shrugged. "Now they come back." He shook his head and his braids flew. "Prob'ly good I didn't catch 'em. They could give me some trouble."

There were a few murmurs from his brothers, but they were murmurs of sympathy, not disbelief. Whatever else these brothers had, lack of confidence wasn't part of it. Rome pondered this latest turn of events. What did it mean, having the Takare back in the picture? He could only assume they would be allies; after all, Kasai had destroyed their home and driven them back to the world they'd left behind after Wreckers Gate. What he needed was to talk to them.

"I want one of you to contact the Takare. Tell them I want to meet, to talk about allying against Kasai."

The brothers chuckled over these words, though it was strange because they made almost no noise. When they had subsided, the gray-bearded one, Tem, said, "You don't have enough liquor for that, Macht."

"Why's that? All I want you to do is talk to them. Are you afraid you can't find them?"

"Oh, we can find 'em all right," Tem asserted. "We can find the lost gods if you give us time. But we ain't fools."

"They're the *Takare*," the tall, skinny brother said. "They find *you*. Not the other way up."

"And you know this how? From ancient legends?"

"Them legends came from somewhere," tall and skinny said. "They always do." The others nodded at his words.

"You're just gonna have ta wait for them to come to you," Tem said, slapping the hand of one of the brothers who was reaching for the flask he was holding. "Ain't two heads on this bear." More nodding greeted his words.

Rome stared at them, knowing there was nothing he could say to change their minds. They were probably right, anyway. He was going to have to wait on the Takare and hope they saw things as he did.

"I want you men back out there tomorrow," he said. "I still don't want Kasai's men to find us."

"We'll be back out, don't fear," the young, braided man said. "But now we're getting paid for honey without any bees, ain't we, brothers?"

"What is that supposed to mean?"

"It means the Takare are back," another brother said. He was missing part of his ear and this was the first time he'd spoken. "They're killing the marked ones. Won't be none left for us to bother with."

"I hope you're right," Rome said.

"Sem's always right," the scarred one said. "That's why he don't talk much."

Rome left while they were still nodding at each other, thinking how glad he was that not all of his soldiers were like those brothers. What he needed now was Quyloc's clear mind on this. He realized that he didn't really know where Quyloc was. In fact, he didn't think he'd seen Quyloc all day. Bad time for his old friend to disappear. A thought struck him. Maybe T'sim could find Quyloc. He took a breath to bellow T'sim's name and there was a soft touch on his elbow.

"Quyloc is up there, on top of that hill," T'sim said, pointing at a hill about a hundred yards away.

Rome stared at the little man. "You are a wonder, you know that, T'sim?"

The little man bowed. "It is what I strive for, Macht."

"I don't know who, or what, you are, or why you're here, but you are useful." T'sim bowed again. "Don't think I don't know about the wigs, though," Rome added. T'sim hung his head. "If the supply wagons ever catch up to us I promise you I will burn those things." The supply wagons were back there, somewhere, making what time they could. They probably wouldn't catch up in time to do any good, but they were coming.

"You may wish to look your best for the victory feast, Macht," T'sim said.

"You think there will be one?"

"It's all in the wind," T'sim replied.

"And that means what, exactly?"

"Whatever you like, Macht."

"Now you're not being so helpful, T'sim."

"It is a difficult job," T'sim agreed.

Rome looked at the hilltop. There was no fire, no sign of movement up there. And he was tired. Time enough to talk to Quyloc tomorrow. Right now he needed sleep. He made his way over to where he'd dropped his gear. When he got there he saw that T'sim had laid out his blanket and arranged his saddle and tack neatly nearby. Rome unbuckled his belt and laid it on the ground, then reached for the black axe hanging on his back. He left his gear unguarded. Partly he trusted the men he led, but mostly he wanted his men as fresh as they could be. He didn't want a soldier missing sleep to stand watch over his gear. None of it was that important. The axe, however, was a different matter. He carried it with him at all times. He wasn't letting anything happen to it.

With a sigh, he lay down, noticing that T'sim had put his blanket on a soft pile of leaves and grasses. The little guy—or whatever he was—wasn't so bad to have along after all.

X X X

Quyloc stood on the hilltop and looked down over the sleeping camp. He saw a figure walking the camp, stopping at fires as he passed and knew it to be Rome. Something about the way he walked and carried himself.

There was no putting it off any longer. He needed to go back to the *Pente Akka* again. He'd already gone three times since leaving Qarath, but so far he'd had no luck even finding the hunter. It was like the creature was avoiding him for some reason. He didn't know whether to be relieved or worried. But he did know he needed to keep trying.

He took the leather cover off the *rendspear*. Since T'sim's tap on the forehead that pushed him into the state of heightened awareness where he could *see* LifeSong, every time he touched the spear he went there. It was, frankly, a little tiring. Fortunately, he'd discovered that if he wrapped the spear in leather, it didn't happen. He carried it that way most of the time now.

He lay down on the ground and clasped the spear to his chest. He visualized the Veil and when he opened his eyes a moment later he was standing in the borderland.

The last time he'd seen a black mesa in the distance, beyond the edge of the jungle. It seemed to him a likely place to find the hunter. Tonight he'd start there.

He visualized the mesa, focusing on the base of it. When he passed through the Veil he found himself standing at its base. Its sides were hundreds of feet high and very steep. Black stones of all sizes littered the slopes. The scree looked loose. Climbing it would be difficult and dangerous.

Fortunately, he didn't have to actually climb it. He picked a spot at the top and concentrated on it until he could picture it clearly in his mind. Then he passed through the Veil, pictured the spot, and passed back through the Veil, arriving at the spot he'd seen.

The hunter was waiting for him.

It was half again as tall as he was. Shadows moved across it like living things. It was shaped like a man, with massive, heavily muscled shoulders, long arms and fingers that ended in claws like knives. Its head was sleek and tapered, smaller than the neck, with protrusions that might have been ears jutting out to either side. There were no facial features other than its red eyes.

With a cry that was both horror and exhilaration, Quyloc charged the hunter, the spear whirling in his hands. He feinted at its chest, then reversed the weapon and slashed at its leg.

It swept its arm downward to block his attack. As it did so, a blade appeared, as long as a short sword. The spear clanged off harmlessly.

But Quyloc was still moving, spinning to the right, the spear dancing over his head. He struck three times in a heartbeat, slashing, stabbing. The weapon was a part of him, controlled by his desperation and ferocity. He had never been faster, deadlier.

Yet, as fast as he was, the hunter slapped all his attacks aside with ease. No matter what Quyloc tried, each time it thwarted him, as if he was no more than a child with a stick. He attacked again and again, using every trick he knew, but none of it worked.

Finally, he had nothing left and stood with the spear hanging loose in his hand, breathing hard.

A blade emerged from the hunter's other hand, this one as long as a sword. Then it went on the attack.

It feinted left, then cut at his legs from the right. Quyloc parried the blow, just barely, but in doing so he left himself open to an attack from its other blade, which came whistling down at his head. There was no time to do anything besides get the butt of the spear up to intercept the blow and inwardly he winced, knowing there was no way the shaft could possibly stand up to such blow. The hunter's blade was going to shear through it. Already it seemed he could feel the hunter's blade tearing into his flesh, crunching through muscle and bone.

But the shaft held. The hunter's blade clanged away harmlessly and the hunter seemed almost as surprised as Quyloc.

It recovered quickly and began to rain attacks on Quyloc. Sword and spear clanged together time and again, the hunter's attacks so fast that Quyloc could not follow them. Yet somehow, each time he seemed to be able to anticipate them, or the spear did, twitching in the eye blink before each attack was launched. He twisted and fought, the spear alive in his hands as he spun and ducked, catching attack after attack on the spear. There was no thought of counter attacking. This was purely survival and he could not have explained how he survived as long as he did.

The hunter flowed around him like a shadow, attacking from one side, then the other. Their battle raged on and time lost all meaning. Quyloc might have been fighting the thing his entire life. No matter how he twisted or how hard he tried, it was always there, ceaseless, remorseless. Inevitably its attacks began to slip by his defenses and he felt lines of pain appear on his body, each wound burning like fire. He cried out each time, but he could not slow, could not do anything but twist and slash and dance as if he danced for death itself.

At last the thing stepped back. It walked a slow, wide circle around Quyloc, while he turned to keep it in front of him. He was unbelievably weary, his limbs leaden. He was a mass of small wounds, arms, legs, torso, even his face. He had nothing left. The next attack would finish him. The end had finally come.

But instead of launching another attack, the hunter pointed at him. Something shot out of its hand, like a small dart. It struck Quyloc in the chest, but there was no pain. He stared stupidly at it, then tried to raise his hand to pluck it free. But he could not raise his arm. Horrified, he watched helplessly as the spear slipped from his nerveless fingers and clattered to the ground. Next his knees gave out. For a moment he hung on, swaying, then he toppled over on his side.

His eyes were open. He could feel the stone, strangely cool, under his cheek, but he could not move. It was almost pleasant there. The battle was over. He had lost. There was no more struggle. The *Pente Akka* had beaten him. His only hope now was that Rome would honor his promise and kill him once he found his body.

He heard the heavy tread as the hunter approached but there was nothing he could do about it. With its foot it pushed him over onto his back so that he stared up at the leaden sulfur sky. It grabbed one of his ankles and began to drag Quyloc away. His head bounced over the uneven ground while his arms dragged uselessly behind him. No matter how he tried, they wouldn't even twitch. He closed his eyes and surrendered to despair. Death was the only thing to look forward to now.

After a period of time that could have been minutes or could have been hours, the hunter stopped. Quyloc opened his eyes. Looming over them was a rectangular stone butte about fifty feet high. As easily as a man might climb a ladder, the hunter laid its free hand against the sheer face of the butte and began to climb up it, Quyloc dangling from one fist.

It climbed nearly to the top, then held him against the stone. Tilting its head back, it shrieked at the sky. From the sky spilled hundreds of black lines. They tumbled over each other, racing toward Quyloc, entwining, seeking. Within seconds they were on him, piercing his body in a hundred places, passing all the way through him and anchoring themselves in the stone underneath.

Quyloc screamed as his LifeSong began to drain out of him. Pulses of light flashed back up the black lines. As they met the sky, holes began to appear, small at first, then growing larger.

Through the holes could be seen the Qarathian army camp.

FORTY-FIVE

Rome opened his eyes to see T'sim standing over him, holding a small lantern. He knew instantly that something was wrong. He could feel it in his gut and deep in his bones.

"It is Quyloc," T'sim said.

Rome came to his feet, gathering up the black axe as he did. A moment later he was following T'sim toward the nearby hilltop, just visible in the slim moon. Nicandro, who was sleeping nearby, woke up as Rome passed and Rome told him, "Get the FirstMother."

Quyloc was lying on the ground with the spear clasped to his chest. Oddly, his eyes were open. Even in the poor light from the lantern it was clear that there was something terribly wrong with him. All his color was gone. His skin looked like wax. Swearing under his breath, Rome knelt beside him and put his fingers on the big vein in Quyloc's throat. His pulse was very weak.

Quyloc jerked, once, twice. His face contorted in a grimace of pain.

"Quyloc!" Rome said, giving him a little shake. "Are you there? Can you hear me?"

There was no response. Rome passed his hand before Quyloc's eyes, but they remained distant and unfocused.

The hunter had him.

Which meant… He didn't want to think about what that meant.

He stood up and turned to T'sim. "Find me Lowellin. Fast."

T'sim bowed. "He is not so well-hidden as he thinks." He hurried away and disappeared into the darkness.

Rome looked down on his friend. "Just hold on, Quyloc. I'm going to get you out of there. I promise you."

The next few minutes seemed to take forever. Rome kept checking Quyloc's pulse and now and then he shook him. It might have been his imagination, but it seemed like Quyloc was fading away. He still felt solid, but he looked somewhat translucent.

Finally, Nicandro arrived with Nalene in tow. She looked haggard, like she'd aged twenty years since they left Qarath. There were new lines in her face and dark bags under her eyes.

She took in the scene at a glance. "What's wrong with him?"

"He's trapped in the *Pente Akka*."

"I only recently even heard of the *Pente Akka*. I sure don't know how to save him from it."

"Use your *sulbit*."

"To do what? Kill him faster?"

"There has to be something you can do," Rome snarled. "Can't you do that thing, what's it called, going *beyond*, and *see* what's happening."

"How do you know about going *beyond*?"

"We don't have time for this right now. Do it!"

Nalene's *sulbit* was nestled in her robe, peering out from her collar. She put her hand on it and her eyes took on a distant, glazed look. A few moments later she blinked rapidly and recoiled.

"What are *those*?"

"What are you talking about? I can't see anything."

"Of course you can't. You're as blind as everyone else. There are hundreds of black lines attached to him. His LifeSong is flowing up them."

"Can you do anything about them? Can you break them?"

"I don't even know how to try."

"Use your *sulbit*, woman!" Rome said roughly, grabbing her arm.

"Take your hand off me," she said icily. Her *sulbit* was standing up on its stubby little legs, its back arched, tiny mouth open, baring fine, needle-sharp teeth. "I won't warn you again," she added.

"Keep that thing under control," Rome warned her. He held the axe poised in his other hand. "Or we'll see how my blade works on it."

Out of nowhere a breeze blew across the hilltop and when it died away a moment later T'sim and Lowellin stood there, T'sim holding onto Lowellin's elbow. Lowellin yanked his arm away, practically spitting with rage. T'sim gave Rome a bow and stepped back.

Rome crossed to Lowellin in two quick strides, the axe gripped in both hands. "Quyloc needs help. Now!"

Lowellin walked over to stand near Quyloc. He looked down at him for a minute, then shook his head. "The hunter has him. There's nothing I can do."

"That's not acceptable," Rome snapped. "There's always something that can be done."

Lowellin scowled at him. "Not this time. Fortunately, we still have the *rendspear*, so this is not a total loss. I'll just have to find someone capable of wielding it." He bent and reached for the spear.

"If you touch that spear, I'll cut you down," Rome growled. He held the black axe at the ready.

Lowellin turned on him, his eyes flashing. "You dare to threaten *me*?"

"I'll dare anything to save him. If it means cutting you in half, then so be it."

"You cannot hurt me with that thing." Lowellin sounded disdainful, but Rome thought he saw a shadow of indecision pass through his eyes. He wasn't entirely sure what the axe would do to him.

"Why don't we find out?" And Rome did want to find out right then. The axe seemed almost to buzz in his hands, as if it were eager to strike at Lowellin.

"Gentlemen, this benefits none of us," T'sim said calmly. They both looked at him. "If you kill each other, Melekath most certainly wins."

"He's right," Nalene said. "You're being foolish, Macht. You can't save him. Accept that."

He swung on her. "I don't accept that. I won't abandon him like that. I won't kill my friend."

"Then I will," Lowellin said. He raised the black staff and stabbed downward at Quyloc's chest.

But Rome had been in too many fights to be caught off guard so easily. The black axe hissed through the air and hit the staff.

There was a spray of sparks and a howl of soundless pain that was felt rather than heard.

Lowellin drew himself to his full height, blazing with fury. "You'll die for that!"

Rome wasted no breath responding. He was on the balls of his feet, adrenalin coursing through his body, a hair trigger away from attacking. He could already see how it would unfold, the feint, Lowellin's attempt to parry, then the axe buried in his neck. Lowellin was old and powerful, there was no doubt of that, but he had no skill in fighting.

"The problem, Macht," T'sim said softly, "is that you can't *see*. Let me help you."

When he acted, it was too fast for even Rome to respond. He stepped in close to Rome and tapped him once, right on the forehead. A light burst behind his eyes and Rome staggered back.

"What did you do to me?"

"Look," T'sim said, gesturing to Quyloc.

Rome shook his head to clear it, then looked at Quyloc. What he *saw* staggered him.

Quyloc was surrounded by a soft, white nimbus of light. Hundreds of black lines pierced him, pulses of light traveling up through them. The lines faded into nothingness ten feet or so above Quyloc.

"I warn you, before you act—" Lowellin said.

But it was already too late.

Rome swung the axe laterally, slicing through the black lines. There was a flash of light and a release of power, an explosion that blew Rome, Nalene and Nicandro backwards and buffeted Lowellin and T'sim.

Gingerly, Rome picked himself up. He was aching everywhere. He felt like he'd run headlong into a stone wall. Nalene was still on the ground, moaning softly. Nicandro stood up somewhat shakily.

"Do you have any idea how idiotic that was?" Lowellin hissed, getting into Rome's path. "You could have killed yourself and half your army—"

"Get out of my way," Rome said, pushing him aside to get to Quyloc. He knelt beside his friend. He slapped his cheeks gently. "C'mon, Quyloc. Come back to us." Whatever T'sim had done to him was gone. He could no longer *see* the black lines or the glow around Quyloc.

"Did it work?" he demanded. "Are the threads cut?"

Lowellin nodded. "They are."

"Why isn't he waking up?"

"I don't know if he will. Most of him is already in the shadow world."

"Help me bring him back."

"There's nothing you or I can do, no matter how badly you want to. It's up to him to find his way out of that place."

"There must be something you can do."

"There isn't, but I see that will not get through to you. So I will leave you." He strode off into the darkness and disappeared. Nalene hurried away as well. T'sim was nowhere to be seen.

"Go back to bed," Rome told Nicandro. "There's nothing more you can do here."

Rome remained kneeling beside his friend, staring at him, willing him to return.

Quyloc's world was red with pain. It was unceasing, filling every part of his being. Nothing else mattered. There was only the pain and the knowledge that it would never end. His old life was gone. Only pain was real.

He could not have said how long he hung there. Time no longer held any meaning. But all at once the pain receded and he had the sensation of falling. He landed hard on the ground and lay there like a broken puppet, looking up at a sulfur-yellow sky.

The memory of the hunter drove Quyloc onto his side, then onto his knees. He had to get away before the hunter returned. He looked around. There was no sign of the creature. But it might be nearby. It might be coming right that moment.

Shakily, he got to his feet. Dizziness swept over him and he stood hunched over, his hands on his knees. When it had passed somewhat he straightened and looked around. There was no sign of his spear, but then the hunter had dragged him for some ways.

Which way should he go? The terrain looked the same in every direction. It was hopeless. He could wander around up here forever and never find his weapon.

He wanted to lie down and give up. Instead he began walking, choosing a direction randomly. He looked for some sign of tracks, but the bare stone showed no traces.

He walked for some time, occasionally glancing over his shoulder, sure every time that he would see the hunter coming for him. But always he was alone. At length he came to the edge of the black mesa. The edge here dropped off in a sheer cliff. At the base was the river.

It occurred to him that he could fling himself off the cliff and end it that way. But would it really? His body was not really here. He might not actually be able to die here. He might just lie broken on the ground until the hunter found him again and then he would be helpless to do anything at all. It made sense that he could not die here;

otherwise, why have so many creatures attack him when the *gromdin* wanted him alive?

An idea occurred to him. He could summon the Veil by visualizing it. Could he do the same with his spear?

He closed his eyes and pictured the spear, remembering every detail as vividly as he could. He opened his eyes.

The spear was hanging there in the air before him, just off to his right.

But when he reached for it, his hand passed through it.

Cold fear gripped him. He tried again. Still the same result. But then he realized something. As he turned, the spear stayed in the same place. He faced it, then took a step toward it. It stayed the same distance away from him. He took another step and another. Each time it stayed right in front of him.

He started to run. As he did, he saw that the image of the spear grew brighter and clearer. He hoped that meant he was getting closer.

All at once there it was, lying on the ground in front of him. He snatched it up, summoned the Veil, slashed it and leapt through. As he did, he could hear a howl in the distance and knew it was the hunter.

Rome knelt by his friend's body, a black sorrow building inside him. He was too late. Quyloc was dead. He was reaching out to close Quyloc's eyes when all at once his friend gasped.

"You're alive!" Rome helped him sit up and had to resist the urge to sweep him up in a bear hug. Even half dead his friend would hate that. He hated all demonstrations of affection.

At first Quyloc said nothing. He sat there, hunched in on himself, his shoulders shaking, his face turned away from Rome.

"Are you okay?" Rome asked.

"No, I'm not okay," he whispered, pushing Rome's hands away. "Just give me a minute, will you?" he said irritably.

"Sure," Rome said, pulling back. "Whatever you need."

In time Quyloc gathered himself and he looked around as if unsure where he was. Last he looked at Rome, just for a moment before turning his eyes away. "What are you doing here?"

"T'sim woke me up and told me something was wrong with you. When I got here you were just staring blankly and you didn't move no matter what I did. You were fading. I didn't know what to do so I got the FirstMother and Lowellin up here to help."

"The FirstMother and Lowellin were here? You let them see me like that?" Quyloc's voice was stronger and his anger was evident in his tone.

"What was I supposed to do? Let you die?"

At first Rome thought Quyloc would say yes, then his friend sagged and shook his head.

"Neither one of them would help you. They were afraid. Then T'sim did something to me, tapped me on the forehead, and all of a sudden I could *see* the lines too."

Now Quyloc did look at him. "You could *see* them *here*?"

"Once he tapped me on the forehead. I'm telling you, it was a weird feeling. Not one I want to go through again. I'll stick to the normal world."

"How did you free me?"

"I chopped the lines with the axe. It caused some kind of explosion and knocked me halfway across this hilltop."

Weakly, Quyloc said, "You're a damned fool, you know that? You could have killed yourself, maybe others too."

Rome chuckled. "I seem to remember Lowellin saying something like that too. Anyway, it must have worked because here you are. I can't tell you how glad I am you're not dead. I don't know what I'd do without you." He held the lantern up so he could better look into Quyloc's eyes. "You're okay now, aren't you? No bites or anything?"

Quyloc nodded. "Just weak. But it will pass."

"Here let me help you up, get you over to your blanket. I'll get T'sim to bring you something to eat."

"No. You've done enough." Quyloc seemed to be struggling to say something else, but Rome couldn't figure out what it was. "Just…leave me alone for now. I need to be alone."

"You're sure?" Rome asked. "You don't look so good."

"I'm sure," Quyloc snapped. "Just go."

"Okay," Rome said, reluctantly rising to his feet. Why in the world was his old friend angry? It made no sense to him. "Maybe we'll start our march an hour or two later tomorrow morning to give you some extra time. I'm sure the men could use it too."

"No," Quyloc replied, sounding even angrier for some reason. "I'll be fine. We're not holding up because of me."

Rome looked down at him for a long moment. He'd never been able to understand Quyloc and he was guessing he never would.

When Quyloc did not look up or speak again, he slowly made his way off the hill.

Quyloc waited until he was sure Rome was gone before he tried to move. He didn't want anybody, especially Rome, to see how weak he was. At first he tried to stand, but after he fell twice he gave up and resorted to crawling over to his gear. The humiliation of crawling was worse than the weakness which disabled him, but he simply had no choice, though it sickened him to give in to his weakness in such a way and the whole time he felt sure there were people nearby, watching him with contempt.

By the time he got there waves of blackness were washing over him and he had to lie against his gear with his eyes closed for a while. After a time, his strength returned so that he was able to sit up. With shaking hands he pulled his blanket out, spread it on the ground and collapsed on it, still clutching the spear to his chest.

He awakened some time later with the feeling that something was terribly wrong. He opened his eyes. In the air above him was what looked like a rip in the air, sulfur light spilling through it.

He closed his eyes, visualized the Veil, and when he opened them again he was standing on the sand under the purple sky. There was a small cut in the Veil, probably the one he'd made when he left. For some reason it hadn't sealed the whole way and the hunter had its hands in it and was trying to force its way through.

Quyloc's first thought was to flee. He was weak from his ordeal, barely able to stand. He needed Lowellin's help.

But he was sick of running, sick of losing to this thing.

His lips peeled back from his teeth in the primal snarl of a desperate, cornered animal and he charged at the Veil, dimly aware that he was screaming incoherently. He raised the spear and stabbed the hunter with every ounce of strength left to him.

He felt the spear meet resistance. A jolt of raw, painful energy surged through him, and the hunter screamed and fell back, one hand clutching its midsection.

Quyloc pulled the spear out and fell back a step, surprised at what he had done. The hunter stood there, staring at him with its red eyes, then it backed away and was lost to sight.

Quyloc left and went back to his world. Lying on the ground, weaker than he'd ever been, still he felt a surge of elation. For the first time, he'd struck back.

FORTY-SIX

They stopped in the small town of Tornith near the Haven so Netra could ask for news about her sisters, but there were only a few people left and they were hostile and suspicious. Even though she'd had Shorn wait for her outside town, they wouldn't speak to Netra until one old man sporting a single tooth pointed east and then hurried away.

She rejoined Shorn. "It looks like they did head for Qarath." There was an old road leading east and Netra set her feet on it then did her best to turn off her thoughts, which swirled and dived around her, each peck drawing a tiny bit of blood.

"How do you do it?" she asked Shorn at one point. "How do you keep on when guilt and regret are all you have left?"

"Anger works," he rumbled. "For a time. Then it doesn't. It's not enough to live on."

She thought long on his words and when the guilt abused her again she thought about Tharn and Melekath and how they had killed those she loved. She thought about making them suffer as they'd made her suffer. She would go to Qarath. She would get one of these weapons that the Protector had brought them, and she would do everything she could to punish those responsible. It did not matter the cost to her. It did not matter the cost anywhere. All that mattered was that they should taste what filled her heart at this moment.

She did not notice Shorn's expression as he observed the grim look on her face.

As darkness fell Jolene awakened at the entrance of the cave that had become her home. The cave was on the southern slopes of the Firkath Mountains, almost overlooking Rane Haven. She did not know how long she had been there. After Netra left, Jolene had started pursuing visions through the dream smoke again. She knew nothing else to do.

The poison was spreading faster than ever and a tiny voice in her mind whispered that if only she could go deeper into the visions she might learn something that could help. It wasn't long before Brelisha caught her and forbade her to use the dream powder. When Jolene appealed to Siena, Siena had reluctantly sided with Brelisha. The dream powder was too dangerous. She was not to use it again.

For a time, Jolene obeyed the order. She busied herself with the numerous tasks that life at the Haven required, sewing, washing, cleaning, and tending the garden. But the tiny voice would not leave her be so finally she left the Haven one night and wandered forth on her own. She took very little with her, stumbling blindly through the darkness, trying to follow the little voice inside, to see where it would lead her.

As morning broke she found herself high up the side of the mountains on the lip of a small cave. It was more of a crevice than a cave, the floor littered with ancient bat dung and small bones, but it would do. She rested only a short while before venturing forth to seek the plants she would need to make more dream powder.

Since coming to the cave she had ventured into the dream world nearly every night, taking greater and greater risks. The dream world was a thin, insubstantial place. If she had tried to explain what she saw there, she would have said it was like seeing reflections on the surface of a lake. The images she perceived were two dimensional and, just as the surface of a lake is disturbed by every breeze so that the images it reflects become choppy and distorted, so the things she saw in the dream world were often confused and meaningless.

On her third trip into the dream world she journeyed to the prison itself. Strangely, the wall of the prison was unlike anything she had ever encountered in the dream world. It was a nebulous, writhing, chaotic mass, shot through with black and purple streaks of some kind of unusual energy that bore no resemblance to LifeSong. She knew with utter certainty that if she tried to pass through the wall that she would never return to her body. Even in this state, disconnected from her body as she was, she could not touch it and survive.

Strangely, finding the wall to the prison heartened her. There seemed no way Melekath could break through that chaotic energy. Perhaps things were not as dire as they seemed. The prison continued to draw her back, over and over, as if there was something there she had missed. Some days later she found a place in the prison wall that was different. It was made of stone, though not ordinary stone. This, then, was where Melekath would break free. The unusual stone proved to be no barrier to her.

What she found on the other side was a scene from a nightmare. A city of ruined buildings, their windows and doors gaping, empty holes, many of their walls streaked black from long-ago fires. The street before her was spiderwebbed with cracks. One of the cracks opened up as it reached the side of the street and the building there was tilted sideways; half of it had broken off and slid into the crack. Something moved in the shadowed depths of the broken building, but Jolene could see no details.

Then a figure came striding down the street and she knew instantly that it was Melekath. Unlike most of what she saw in the dream world, Melekath appeared solid, three dimensional. He looked up, his eyes fixing on her and she went cold inside. He reached toward her with one hand and she panicked and fled.

Periodically during the next days she felt unseen eyes on her, but whenever she looked up she saw nothing. In her heart she felt certain it was Melekath, that he had marked her and perhaps had followed her somehow.

It was days before she again mustered the courage to use the dream powder. She knew that if she entered the prison Melekath would be waiting for her. He would trap her there and she would never escape. But finally she had no choice. The prison drew at her. She had to know more. Perhaps she could get some glimpse of his plans. Maybe she could learn something that would help defeat him.

That night she used the dream powder once again and entered the prison. There was no sign of Melekath, though she thought she could sense his presence, somewhere in the middle of the city. She passed over the city, looking down on it from above. Everywhere she saw shattered buildings and signs of old fires. The roof of one huge, domed building had fallen in and in the depths of the interior she saw movement, but she did not linger to see what it was.

In the center of the city was a huge spire, made of some kind of bluish stone. Balconies encircled each level, doors and windows opening onto them. It was so large that she gaped at its scale and wondered at the power required to erect it. Gathering her courage, she passed through one of the doors, and followed the stairs downward.

At the base was a massive amphitheater with a stone tiled floor. Seating lined the entire circumference of the theater, angling up and back. In the center, at ground level, was a stage made of a single large block of stone.

On the stage stood Melekath, his back to her. He was staring at a tall, rectangular box. The box appeared to be made of stone.

He turned and his gaze locked on her. As she started to flee he held up his hand and spoke.

Stay. There is something you want to see first. His words made no sound. It was as though he spoke directly to her mind.

She hung there, unsure.

I have someone you have been looking for.

He laid his hand on the rectangular box. When he did, it changed, becoming transparent.

Jolene gasped, her world spinning wildly.

A woman was trapped in the box, her eyes wide with fear. She looked at Jolene and her mouth moved with silent pleas. Then Melekath lifted his hand and the box was once again opaque.

Tell them. Tell them I have your god and now there are none in your world who can stop me.

He made a flicking motion with his hand and Jolene was thrown backwards, tumbling over and over. There was a painful jolt and when she opened her eyes she was back in her body, staring at the roof of the cave.

Xochitl was Melekath's prisoner.

She had to tell the others. Slowly she climbed to her feet. It was dark outside and she was painfully weak—she'd eaten very little since leaving the Haven—but what she had learned could not wait. She tottered out into the darkness.

Netra stopped, tilting her head to one side. She had just caught a faint echo of a familiar Song, but it was gone too fast for her to be sure who it was. Shorn stopped as well and turned toward her, a question in his eyes.

"I'm not sure, but I think…" She turned and looked up toward the Firkath Mountains on their left. There it was again. She felt herself smiling. "It *is* her! I can't believe it!"

She left the road and ran off into the desert, Shorn thundering along behind her. In the distance a worn figure appeared, making her way slowly down a rocky slope. Netra yelled and ran to her.

"Jolene! Jolene, it's me, Netra!"

The black-haired woman looked up as she approached and for a moment Netra faltered. Jolene had always been thin, but now she was a scarecrow. Her brown robe was dirty and torn and it billowed around her frail frame like a sail. Her eyes were sunken and lined with darkness. At first there was no recognition in her eyes, but then she said, "Netra?"

Overcome, Netra wrapped her up in a hug and squeezed her tightly. At length she let go of Jolene and stepped back, but she kept one hand on her, as if afraid she might disappear.

Shorn came up then. Jolene's eyes grew very wide and she stepped back, her hand coming to her mouth.

"It's okay," Netra reassured her. "He's my friend. He won't hurt you."

Jolene looked unsure, but she nodded slowly.

"What happened to you, Jolene? Why didn't you go with the rest to Qarath?"

"Qarath? Who went to Qarath?"

"All of them, all but Siena and Brelisha." Netra stopped and swallowed, a fresh pain stabbing her. "At least, I think they went to Qarath. I thought you'd gone with them."

"No," Jolene said softly. She wavered and might have fallen if Netra didn't grab her.

"Here. Sit down. You look awful." Netra realized what she'd said and mentally kicked herself. "I didn't mean it like that."

"I suppose I do look awful," Jolene replied, looking down and patting some dust from her robe.

Once she was seated, Netra dug some food from her pack and gave it to her. "How long has it been since you ate?" she asked as Jolene reluctantly took the food.

"I left the Haven…" Jolene paused, thinking. "I don't know how long ago it was. After you left. The others were still there. Why did they leave?"

"I don't know for sure," Netra replied. "They must have gone to join the FirstMother in Qarath. Where have you been? Why did you leave?"

"The dream powder. Brelisha caught me using it. She forbade it. I tried to obey, but I had to know more. I had to help." She grabbed Netra's sleeve, her dark eyes searching Netra's face. "You have to believe me," she whispered.

"Believe you? About what?"

Jolene let go of her sleeve and rubbed at her face with shaking hands. "It seems impossible, but it's not. In my heart I know it's true."

"Jolene, what are you talking about? What's going on?"

"It's the Mother. I found her."

Netra gaped at her. Then she broke into a huge smile. "But that's wonderful! Where? Where is she?"

Jolene's next words were nearly inaudible and there were tears in her eyes as she spoke. "In the prison. Melekath has her."

Netra's sudden joy died. She had to put a hand out to steady herself. "But...that can't be," she croaked. "How do you know?"

"In the dream I traveled to the prison. I...went inside. He has her, in a stone cage. I *saw* her."

"But maybe...you don't know for sure," Netra said desperately. She felt suddenly, irrationally angry at Jolene.

"He spoke to me. He told me to tell everyone he had her and there's no chance we can defeat him. That's why I left the cave." Jolene slumped over as she finished speaking, as if the words had taken the last of what she had left.

Netra stood and backed away. "You must have imagined it. It can't be true." She realized that she was breathing hard, but she couldn't seem to get enough air.

"I wish I was," Jolene said sadly.

Netra looked at Shorn, but his thoughts were hidden behind the wall of his stone face. There was a sick feeling growing in the pit of her stomach.

Then Jolene stood up and made her way unsteadily to Netra. There was something different on her face, a strange sort of certainty. "It's no accident that I met you here, now," she said. Netra looked at her with confusion. "Don't you see? I was guided to you. This is all for a reason. It's you. You're the one. The only one who can help Xochitl."

"That's crazy," Netra said. Jolene's eyes were very bright. "What can I possibly do?"

Jolene shook her head. "I have no idea. But I know this to be true."

Again Netra looked to Shorn for help, but she found none. She looked back at Jolene.

"You have to go to the prison. You have to help her. It's our only chance."

"I don't…" Netra's words trailed off. Jolene was surely crazy. All she had to do was look at her to see that. What could she possibly do? But then…

"Maybe it's not so crazy," she said slowly. "After I escaped from the burned man I remember thinking that maybe the reason Xochitl hadn't appeared was because she *couldn't*. I even thought that maybe the reason I'd survived all three Guardians was because she was guiding me, that maybe she needed *me* to help her." Wonder filled her voice. She turned to Shorn. "It's possible, isn't it? That I'm the one?"

There was an expression on Shorn's face, but she couldn't read it. She turned away from him. This wasn't something he'd know anything about.

There was awe on Jolene's face. "You encountered Kasai as well?"

"Not directly, but through one of his minions."

"How did you escape?"

"It was my spirit guide, just like when I encountered Tharn. With its guidance I…opened my captors' *akirmas* and used their own Song against them. I used it to break my bonds and flee."

Jolene put her hand to her mouth. "No Tender has done that in a thousand years." Tears began to flow down her face. "Don't you see, Netra? It *is* you. The Mother has been guiding you all along. She sent me that vision and guided me down here today, at this exact time, just so I would find you and tell you."

"It seems impossible…"

"No, what's impossible is that all these things should be only a coincidence. The Mother's hand has been in this all along. How else do you explain all the events that led to this moment? Think about it. I have a vision that we need to go to Treeside. Why? At the time it seemed pointless. All that happened was Gerath was killed. But now I can see that it was a test. Xochitl wanted to see if you were the one and when you survived it increased her faith in you."

"She sent us there just to test me? But Gerath—"

"Don't," Jolene said sternly. "It is not our place to question the Mother's plan. So much is at stake and we all have our roles. Gerath had hers, just as I have mine and you have yours."

"You really believe that, don't you?"

"With all my heart."

"But…what am I supposed to do?"

"I don't know. But I think the first step is to go to the prison. Trust that the Mother will guide you. After all, she has guided you this far."

"Right now?"

"Yes, now."

"Okay," Netra said, giving in suddenly. "I have no idea what I can do, but I will go. But I can't leave you here, by yourself."

"Don't worry about me. I will go back to the Haven."

"There's nothing to go back to. Tharn came. After the others left for Qarath or wherever." She put her hand on Jolene's arm. "It destroyed the Haven. It killed Siena and Brelisha."

Jolene closed her eyes and a took a deep breath. Then her eyes opened and they were filled with resolve. "This is only more proof. Melekath must have learned of you through his Guardians. He sent Tharn there to kill you."

"But where will you go?"

Jolene drew herself up straight. "I don't know. But what happens to me doesn't matter. All that matters is freeing the Mother. Surely you, of all people, can see that?"

"At least let us go with you to Tornith."

Jolene shook her head. Though her face was pale her words were strong. "I can make it there on my own. Now go."

"Let me give you some of my food."

"No. You need it more than I do. Go. Now. Help her." As Netra began to turn away, she grabbed her arm.

"You must hurry. Time is running out."

FORTY-SEVEN

Netra and Shorn struck off across empty desert to the south, toward the Gur al Krin desert. Netra's thoughts were whirling. Was this really happening? Had Melekath really trapped Xochitl? But how? Was it possible that when she realized the prison was breaking she'd gone there to check on it and that somehow he'd been able to capture her then? It seemed farfetched, but what other explanation was there?

"I don't understand," Shorn said out of nowhere, after they had been walking for about an hour. "How does she know your god is held in this prison?"

"She saw it in a vision."

"What is a vision?"

"It's hard to explain. It's like a dream, but real."

His heavy brows drew together. "You are sure of what she says? She did not look...well."

"I am." But suddenly she was seeing Jolene again in her mind—disheveled, tattered, skinny—and her steps faltered. The dream powder was known to be dangerous and Jolene had always been a little strange. Netra shook her head, trying to drive the thoughts away. Jolene was perceptive, more perceptive than anyone she had ever known.

"What will you do when we get to the prison? Do you have a plan to fight this Melekath?"

Netra sagged. "I don't know what I'm going to do. I guess I'll figure that out when I get there."

"It is not good, to go without a plan."

"What else are you proposing I do? Just sit here and do nothing?"

"No. It is not your way. But to rush blindly is not good."

"It will be days before we get there. I just have to have faith that something will come up."

He scowled. "What is faith?"

Netra thought about it. She'd never tried to define it before. "It's doing something that you know is right, even when there's no proof it's right."

"I do not understand."

"That wasn't a very good definition. How about this: Faith is trusting in your god no matter what."

"What if your god is wrong?"

"What? That's ridiculous. Xochitl could never be wrong."

"Are there not other gods? People who believe in them? They cannot all never be wrong."

"That's different. Those are false gods. Only Xochitl is the true god."

"And she is never wrong."

"She…" Netra trailed off. She had spent her childhood arguing with Brelisha about the Book of Xochitl. She had spent the last months doubting everything. She wasn't sure what she believed anymore. "Maybe I can explain it better. Faith is trusting you are doing the right thing, even when you can't know for sure that you are."

"Faith is trusting in yourself?"

"What? No. It's trusting in your god."

"That is what you said."

"Stop twisting my words. That's not what I just said."

"But this is what you take to the prison? Faith?"

Netra stared at him. His expression was blunt. He was not judging her. He played no games. He was asking simply because he needed more information.

"I cannot protect you if I do not know what is going on," he said at last.

Netra felt very small and uncertain. In a small voice she said, "It means I don't know what I'm going to do. I'm just going to try."

He nodded. "Okay. Let us have faith then."

All day they walked, pausing only briefly to dig food from their packs, then eating while they walked. Netra noticed with dismay that her food was nearly gone and that Shorn did not have much either. She didn't want to waste time scavenging for food or cooking it. They needed to find something they could take without slowing them down.

She knew what the solution was, but she didn't want to take it unless she had to.

By the end of the day she was certain they had to do it. The land was flattening out, broken only by clumps of greasewood and twisted cacti. In the distance were the black humps of small volcanic hills. At the base of one she saw the green of a mesquite thicket.

"See how green that is?" she said, pointing. "I'm thinking there's water there." She looked at the sky. "It's getting down to the end of the day. If there's water there, wildlife will be coming in to drink."

Shorn stared in the direction of the hill and nodded. Then he said, "I have no bow to hunt with."

"Leave that to me," she assured him. "I know what to do."

She led them in an arc that swung around the hill so that it blocked them from the water and they were downwind. Then she led them slowly up to it. When they reached the hill, they crept forward over the jagged black boulders, taking care not to dislodge any stones. The sun was just about to set by the time they got there.

At the water's edge were three antelope. Two were drinking, while the other kept its head up, watching the surroundings. Closing her eyes, Netra went *beyond*. In that nether place she *saw* the glow of the animals' *akirmas* and the flows of LifeSong that sustained them. The flows were too far away to reach and she didn't think she could get closer without frightening the animals.

But there was another way, if only her will was strong enough. She focused Selfsong in her hand, so that she would be able to grasp the flow once it was close enough. Then she concentrated on the nearest flow, willing it closer. After a few moments it began to drift nearer.

The moment she took hold of it one of the antelope stiffened. It threw its head up, muscles bunching as it prepared to flee. But Netra clamped down on the flow, pinching it off, and the animal was only able to take two steps before it went to its knees, kicking and contorting its body, its eyes rolling. Netra clamped down harder. The other two fled.

Shorn leapt over the boulder they were hiding behind and ran toward the animal, drawing a sword as he went. But by the time he got to the animal it was already dead.

Stunned, Netra made her way around the boulder and towards the animal. She paused partway as a spasm of nausea passed over her and she bent over, her hands on her knees. She cleared her throat and spit, closing her eyes until the worst of it had passed. Feeling Shorn's eyes on her, she straightened and gave him a weak smile.

"It worked. Now we have food."

Was it her imagination, or did he look worried? Before she could be sure it was gone, replaced by his normal impassivity.

Her stomach turned over again as she relived the animal's panic and desperation. She'd felt it all as if it was her own. She swallowed hard. "We had to have food. It's no different than hunting."

Slowly, Shorn nodded.

"I'll gather wood for a fire while you clean it," she said shakily. She hurried off into the trees and once she was out of his sight she fell to her knees and vomited. For a time she knelt there, grappling with what she had just done. *I had no choice,* she told herself, over and over, trying to force herself to believe it.

When she felt better she stood and began gathering wood. Shorn had the antelope skinned when she returned and she lowered her eyes, trying not to see the animal's carcass glistening nakedly, trying not to think about how recently it had been a living creature. Again, doubt and weakness assailed her, but she fought it off. It was a war. In war one killed. That was the way it was. Without food she could not help the Mother. What she had done was the right thing. There was no question about it.

She had to stand upwind when Shorn put the carcass over the flames, fighting the sickness in her gut and staring out into the darkness. Whenever the wind shifted she did also and what little appetite she had was completely gone by the time he thrust a chunk of meat her way. However, she forced herself to eat some of it, fighting down each bite as it tried to come back up. She ate only a few bites before giving the rest back to Shorn.

"I guess I'm just not that hungry." He made no reply, but she knew he did not believe her. For some reason that made her angry. "I had to do it. Can't you see that? We don't have time to waste. We have to move."

Then she stomped off into the darkness, angry at Shorn, angry at herself. She sat on a rock and drew out her *sonkrill*, hoping for some reassurance there. But there was nothing.

Sighing, she was putting it away when she thought she heard something. It was like a distant voice, carried on the wind. She froze, straining to hear more. There it was again. It sounded like a cry for help.

Netra hurried back to their camp, where Shorn was sitting, staring into the fire. "Let's go," she told him. "We're going to walk a few more hours." Without hesitation Shorn stood and gathered his gear.

"I think I just heard her," Netra said to him, when they had started walking. "I was holding my *sonkrill* and I heard a cry in the distance. It sounded like a cry for help. It has to be Xochitl. Somehow she is speaking to me through my *sonkrill*."

"You are sure it was her?"

"Of course I'm sure! Who else would it be?"

Shorn shrugged but did not reply.

Over the next few days Netra heard the distant cry a number of times. Sometimes she heard it when she was holding her *sonkrill*. Other times she heard it when she wasn't. Once she woke up sure that she'd just heard it in her dreams. As the days passed the cry grew louder, making her sure they were going in the right direction. It also seemed to her that it grew more desperate.

She kept them moving fast, jogging as often as she could, and only stopping for a few hours at night to rest, rising in the early morning darkness to push on south. The pace didn't seem to bother Shorn, but Netra felt her fatigue growing and knew she could not keep up this pace much longer. She was not far from collapsing.

The solution came to her one afternoon after she fell and cut her knee on a rock. As she sat there, catching her breath and trying to staunch the flow of blood, it occurred to her that there was Song, pure energy, all around her. It pulsed within the animals and birds of the desert. What if she took some from them, to give herself the energy she needed to continue on? She remembered the burst of energy she got when she took Song to escape from the burned man, and again when she killed Bloodhound.

The idea scared her at first and she discarded it. Brelisha had taught them about the Tenders of the Empire keeping slaves for their Song and the idea of it had always horrified Netra. How could one person do that to another? It was unimaginable to her.

Wearily, she got to her feet and continued on. But as the time passed and she grew weaker and weaker, she kept thinking of it. She would not take enough to kill anything. Only enough to keep her going, and she wouldn't be taking Song from a person, just an animal. Besides, if she didn't do something, she was going to have to stop and rest. Who knew how long they had? Who knew what Melekath was planning?

Finally, she just stopped. "I can't keep this up any longer. I'm exhausted."

Shorn looked down at her. He looked elemental, indomitable. Then he said something that surprised her. "I will carry you."

She was strangely touched by his offer and she felt tears in her eyes. "Thank you," she said simply. "That is very kind of you. But I think there is a better way." Shorn raised one eyebrow, but said nothing.

"I'm going to take Song from an animal and use it to strengthen myself. It's similar to what I did when the burned man's minions caught me." Now that she had decided to do it, she found herself strangely excited by the idea. The rush of energy she'd felt had been unbelievable.

Shorn thought on this for a minute. Then he said, "Are you sure? You said Tenders do not kill animals."

"Listen to you. What happened to the man who just wanted to kill everything?"

Shorn's heavy brows drew together, but he did not reply.

"I'm not going to take enough to kill anything anyway," she added. "Just enough to keep myself going."

He stared at her with his amber eyes. His scars were dark lines across his face. Then he looked at the sun. It was less than an hour until sunset. "We could stop now. Make camp. In the morning you may feel different."

"We can't do that, Shorn," Netra replied irritably. "When did you decide to start questioning me? Didn't you make a vow or something to follow me, no matter what?"

Shorn lowered his head in acknowledgement of her rebuke.

"We can't stop. We can't afford to waste the time."

Shorn stared into her eyes once more, as if trying to find something there. "Your god tells you this?"

"Not in so many words. But she's afraid. I can feel it. She wants us to hurry."

Slowly, Shorn nodded. "What do you want me to do?"

"You don't need to do anything. Just stay back and be quiet. I have to concentrate."

Netra moved to a flat rock and sat down. It felt good to sit. She was so tired. She closed her eyes and had to fight to keep from falling asleep. Lying down on a stone, even a bunch of broken stones, would feel as good as a bed right now. When had she last slept in a bed, a real bed?

Netra shook herself. She had to stay focused. She deepened her breathing and let her inner senses flow outward, taking it all in. The cold emptiness of the stone underfoot. The soil with its tiny inhabitants squirming and crawling through darkness. Birds flying overhead. A rabbit crouched behind a bush. Then, further out, what she sought. A coyote curled up in the shade, waiting for night.

Slipping *beyond*, she looked outward and there it was, its *akirma* brown and gold. The flow of Song sustaining it shimmered in the darkness. For the first time in ages she thought of something Brelisha had tried to teach her: that distance didn't really exist *beyond*. It was not a physical place at all, but rather a construct built by the mind to make sense of something that was beyond sense.

It was true. The flow of Song sustaining the coyote seemed far away at first, but then she changed her mind about it, gave up the idea of it being distant—

And all at once it was right there, next to her.

Focusing Selfsong in her hand, she reached out and took hold of the coyote's flow.

She heard it yelping in the distance and felt it struggle. She began to pull it to her. It came unwillingly, its ears flattened against its head, its lips peeled back in a snarl. Its legs scrabbled at the ground as it fought to free itself from the invisible hand that held it.

"It's okay," Netra told the animal softly. "I won't hurt you."

When she reached out with her other hand to touch it, it snapped at her and she barely pulled her hand back in time to avoid being bitten. Frowning, Netra clamped down harder on its flow and the coyote crumpled to the ground, whining.

Trembling slightly, Netra laid her hand on the coyote's back. She concentrated and a tendril of pure will flowed out from her *akirma*. With it she easily pierced the animal's *akirma*. Immediately, its Song began to rush into her.

The effect was immediate, electric. Every nerve ending, every fiber of her being, was instantly aflame. It felt like her hair was standing on end. The pain and exhaustion were flushed away, replaced by a tingling feeling of alertness and possibility. She wanted to sing and laugh out loud. It was amazing and invigorating. She couldn't imagine why she hadn't done this before. For a time she lost herself in the feeling, all the fears and worries of her life slipping away into the distance.

But then there was a hand pulling on her shoulder. She tried to shrug it away. The interference became stronger and now a voice was saying something. Finally, it resolved into a single word:

"Stop."

Netra opened her eyes. She was kneeling on the ground and the coyote was lying stretched out before her, its eyes glassy, its breathing ragged. Shocked, she pulled back from it and jumped to her feet. The coyote whined once, then pushed itself unsteadily to its feet. She started to reach out to it, to calm it, but it bolted, weaving badly. Before it had gone two steps it fell sideways, its hindquarters ceasing to work. But it did not give up and used its front legs to drag itself into some bushes and disappear.

Netra stared after it. "What have I done?" she asked. Shorn gave no reply. After a long moment, Netra turned away and started south once again.

Her concern for the coyote and her guilt over her treatment of it did not last long. She felt better than she had since she could remember, the stolen Song coursing through her veins. She felt strong and confident, rested and fit. On impulse she started running and almost laughed at the ease of it. She could run clear to the Gur al Krin if she wanted to. Nothing was too difficult. She heard Shorn's heavy steps behind her and she increased her pace, wanting to see him tired and gasping for air.

"This is incredible!" She laughed and twirled in a circle, then ran on again.

Sometime after dark she started to tire once again. Her steps slowed, she stumbled once or twice, and then weariness began to draw its blanket over her. Each step became an effort. There were pains in her legs and a sharp stitch in her side. She tried pushing them out of her mind and continuing on, but they grew worse. Her very bones seemed to ache and her eyes tried to close of their own accord. She felt as if there were great empty spaces inside her with cold winds howling through them. Finally, she came to a stop.

"I can't go any further," she mumbled, then simply lay down on the spot, asleep before she hit the ground.

FORTY-EIGHT

Netra woke up the next morning horribly weak and consumed with guilt. Over and over she saw the coyote, a twisted clump of yellow-brown fur, dragging itself into the bushes. Had it survived? Was it lying dead in those same bushes? How had she done such a thing?

Did she do the right thing?

Wearily she sat up, the exertion enough that she had to close her eyes while she fought off the dizziness. Her limbs were made of stone. She didn't think she had the strength to stand up, much less walk. She wondered how she would make it through another day.

She pulled the *sonkrill* out and clasped it in both hands, lowering her head and pressing the *sonkrill* to her forehead. Then she waited.

At first there was nothing. She heard Shorn sit up. She became acutely familiar with her own weakness, the tremor deep in her muscles that made even sitting up hard.

Still nothing.

She squeezed her eyes tightly shut, praying hard.

Nothing.

Sagging, she put the *sonkrill* away.

Help me. Hurry.

Netra raised her head, her eyes opening wide. She rolled to her knees and began struggling to her feet. Shorn hurried to her, catching her as she started to fall.

"You need rest," he said.

"I know." She slumped against him, her heart pounding hard. "But we have to keep moving." She lifted her head, stared into his eyes. "She spoke to me this time."

The lines around Shorn's eyes deepened, but he did not move.

"I don't have time for this," she snapped, suddenly irritated. "We have to go, and we have to go now. Are you with me or not?" She made no effort to soften her tone and she thought he winced slightly.

"I am with you," he rumbled. "I only..." He hesitated. "You do not seem...well."

Netra's anger blazed forth like a sudden fire. She pulled away from him and drew herself up to her full height. "Of course I'm not well!" she yelled, glaring at him. "Look around you. The *land* is not well. Nothing is *well*! It's all dying. Can't you see that?"

He held her glare for a moment, then looked away.

"*I* don't matter in this," she continued. "*You* don't matter. That coyote doesn't matter. All that matters is getting to Xochitl and setting her free. She's the only one who can save us now." She was standing there, her chest heaving, when blackness began to crowd her vision. She put out a hand and would have fallen if Shorn hadn't caught her again.

She must have lost consciousness then because when next she opened her eyes she was lying on the ground and Shorn was bending over her. Concern showed in his eyes and she immediately felt sorry. After the way she'd yelled at him, it would be only fair if he turned his back on her for good.

"I'm sorry, Shorn," she whispered. "I didn't mean to take it out on you. I'm just...afraid."

Awkwardly, yet gently, he reached out with one huge hand and patted her on the shoulder.

Netra's eyes filled with tears. "I'm going to have to do it again. There's no other way." She drew a deep breath. "Is there?"

Shorn opened his mouth, but then closed it again. He had no answer for her.

Netra lay there with her eyes closed for a while, then said, "Help me sit up, Shorn." The fear and the indecision had been pushed back for a time and her tone was resolute. Still with her eyes closed, she reached out with her inner senses, probing the land around her. She found what she was looking for in a small herd of shatren grazing in the next ravine. At the same time she felt the presence of a person. She narrowed her focus and a moment later realized it was a boy, probably around ten. He must be out there to keep watch over the shatren. Which meant there was a farm house somewhere near.

This was rough country and getting rougher as they drew closer to the Gur al Krin. The canyons were getting deeper, their sides steeper.

Grass and forage was intermittent at best and even the cactus seemed smaller, sapped by the struggle to survive. Life out here was harsh, between the rigors of the desert and the threat of raids by the Crodin nomads. Losing even one shatren would be tough on the boy's family.

Netra pushed the thought away. The time for regrets and doubts had passed, ended by Melekath's reemergence into the world. Slipping *beyond*, she located the shatren and chose one, a cow with a calf beside her. She erased the idea of distance and the next moment the cow's flow was right there in front of her. The next step was to focus Selfsong in one hand, but when she did, nothing happened.

Netra opened her eyes. "I need help, Shorn. I'm too weak to do this."

Shorn looked around, unsure what she wanted him to do.

"I need..." Her voice cracked. Why were there no easy choices anymore? "I need some of your Song."

To his credit, Shorn barely hesitated before nodding.

"Sit down beside me, where I can put my hand on you." Shorn sat down on her left, his head turned so that he could look into her eyes, and Netra put her left hand on his forearm. As she did, her sleeve pulled back and she saw the faint mark where the yellow flow had touched her that night outside the Haven, when Jolene had her first vision. *Was I marked then?* she wondered. *Was that when all this really started?*

Then she felt Shorn's Song coiled within him and all thoughts of the past disappeared before the sudden hunger that blossomed inside her. She was so empty, so drained, and he had so much. With a tendril of her will she tore a small hole in his *akirma* and began to drink.

Shorn's eyes widened and his arm twitched, but he held himself still.

It took every bit of Netra's willpower to stop herself after a few moments. The desire to widen the hole, to drain every bit of Song he held, was nearly overwhelming. She was shaking when she pulled away.

But now it was easy to take hold of the cow's flow and draw her in. The animal made a startled sound and started walking toward her. The boy rose to his feet from where he crouched in the shade of a rock, moving to intercept the shatren. He waved his arms and shouted, then threw two stones that bounced off the animal's side.

The cow walked over the ridge on stilted, wooden legs, followed by her calf and the boy. He shaded his eyes, not believing what he was seeing, then disappeared back over the ridge with a yelp.

Netra stood and placed a trembling hand on the cow shatren's head, while the calf bawled nearby. The tendril of will that burst from her was larger and stronger than she meant it to be and the hole it tore in the animal's *akirma* was huge. Song fountained out of the animal and some of it she lost, but most she was able to take in.

The effect was instantaneous. Weakness and pain disappeared, replaced by strength and a warm glow that spread over her entire body. It felt wonderful. It felt *right*.

The animal's legs folded under it and the shatren collapsed in a heap. Netra followed it down, never losing contact. She felt Shorn's hand on her shoulder and heard his voice as if from the bottom of a well, but she ignored him and when he persisted she shoved him away angrily.

Then there was no more. Netra knelt there, panting. She could feel every individual grain of sand under her hands. She could feel the fine hairs on the backs of her arms moving in the faint breeze, smell a thousand odors she'd never known existed, hear ants crawling in their underground vaults. It was exhilarating and agonizing at the same time. It rushed over her in a flood and she knew no feeling in the world could ever compare to this.

Effortlessly, Netra came to her feet, all aches and doubts gone completely. She took a deep breath and stretched. She felt elemental, powerful. She glanced at the dead shatren in a heap at her feet and her confidence wavered, just for an instant, but then she shrugged it away. She was Netra and Xochitl was calling her.

Nothing else mattered.

They raced through the morning and on into the afternoon. She heard the Mother calling again and again and there was only the need to answer and the wondrous rapture that surged within her. She, Netra, would find Xochitl. She would free her and Xochitl would destroy Melekath. Then Xochitl would walk amongst them once again and all the Tenders of the future would know Netra's name and revere her, the one who saved Xochitl.

It was a wonderful dream and the only hiccup came from the dour presence that paced her through that long day and the twinges of guilt she felt when she looked at him. Shorn was judging her; she was sure of it. From behind those cold, distant eyes he looked down on her, condemning her. She found herself beginning to hate him and watched him surreptitiously whenever possible, waiting for him to make a move against her. She could handle him, of that she had no doubt. She would drain him as effortlessly as she did the shatren if he raised as much as a finger against her. He would see. He would know how wrong he'd been.

But Shorn did nothing, said nothing. He ran beside her when he could, behind her when he could not, as they moved ever south. His features were utterly closed, his will iron. When Netra mocked him or taunted him he said nothing, betrayed nothing. When that happened Netra cursed him and put on extra speed, thinking to leave him behind, but each time he matched her, his strength seemingly endless.

Netra's strength, however, was not endless. The sun was beginning to drop when she felt herself weakening yet again. This time she did not wait until she collapsed to do what had to be done, but began scanning the land around her for animals. The terrain was harsher and dryer and game was surprisingly scarce, only small birds and rodents. Finally, she felt the presence of an old badger, hunkered in his burrow. With a gesture she dragged him forth, as he snarled and snapped. She realized that she didn't need to touch him and drained him from a distance, so swiftly and completely that he simply dropped on the spot between one snarl and the next, a shrunken thing that might once have been alive.

Then she moved on, but her hunger was not sated. If anything it was stronger. She longed for the clarity and sense of power that she had felt after draining the shatren. The surge she received from the badger was only a shadow of that glory.

Desperately, she reached out further and further, taking every scrap she found, regardless of how meager. Birds fell from tree limbs in her wake, dead before they hit the ground. Rabbits crouched under bushes toppled over and were still. Mice and gophers collapsed in their tunnels. Lizards withered and died. At one point a buzzard soared overhead, perhaps sensing the presence of death with that preternatural sense all carrion eaters seem to have. It stiffened and nosedived to the earth in a rush of black feathers.

So Netra and Shorn passed the next two days, a trail of death marking their passing, Shorn tireless, Netra drawn on by a distant voice, always reaching desperately for the next scrap of Song she could steal, reaching for something she could not quite seem to grasp.

It was dawn when the dunes of the Gur al Krin became visible in the distance for the first time. Netra stopped on the crest of a ridge, gazing at it. The legendary Gur al Krin, mountainous dunes of red and orange sand extending beyond the horizon. It was quiet in the stillness of dawn, but Netra could feel the malevolent heart that beat within its depths. Somewhere under there Melekath clawed his way to the surface. Somewhere under there he had imprisoned Xochitl, their only hope for stopping him. She would find the Mother and free her. She knew she was capable of it.

Shorn pointed wordlessly and she lowered her gaze. They were in a land of steep canyons and sharp spires. Sandstone ruled here, layers of white, yellow, red and black that spoke of ancient, shallow seas, beaches and mudflats. There were cliffs everywhere, some smooth and soaring for hundreds of feet into the air, others squat and toothy. Here and there were patches of soil, lining the bottoms of the canyons or gathered in clefts. From the sparse soil sprouted scraggly bushes with hooked, yellow thorns and iron-gray tufts of grass.

Down at the bottom of the canyon at her feet, huddled at the foot of a cliff by a pool of brown water, Netra saw a village of rough hide shelters and her heart soared. An oasis in the desert. But not an oasis of water, an oasis of Song. Beautiful Life-energy. Tears dimmed her eyes. Xochitl must have guided her here, knowing that she would need to drink deep before crossing the desert, before tearing away the chains that kept her bound.

Netra started down the hill.

"Netra, wait." Shorn grabbed Netra's arm. She spun on him, eyes flashing. "They are people."

She cast a contemptuous glance at the village. "They are little more than animals. They should be honored to sacrifice everything for Xochitl." She jerked her arm away from him. "Everything I do, I do for the Mother."

Now Shorn blocked her path. "Do you do this for your god, or for yourself?"

Netra hissed at him. "How dare you ask me that, after the suffering I have gone through? I have lost my family!"

"Not all of them. Not yet."

"And I will make sure I do not lose the rest." She tried to go around him, but he moved into her path again.

"What about all you told me, your love for all life? How is this…how does this fit?"

Netra wavered, just for a second, then set her jaw. "I do this for life. *All* life."

"Are you sure?"

At that, Netra struck him. Across the face with the back of her hand. A trickle of blood appeared at the corner of his mouth.

"Please," he said. "You are not well."

"You said that already," she grated. "Now get out of my way."

Shorn took a deep breath, then shook his head. "I cannot let you do this."

"Wrong answer." Netra shoved him, putting everything she had into it. Shorn staggered backward, off balance, and she ran past him before he could recover.

A sentry dozing on top of a knob of rock saw Netra before she was halfway down the steep slope. He called out a warning and in one smooth motion brought his bow up, already bending it back.

Netra held out her hand and he froze, his eyes bulging. His mouth worked, but no sound came out. Netra curled her fingers and he collapsed like a puppet with its strings cut. The air between them shimmered as if from heat waves and Netra closed her eyes briefly, drawing in a deep breath, her arms coming up involuntarily. A gasp came from her as the full force of his Song entered her and then she laughed out loud.

It was amazing, beyond anything she had ever imagined. The Song she had been taking from the animals could not compare to this. Nothing could. His Song exploded within her, a brilliant burst that lit every corner of her being. She would not have been surprised to look down and find that her feet had left the ground. Such strength, such *power*. Why had she not done this before? She felt like a god.

Shouting voices intruded on her wonder and she opened her eyes, unaware of the cold smile that stretched her face. Below her the Crodin were swarming like ants, pouring out of their crude shelters, waving weapons, faces turned up to her. As they should. She stood so far above them, was so much more powerful than they were, that she felt she could reach out and scoop them up like toys. A few arrows flew towards her. The range was great and they were firing uphill, so most bounced harmlessly off the rocks around her. But one lucky shot stuck in her leg and she flinched as the pain intruded on her wonder. It was not deep and she bent and pulled it out easily, then watched as the wound began to close before her eyes, the torn edges drawing together.

Another arrow hissed by her ear and now she was angry. "You *dare!*" she shouted at them. "I am the chosen of the Mother! You strike at *her!*"

She began to run, each stride a superhuman leap that cut the distance between her and the Crodin with astonishing rapidity. Behind her, Shorn struggled to keep up, but his speed was no match for hers, and the slope was steep, the footing treacherous, so that he fell more than once and was far behind when she reached them.

Many of the Crodin threw down their weapons and turned to flee as what could only appear to their superstitious minds as an avenging god roared down the slope toward them. But others had more courage and continued to fire arrows and throw spears as she approached. One struck her solidly in the stomach and she cried out, but she did not stop, ripping the spear free as she advanced and flinging it down.

When she was only a few dozen paces away, Netra flung one arm forward with a scream of rage, releasing just a fraction of the Song she had taken. The air shimmered and a handful of Crodin were flung backwards, bones breaking, falling scattered across the desert floor. Now the rest of them panicked, fleeing in all directions while Netra waded among them, reaching out again and again, each one she chose falling bonelessly to the ground. It lasted only moments, but it seemed like hours and when it ended a dozen Crodin lay scattered around her. The rest had fled, dogs and goats with them. Hide tents lay on their sides and one body lay face down in the pool of brown water, unmoving.

Netra threw her head back and screamed, a triumphant, animal sound that made the fleeing survivors run harder. She glowed with a brightness that made it hard to look at her.

"I'm coming!" she yelled and, without a backward glance at Shorn, still struggling to catch up, she raced down the canyon and into the dunes. She moved with impossible speed and in less than a minute she was lost to sight.

Shorn reached the remains of the village and stood there for a moment, staring at the bodies. His face tightened and there was sorrow in his eyes.

Then he went to the pool of water, took a long drink, and refilled his water skins. Moving to one of the ruined shelters, he kicked through the tattered remains until he came up with a quantity of dried meat. He put some in his mouth, then took off after Netra, following the traces of her passage into the trackless wastes.

FORTY-NINE

Three thousand years ago

"We're not going to win this way," rumbled Sententu. The form he wore this day was like a man in some ways, but twice the height of any man, and seemingly cut from a slab of living white rock. He clenched his huge fists in frustration.

"The shield is too strong," agreed Gorim. His form was slightly shorter than Sententu, but reddish and broader, with fierce, craggy features and deep holes where eyes and nose should have been. "To destroy it we will crack this entire continent."

"So what?" interjected Khanewal. She favored female form, lithe and dusky-skinned, but she was clearly not human. Even if she had bothered to copy the human form exactly, there was something too sharp, too feral about her. "In the old days we tore these continents apart and put them back together for nothing more than our own amusement."

"The humans," Sententu replied. He did not need to say more. All the Shapers knew how Xochitl favored them. Sundering a continent would kill a great many of them and Xochitl would never allow it.

The Shapers stood on a low hill overlooking Durag'otal, a starkly beautiful city of multicolored stone. Graceful spires soared over gossamer stone bridges connecting high towers. Melekath had drawn on all his considerable power and skill to shape the perfect home for his Children, as he called those humans who had accepted his Gift.

Around the city shimmered a sphere of orange light that for three years had resisted everything the attackers had thrown at it. Even now a ring of lesser Stone Shapers surrounded the city and were throwing focused orbs of Stone power at the shield. Interspersed among them were a number of humans, males and females alike, who were pounding the shield with LifeSong. There were a great many humans engaged in the siege. They had come from far and near, answering Xochitl's call to war.

None of the attacks were having any effect on the glowing sphere. The lands around the city had suffered though. When the army led by eight of the most powerful Nipashanti—as those Shapers of the First Ring called themselves—had first arrived, the lands had been green and fertile, with a placid river and a thick, hardwood forest. It was a beautiful place. Melekath had chosen the site well.

Now the river was gray sludge that barely flowed. The forest had been burned to ash early on by an errant burst of power. The wildlife had long since fled and nothing green grew for miles in every direction.

Overhead several of the *aranti* raced and shrieked, drawn by the excitement as their kind always was. Before too long they would grow bored and leave, then be replaced by others who would also grow bored and leave. Alone of the Shapers the *aranti* had never warred. They angered easily, but soon forgot their anger and raced away. It took the slow, simmering rage of the *pelti*, the Shapers of Stone, and the powerful, swollen rage of the *shlikti*, the Shapers of Sea, to build and sustain a real war.

With the Shapers on the hill stood others: Protaxes, slender and regal, very like a human except for the gold cast to his skin; Tu Sinar, more like a blade than a human, all sharp edges and dour features; Golgath, the only one to come from the *shlikti*, changing as easily as the face of the ocean, one moment calm and pale, the next stormy and dark; and Bereth, standing on his four stout legs, his face hidden in shadow.

They all turned as Xochitl approached, in form a tall, graceful woman with alabaster skin. She could have passed for human except for the unnatural perfection of her beauty. With her came the one who called himself the Protector, Lowellin of the Second Ring. He looked more like a human than the rest of them, with smooth skin and long, unbound hair. Something frightening danced behind his eyes.

"You'll be bringing a solution," Khanewal declared sarcastically. "Something to keep the rest of us happy before we grow bored and leave."

"I don't know why we're here anyway," Protaxes said. "Melekath has harmed none of us."

"When Melekath first took from the three Spheres to make the new Circle of Life, he vowed that the theft was only temporary. 'All

Life dies,' he said. 'The life always dies and returns what was taken.' Yet now he has gone against this. This is why we are here. What he has done threatens all of us." Sententu towered over Protaxes, stabbing a finger the size of a small boulder at the smaller Shaper as he spoke to him. Protaxes fluttered his hands but spoke no more.

"The power for his shield comes directly from the Heart of Stone," Xochitl said. "I am certain of it now." All power that flowed through the Sphere of Stone originated from the Heart.

"Ever was he the most powerful among us," Gorim said. He sounded appreciative. He had sided with Melekath more than once in past wars.

"You are certain of this?" Sententu asked.

Xochitl nodded. "I went there. I *saw*. Lowellin will vouch. He accompanied me."

"He really did it," Khanewal said, looking at the city and smiling slightly. "I *am* impressed."

"Then there is nothing we can do," Protaxes said. The sunlight glinted off his gold skin, but then it always did. He was the vainest of all of them. "It is time for me to go then. Farewell, my brethren. I wish I could say it has been a pleasure." The stone at his feet liquefied and he began to sink into it.

"Hold!" Sententu barked, reaching out with one massive hand and grabbing the smaller Shaper. "We are not done here!"

Protaxes looked deeply offended and he raised his hands, Stone power beginning to glow there.

Quickly Xochitl stepped forward. "Let go of him, Sententu. Protaxes, this alliance is not yet at an end. There is still another option."

The two glared at each other, but Sententu released his hold and Protaxes lowered his hands, the Stone power dissipating. The alliance was fragile at best, held together largely by Sententu and Xochitl. Several times they had had to fetch those who had slipped away or break up conflicts before they became serious.

"We build a prison around him and his city," Xochitl said. "One he will never break out of."

"That's ridiculous," Protaxes retorted. "There is nothing on this world we could imprison him in that he could not eventually free himself from."

"There is one thing. We open the abyss, use chaos power," Xochitl said, looking at Bereth.

"Utter foolishness," Bereth hissed, shadows shifting around him. None ever saw his face. He made certain of that. "I am proof of that."

Khanewal laughed. "We could find the remains of Larkind if we need more convincing."

Eons before, Bereth and Larkind went too deep. At the center of the world they found an abyss filled with a chaotic power of a kind never seen before. They tried to shape it…with disastrous results.

"It is chaos, and it cannot be controlled," Bereth insisted. He was growing larger as he spoke, drawing stone from underfoot and pulling it into himself. He seemed to have more legs now, but the shadows were growing as well and it was hard to tell for sure.

"Because you were not prepared," Xochitl countered. "Lowellin and I have been studying this and we believe we have found a way."

"I will be no part of this," Bereth grumbled and walked away.

"We can do it without him," Lowellin said. He stood closest to Xochitl and there was something possessive in his manner. In all the wars, through all the shifting alliances, he had always stood with her. "If we only scratch the surface, just enough to release a tiny amount, and we all join our strength, we can control what spills forth. We shape it around Durag'otal, and then we seal the crack. Melekath will never be able to break through it."

"And everyone always says I have the bad ideas," Protaxes said sardonically.

"An eternal prison," Khanewal mused. She was smiling as she said it, clearly liking the idea.

"It had better work," Tu Sinar said, speaking for the first time. "If he ever gets free, he will show us no mercy."

"We can agree on that," Gorim said grimly.

Golgath had turned dark, tremors crossing his form like waves. In a voice that was surf and seagulls he said, "There is nothing else we could possibly shape that would hold one of the First Ring."

"It's risky—" Protaxes began.

"Do you ponder the risks to rising from your slumbers in the morning?" Khanewal asked sarcastically. "Do you shiver there, wondering whether to start with one foot or the other?"

"Enough!" Xochitl snapped before the argument could proceed, and Sententu added a warning growl. Both knew how fragile this coalition was. The First Ring had feuded for countless millennia. They could easily stand here for a hundred years trading barbs and not realize it. When life is endless, time means little. Yet Melekath would not waste that time. He would plan and he would act and they might not pin him again.

"It would solve many problems," Sententu conceded.

In the end they agreed because there were no better ideas. The lesser Shapers and the humans were ordered to cease their assault on the city, move back, and make ready to share their power. The rest lined up in front of the city, only a few dozen paces from the edge of the shield that protected it. Lowellin stood next to Xochitl.

"You are not beginning to doubt now, I hope," he said as the rest were moving into place. "You know there is no other way. What he has done threatens Life itself, and even the Spheres. If Life is allowed to spread unchecked, it will eventually consume everything."

"I know, I know," Xochitl said tiredly. It was a conversation they had had many times during the siege. "You are right, but that doesn't mean I have to like it."

"I only want to be sure you will not waver," Lowellin said.

"Your only concern is for them, right?" Xochitl said, gesturing to the humans. "This has nothing to do with your hatred toward Melekath?"

Lowellin stiffened. "If you think that my decision is—"

"Stop," Xochitl said, placing her hand on his arm. "I am sorry. I only want this to be over." She looked at the city. Sensing something different coming, a number of Melekath's Children had gathered near the shield and were watching intently. Something passed over her features and she turned her face away, not wanting to look at them.

Sententu stood in the middle of the line. At his signal, they bent and reached into the stone underfoot. It yielded before them as if it was only mud. Then they pulled back. A long crack opened, quickly growing deeper and wider while the earth groaned as it was torn apart. Down and down they went, opening a chasm around the city, its bottom far beyond the reach of sunlight. By then the inhabitants of the city had all gathered at the shield, staring on in fear and awe. Cries arose from some and Xochitl shuddered when she heard them, keeping her eyes averted.

The chasm deepened. Inside the city, the cries grew louder. A figure had appeared among the inhabitants. They beseeched him, some going so far as to pull on his robe, but he was staring fixedly at Xochitl. "Do not do this, Xochitl," he said, his voice cutting through the din. "I implore you."

Xochitl faltered and looked up into his gaze.

At that moment they broke through into the abyss. There was a shriek, followed by a whistling sound, and the ground tilted crazily beneath them.

"It's coming!" Protaxes yelled. The whistling noise was drawing closer fast.

It almost got away. Distracted by Melekath, Xochitl missed the first time she grabbed at the chaotic energy. It slipped through her grasp and surged upwards. At the last moment she was able to get a hold of it—drawing heavily on the Shapers and humans gathered behind her—and wrest it under control. Even as she fought to get it under control, she knew that some had gotten away, but there was no time to think of it now. Nor could she think of the people in the city who were screaming in terror, falling back as a wave of purple blackness boiled up out of the chasm.

The Shapers threw everything they were and everything they could get from the army behind them into hanging on. It was like trying to hold onto a flood. But somehow they did. Somehow they bent it to their combined will, just enough to divert the flood over the doomed city.

"Xochitl! Gorim! Help me seal the abyss!" Sententu roared.

As the others fought to hold back the flood of chaotic energy, the three Nipashanti jumped down into the chasm. For long moments they could not seal the abyss and the Nipashanti up above cursed and screamed, but at last they were able to close the crack they had made.

The whistling shriek died away and the Nipashanti fell back from the chasm. Xochitl had a long burn along one arm. Protaxes was unable to stand. Gorim was on one knee. For once Khanewal had nothing to say.

The purple blackness was spreading rapidly over the shield protecting the city. The people in the city were panicking, trying to flee. But it was too late. In moments the blackness covered everything, thinly at first, then thickening and hardening. In the last moments Xochitl looked up and saw Melekath staring at her. Then he was gone, the city of Durag'otal and its inhabitants sealed in blackness.

"It is flawed," Sententu said, pointing.

There was a hole, high up on one side.

"It was you," Lowellin said, turning on Xochitl. "He distracted you and you lost hold. Some got away and now the prison is incomplete." Xochitl lowered her head. "You did it on purpose," he whispered, his features twisted with rage.

"I will seal it," Sententu announced. The rest turned to him, surprised.

"You don't know what you're saying," Xochitl said. She was cradling her injured arm, but the pain in her eyes was not from that. "It is forever."

The massive Nipashanti shrugged. "I tire of this world. There is nothing left for me. It is decided."

"The Guardians escaped before the prison was complete," Gorim observed, looking off into the distance.

"It does not matter," Sententu replied. "They cannot help their master now." He walked to the prison wall and began to climb the side. Each time he touched the wall, his skin sizzled and he seemed to melt away, as if the wall was dissolving him. When he reached the opening, he paused for a moment, looking around at the world he had known for countless millennia. Then he began to lose shape, as if he was melting. He flowed into the hole, filling it.

"We need to sink this cursed place underground," Gorim growled. "I do not like to look upon it."

The Shapers spread out and encircled the city. They peeled the stone back and the prison began to sink out of sight. Only Lowellin was watching the opening that Sententu had filled. Only Lowellin saw something slip up the side of the prison and sink into Sententu's now-formless shape. He said nothing, a thoughtful look on his face.

FIFTY

"There it is," Rome said. It was about an hour after sunrise and the army, or at least part of it, had finally reached Guardians Watch. Most of the army was still strung out down the hill behind him. They'd marched through the night, stopping only for an hour around midnight, and the men were exhausted. Rome's horse stood with its head down. Quyloc's and Tairus' horses didn't look any better. There was an ache in Rome's lower back, courtesy of a spear he'd caught a few years back, and he wondered when he'd gotten so old. He felt like he could topple over and be asleep before he hit the ground.

To Rome's left was the long, high ridge of broken granite that sloped down from the Firkath Mountains, blue in the distance. To his right loomed the bulk of the Landsend Plateau. A mostly-intact stone wall stretched across the pass, which was about a hundred yards wide. On the left end of the pass stood a crumbling tower. The right end was a massive tangle of broken stone, with one huge stone about sixty feet across lying on the edge of it. That stone would be what Tu Sinar dropped on the fortress, once he decided his followers were betraying him. The rest of the stone was the remains of the fortress itself.

Enemy soldiers were visible on top of the stone wall. Not a large force, but enough to put up a fight.

"Looks like the brothers were right," Tairus said, his gaze taking in the enemy position. He yawned and rubbed his eyes as if he was having trouble focusing.

The brothers had reported back to Rome the day before near dusk. One minute Rome was riding along beside a double column of marching soldiers, thinking of Bonnie, and the next there was one of the brothers beside him, seemingly rising up out of the ground. It was the scarred one with the long beard. Was his name Clem? Rome was pretty sure he'd heard one of the brothers call him that a couple days ago. Sem, Rem, Tem, Clem and Lem. Those were the names he'd heard so far, though it wasn't always clear who was being referred to by what name. When Rome had remarked that all their names were pretty much the same, the gray-haired one—he thought it was Tem—told him their pa wasn't interested in wasting his time on names and ma was too busy being pregnant to care.

"You're slow," the scarred one drawled, spitting on the ground. "But it could be you'd make it before Kasai's army if you didn't sleep so much." He hitched his pants up and scratched an armpit. He, Rome and Tairus stood off to the side of the trail as the line of exhausted, footsore soldiers marched by. Three more brothers drifted up right then. There were a couple of small bushes nearby—the only things the brothers could have been hiding behind—but they sure didn't seem big enough. Whatever else they were, the brothers were good.

"What?" Tairus said, disbelieving. He turned on the scout. "We haven't stopped for more than four hours in three days!"

"Easy, Tairus," Rome said, putting a hand on his arm. Clem had not looked up at Tairus' outburst and looked, to all outward appearances, as if he hadn't even heard him. But Rome knew that looks could be deceiving. He remembered the long knife the man kept in his boot and how quickly he could draw it out.

"So the main forces haven't reached the pass yet?"

Clem was digging around in one filthy ear with a finger and appeared at first not to have heard him. He pulled something out of his ear and looked at it with interest before flicking it away. Rome heard Tairus curse under his breath and tightened his grip on the shorter man's arm. The brothers were impossible to work with, but they were very good at what they did. Their information had been spot on so far.

"No," Clem said. "They ain't there yet, but they're close. Probably get there about the middle of the day tomorrow. The ones who are there are holding the wall, waiting for you."

"I thought you were going to take care of them," Tairus said.

Clem finally looked at him. "Said we'd try. And we did. But they brought up more men. Built some big fires for light at night. We didn't sign on for soldiering, signed on for drink." He gave Rome a meaningful look.

Rome nodded. "I'll have some brought up." He turned to call for an aide but T'sim was already there, two clay jugs in his hands. The brothers perked up at that.

"What else can you tell me? Any sign of the Takare?" Rome asked.

Clem shook his head. "They gone to ground."

"Does Kasai have any scouts on this side of the pass?"

Clem gave him a flinty look. "I thought you said to kill them if they came through."

"I did."

"Well, then there ain't any." He looked at his brothers and hand signals flew. Rome had a feeling if he knew what they were saying about him he'd have to kill a couple of them.

"How about on that high ridge?" The high ridge Rome spoke of was the one that jutted north from the Firkath Mountains. It was already visible far ahead on the left. "Have any more tried to position themselves up there? They could see a long way from up there."

The youngest brother with the twin braids shook his head. "They found out it's too dangerous. Seems they kept falling off."

"Stay close," Rome said, as T'sim handed over the liquor. "I'll need you some more."

"We'll be by," Clem said laconically.

"Give a coyote call when you need us," twin braids—Rem?—put in. "That works."

"Idiot," another one said, poking him in the ribs. "Not a coyote. A hoot owl. That's our call."

"No it ain't. We voted and it's a coyote." They were still arguing as they moved off. Rome hadn't seen them since.

"If we don't take that position fast," Tairus said, "we've come a long way for nothing."

"We'll take it," Rome replied confidently. Privately he was somewhat concerned. Charging uphill, after marching so hard? It was a lot to expect from the soldiers. "Form up the men."

The FirstMother rode up then. "They won't be necessary."

Rome turned to her. "Who won't be necessary?"

"Your soldiers. My Tenders will handle this."

Rome looked at Tairus, who shook his head and frowned. Then he turned to look at Quyloc, sitting his horse on the other side of him. "What do you think?"

"We need to know what they can do. This could be a good chance for that."

"I know you think us helpless women," the FirstMother said stiffly.

"I've heard the reports," Rome said. "I have some idea what you're capable of. But practicing on a target is far different from real soldiers with real weapons."

"We killed the monster that rose out of the sea."

"I know you did. I hope you do as well here, I really do," Rome told her. "My men are tired and if we have to charge that wall, some of them will die, maybe a lot of them. I'd like to avoid that."

She stared at him as if gauging his sincerity, then nodded. "We will take care of this for you. Just give us a few minutes to feed our *sulbits*." She turned her horse and rode away, calling orders as she went.

"I almost feel sorry for those men," Tairus said, looking up at the wall.

"I don't," Quyloc said.

"I feel sorry for those shatren too. I hate watching them do that."

"I try not to," Rome said.

"Is this what the world is coming to?" Tairus asked. There was no answer to that.

A few minutes later Nalene and the other Tenders approached, their guards trailing them. By then Rome had all the soldiers who had made it this far formed up, facing the wall. Nalene looked at them and then gave Rome a sour look.

"You don't need them."

"I hope not. Better to have them and not need them, don't you think?"

When the order came from the FirstMother to line up, Larin turned to Haris.

"I can't do it," he said. "I'm too scared."

"Sure you can do it," Haris replied. "Just don't think about it too much. You ought to be good at that."

Larin shook his head. "I can't stop thinking about it."

"C'mon," Haris said, grabbing him by the elbow and propelling him forward to where the rest of the guards were starting to line up. "It won't be that bad. It's not gonna kill you."

"But I've seen what they do to the shatren," Larin moaned.

"They'll stop before that. The FirstMother said so."

Larin was still complaining when Haris pushed him into line. The Tender he'd been assigned to was named Donae. When he'd first been assigned to her, he'd thought that she was a fine looking woman, even with all her hair shaved off. Then she'd looked up, caught him staring and gave him a cold look that changed his opinion forever. He hadn't looked at her above her knees since then.

The FirstMother ordered them to advance and Larin and the other guards shuffled forward holding the shields up. Right behind him came Donae, so close she stepped on his heel. More than anything Larin wished she was far away. No, that wasn't right. More than anything he wished *he* was far away. He was so scared he was shaking.

It wasn't fair. No one told him when he signed up that some horrifying little beady-eyed creature was going to eat him. He wanted to bolt and run right then, but he was afraid to do that too. Probably the FirstMother would use her *sulbit* on him and he'd end up like all those poor, dead shatren.

It didn't make him feel better that the FirstMother had told them they would be all right. They'd just feel a little weak, she said. But it wouldn't hurt and they'd be in no danger.

He didn't believe her. There was something mean in her eyes and he'd seen firsthand how ruthless she was. If taking a little bit of his LifeSong—he had no idea what that was, just that he needed it to live—wasn't enough to kill the enemy, he had no doubt she'd order them all bled dry if that was what it took.

"Easy," Haris whispered, from his spot to Larin's left. "Just keep your shield up and hold fast. That's all you have to do."

Larin swallowed and tried to nod. It didn't sound all that easy to him. At least the men on the wall weren't shooting arrows at them. That had to count for something.

"Closer," the FirstMother called from her spot in the center of the line. "We're still too far away. And close up this line."

Larin shuffled forward, his heart pounding. He was sure he could feel Donae's *sulbit* staring at his back, probably licking its lips. Did it know it was about to eat him? Why had he ever left the farm?

"Stop. Meld with your *sulbits*," the FirstMother called.

Larin stopped and held his shield steady. He was sweating profusely. His vision had gone funny and he thought he might be about to pass out.

"Find your guard's flow and take hold of it."

Larin shot Haris a desperate glance. Haris tried to give him a reassuring smile but it was sickly and weak. He was afraid too.

Then all thoughts of fleeing were rendered moot as a sudden, sickening feeling washed over Larin. It was as if the ground disappeared beneath his feet and he was falling into a bottomless abyss. Light and hope disappeared and Larin threw out his arms, trying to find something, anything to grab onto. He thought he was screaming, but there was no sound.

Rome had heard reports of what the Tenders could do with their *sulbits*, but this was the first time he'd actually seen it himself and he was surprised.

The air shimmered as blue-white bolts of energy shot out from the Tenders. Every bolt struck home, ripping holes in chests and stomachs. Blood spurted everywhere. The men who were struck screamed and were thrown backwards, off the wall.

"Attack as you will!" the FirstMother screamed.

More bolts shot out, with the same deadly effect. Then more. The successive volleys were not as powerful, but it didn't really matter. They were still plenty powerful enough to kill.

In less than two minutes it was over. There were no more enemy soldiers on the wall. Even the ones on the tower had fled.

"Stand down!" the FirstMother yelled.

Slowly the gathered energy dissipated. The Tenders stood looking at each other in astonishment. Then the ranks of soldiers formed up behind them broke into cheers. Even Tairus joined in.

"Secure the wall!" Rome yelled, and the cheering died off as the men ran forward to take possession of the wall.

"What happened to them?" Tairus asked, just noticing the Tenders' guards. Some had managed to remain on their knees, but the rest were on the ground. One big fellow was curled up in the fetal position. A couple of them looked to be unconscious.

Rome looked at Quyloc, who said, "The Tenders used them."

"What do you mean, used..." Tairus broke off as the meaning came to him. "You mean...?"

"The power in those Song bolts had to come from somewhere."

"I thought that's why they had the shatren," Tairus said, his face darkening.

Quyloc shrugged. "I guess it's not enough."

"Did you know they were going to do that?" Tairus asked Rome.

"I never really thought about it."

"What are you going to do about it?"

"What do you want me to do about it? Force them not to do it? They just drove off the enemy and we didn't lose a single man."

"Unless some of those guards are dead."

"Even if some are, it's a lot fewer men than we would have lost." Rome sighed. "I don't like it any better than you do, but what choice do we have?"

"There has to be something. It's just not right, doing that to a man."

"Well, if you think of it, let me know," Rome said wearily, turning away.

Just then the FirstMother walked up. Her eyes were alight with victory. Her *sulbit* was standing on her shoulder, its beady eyes darting this way and that.

"I told you we could do it," she said triumphantly. "I told you."

"Well done, FirstMother," Rome said. "We'll take it from here." He gestured at the guards. "Are they going to be okay?"

The FirstMother turned and looked at them as if noticing them for the first time. She stared at them for a long moment, then said, "They just need some time to recover."

"Did you have to do that?" Tairus asked her.

"Do what?"

"Use them like that? Couldn't you have used shatren or something?"

Her tone grew very icy. "I understood that this was war, General. I understood that sacrifices had to be made. Was I incorrect?"

"Let it go, Tairus," Rome said.

"Couldn't you have used the flows from the enemy?" Quyloc asked.

"Don't you think I would have if I could?" she retorted. "We're not strong enough yet to reach that far. In time we will be, but we weren't given time."

She stalked away. Rome turned to Tairus. "Get some men up on that tower. I want to know how far away the rest of Kasai's army is. Put some men on building up the wall as much as possible." The wall was crumbly and in several places had mostly fallen down, but there were plenty of stone blocks lying around. "Send some men down the other side to chop down as many trees as they can. I want a clear field of fire for the archers."

To Quyloc he said, "Come with me. See that huge stone on the right? I'm thinking that would be a good vantage point from which to oversee the battle. Some archers would be good up there too."

When they were up on the block of stone they saw that the west side of the pass was much steeper than the way the Qarathian army had approached, and far more heavily wooded. Down in the valley beyond a cloud of dust was rising as thousands of soldiers marched toward them.

"Looks like we got here just in time. They'll be here before the end of the day."

Quyloc turned to look back at their own army, a long line of exhausted men strung out for several miles back the way they'd come. Then he turned back to Kasai's army. "There are a lot more of them than we expected."

Rome nodded. He'd noticed the same thing. "Do you think we can hold them?"

Quyloc shrugged. "This is a strong position. They won't be able to bring their full weight to bear on us."

"If only we knew what else Kasai is bringing to the party," Rome added, peering into the distance. "What is Kasai capable of? Will any of the other Guardians be here?"

FIFTY-ONE

It was late afternoon when Kasai's army finally reached the pass. The soldiers who had been chopping down trees ran to the wall, which had been patched as much as possible, and their comrades helped them climb up and over. Most of the rest of the Qarathian army had arrived by then and the top of the wall was packed with soldiers. Thousands more waited in reserve behind the wall. Without room to maneuver in the tight confines of this battlefield, the ranks of cavalry waited further back. The Tenders were positioned on the end of the wall near the crumbled tower, standing back for the moment to give the archers room to fire.

"Do you think they'll attack this late in the day?" Tairus asked. He, Rome and Quyloc were on top of the huge block of stone that lay across the north end of the pass, looking down on the battlefield.

"I guess we'll find out," Rome replied.

The answer came a few minutes later. There was no order given that anyone could hear; suddenly Kasai's soldiers just started running up the slope, jumping over recently felled trees and climbing over loose stones. They were eerily silent as they came, with none of the shouting or cursing that soldiers usually used to help prepare them to face death. Most of them were men, but quite a few were women and they were all ages, from twelve or so up to gray-haired. They had no uniforms and carried a motley assortment of weapons; some had no more than pitchforks or clubs. Only a few wore armor. There were no flags, no banners. The only thing they had in common were the black marks on their foreheads. They all seemed unnaturally pale and the black marks stood out starkly.

They had no order but attacked like a mob. Arrows flew out to meet them and they fell by the score, but the survivors did not slow; they simply jumped over the fallen and came on with silent ferocity.

"Whatever is behind them is more frightening than we are," Tairus remarked.

Though the arrows killed a great many, the attackers' numbers were not significantly reduced and it was a solid wave that crashed up against the wall. The archers on the wall stepped back and were replaced by soldiers bearing axes and swords. Heedless of their own lives, the attackers flung themselves at the wall. They had no need of ladders or grappling hooks. The stones that made up the walls were pitted by time and easy enough to climb, and in the places where the wall had crumbled, they didn't even need to do that, but could jump, grab the edge and pull themselves up. They died in greater numbers now, but still they did not hesitate.

Quyloc was watching the Tenders closely, the spear naked in his hand. He wanted to *see* what it was they did.

When the archers stepped back, the Tenders moved forward, their *sulbits* perched on their shoulders. None of their guards were with them; most were asleep in the Tender camp, the others too weak to do much of anything. But now the Tenders didn't need them anyway. There were plenty of enemy soldiers within easy reach.

The FirstMother called out an order, her words lost in the din of battle. Each of the Tenders reached out with one hand, grabbing hold of an attacker's flow.

Even from this distance, Quyloc could feel the buildup of energy as the Tenders bled Song. It was easy to see who they took the Song from; they faltered and stumbled as Song sustaining them was suddenly snatched away.

"Here it comes," Quyloc said.

The FirstMother shouted and a volley of Song bolts lanced out from the Tenders, tearing through the front wave of attackers as if they were made of straw. Those who were struck were lifted off their feet and thrown backwards into the ones running up behind them, slowing the attack on that whole side of the line.

More Song built up and a few seconds later another volley shot out, this one not as coordinated as the first, but no less deadly as two dozen more attackers were thrown backwards. Those that were not struck had difficulty continuing their advance, as they were either knocked back by the bodies, or tripped over the soldiers who were being bled by the Tenders, all of whom were now down on the ground, some of them unmoving, their *akirmas* now faded to a barely discernible glow.

There was a slightly longer pause before the next volley, as the Tenders reached for new flows to grab onto.

"I never thought I'd say this, but I wish we had a lot more Tenders," Quyloc said. "I wish we had a thousand of them."

"If Kasai's men had any sense at all," Rome said, "they'd bring up some archers and take the women down. But I don't see anyone in charge. They're a mob, not an army."

"That's good for us," Tairus said. "Maybe this won't be so bad after all."

No archers appeared, but a few minutes later others did.

Down the hill, out of bow range, five people appeared amidst the mob, all clad in gray robes with the hoods pulled over their heads. They spread out across the battlefield until they were equally spaced across the entire width, facing the wall. Wooden platforms were brought forward and each gray-robed figure stepped onto one. Surrounding soldiers lifted them into the air and supported them on their shoulders. The robed figures raised their hands in the air.

"I take back what I said. I have a bad feeling this is all about to get a lot worse," Tairus said.

"I believe those are the blinded ones," Quyloc said.

Their hands burst into gray flames.

"Get word to the Tenders to target them," Rome said to Nicandro, who was waiting nearby. A chain of messengers had been set up ahead of time, one at the top of the ladder that had been set up to allow access to the top of the block of stone, and others stretched across the line behind the wall.

"No need," Quyloc said. "She sees them."

The FirstMother had ceased her attacks and was staring down the hillside. She turned her head, clearly giving orders to the other Tenders, and others raised their heads to look at the gray-robed figures as well. By then the gray flames had spread, down the robed figures' arms, over their torsos, and down their legs, completely covering them. They were only hazily visible behind the flames.

Song bolts shot out at the robed figures—

And sizzled harmlessly in the flames.

"Why did I have to say anything?" Tairus groaned. "Aren't these guys known for burning people?"

The gray flames continued to spread, reaching out to the sides of the robed figures. The enemy soldiers touched by the flames were not affected. Soon the flames had spanned the distance between the robed figures and connected in a solid wall of flame. The flames grew stronger, higher, the wall extending upwards, reaching a height of ten, then twenty feet. Now there was a solid wall of gray flames stretching clear across the battlefield.

The robed figures thrust their hands forward…

And the wall of flame began to move up the slope toward the wall.

Rome turned to Quyloc. "I need ideas. How do we counter this?"

Quyloc didn't answer at first. Then he said, "Unless the Tenders come up with something, there isn't anything we can do except run."

"That's it? The best you have is run away?"

"Or we could stand and die. When those flames hit our soldiers, they're going to burn. There's no way to fight that."

"There has to be something else we can do." Rome walked over to the edge of the stone and looked down. "If we could take out the ones causing it…"

Quyloc knew Rome well enough to know what he was thinking of. "Don't do it," he said, grabbing Rome's arm. "It must be a twenty foot drop at least. If you don't break a leg jumping down there, you'll never fight your way through all those soldiers in time."

"Shall I give the order to retreat?" Tairus asked. At the speed the flames were moving, they'd be on the wall in less than a minute.

"Wait," Quyloc said. "The FirstMother may come up with something."

Rome looked at the wall of flames, then at the defenders, gauging the distance between them. "We'll hold as long as we can."

"Send word to have every available archer focus their fire on the enemy in front of the Tenders," Quyloc said. "They can't do much if they have to concentrate on defending themselves."

"Cease fire!" Nalene yelled. She'd noticed that all the archers were firing at the enemy before them. Rome was giving them breathing room to try and find some way to defeat the robed figures. But what could they do? It was clear that none of their Song bolts were strong enough to pierce the flames. She'd even taken hold of two flows at once to see if she could bleed off enough power to get through. Her hands felt burned from the effort.

Her mind raced as she considered possibilities and discarded them. The wall of flames wasn't very thick. Beyond it the air was clear. If only they could get past it and then attack the robed ones, the bolts would probably work; the robed ones were no longer sheathed in flames.

The flames were getting closer. Already she could feel the heat on her skin, like getting too close to a bonfire. Emboldened by it, Kasai's soldiers were attacking even more fiercely, while the defenders were glancing at each other nervously. Many were looking to the their macht, waiting for the order to retreat. Nalene could sense their fear and desperation. If the order didn't come soon, they were going to break and run.

What if she used Song to protect them? The Tenders of old had been capable of doing such a thing, their wills so strong they could contain free Selfsong in a bubble around them.

Which didn't mean she could do it. Was she strong enough? Was her control good enough? She'd spoken to Lowellin about it, but he'd said she wasn't ready to try it. If she faltered in the slightest, all that energy would get loose at once and she—and everyone near her—would probably be killed.

But what other choice did she have?

The Tenders were all looking to her, waiting for her to tell them what to do. They were frightened, close to fleeing themselves. Time was running out.

Mulin and Perast both stood to her immediate right. She turned to them and quickly told them what she planned. They looked shocked, uncertain, but both nodded.

"Bleed off as much Song as you can and direct it to Mulin and Perast!" she shouted at the others. "Grab two flows at once if you can. Don't hold back."

Moments later Song began to rush into the two Tenders. "Don't try to hold onto it," she told them. "Release it into the air in front of you, in as fine a stream as you can manage."

When they released the Song, she was ready. With the help of her *sulbit*, Nalene corralled the streams of energy, picturing her will as a bubble extending completely around her Tenders. It was dizzying, trying to hold onto so much power at once, and she had to fight for balance as she was stretched beyond anything she thought she was capable of. She had to completely tune out everything happening around her and focus everything she had on keeping the free Song contained.

When the wall of flames was a dozen feet away, one end—the end opposite the Tenders—skipped forward suddenly, enveloping dozens of Qarathian soldiers. Instantly, they burst into flames. Screaming, arms flailing, they staggered back, spreading the flames to their comrades and spreading panic to every soldier on the wall.

The Qarathian army abandoned its position and began to flee. Kasai's soldiers surged after it with a shout of triumph, hacking and stabbing at the fleeing men.

FIFTY-TWO

The flames roared and crackled and the heat grew ever more intense as the wall of fire drew closer. It felt to Nalene like her skin was starting to blister. The pain intensified to the point where she began to lose her focus and when that happened, her control slipped. A rip appeared in the bubble she'd erected and Song began to spray out wildly. The rip widened quickly. Imminent disaster loomed.

Then all at once a steadying hand reached in, helping her. It was Bronwyn, standing to Nalene's left. The tall young woman's teeth were bared as she poured everything she had into closing the rip.

The heat diminished, but Nalene knew the barrier was not yet strong enough. If would evaporate when the flames touched it, like a drop of water on a hot skilled. "More," Nalene gasped to Mulin and Perast. "Give me more."

More Song poured into the air around them as Nalene and Bronwyn clamped down on the barrier with their wills. Nalene braced herself for the impact.

A heartbeat later the wall of flames struck the barrier. The force of it was such that Nalene nearly lost her hold and again it was Bronwyn's steadying strength that saved her. It wasn't much, just enough to tip the scales in her favor.

The pressure from the flames built; Nalene could feel it on her eardrums, as if she were deep underwater. Even through the barrier the heat was incredible. Several of the Tenders cried out. Under the onslaught, the barrier began to fray rapidly, tiny holes appearing in it. Gray flames leapt up on Nalene's sleeve and she slapped at them, further loosening her control. In seconds the barrier would collapse completely.

Then, all at once, the flames passed.

"Stop," Nalene gasped. The Song coming from Mulin and Perast stopped. Nalene released the barrier, straightened and looked around.

The gray wall was now behind them. On all sides enemy soldiers were surging over the wall, butchering everyone they could reach.

The enemy soldiers who had been held back by the barrier charged at the Tenders. Most of the archers who'd been firing at them had fled.

A huge man with a mace ran at Nalene. The weapon came crashing down at her head…

If she'd hesitated for even a heartbeat, she would have been killed.

She threw up one hand. A Song bolt exploded out of it, hitting the man in the face. Blood and fragments of bone sprayed everywhere. He was knocked backward.

Around her Song bolts exploded on all sides, tearing into the soldiers bearing down on them. One Tender was too slow and she screamed as a sword chopped away most of her arm. She went down and the Song built up inside her exploded outwards in every direction, knocking several other Tenders down.

Utter chaos reigned, as Tenders were forced back as far as they could go, firing wildly into the mass of soldiers the whole time. Some went to their knees, firing blindly.

Nalene hit another man with a bolt in the hip. A fist-sized chunk of flesh was torn away and the impact spun him halfway around, but he didn't drop and somehow continued forward, half-falling against her so that she staggered back and almost fell off the wall.

Near panicking, Nalene grabbed flows with each hand, paying no attention to whose they were, and began to spray stolen Song indiscriminately in front of her. It came out as a narrow band of pure energy and she scythed it side to side. A woman with a short sword was cut in half. Another man lost both legs in a spray of blood.

A moment later Nalene realized there was a gap in the enemy in front of her. She had breathing room.

Panting, she looked around. The carnage was unbelievable. Corpses lay everywhere on the wall around them and piled up at the base of it. More were already coming, but they still had to climb the wall. That gave them a few precious seconds and she knew she had to take advantage of it.

Ignoring the oncoming soldiers, she turned to Mulin and Perast.

"Target the robed ones!" Nalene shouted to them. "You too!" she said to Bronwyn.

Then she once again grabbed onto two flows, bleeding the Song off them greedily. Fear had turned to rage and all she wanted in the world right then was to see the robed ones dead.

It was the worst defeat Rome had ever witnessed. His army was in complete rout. But what else could they do? How could a soldier fight a flaming wall? Horrified by the men they saw burning, and infected by the panic of those who fled the wall, the soldiers held in reserve behind the wall simply turned and scattered, many of them throwing down their weapons as they ran.

"What's that?" Tairus said, pointing.

Rome looked up from the devastation and felt a glimmer of hope. Around the Tenders was a bubble of flickering golden light. He held his breath as the wall of flames struck the bubble—would it hold?—then pumped his fist in the air as the flames parted around it.

The gray flames passed over the Tenders and as it did he could see that the Tenders were still alive. A moment later the bubble flickered and disappeared.

The enemy soldiers who had been held back by the barrier charged forward and Rome held his breath as they struck the Tenders' fragile line. To survive the flames only to perish like that...

But somehow, in the midst of the chaos, Song bolts continued to flash out from the Tenders, just barely keeping the enemy back. Still, he didn't see how they could survive long when suddenly from the FirstMother came a bolt of glowing power that didn't flash and disappear like the rest. Instead it held steady and as the FirstMother swept it back and forth it caused terrible destruction to the enemy, so much that an opening ten or fifteen feet wide appeared front of her.

"Hit the ones in robes," Rome urged her. "Come on."

As if she heard him, the steady bolt went out. She turned to the Tenders on either side of her and shouted something.

Moments later the FirstMother fired, the bolt larger than any Rome had yet seen. It struck the robed figure in the middle with such force that he practically disintegrated. One moment there was a person there, hands held out, a line of gray flame running from him to the wall of flames...

And the next he was a spray of bloody flesh.

The whole middle section of the wall of flames flickered and went out.

A heartbeat later bolts struck three more of the robed figures and all three were killed. One more bolt from the FirstMother and all the blinded ones were dead. The wall of flames collapsed completely.

The wall of gray flames was gone, but most of Qarath's forces didn't know it and continued to flee. The mounted soldiers, positioned further back, fought to hold their formations but the flood of fleeing soldiers was too great. Making it worse was the fact that their horses could sense the chaotic energies seething nearby and many reared and snorted with fear. Some bucked their riders off and fled as well, trampling men as they went.

Rome stared down at the chaos, his fists clenched. There was nothing he could do from here. The army he had worked so hard to build, that he had marched so far, was dissolving before his eyes. Even if Kasai's soldiers could somehow be driven back—and the Tenders were once again busy cutting down large numbers of them in the area around them—soon his men would be so scattered it would be impossible to reassemble the army.

Then he noticed something. Dargent and the other mounted soldiers with him—a force consisting of noblemen's sons hoping for glory and hired guards—were not caught in the rush of fleeing men. They had been stationed on higher ground on the left wing and so were out of the path of the stampede.

As Kasai's soldiers passed below Dargent and his men, Dargent raised his sword, shouted, and plunged down the hillside into the flank of the enemy, all his men following. There were no more than a hundred of them, but they cut deep into the enemy's flank, slashing through them and cutting them down like wheat.

Caught off guard, Kasai's soldiers offered almost no resistance to the mounted and armored men who hacked at them mercilessly. The enemy's charge faltered and for a moment all hung in balance. They had Dargent's force vastly outnumbered and if they'd had a true leader to rally them, they could have quickly surrounded them and crushed them, but they were largely untrained conscripts, farmers and townsfolk forced to fight by fear, while Dargent's force were, one and all, well-trained and well-equipped. As nobility they had benefitted from the best training since boyhood and the hired guards were the best money could buy, the horses all well-trained as well.

Dargent's men cut them down furiously and suddenly the whole flow of the battle changed. Like a fear-maddened animal, Kasai's forces turned and ran back the way they had come.

Hearing the shouts behind them change, Qarath's fleeing forces turned, saw what was happening, and joined in, falling on and slaughtering those too slow to make it back through the pass in time.

Now a different danger loomed. In their battle madness and lust for revenge, Qarath's forces chased the enemy back through the pass and would have pursued them down the far side as well, into the trees. But Rome could see what they could not: those that fled were only a small part of Kasai's army. The bulk of it was still down there, moving forward. If they continued their pursuit, they would run into the rest of that army. Disorganized as they were now, they would be mauled.

Tairus and Quyloc realized the danger at the same time and all of them began shouting orders. Horns were blown, calling the soldiers to return to their lines.

It was close, and a few hundred men—mostly levies from the conquered cities who were not as well-trained—continued on down the hill, but the rest slowed, then stopped and returned to their places.

FIFTY-THREE

Rome wiped the sweat from his forehead and turned to Tairus and Quyloc.

"That was way too close."

"I thought we were done for," Tairus said. "If the Tenders hadn't done…whatever it is they did, we'd all be running for Qarath right now."

Rome clapped Tairus on the back. "And if it wasn't for your brilliance, posting Dargent and his men in that spot…"

Tairus' bearded face split in a grin. "Brilliance?" he snorted. "I just wanted to keep them out of the way. I figured they were useless."

Rome turned to Nicandro. "Get me Dargent up here. I want to talk to him." Nicandro saluted and ran off.

Rome turned to Quyloc. "Did you know the Tenders could do that?"

Quyloc shook his head. "I have read that they were once able to, but I had no idea they could do it now. My guess is they didn't know they could do it either, until just now."

"I think we're going to have to be nicer to the FirstMother from now on, don't you?" Rome walked over to the edge of the stone and looked down to the west. Dust hung in the air from those elements of Kasai's army that were yet to make it to the pass. He looked at the sun. It was still almost two hours until sunset.

"Do you think they'll attack again today?"

Tairus shrugged. Quyloc said, "I think it is clear that the enemy we are facing will not respond in the ways we expect. We need to remember that they are led by a creature that is millennia old, who thinks nothing like we do, and has no qualms about wasting however many men it takes to achieve its goals."

"So you think they'll attack."

"I think no possibility should be discarded."

"I sure hope they don't attack. The men are exhausted."

The Qarathian army resumed its positions. Dargent climbed the ladder and walked over to them. There was blood on his armor and something different in his manner that Rome noticed right away. He'd seen it before in men who survived their first battle. It wasn't something you ever got completely over.

Rome stuck out his hand. "Congratulations, Dargent. You and your men came through when we needed it most."

For a moment Dargent looked at his hand and Rome thought his habitual sneer would return to his face, but then he reached out and took it. "Thank you."

"In recognition of your efforts, I am giving you a battlefield commission, Colonel Dargent, and naming you commander of your men. We'll discuss the permanence of your rank later, but for now you are in charge of them."

Dargent nodded, looked like he was about to say something, then just turned and walked away.

"Maybe some of them aren't so bad," Tairus said as Dargent climbed back down the ladder.

"We just have to break some of their bad habits," Rome said. "But there's hope."

The three men stood there watching and waiting, then, as the sun moved toward the horizon and Kasai's army reformed down the slope, just out of bowshot.

"It feels to me like they're waiting for something," Tairus said.

"And there it is," Quyloc replied, pointing.

The ranks parted as a small group of people came forward through Kasai's army. There were no more than a score of them and they did not look dangerous. They bore no weapons, wore no armor. They were a mixed group, males and females, some looking to be as young as ten, others clearly well into old age. Despite the growing chill, they were barefoot, dressed in ragged clothing. Some of the men were shirtless. Their skin was very pale and on their foreheads the black marks stood out starkly.

"What's this all about?" Rome wondered.

"There's something wrong with them," Quyloc muttered. He had the spear bare in his hand and his eyes had a distant, unfocused look in them. "I don't know what it is, but I can feel it."

"Pass the word to the archers," Rome said to Nicandro. "I don't want them getting any closer."

Before Nicandro could respond, the Tenders did. They reached out and began to bleed off Song, readying for a new attack.

"No!" Quyloc suddenly yelled. "Don't do it! Hold off!"

But it was too late.

Song bolts lanced out from the Tenders, striking the ragged band. They fell quickly, just a handful of dead bodies on a slope covered with them.

"Whatever Kasai had planned there, it didn't work," Tairus observed.

Quyloc groaned. "But it did. It worked exactly as Kasai planned. Look."

There was something wrong with the Tenders. They were staggering about, bumping into each other. Several of them fell down. Two began to vomit uncontrollably. Even the FirstMother was bent over. In less than a minute all the Tenders were down. The soldiers on either side of them drew back in alarm.

"What just happened?" Rome asked.

"I don't know for sure," Quyloc replied. "But if we don't find some way to help them, we just lost our best defense."

"Let's get those women back to their camp!" Rome yelled to the soldiers who were nearest the Tenders, while heading for the ladder.

When some of them hesitated, Quyloc yelled, "They're not contagious." He was right behind Rome and they were quickly down off the stone and making their way through the mass of soldiers toward the far end of the wall.

When they got there, men were carrying the unconscious women and helping the others off the wall. Except for the FirstMother, who was climbing down off the wall on her own.

"Let me help you," Rome said, trying to take her arm.

She pushed him away. "I don't need help."

"What happened?"

"I don't know. They were poisoned somehow. The poison fed back up through the Song bolts." She didn't look good. She was swaying. Her skin was very red and blisters were already forming. Her *sulbit* looked worse. It was shivering uncontrollably and there was foam coming out of its mouth. Its skin had turned a jaundiced yellow.

The Tenders were camped on the army's right flank, amidst the debris from the crushed fortress, up against the huge block of stone from which Rome had watched the first battle. The camp was partially screened from the rest of the army by a line of bushes. In a few minutes all the Tenders were in their camp, stretched out on their blankets. The FirstMother was sitting on hers, cradling her *sulbit* in her lap.

"Hold on," Rome told her. "We have a healer coming."

"He won't be able to help." She seemed to gag on something, then began coughing and spat on the ground. "We need Lowellin."

"I'll see if T'sim can find him," Rome said.

But there was no need. Out of nowhere, Lowellin was there. He stood over the FirstMother and looked down on her. She seemed unaware of his presence, she was so sick. Her eyes were closed and she was shaking. Her blisters were visibly worse.

"How do we heal them?" Quyloc asked Lowellin.

"The only thing that might work is clean Song. Lots of it. It might flush the poison out of them."

"I don't understand—" Rome began, but Quyloc got it instantly. He turned to Rome.

"We have to let the *sulbits* feed on the men. That's the only way we can get enough Song to do this."

"No," Rome said, automatically repulsed by the thought. "I can't order them to do that."

"Then they'll die and so will your only hope of beating Kasai," Lowellin said coldly.

"There has to be another way."

"I know how you feel," Quyloc said. "I don't like it either."

"I've seen those things feed. Without the women to control them, they'll feed until death."

"Without these women, many of your men would already be dead," Lowellin said ruthlessly. "You know this to be true."

"But this is suicide."

"I don't like agreeing with him," Quyloc said. "But he's right. We have to have those women. They're the only reason we're still in this fight." When Rome still hesitated, he added, "At least ask them. Give them a chance to volunteer."

Rome thought about it, looking around at the other Tenders. They didn't look like they had long. On some the blisters were the size of a fist and a few had burst and were leaking yellowish fluid. Over half were unconscious. Their *sulbits* crawled over them, making painful mewling sounds. As he watched, one went into convulsions.

"Okay," he said. "I'll ask them." As he started to walk away, Lowellin did as well. "Where are you going?" he asked him. "Aren't you going to stay and help?"

"I've already risked too much by coming here. Kasai may have sensed my presence already."

"Are you that afraid of him?"

"You're an idiot. Haven't you ever heard of the element of surprise? Do you want Kasai to report to Melekath that I am helping you? Do you think that will make it easier to defeat him?" He stalked off before Rome could reply.

Rome hurried to the wall and climbed up on it. "The Tenders are sick," he called out, loud enough that the soldiers on the wall and those waiting in reserve behind the wall could hear him. "I think they're dying."

A numbed silence spread over the soldiers at his words.

"We might be able to save them though. It's not for sure, but it's a chance." He took a deep breath. "They need clean Song to wash out the poison. The short of it is this: their *sulbits* need men to feed on."

He barely had the words out of his mouth before dozens of men were putting up their hands and stepping forward.

"I have to warn you, you may die."

"I'd be dead already if it wasn't for them," said Felint, who'd pushed his way to the front. Others voices echoed his sentiment.

A long line of men followed Rome back to the Tender camp. "Here they are," he told Quyloc. "What do we do now?"

"We start with the FirstMother. We're going to need her." Nalene was no longer sitting up, but lying flat on her back. Her breathing was shallow.

"Come here," Rome said to Felint. "You better sit down."

The old veteran unbuckled his sword belt and laid it down. He seemed steady, calm. He sat down on the ground beside Nalene. Rome crouched down beside him.

"Are you sure you want to do this?"

"Whatever happens," he replied, "it was my choice."

"Put your hand on her *sulbit*," Quyloc told him.

Felint leaned forward and put his hand on the creature, which was lying still on the FirstMother's chest. At first the thing didn't respond, and Rome wondered if it was already too late. But then it twitched. Its head came up and swiveled around. The tiny mouth opened and latched onto Felint's hand.

Felint went rigid at the contact. "Oh," he said softly.

As the *sulbit* fed on him, Felint's eyes rolled back in his head and he flopped over on his side. He began twitching, his legs kicking out.

After a minute his twitching stopped and he went very still.

"That's enough! He's going to die!" Rome grabbed onto Felint and tried to pull him back, but when he touched him a powerful shock went through him. He tried to jerk away and realized he couldn't let go. A terrible feeling went through him. He felt as though he was falling into a bottomless pit. A sense of desperate emptiness enveloped him. He could see Quyloc reaching for him, but his friend seemed very distant and small. He couldn't speak.

Then he was free and lying on his back, gasping. Quyloc was bent over him, the spear in his hand. Quyloc helped him sit up.

"What did you do? How did...?"

"I used the spear to break the connection."

Rome remembered Felint suddenly and rolled up onto his knees. The old veteran was laying nearby, his eyes open and staring sightlessly at the sky. A heaviness settled on Rome. "I'm sorry," he whispered, closing his eyes.

"It's working," Quyloc said. "Look."

Rome turned to the FirstMother. Quyloc was right. Her breathing was better and the blisters had begun to recede. Much of the yellowness was gone from the *sulbit*'s skin. She turned her head to the side and her eyes opened.

"Where...?" she murmured.

"She needs more," Quyloc said, waving the next soldier in line forward. He was a young man, with a pale wisp of a beard and narrow shoulders and he hesitated, but then he clenched his fists and came forward.

"Let me go next," Rome said, trying to move over and sit beside the FirstMother. But he was weak as a kitten and Quyloc easily pushed him back.

"Don't be ridiculous. We can't take a chance on losing you."

"He's right, Macht," the young soldier said. "Be no army without you."

So Rome had to sit and watch while the drama repeated itself. But this time the FirstMother was conscious while it was happening, and when the young soldier flopped onto his side she grabbed onto her *sulbit* with one hand.

"Stop," she told it, then repeated it more loudly. Reluctantly, the creature let go. Quyloc motioned to a couple of soldiers and they dragged the young soldier off to the side. His eyes were closed, but he was still breathing.

The FirstMother sat up. The blisters were mostly gone and her breathing sounded normal. "One more," she said. When the next soldier in line didn't move fast enough she snapped at him, "Quickly! We have to help the others!"

She pulled her *sulbit* away before the man was unconscious and pushed herself to her feet. Her color was again normal and her *sulbit* had resumed its ivory hue. She turned toward the waiting soldiers. "One of you to each Tender. Now!"

They nearly tripped over each other, hurrying to obey. "You know what to do!" she called out to them.

"One at a time would be better," Rome said, standing and moving up to her. "That way—"

"Get out of my way," she snapped. "I don't have time to argue with you. I'll save as many as I can. That's the best I can do." She hurried over to one of the unconscious women.

"I'll do what I can too," Quyloc said. "Maybe you should go lie down. You don't look well."

"I'm not going anywhere until this is done."

Quyloc shrugged and walked off.

Rome stayed until the end. It hurt to watch, but he didn't look away. Despite Quyloc's and the FirstMother's efforts, a half dozen men died saving the Tenders.

"But only one of the Tenders died," Quyloc said, as they walked away from the Tender camp. The sun had gone down. Fires were burning around the Qarathian camp. The silhouettes of men on the wall on watch were visible against the starry sky. "That's what matters."

"I know you're right," Rome replied. He felt mostly normal once again, though terribly tired. "But it doesn't feel that way."

As they passed by one of the fires a soldier called out to him. "Are they going to be all right, Macht, the Tenders?"

Rome walked over to the fire and looked down at the men sitting around it. "We only lost one. But not all of the soldiers survived." He started to say something more, but the man spoke first.

"That's war for you. Some die. It ain't the worst way to go, is it? They died to save a lot of people. We'd have already lost if it wasn't for them women." The other soldiers nodded their agreement.

Rome just stared at them for a moment, then turned away.

"See?" Quyloc said. "I told you so."

FIFTY-FOUR

It was late in the day and Netra was in the heart of the Gur al Krin. Huge red and orange sand dunes loomed all around. The wind had died, but earlier the gusts had been fierce and twice she had seen whirlwinds of fire in the distance, though they had not come close to her. She was in an area where the dunes gave way to a large, flattened area, almost a depression. Huge stones were sprayed around a gaping crater in the ground; clearly something of great size and power had burst up from underneath. The stones were too regular to be natural.

She walked to the lip of the crater and looked down. No light made it to the bottom. She looked around, wondering why the Mother had come to this place. Had she been checking on the prison? Had Melekath lured her here?

Come to me, my daughter, my chosen. Quickly. Free me and we will defeat Melekath together.

The urgency in the Mother's voice went through Netra like a jolt of electricity. Her questions forgotten, she began her descent.

Far behind her, still lost in the distance, but slowly closing the gap, came Shorn, his head down, running through the heavy sand with his tireless gait. He had lost Netra's tracks long ago, when the wind started blowing, but strangely he had found he did not need them. He could *feel* which way she had gone. It was as if they were connected on some level he could not fathom. Perhaps it was a result of when she saved his life.

Ultimately, though, it did not matter. What mattered was that he be there. She was going to need him. He knew it as surely as he had ever known anything in his life.

He would not fail her.

FIFTY-FIVE

Nalene awakened the next morning with a headache. She sat up. The sun was not yet up, but it was light. She looked at her *sulbit* and was surprised at how much bigger it was. Its body was thick enough that she would have had trouble encircling it with both hands. Its head wasn't as blunt, a narrow snout starting to emerge. Its legs and tail were longer too. It looked somewhat like a hairless rat, but with no ears and the toes on its front legs were so long they were almost fingers.

It must have been all the Song that made it grow so much. Not for the first time she wondered what it would become when it finished growing. She shook the thought away and got up. There were bigger things to worry about now.

Other than the headache, she felt surprisingly good. There was no sign of the poison at all. She thought of the man who had died to save her and felt a stab of guilt that made her angry. He was a soldier. It was his job to die if necessary. Her death would have been a terrible defeat in the battle against Melekath. All that mattered was winning the war, not who died along the way.

But for some reason he made her think of Lenda and she could not escape the feeling that if she'd only been smarter, what happened to both could have been avoided. She should have known Lenda was too weak for a *sulbit*. She should have known those people were poisoned.

She saw the tall young Tender, Bronwyn, sit up, rubbing her eyes, and she walked over to her. "You did well yesterday," she said. "Without your help I would have dropped the barrier."

Bronwyn stood up. "Thank you, FirstMother."

"You're stronger than the rest of them, except for perhaps Mulin. Stay close to me. I may need you again."

"I am only happy to serve, FirstMother."

One of the guards came running up then. "They're coming again," he said simply.

"Get them up," Nalene told Bronwyn. Bronwyn hurried off, calling to the others, shaking those who were slow to move.

Nalene looked up. Looming over the Tender camp was the huge block of stone that Rome commanded from. She could just see several figures on it. Off to the left, past a line of low shrubs, was the wall. Soldiers were clustered on top of it. She saw archers bend their bows and release.

She lowered her defenses and melded with her *sulbit*. With its help she stretched out her inner senses toward the battlefield, wanting to know what awaited them, if there were any more blinded ones approaching.

What she sensed made her heart start pounding suddenly.

A Guardian had come.

"What in Gorim's blackest nightmare is that?" Rome said.

Something had appeared in the fringe of the forest, shouldering aside full grown trees as if they were saplings. The grating crunch of stone on stone accompanied its movements. Rome's first thought was that if a granite boulder was shattered, and then the pieces put back together very roughly, it would look like this, a thing made from shards of broken stone. Its fists were the size of a man's torso, its head the size of a boulder. A deep gash ran diagonally across its rough features, cutting across one deep set eye. From the depths of the gash came the reddish glow of molten rock.

"From its appearance, I think that is Tharn, the Guardian known as the Fist," Quyloc said.

Kasai's soldiers scrambled to get out of its way and those who were too slow were stepped on as the thing made its way uphill toward the wall.

Arrows and spears arced out from the wall as Tharn drew near, but they had no effect. The soldiers massed on the wall shifted nervously and more than one looked to their leader up above.

"It looks like it's made out of stone," Tairus said.

"Stone is good," Rome said, an idea forming. "I have something that works on stone."

"Get up, get up!" Nalene was yelling. "A Guardian is coming!"

The rest of the Tenders were scrambling to their feet, gathering in a loose group near Nalene. They were wild-eyed, close to panicking. Nalene felt the same way herself. The sense of hatred radiating off the creature, even from a distance, was nearly overwhelming.

"Break into four groups! Meld with your *sulbits* and bleed off as much Song as you can! Hold for my command!" she shouted at the Tenders. She pointed at Mulin, Perast and Bronwyn. "You three up here with me!" To the guards milling around she said, "Stand close to your assigned Tenders!"

The Tenders and guards were just reaching their assigned places when the end of the stone wall nearest them essentially exploded, shards and chunks of stone flying everywhere. Soldiers screamed as they were tossed into the air like rag dolls. When the debris settled enough to see, there was a gaping hole in the wall.

Nalene spun. "Tharn," she whispered.

Tharn stomped through the gap, enemy soldiers surging in its wake. It paused in the opening for a moment, the massive, lumpy head swiveling side to side. The lone remaining eye found the Tenders and fixed on them.

"Tenders!" it roared, its voice easily carrying across the din. "Time to die!"

Several of the Tenders bolted, but the rest held firm, though they fell back several steps.

"Give us all you have!" Nalene screamed.

The Tenders began recklessly bleeding Song off the guards' flows, so much that within a couple of seconds every one of the guards was on the ground. Song began to stream from the Tenders to Nalene and the three others standing in front with her. She shot them a sideways look. "Don't release until I tell you to."

Nalene felt her skin tingling as the Song diverted to her increased with each passing second. It was more than she'd expected and at first she worried that she couldn't control it. But there was no time for caution. They would get only one chance and they had to make it count. Nalene fought to tune out the fast-approaching Tharn, the screams of dying soldiers, the frightened women around her, focusing everything on keeping her grip on the Song.

But even as the power built, she knew that no matter what they did, it would not be enough. Tharn was huge, powerful, a force of nature. Its sheer size was astonishing. The soldiers around it only came up to its waist. Even if she and the other Tenders had ample time to prepare, it wouldn't make any difference. Tharn would kill them without slowing down.

Tharn came fast, like a boulder rolling downhill. Its eye was fixed on her, its mouth open in a snarl. It waded through the soldiers in reserve as if they were made of straw, slapping them aside with its huge hands, each blow sending a dozen men sprawling. Some it merely stepped on, crunching their bones like twigs and mashing them into pulp. Those who survived long enough to strike it with swords or axes saw their attacks bounce off and their weapons shatter.

Nalene stood in a growing nimbus of power, Song racing through her like fire, more and more every second. Already she was dizzy with it. Tharn was only heartbeats away, but still she did not give the order to fire.

Strangely, she was not afraid. Or rather, the fear she felt was distant, almost alien. Her strongest emotion was a growing anger. She welcomed the anger, let it flow through her and fill her. Anger had ever been her defense against a world that derided and mocked her at every turn. This thing bearing down on her became the epitome of all she hated. It was as if the years of helplessness and frustration all boiled up within her at once, finding focus on Tharn. At that moment she cared nothing for the growing darkness over the land, for Melekath, for Xochitl even. The only thing that mattered was to destroy this thing, to see it crushed and dying.

"Come on," she growled, her teeth clenched tightly. "Come and get me. Just a little closer."

It loomed over her. She was vaguely aware that Perast was screaming. Her *sulbit* was glowing like a small sun. She held back a flood with only her hands. There would be no fine control when she released this time, only a massive flood of power.

She threw up her hand. "Now!" she howled.

Four huge Song bolts shot out nearly simultaneously. They struck Tharn square in its massive chest. It howled and staggered back a step. One massive hand went to its chest. Where the bolts had struck chunks were torn out and red light flickered in the depths of the holes. For a moment it just stood there, looking down at the wound in disbelief.

Then it raised its head, threw its arms wide, and bellowed. Nalene and the others staggered back, so weak they could barely stand. Within Nalene, anger gave way to despair. They had failed and now they would all die.

Bellowing again, Tharn crouched and slammed both fists to the ground. The ground split open with a loud cracking sound and Nalene and the other Tenders were knocked sprawling.

Stubbornly, Nalene rolled over and made it to her knees. She hurt everywhere. There was blood running down her face, running into her eyes and blinding her. The other Tenders moaned around her. She wiped at the blood, determined to face Tharn as it killed her.

Tharn's shadow fell over her and she braced herself, wondering if she would feel the blow when it came or if she would simply die instantly. Would the Mother be waiting for her? Was there anything on the other side?

Tharn raised its massive fists.

Then she saw something over Tharn's shoulder and her eyes widened in surprise.

Rome was already running when Tharn destroyed the wall. The black axe was in his hands, though he could not remember drawing it. It was light and powerful. It felt like a living thing in his hands.

He saw Tharn turn towards the Tenders, who were gathered in a group not far from the edge of the block of stone he stood on. As he ran, he gauged the distances, how far he had to go before he could make his leap, how fast Tharn was moving.

He wasn't going to make it. Tharn was moving too fast. By the time Rome reached the jumping-off point, Tharn would be too far away.

Then four Song bolts shot from the FirstMother and the three Tenders beside her, striking Tharn. The Guardian staggered back and paused. It was only for a moment, but it was enough to give Rome his chance.

As Tharn raised its huge fists to finish off the FirstMother, Rome reached his spot and jumped.

Nalene looked up from her impending death just in time to see Wulf Rome launch himself from the top of the cliff.

Tharn roared and swung.

Rome was in full swing when he reached Tharn, the axe coming around in a whistling arc and striking the Guardian with his full weight behind it. There was a high-pitched shriek from the black axe as it hit Tharn at the base of the neck and bit deep. Tharn howled.

Something that looked like lava gouted from the wound, sparking as it hit the air.

Rome's feet hit Tharn's back a fraction of a second after the axe bit. His momentum carried him forward and with his left hand he grabbed onto the top of Tharn's head to balance himself. With his other hand he pulled the axe back and swung the weapon wildly at the side of the Guardian's head, striking once, twice, each blow drawing new howls from Tharn, along with sparks and blood like lava.

Then a fist like a stone wall hit him in the side and Rome went flying. He landed on his shoulder and lost his grip on the axe. He rolled and came to his knees. The day pitched and tossed around him, but he fought to hang onto consciousness, looking around for the black axe.

He found it and struggled unsteadily to his feet. Tharn was staggering away, bleeding from huge gashes in its neck and head. Nalene had gotten up and was stumbling after it, hitting it with one Song bolt after another.

With a last bellow of pain, Tharn went back through the pass, wading through the soldiers that had surged through in its wake, killing dozens of them, and tearing a new hole through the wall. After it came a throng of Qarathian soldiers, heartened by Rome's victory, shouting and killing as they drove Kasai's forces back.

Once again Qarath's army had survived certain defeat.

FIFTY-SIX

Netra stood at the edge of a huge cavern. She had lost all sense of time and direction and had no idea how long she had been wandering underground in the absolute darkness. But it did not matter. All that mattered was answering the Mother's call. All that mattered was that she was almost there. She looked around, wishing there was something living nearby that she could draw Song from. The ecstasy that had filled her after draining the nomads was dissipating. Emptiness was once again stealing back into her. But there was nothing and so she had no choice but to move forward.

Across the cavern stretched a massive wall. It was the white of old, rotted ice, but with a hint of purple so dark it was almost black under the surface. A harsh, discordant buzzing emanated from it, as if millions of angry wasps were trapped within it. The sound clawed inside Netra's mind, painful enough that she stopped, suddenly unsure. Like someone awakening from a dream, she looked around. How did she get here? Where was Shorn?

"Shorn?" she called. The word echoed in the darkness and there was no answer. She tried to remember what had happened to him. Had she hurt him? She remembered the Crodin village then and cringed inwardly. It seemed like something done by another person, long ago.

"What do I do now, Xochitl?" she asked the emptiness. "Are you really here?"

Come to me, my chosen. Free me.

Netra approached the wall hesitantly. Chaotic, unnatural power radiated from it and she knew instinctively that if she touched it she would be killed.

This way.

Netra walked along the wall. Something deep inside her cried out to her to run away, flee before it was too late, but it was very small and she was gripped by something larger than she was. Every step she had ever taken had led her to this place, this time. It was what she was chosen to do. She could not turn away now.

Ahead was an oval section of the wall that looked different. It seemed to be made of dirty granite and there was a vertical crack in it. Just beyond, lying beside the wall, was the body of some huge, black-shelled creature.

Netra walked up to the crack. Was this, then, how Xochitl got into the prison? She held her hand out, close to the stone. There was something different about it; she could tell that much. A deep hum of something lurking within it. But there was none of the painful wrongness she felt from the rest of the wall.

She laid her hand on the stone.

A vision flashed into her mind and she quickly pulled her hand back, alarmed.

Cautiously, she put her hand back on the stone. The vision returned. She was looking at some kind of amphitheater. There were rows of seats along the walls, sloping sharply upward. In the middle was a large stone slab, and on the slab was a rectangular stone, set on its end. There was something unusual about the rectangle of stone, but she couldn't tell what it was. Suddenly it flickered, as the stone temporarily became transparent. Inside stood a tall woman of porcelain beauty. The woman raised her head and stared into Netra's eyes.

Netra knew her at once.

It was Xochitl.

You came. I knew you would.

Netra nodded, breathless. She glanced at her hand where it rested on the stone. Was this really happening? Netra looked back into Xochitl's eyes. "I came as fast as I could."

Are you ready?

Netra shook her head. "I don't think so. I don't know what to do."

Xochitl smiled and Netra felt something flip over in her heart. *I am weak and cut off from my power. All you have to do is return my power to me. I will handle the rest. I will stop Melekath.*

"What do I do?"

A trunk line.

Netra gaped at her. Trunk lines branched off the River directly, before branching off into feeder lines, then down to the flows that sustained individual lives. The smallest trunk lines carried LifeSong enough for a small city. "I can't. I...I'll be torn apart." No person could hope to so much as brush against that much power.

The Songs of those nomads fill you. While they are in you, you possess the strength to do this.

Netra flinched. Scattered images of people running from her, dying. "I killed them," she said softly.

It was all to free me. You did what you had to do.

Netra straightened. "You're right. I had to do it. I had no choice."

Now I need only one thing more from you. Xochitl pointed. *There. Do you* see *it?*

Netra turned her head. There, underneath the mists of *beyond*, pulsed a thick flow of LifeSong, as big around as the trunk of a large tree.

"I can't do this."

You can. Xochitl looked over her shoulder. *Hurry! He comes.*

Netra raised one hand, focusing Selfsong there. In a second it glowed like a small sun. She took a deep breath, then barely brushed the trunk line.

The shock that ran through her should have torn her to pieces. Golden fire played across her skin. She cried out and jerked her hand away.

It's too late! Xochitl cried.

A figure emerged from the shadows and approached Xochitl.

FIFTY-SEVEN

It was afternoon and the battle had not let up all day, as the attackers surged forward and the defenders pushed them back. Rome had spent most of the day in the thick of the fighting. He was bleeding from a half dozen minor wounds, and he was sore everywhere from his fight with Tharn, but none of it was serious.

They were going to win this battle; Rome was confident of it. The pass was an excellent spot to defend against a larger army, even with the holes Tharn had torn in the old wall. It was narrow enough that only a small part of Kasai's army could attack them at once. As men grew tired, they could step back and be replaced by fresh troops.

Nor were the Qarathians losing very many men, while Kasai's losses were horrendous. The dead were piled in heaps before the old wall, so high that they practically formed a wall of their own. Kasai's soldiers were fanatical and unrelenting, but they were also poorly equipped and poorly organized. It was only a matter of time until they gave up—or until the Qarathians slaughtered the lot of them, if that was what it took.

Then Rome felt a new presence arrive and a chill swept over him. Something was coming. All up and down the line Kasai's men ceased their attack and turned around to look back down the slope. The defenders paused as well, looking to the line of trees, every one of them feeling it.

A hush fell over them all as a figure strode out of the trees. It was impossibly tall and thin, with hairless white skin. There were no eyes visible, two slits where the nose should have been and a vertical slash for a mouth. It moved oddly, as if it walked in a body it had never become comfortable with, the joints in its arms and legs bending the wrong way.

Kasai.

The name whispered through the air, muttered by thousands of the enemy soldiers. For a long, awful moment everyone stood there as if frozen, every eye fixed on the Guardian.

Kasai raised its hands, palms upward. Gray flames sprang up from each palm. It drew back one hand.

"Get down!" Rome yelled, running along the top of the wall. "Get down!"

The first fireball struck the middle of the wall. It exploded on impact and soldiers flew everywhere. They hit the ground screaming, many with limbs torn off in the blast. All those within a dozen feet of the blast caught on fire, and when they slapped at the flames or rolled on the ground they discovered that they wouldn't go out.

Most terrifying of all was that the wall itself, the very stones, began to burn. The heat was so bad that the soldiers waiting in reserve behind the wall had to move away or risk catching on fire themselves.

Kasai threw another fireball. Another explosion, more soldiers flew through the air screaming, and another section of the wall caught on fire. As it threw the fireballs, Kasai continued to move up the slope, its stride odd and jerky, but deceptively fast. Arrows arced out to strike it, but all of them burned to ash before they struck.

The Tenders, initially scattered by the attack, reformed under the FirstMother's shouted commands and Song bolts began to fire at Kasai, striking it in numerous places.

But they made no difference. It was like shooting at a stone. Small blackened marks appeared on Kasai's hide, but the Guardian did not appear injured at all.

Kasai hurled two more fireballs and after the second one the last of the soldiers gave up and jumped off the wall. Kasai's forces swarmed up onto and through the wall, hacking at any they could reach.

Quyloc looked at the spear in his hand and thought of the plan he'd been mulling over for days now. It seemed outlandish at best, and might just get him killed while accomplishing nothing. More screams rang out as Kasai reached the wall and threw two more fireballs, lobbing them into the midst of the fleeing soldiers, killing scores outright and lighting dozens of others on fire. Quyloc was out of options. He had no other choice but to try.

He backed away from the edge of the stone and lay down. Tairus shouted something at him, but he ignored it. He closed his eyes and visualized the Veil. When he opened his eyes a moment later he was in the borderland.

Now came the hard part.

Instead of passing through the Veil, he planned to return to his own world, but at a different point than where he entered. Would he be able to do it? When he passed through into the *Pente Akka* the body he carried with him, formed of his thoughts, was solid enough, but would it be in his own world?

Another problem: How could he be sure he would emerge in the right spot? There were no directions here, no way to determine distance.

He walked along the sand, concentrating. After a dozen paces he sensed something, a powerful presence. It didn't seem like he'd gone far enough to be there already, but what else could the presence be?

He closed his eyes and pictured Kasai in his mind.

When he opened his eyes he was standing on the battlefield, Kasai about twenty feet away, right up against the wall.

Without hesitating, he ran at the Guardian.

"What are you doing?" Tairus yelled disbelievingly at Quyloc as he suddenly just laid down and closed his eyes. "You need to use the spear!"

He spun back toward the battle. Kasai was at the wall, readying yet more fireballs. Frustration welled up in him. All his years of experience, all his knowledge of battle, and yet what faced him was completely beyond anything he knew how to fight. Nothing they'd done had made any difference. Two minutes after arriving, Kasai was ending the battle.

Then, suddenly, Quyloc was down on the battlefield, just downhill from Kasai. Disbelieving, Tairus spun.

Quyloc was still lying there on the stone.

He turned back, wondering if he was seeing things. But there was Quyloc on the battlefield as well, running up behind Kasai. Two of Kasai's soldiers saw him and tried to strike him, but he dodged their clumsy attacks easily and kept going.

At the last moment Kasai became aware of him and the Guardian turned.

Quyloc was drawing the spear back to strike when Kasai suddenly turned. The red-rimmed eye fixed on him and he felt his entire being grow cold.

But he'd been to the *Pente Akka* too many times. He'd faced the hunter. He'd been trapped and helpless in that other world.

As Kasai swung one flaming hand toward him, Quyloc stepped in close and drove the *rendspear* deep into its gut.

Kasai screamed, a high-pitched, unearthly wail that echoed off the stone face of the Plateau. Its soldiers stopped when they heard the sound, and turned toward it, mouths dropping open at what they saw.

Quyloc jerked the spear back and stabbed again, up under where the rib cage would be if this was any kind of normal creature, seeking the heart.

Kasai screamed again and this time fire came from its mouth.

FIFTY-EIGHT

Melekath laid his hands on Xochitl's prison. Bolts of reddish light flashed from his fingertips and struck Xochitl, wrapping her in a crackling web of energy. She convulsed and began screaming.

"No!" Netra screamed.

She flung caution to the winds and threw herself at the trunk line, wrapping her arms around it. The massive flow of raw energy struck her like a raging flood, staggering her. Compared to the trunk line everything she had taken from the Crodin was nothing. Never had she dreamed of such power. Never had she felt such pain. Flames engulfed her entire body as the power burned through her. Without the stolen Crodin Song protecting her, she would have died instantly. The stolen Song kept her from being instantly torn apart by the flood; it kept her body from being consumed by the fire. But it did not stop the pain and it would not protect her for long.

Netra was dimly aware that she had fallen to her knees. Her screams echoed throughout the cavern. A detached part of her mind, the part that calmly counted the seconds until her death, noted the screams and recorded them as if they were coming from someone else.

It would be so easy to give up. All she had to do was quit fighting and in a few seconds it would all be over. All the pain and uncertainty and fear gone, just like that.

But quitting was not in her nature. Blinded by the pain, Netra somehow fought her way back to her feet. There was no longer any need to hold onto the trunk line. She was immersed in it. She could not have gotten free of it if she'd tried. Unconsciousness threatened.

She reached for the crack in the stone, knowing she had only seconds to unleash the power of the trunk line before she was ripped apart.

"Stop."

The voice was deep and ancient and powerful. From the broken granite two huge stone hands emerged, clamping onto her wrists with a merciless grip. A crude face formed in the stone, the empty eyes staring at her. The lips moved and it spoke again.

"Stop. It is a trick."

Netra tried to pull free, but she was less than a child in its grasp. She looked back into the vision and once again saw Xochitl in her prison, still writhing in the web of energy.

Please, Netra! You're my only hope!

"I can't!" Netra cried. "The wall! The wall has me! I can't get free!"

From within the energy web Xochitl's eyes locked on her own. *You have the power of Life in your grasp. Use it!*

It was true. Netra's hold on herself was crumbling. She was seconds from death. But until then a vast power still lay at her command. She could use it as she wished.

Gritting her teeth, she dug deep and found the strength to fight back one more time. She looked down at the stone hands which gripped her. Instead of flexing her muscle, she flexed her will and diverted some of the power from the trunk line into the stone.

The hands exploded into bits. The power almost got away from her then, and most of the crude face was sheared away as well. There was a deep, desperate cry from the depths of the granite.

Freed, Netra reached into the crack, gathering the power of the trunk line as she did so.

Then she let go.

Unleashed, the flood of raw LifeSong slammed into the crack.

The vision of Xochitl wavered and disappeared. For a moment Netra still saw the floor of the amphitheater, the stage empty, then that disappeared as well.

There was a groan like the end of the world. The cavern began to shake. Stones fell from the ceiling, narrowly missing her. A network of cracks raced across the entire granite section of the wall.

The granite exploded.

The concussion blew Netra backwards, and only the remnants of power that remained inside her kept her from being torn completely apart. As it was she was knocked unconscious, and blood poured from her mouth and the back of her head.

Dust filled the cavern, and as it began to settle, movement could be seen in the darkness beyond the wall. Scores of misshapen creatures surged forward, wordless cries arising from them, a terrible eagerness. At their head came Melekath.

It was then that Shorn arrived. Taking in the scene at a glance, his eyes fell on Netra's crumpled form, lying on the ground. Instantly he sprang into action, racing toward her. He reached her just as the Melekath stepped out of his prison of three thousand years.

Snatching Netra up, he turned and ran back toward the surface.

FIFTY-NINE

Tairus saw the flames come out of Kasai's mouth and engulf Quyloc and he winced, knowing there was no way Quyloc could have survived that. But then the flames died away and there was nothing there. He turned, saw Quyloc still lying on the stone motionless.

He turned back just in time to see Quyloc reappear on the battlefield, this time to Kasai's right. He stabbed once, twice, in quick succession and then, before Kasai could react, he disappeared once again.

Almost instantly he popped up behind Kasai and stabbed the Guardian in the back.

As Quyloc gathered for another strike, Kasai seemed to shimmer, then the Guardian flowed down into the ground and was gone.

As Kasai disappeared, a howl of despair came from thousands of throats. Kasai's soldiers held for a moment longer, then they broke and ran.

The soldiers of Qarath chased them back through the pass and then down the steep slope, howling and killing. Qarath had won the first great battle of the war.

But their triumph was short lived.

One minute they exulted and the next something tore open inside each one of them.

As one, the Qarathian army stopped and looked to the south, all of them knowing instinctively what had just happened.

The prison was broken.

Melekath was free.

The story continues in *Hunger's Reach*.

Before you go!

I'd like to thank you for reading *Guardians Watch*. As much as I love writing, it takes readers to make the experience complete. A journey shared is a much more powerful experience.

You may not be aware of this, but reviews are vitally important to unknown authors like me. They give other potential readers an idea of what to expect. So, if you have the time to leave one, I'd very much appreciate it. If you're busy (and who isn't?) leave a short one. Even one sentence is enough!

Glossary

abyss – place deep in the earth that is filled with unknown entities. It is the home of chaos power. Gulagh drew chaos power from the abyss and released it into the River, which is what is causing the strange diseases and mutations plaguing the land.

Achsiel — (AWK-see-el) blinded one who went with Kasai to get *ingerlings* from the abyss. He also led the first group of raiders onto the Plateau.

akirma – the luminous glow that surrounds every living thing. Contained within it is Selfsong. When it is torn, Selfsong escapes. It also acts as a sort of transformative filter, changing raw LifeSong, which is actually unusable by living things, into Selfsong.

Ankha del'Ath — ancestral home of the Takare. Empty since the slaughter at Wreckers Gate.

aranti — Shapers of the Sphere of Sky that dwell within the wind. They are the only Shapers never to war against the others.

Arminal Rix — ruler of Qarath before Rome and Quyloc took over.

Asoken — the Firewalker for Bent Tree Shelter, killed by the outsiders.

Atria — (AY-tree-uh) name commonly used to refer to the landmass where the story takes place. It is a derivation of the name Kaetria, which was the name of the old Empire.

Azrael — (AZ-ray-el) the one the Takare call the Mistress, protector of wildlife on the Landsend Plateau. If a game animal is not killed cleanly by a hunter, it may cry out to her and she will bring violence on the one who killed it. She killed Erined, mate to Taka-slin.

Banishment – when the Eight created Melekath's prison and sank the city of Durag'otal underground.

barren — area of bare stone on the Plateau. Nothing lives on the barrens except occasionally a tani or a poisonwood. The barrens actually seem to repel LifeSong.

Bent Tree Shelter — village on the Plateau where Shakre lived after being exiled from the Tenders.

Bereth – a Shaper of the Sphere of Stone, one of the Eight, who together with Xochitl laid siege to the city of Durag'otal. Along with the Shaper Larkind, he discovered the abyss and tried to enter it. Larkin was destroyed and Bereth was permanently damaged. He is the primary god in Thrikyl.

beyond — also known as "in the mists," the inner place where Tenders can *see* Song.

Birna — woman of Bent Tree Shelter who recently gave birth. Wife of Pinlir.

Bloodhound — one of Kasai's followers. He chased Netra up onto the sides of the Landsend Plateau and nearly caught her.

Bonnie — Rome's girlfriend, pregnant with his child.

Book of Xochitl – the Tenders' sacred book.

Brelisha — old Tender at Rane Haven who taught the young Tenders.

blinded ones – those people who have had their eyes burned out by Kasai. They gain the ability to use Kasai's gray fire and are in direct contact with the Guardian.

Caller — shortened form of Windcaller.

Cara — Netra's best friend.

chaos power – The power that comes from the abyss. It is completely inimical to all power in the normal world, including LifeSong, Stone force, Sky force, and Sea force. Chaos power was drawn from the abyss by the Eight to form Melekath's prison.

Children — the ones who followed Melekath to the city of Durag'otal and were Banished with him.

cla'sich — a Themorian term, applied to military leaders who are cowards, who hide behind others, then hide their cowardice from themselves.

Clem — one of the ten Telinar brothers, hired by Rome to scout for his army. Rome thinks it is the scarred one with the waist-long beard.

Crodin — nomadic people who live along the edge of the Gur al Krin desert. After they die the Crodin believe that their spirits are drawn into the desert, to the gates of Har Adrim, the dread city where their god awaits: Gomen nai, the Faceless One.

Dargent — nobleman who leads the soldiers raised by the nobility. Nearly thrown into chains by Rome.

Donae — (DOE-nay) Tender from Rane Haven.

Dorn — Windcaller that Shakre had an affair with as a young woman. Netra's father.

Dreamwalker — the Dreamwalkers are those who are responsible for guiding the Takare in spiritual and supernatural matters.

Durag'otal — (DER-awg OH-tal) city founded by Melekath as a haven for his Children. It was sunk underground in the Banishment.

Eight — eight Shapers of the First Ring who besieged the city of Durag'otal, formed a prison of chaos power around it, and sank it underground.

Elihu — (eh-LIE-who) the Plantwalker for Bent Tree Shelter and Shakre's closest friend.

Fanethrin — (FAIN-thrin) city to the west. Part of the old Empire.

feeder lines – the intermediate sized current of LifeSong, between the trunk lines, which come off the River directly, and the flows, which sustain individual creatures.

Felint — grizzled veteran in the Qarathian army.

Firkath Mountains — mountains just to the north of Rane Haven.

FirstMother — title of the leader of the Tenders.

First Ring — the oldest and most powerful of the Shapers, the first to arrive on the world.

flows – the smallest currents of LifeSong. One of these is attached to each living thing and acts as a conduit to constantly replenish the energy that radiates outward from the *akirma* and dissipates. If the flow attached to a living thing is severed, it will only live for at most a few hours longer.

Gerath — Tender who went with Netra to the town of Treeside. She was killed by Tharn.

Gift — something that was given by Melekath to his Children. The nature of it is not known, but whatever it was it led the Eight to besiege Durag'otal.

Godstooth — a tall spire of white stone near the center of the Landsend Plateau. It used to mark the hiding place of the god Tu Sinar.

Golgath — one of the Shapers that stood with Xochitl at the siege of Durag'otal. He was the only one of the Eight who was a Sea Shaper.

Gorim – one of the Shapers that stood with Xochitl at the siege of Durag'otal. Worshipped in Veragin, the dead city Rome found at the end of the summer campaign, where T'sim was found.

gromdin — a denizen of the *Pente Akka*. According to Lowellin, it seeks to shred the Veil, thus allowing the *Pente Akka* to spill over into the normal world.

Gulagh – one of the three Guardians of the Children, also known as the Voice, in control of the city of Nelton. It has discovered a way to make a small opening into the abyss and when chaos power leaks out, use a living person to feed that power back up the flow of LifeSong sustaining that person and ultimately into the River itself. It is this poison in the River which is causing the strange diseases and mutations plaguing the land.

Gur al Krin — desert that formed over the spot where Durag'otal was sunk underground. Means "sands of the angry god" in the Crodin language.

Has Trium'an — in Themorian belief, the Keepers of the Blessed Land.

Heartglow – the brighter glow in the center of a person's *akirma*. Like concentrated Selfsong. When it goes out, the person is dead.

Huntwalker — the Huntwalkers are those responsible for guiding the Takare in the hunt.

Ilsith – Lowellin's staff. Nothing is known of this creature or why it obeys Lowellin.

ingerlings – ravenous creatures Kasai took from the abyss.

Intyr – Dreamwalker for Bent Tree Shelter.

Jehu (JAY-who) — young Takare who took the black mark from Achsiel rather than be burned alive.

Kasai — one of the three Guardians of Melekath, also known as the Eye. Kasai discovered a way to take the *ingerlings* from the abyss and use them against Tu Sinar. It was badly injured by Quyloc with the *rendspear* at the battle of Guardians Watch.

Kaetria — (KAY-tree-uh) capital city of the Old Empire.

Karthije — (CAR-thidge) kingdom neighboring Qarath to the northwest.

Karyn — (CARE-in) Tender at Rane Haven.

kelani — a Themorian warship.

Khanewal — one of the Eight, who together with Xochitl laid siege to the city of Durag'otal.

Koni Anat — true Themorian warriors are allowed to meet him in single battle after death.

krenth-an — Themorian word for one who is no longer seen by his people, an exile.

Landsend Plateau — place where the Takare lived before it was destroyed in Tu Sinar's death throes.

Larkind — a Shaper of the Sphere of Stone. He was destroyed eons before when he and Bereth tried to Shape chaos power from the abyss.

Lem — one of the ten Telinar brothers, hired by Rome to scout for his army.

Lenda — simpleminded Tender from Qarath. Something went wrong when she received her *sulbit* and she went crazy and disappeared. It now appears she has two *sulbits* instead of one.

LifeSong – energy that flows from the River and to all living things. It turns into Selfsong after it passes through the *akirma*, which acts as a sort of filter to turn the raw energy of LifeSong into something usable by the living thing.

Lowellin — (low-EL-in) known by the Tenders as the Protector, he guides them to the *sulbits.*

macht — title from the old Empire meaning supreme military leader of all the phalanxes. Adopted by Rome for himself instead of king.

Mak'morn — Shorn's family name.

melding — when a Tender allows her *sulbit* to join with her on a deep level. In order for a Tender to meld with her *sulbit* she has to lower her inner defenses and allow the creature into the deepest recesses of her being. Her will must be strong to keep it from taking over.

Meholah — Huntwalker for Bent Tree Shelter. He was killed by Achsiel for saying no to the question.

Melekath — powerful Shaper of the Sphere of Stone, one of the First Ring.

Musician — one of a highly secretive brotherhood who can manipulate LifeSong to create Music that transports the listener. Rumor has it that there is a pact between them and their god, Othen, which is where they get their power.

naak'kii — Themorian term for warriors.

Nalene — FirstMother in Qarath.

Nelton – small city where Netra and Siena encountered the Guardian Gulagh.

Nicandro — aide to Wulf Rome.

Nipashanti — what the Shapers of the First Ring call themselves.

Oath — when the Takare first arrived on the Plateau, all life there turned against them and they were nearly all killed. Taka-slin, the legendary hero, traveled to the Godstooth and challenged Tu Sinar to come out and answer for his crimes. When the god did not answer, Taka-slin spoke the Oath, that the Takare would build no cities nor allow outsiders on the Plateau, and in exchange, Tu Sinar would call off his minions.

Othen's Pact — agreement made between Musicians and the god Othen.

Owina — one of the Tenders from Rane Haven.

Pastwalker – the Pastwalkers are entrusted with remembering the past. They can take others to actually relive past events from the history of the Takare.

pelti — Shapers from the Sphere of Stone.

Pente Akka — the shadow world that Lowellin showed Quyloc how to access.

Perganon — palace historian/librarian. He meets with Rome to read to him from the old histories. Also runs an informal network of informants.

Perthen — king of Karthije.

Pinlir — Takare man who was opposed to the use of violence until his father was killed by the outsiders.

Plains of Dem — where the Takare defeated the Sertithians.

PlantSong — the Song found within plants.

Plantwalker — the Plantwalkers are Takare who are sensitive to plants and can even communicate with them in a fashion.

Protaxes — one of the Eight, who together with Xochitl laid siege to the city of Durag'otal. Worshipped in Qarath by the nobility.

Qarath — (kuh-RATH) city ruled by Rome and Quyloc.

Quyloc — (KWY-lock) Macht Rome's chief advisor.

Rane Haven — where Netra grew up.

Rehobim — (reh-HOE-bim) Takare who wants to fight the outsiders.

Rekus — (REE-kus) Pastwalker for Bent Tree Shelter.

Rem — one of the ten Telinar brothers, hired by Rome to scout for his army. Rome thinks it is the youngest one with the two braided beards.

Reminder — a many-pointed star enclosed in a circle, the holy symbol of the Tenders.

rendspear — weapon Quyloc made in the *Pente Akka* from a tooth of the *rend,* lashed to a tree limb from the jungle, then doused in the River. It is capable of slicing through the flows of the three Spheres, as well as those of Life.

Ricarn — Tender of the Arc of Insects who shows up with two others in Qarath.

River — the fundamental source of all LifeSong, deep in the mists of *beyond.*

Seafast Square — place where Nalene defeated the creature that crawled out of the sea. The new Temple is being built there.

seeing – the act of perceiving with inner, extrasensory perception. It has nothing to do with the eyes yet what the mind perceives while *seeing* is interpreted by the brain as visual imagery.

Selfsong – when LifeSong passes through a person's *akirma* it becomes Selfsong, which is the energy of Life in a form that can be utilized by the body. It dissipates at death. It is continually replenished, yet retains a pattern that is unique to each individual.

Sem — one of the ten Telinar brothers, hired by Rome to scout for his army. Rome thinks it is the one who is missing part of his ear.

Sententu – a *pelti*, Shaper of the Sphere of Stone, one of the Eight who joined with Xochitl to besiege Durag'otal. He sacrificed himself to be the door of the prison.

Sertith — high grassland area to the north of Qarath. Nomadic horse warriors live there. It is believed they toppled the old Empire after it grew weak.

Shakre — Netra's mother. She lives with the Takare, having been driven to the Plateau by the wind after being exiled from the Tenders.

Shapers — powerful beings inhabiting the world long before life. Each belongs to one of the three Spheres, Stone, Sea or Sky, though some left to be part of the Circle of Life.

shlikti — Shapers of the Sphere of Sea.

Shorn — powerful humanoid from Themor who was exiled and crashed to earth near the Godstooth.

sklath — demons that the Crodin believe inhabit the Gur al Krin. They are believed to be responsible for raising the pillars of fire when the wind blows.

snek — Themorian term for leaders who waste their men in foolish battles.

Songquest — ritual that Tenders go through to acquire their *sonkrill*. They fast and wander the land until a spirit guide appears and leads them to their *sonkrill*.

sonkrill – talismans that the Tenders receive/discover at the end of their Songquest. The use of *sonkrill* came about after the fall of the Empire, as the Tenders sought to recover their lost power.

Sounder – one with an affinity for the Sea and its denizens. Due to the ancient wars between the Shapers of the Sea and those of the Stone, in which many people died and the seas and coastal areas abandoned, the people of Atria have a long history of fearing the Sea. As a result Sounders risk injury and death if they are found out.

Spheres — Stone, Sea and Sky.

spirit-walking — an ability that the Tenders of old had, a way of separating the spirit from the body, the spirit then leaving the body behind to travel on without it. A thin silver thread connects the spirit to the body. If the thread is broken, there is no way for the spirit to find its way back to the body.

stitcher — army surgeon.

sulbit – creatures that dwell in the River, living on pure LifeSong. In an effort to gain allies in the fight against Melekath, Lowellin gives them to the Tenders. When a Tender melds with her *sulbit*, she gains the creature's natural affinity for Song. As the *sulbit* becomes larger and stronger, the Tender can use its ability to touch and manipulate Song.

T'sim — (TUH-sim) unusual man Rome finds in the dead city of Veragin.

Tairus – (TEAR-us) General of the army.

Taka-slin — legendary hero of the Takare. He led them to the Plateau and defeated Azrael when she attacked his people. After that he traveled to the Godstooth and made the Oath which allowed the Takare to remain on the Plateau.

Takare — (tuh-KAR-ee) the greatest warriors of the old Empire. After the slaughter at Wreckers Gate they renounced violence and migrated to the Landsend Plateau.

tani — (TA-nee) huge, lion-like predator that lives on the Plateau.

Tem — one of the ten Telinar brothers, hired by Rome to scout for his army. Rome thinks it is the gray-haired one.

tenken ya — Themorian life debt.

terin'ai — it is the hidden, the shadow of a self. To face it is to face one's self honestly, without excuses or regrets. It is the greatest battle a Themorian can fight.

Tharn — one of the three Guardians charged with protecting Melekath's Children, also known as the Fist. Rome badly wounded it with the black axe in the battle at Guardians Watch.

Themor — Shorn's home planet.

Thrikyl — kingdom south of Qarath where Rome used the black axe to bring down the walls.

tiare — peppery liquor made in Karthije.

Treeside — small village in the Firkath Mountains where Netra and Gerath encountered Tharn.

Treylen — Sounder who wrote about the arrival of Shapers on the world.

trunk lines – the huge flows of LifeSong that branch directly off the River. From the trunk lines the feeder lines branch off, and off the feeder lines come the individual flows that directly sustain every living thing.

Tu Sinar — a Shaper of the Sphere of Stone and one of the Eight who stood with Xochitl at the siege of Durag'otal. He was destroyed by the *ingerlings* — creatures brought from the abyss — that the Guardian Kasai unleashed on him. Though not actually dead, since the Shapers are immortal, Tu Sinar is dissipated to the point where he will never reform.

unserti — Themorian word for wisdom.

velen'aa — Themorian term. "*Velen'aa* is not just war. It is any fight which fills a warrior's life. To embrace it is the beginning of *unserti* (wisdom)."

Velma — Tender that Nalene leaves in charge when she leaves with the army.

Veragin — dead city the Rome's army found at the end of the summer campaign. The people there worshipped Gorim.

Werthin — young Takare man who carries Shakre off the Plateau and keeps an eye on her.

Windcaller – men reputed to be able to call the wind and make it serve them. They are considered blasphemers by the Tenders.

Windfollower — name given by the Takare to Shakre.

Windrider — name given by the Takare to Shakre after she rides the wind to save the people of Bent Tree Shelter when the Plateau is tearing itself apart.

Wreckers Gate – the name of the main gate protecting Ankha del'Ath, ancestral home of the Takare. According to the Takare, the wealth and acclaim they received as the Empire's greatest heroes blinded them. Eventually a rogue Takare led the Takare still living at Ankha del'Ath to rebel and the great gate was shut. The Takare legions returned home and slaughtered their kinsmen. When they realized what they had done, they threw down their weapons, forswore violence, and moved to the Landsend Plateau, where the affairs of the world could no longer tempt them.

Wulf Rome — leader of Qarath.

Xochitl (so-SHEEL) — the deity worshipped by the Tenders. She is a Nipashanti of the First Ring and was a Shaper of the Sphere of Stone before moving to Life.

Yelvin — name of the two Insect Tenders who accompany Ricarn.

Youlin — (YOU-lin) young Pastwalker from Mad River Shelter. She awakens the Takare warriors to their past lives.

ACKNOWLEDGEMENTS

I would like to take this opportunity to thank some people who made valuable contributions to this book. They are my select team of trusted reviewers, reading the first draft of *The Broken Door* and pointing out misspellings, sentence errors and places where things just plain didn't make sense.

Thanks to my wife Claudia and my son Daniel (can I please have more than five weeks to write the next book, Daniel?). Thanks also to my brother, Scott. Last, but not least, thanks to Stormy and Paul Hudelson for their valuable input (and an extra thanks to Stormy for getting me back on track when I had lost faith in the story).

ABOUT THE AUTHOR

Born in 1965, I grew up on a working cattle ranch in the desert thirty miles from Wickenburg, Arizona, which at that time was exactly the middle of nowhere. Work, cactus and heat were plentiful, forms of recreation were not. The TV got two channels when it wanted to, and only in the evening after someone hand cranked the balky diesel generator to life. All of which meant that my primary form of escape was reading.

At 18 I escaped to Tucson where I attended the University of Arizona. A number of fruitless attempts at productive majors followed, none of which stuck. Discovering I liked writing, I tried journalism two separate times, but had to drop it when I realized that I had no intention of conducting interviews with actual people but preferred simply making them up.

After graduating with a degree in Creative Writing in 1989, I backpacked Europe with a friend and caught the travel bug. With no meaningful job prospects, I hitchhiked around the U.S. for a while then went back to school to learn to be a high school English teacher. I got a teaching job right out of school in the middle of the year. The job lasted exactly one semester, or until I received my summer pay and realized I actually had money to continue backpacking.

The next stop was Australia, where I hoped to spend six months, working wherever I could, then a few months in New Zealand and the South Pacific Islands. However, my plans changed irrevocably when I met a lovely Swiss woman, Claudia, in Alice Springs. Undoubtedly swept away by my lack of a job or real future, she agreed to allow me to follow her back to Switzerland where, a few months later, she gave up her job to continue traveling with me. Over the next couple years we backpacked the U.S., Eastern Europe and Australia/New Zealand, before marrying and settling in the mountains of Colorado, in a small town called Salida.

In Colorado we started our own electronics business (because, you know, my Creative Writing background totally prepared me for installing home theater systems), and had a couple of sons, Dylan and Daniel. In 2005 we shut the business down and moved back to Tucson where we currently live.

Made in the USA
Lexington, KY
22 July 2018